To Jason and our son:
You both teach me, day after day,
that love can be bigger, stronger, and more beautiful
than I ever could have imagined.
As long as there are stars in the sky, I will love you.

WHEN WE MEET AGAIN

KRISTIN HARMEL

GALLERY BOOKS

NEW YORK   LONDON   TORONTO   SYDNEY   NEW DELHI

G

Gallery Books
An Imprint of Simon & Schuster, Inc.
1230 Avenue of the Americas
New York, NY 10020

First Gallery Books trade paperback edition June 2016

GALLERY BOOKS and colophon are registered trademarks of Simon & Schuster, Inc.

For information about special discounts for bulk purchases, please contact Simon & Schuster Special Sales at 1-866-506-1949 or business@simonandschuster.com.

The Simon & Schuster Speakers Bureau can bring authors to your live event. For more information or to book an event, contact the Simon & Schuster Speakers Bureau at 1-866-248-3049 or visit our website at www.simonspeakers.com.

Interior design by Davina Mock-Maniscalco

10   9   8   7   6

Library of Congress Cataloging-in-Publication Data

Names: Harmel, Kristin, author.
Title: When we meet again / Kristin Harmel.
Description: First Gallery Books trade paperback edition. | New York : Gallery Books, 2016.
Identifiers: LCCN 2015047544
Subjects: LCSH: Women journalists—Fiction. | Family secrets—Fiction. | Domestic fiction. | BISAC: FICTION / Contemporary Women. | FICTION / Family Life. | GSAFD: Love stories.
Classification: LCC PS3608.A745 W48 2016 | DDC 813/.6—dc23
LC record available at http://lccn.loc.gov/2015047544

ISBN 978-1-4767-5416-1
ISBN 978-1-4767-5418-5 (ebook)

WHEN

WE

MEET

AGAIN

WHEN WE MEET AGAIN

CHAPTER ONE

The phone rang on a Friday morning as I was lying in bed, feeling sorry for myself and trying to figure out what I was going to do with the rest of my life.

"You're wallowing, aren't you?" Brian Mayer, who'd been my managing editor until last week, said when I picked up.

"You fired me." I pulled the covers over my head, blocking out the morning sun. "Wallowing is my right."

"Emily, you and I both knew this was coming. And you weren't fired; your column was canceled for budgetary reasons." He sighed, and I could hear him shuffling papers. "Besides, it was just a part-time thing. You have plenty of other freelance work to keep you afloat."

"Yes, magazines and newspapers across the world are just throwing money at journalists these days." I'd been a freelance magazine writer since my early twenties. Publications were flourishing then, and freelancing was an easy way to make a living if you were willing to work hard. But over the last decade, the market had become flooded with laid-off staff writers and editors, and now there were more journalists than jobs.

"Anyhow, I'm not calling to talk about the current state of journalism," Brian continued after a moment. "I'm calling because I have something for you."

I kicked the covers back and sat up. "Another writing gig?"

"Right, because our budget suddenly opened up for no particular reason." He chuckled. "No, I mean, I have a package for you. It arrived today."

"Is it from a PR firm?" I was constantly getting random mailings—jars of peanut butter to taste, CDs to review, clothing samples that never seemed to be my size—despite the fact that I'd made a career out of writing personality profiles in addition to my now-defunct column about relationships. It wasn't like I was suddenly going to write a glowing piece on peanut butter choices. "You can just throw it out or pass it along to an intern."

"No, I think this is something different." I could hear more paper shuffling. "It's a big, flat cardboard box, a poster or something. And it's hand-addressed to you. Doesn't look like it comes from a PR company."

"What's the return address?"

"It's from an art gallery in Munich, Germany."

"Germany?" I was perplexed; my column was only circulated to U.S. papers. Who would want to reach me from Germany?

"I'll FedEx it over to you, okay? Just wanted to give you the heads-up. And listen, hang in there, okay? Things are going to turn around for you. You're very talented."

"Sure," I said. I hung up before I could tell him what I really thought, which was that "very talented" people didn't get fired from jobs they'd held for the last three years. Granted, I'd never been a full-time employee of the Craig Newspaper Group, but they'd syndicated my column, Relating, to twenty-three newspapers across the country, where it had a readership in the millions. I'd been paid relatively well, enough that I was comfortable with my income as long as I supplemented it with a couple additional assignments each month. I'd thought I was surviving the collapse of the freelance marketplace, but apparently I'd only been treading water until the sinking began.

I supposed it was about time for me to lose my column anyhow. After all, there's only so much blind-leading-the-blind that one person can do before someone calls foul. And although I always put a lot of work into whatever I was writing, citing scientific studies or providing quotes from well-adjusted friends and colleagues, the idea of the endlessly single woman with the dysfunctional family history writing authoritatively about relationships was, to some people, laughable. In fact, I secretly kept a file of e-mails and letters from readers who accused me of being a washed-up, bitter old maid. Maybe they were right. Of course there were also plenty of complimentary letters from readers telling me I'd helped them through a divorce or encouraged them to reconcile with an estranged family member, but I'd found that people tended to write more when they were peeved at you than when they were thrilled. Also, they used more four-letter words.

The package from Germany was probably a sarcastic how-to-get-a-man poster from a snarky reader who'd seen my column online. It wouldn't be the first—or even the fifth—I'd received. However, it might be the first insult I'd gotten in German.

I pulled the covers back over my head and tried to retreat back to sleep. Today was the day my very last piece would run, and I didn't particularly want to be awake to witness my column's funeral.

Four hours later, despite my best intentions, I was sitting across the table from my best friend, Myra, at a restaurant overlooking downtown Orlando's Lake Eola as she dramatically waved the current *Orlando Sentinel* at me.

"You should be proud," she said firmly. "Seriously, Emily, you did a lot of good work with this column, and your good-bye was totally classy."

"I told you I didn't want to talk about this today." I took a sip of sauvignon blanc. Wine at two in the afternoon was perfectly acceptable when you no longer had a job. So was the fact that I was already on my second glass.

"Too bad. We're going to talk about it, because denial never did anyone any good. In fact, I'm pretty sure that's a direct quote from one of your columns."

"I'm not denying anything." I raised my glass in a mock toast. "I'm just pointing out that my whole career so far has been pointless."

"Self-pity is not attractive on you." She gestured to the waiter and ordered another Diet Coke. Unlike me, she had a job to get back to. She worked in community outreach for Easter Seals Florida, which meant that she was actually helping people all day long. "Fortunately, you manage to keep all that self-doubt out of your columns."

I shrugged. She was right; I was much more well adjusted in print than in the real world. If only I could live my whole life behind the protection of a computer screen.

"As I was saying," she continued after her soda arrived, "this last column was great. And you're going to land on your feet."

"I know I will. I just wasn't planning to be basically unemployed at thirty-six."

"But look at it this way. You have no obligations, nothing holding you back. No husband, no kids. You can literally do anything. Total freedom."

I forced a smile. "Yes, lucky me. Perennially single and childless. Every woman's dream."

Myra's brow creased in concern. "That is *so* not what I meant."

"I know." Still, the words stung, especially since Myra knew the statement wasn't exactly true. I *did* have a child—but I'd given her up for adoption half a lifetime ago. Now that she had just turned eighteen, an adult herself, the futility of my own life was really hitting home. What had I done with all the supposed freedom that giving a baby up had granted me? A whole lot of nothing, while my child had presumably blossomed under someone else's roof into a full-grown woman.

Myra's expression changed, and I could tell that she was now thinking about Catherine—that's what I'd named my daughter before a nurse whisked her away—too. I'd confided in her four years ago, and it had felt good to finally unburden myself. I'd been carrying the story of my daughter's existence in some subterranean spot in my heart, in a place where I stored those pieces of my life I wanted to remember and forget at the same time.

"I didn't mean to say you didn't have a child," Myra said quietly. "That was really thoughtless of me."

I shook my head and tried to look unfazed. "No worries. I mean, hey, you're right. I gave her up, didn't I? She's someone else's child now, not mine."

But although I hadn't seen Catherine since the day I gave

birth to her—and although I knew that her new parents had undoubtedly given her a different name—she was still mine in some basic, cellular way. I would always love her; I would always wonder about her; I would always fear that I'd hurt her rather than helped her by giving her away. She was in my blood, in my bones, and even all these years later, she was almost always my first thought when I awoke in the mornings. I had posted queries on an embarrassing number of adoption search sites and chat rooms online in the hopes of finding her one day, just to know she was all right. But she hadn't surfaced yet.

"So did you mean the things you said here?" Myra asked. She was waving my column around again. "About forgiveness?"

I blinked, drawing myself back from the edge of the self-pity cliff. "I always mean what I write." It was a glib answer, not exactly untrue, but not the whole truth either. My farewell column had been about moving forward and moving on, and I had written that the key to doing so in a healthy manner was to release past grievances. *Grudges stand in the way of building and repairing relationships,* I'd said. It was just that letting go wasn't always as easy as it sounded.

"Then maybe it's time to take your own advice and forgive yourself," Myra said. "Maybe you're feeling stuck in place because you're still feeling guilty over giving your daughter up."

"No, I'm not." My answer was instant, and I knew that my lack of eye contact told Myra everything she needed to know about the veracity of my words.

"Emily." Myra sighed and shook her head. "Look, we've been through this. You made the best decision you could at the time. It wasn't a selfish act; it was a selfless one. You weren't equipped for a child at eighteen, especially right after your mom had died. You made a choice to give her a better life."

I looked down at my wineglass, which was somehow empty. "I know." And I *did* know. I'd made the decision for the right reasons. But that didn't mean I didn't question it all the time. Besides, there was more to the story than what I'd told Myra. No one in the world—except for my grandma Margaret, who had died earlier this year—knew the whole truth. "In retrospect, it turns out that writing a relationship column might not have been the best choice in the world for a person who wants to bury her head in the sand," I said when I looked up to find Myra still staring knowingly at me.

She smiled. "Or maybe it was the best thing you could have done, because it forced you to start confronting some of your own demons. But now the hard work begins."

"The hard work?"

She laughed and glanced down at the column. "I'm going to quote the very wise Emily Emerson here, so get ready: *You may have been wronged in the past, but if you don't find a way to let those grievances go, you're responsible for dragging yourself down. So find a way to forgive, even if it's hard.*'" She paused and smiled at me. "So I'll ask again. Did you mean the things you said here?"

I looked at my lap and nodded.

"Good. Then put your money where your mouth is, my friend. Start forgiving yourself."

"Aye-aye, Captain," I said weakly as I gestured to the waiter for another glass of wine. "I'll get right on that."

But the truth was, I didn't know where to begin.

Two days later, the doorbell rang just as I was finishing up a profile of a local triathlete for *Runner's World* magazine. The publication was one of my semiregular clients, and I especially enjoyed assignments like this one, in which the subject of the piece was doing something good for the world. In this case, the woman I was writing about was a three-time breast cancer survivor who ran to raise awareness, and I had thoroughly enjoyed interviewing her over lunch in the Orlando suburb of Winter Park last week.

"Coming!" I called, but by the time I got to the door, a FedEx truck was pulling away and there was a flat cardboard box on my front porch. It took me a moment to remember that Brian had promised to forward the package from Germany. I picked it up and carried it inside, still convinced it was just another joke from an unkind reader. But my curiosity got the best of me, so I peeled the tape back and slid the contents out.

Even before I finished taking off the protective wrapping, I knew that what I was holding wasn't a poster. The paper was thick and textured, and as I peeled back the thin piece of parchment covering it, a small, sealed envelope tumbled out. I grabbed it from the floor and then propped what was actually a small painting against the wall, atop my kitchen table.

And then, frozen in place, I simply stared.

It was a richly textured watercolor of a woman standing in the middle of what looked like a cornfield, her face clearly visible as she stared into the distance. She was wearing a red dress, tattered at the edges and ripped on the right sleeve, and her expression was resolute and wistful at the same time. In the background, the sky was a strikingly deep violet. "What the . . . ?" I murmured as my fingers traced the woman's face.

She looked exactly like a younger version of my grandma Margaret. I'd written about her death in my Relating column just two months ago, and in the old family photo that had run with the piece—a shot of my grandmother holding my dad's hand when he was a little boy—she couldn't have been more than a few years older than the woman in the image before me now.

Feeling strangely breathless and shaken, I reached for the envelope that had accompanied the painting, tore it open along the seam, and removed the small note card inside.

I read your column, and you're wrong, it read in elegant cursive. *Your grandfather never stopped loving her. Margaret was the love of his life.*

The note was unsigned, and its weighty, expensive-looking cardstock was nondescript. There was no clue to who had written it, though it was obviously someone who wanted me to believe that he or she knew my grandfather. But that was impossible. The man had vanished before my father was even born. Grandma Margaret had gone silent each time I asked about him, but I knew he had abandoned her, just like my father abandoned my mother and me.

That's what my column two months ago had been about: the way the decisions of a parent trickle down through the generations. I had written about how my grandmother was a loving person, but how there'd always been a piece of her missing, a part that felt removed. I speculated that my father—who'd been raised without knowing who his own father was—felt both the absence of the man and the absence of his mother's full attention. Grandma Margaret always seemed to be on the verge of drifting away, and even her death left things feeling somehow unfinished. In fact, it was only after she died that I'd received a final voice mail from her. *I need to see you, Emily,* she'd said, her voice weak and rasping. *Please come as soon as you can, dear.* She'd left it before dawn on Valentine's Day, only hours before she took her last breath, and I'd slept right through it.

I'd ended the column without mentioning my own following

of the family footsteps, but in the depths of my own heart, that was really what the piece was about: my fear that, unwittingly, I was walking the same path as my father and grandmother. After all, I hadn't been in a real relationship for years, and I'd walked away from my own daughter, hadn't I? Was I fated to become just like them? Was it in my blood? I'd concluded by encouraging readers to think through their own family histories and to confront the things that affected their own relationships before it was too late. It hadn't escaped my notice that the column was yet one more example of me neglecting to practice what I preached.

I tried to think logically as I stared at the painting. Perhaps it had been painted *after* my column had run, by someone who used our family photo as a model? But I knew that wasn't true; the thick paper was slightly yellowed at the edges, suggesting that it was many years old, and the expression on the woman's face was exactly like my grandmother's when she was deep in thought, though in the photo that had run with the column, she'd been softly smiling. I was almost certain that it had been painted by someone who knew her. But was the note implying that my long-lost grandfather had been the artist?

I had to figure out where this painting had come from. Walking over to my computer, I googled the name of the gallery, then dialed the phone number posted on its website.

But as the phone rang several times I quickly did the math and realized that it was already nearly 9 p.m. in Munich. I wasn't surprised when an answering machine picked up. I didn't understand a word of German, so I had no idea what the outgoing message said, but after it beeped, I began to speak, hoping that someone there spoke English.

"Hi. My name is Emily Emerson, and I just received a painting from your gallery with no indication of who the sender is. It's a portrait of a woman standing in a field with a beautiful sky behind her. Could you please call me at your earliest convenience?" I left my number, hung up, and spent the next ten minutes in my kitchen, simply staring at the familiar face of my grandmother. Finally, I picked up the phone again, took a deep breath, and called the last person I wanted to talk to.

"Hi," I said when my father answered. His deep voice was achingly familiar, though I hadn't spoken with him in nearly eight months. "It's Emily. I—I need to show you something."

"Emily?" I hated how hopeful he sounded. It was as if he thought I was finally opening the door to a relationship. But that wasn't what this was. "Of course. I'll be right over."

CHAPTER TWO

"Emily?" I heard how hopeful he sounded. It was as if he
thought I was finally opening the door to a relationship. But that

My father arrived thirty minutes later, dressed in crisp charcoal pants, a pale blue shirt, and a gray tie. It appeared he'd
just come from the office. He looked thinner than he had the last
time I'd seen him, at my grandmother's funeral in February, and I
was struck by how much he'd aged. His hair had gone almost completely white, and the creases on his face were deeper than ever.

"Hi, sweetheart," he said, gazing at me hopefully from the
doorstep.

"Come in," I said, turning away and walking toward the
kitchen before he could try anything embarrassing like a hug.

My father lived in Orlando now too; he'd come here from
Miami seven years ago, apparently in hopes of reestablishing a relationship with me. He'd even opened a branch of his firm, Emerson Capital Investments, on Orange Avenue downtown so that
he'd have a reason to be close by. *I wanted to be in Orlando more
often so that we could have a shot at getting to know each other,* he'd
told me when he first called out of the blue. Since then he had
telephoned dutifully every two weeks, but I almost always let his

calls roll over to voice mail and deleted most of his messages without listening. After all, what was there to say?

He'd left my mother and me when I was eleven to marry a twenty-four-year-old assistant at his firm. Her name was Monica, and the first time I'd met her, I'd told her I hated her and that she had no right to break up my parents' marriage. She, in turn, had told my father that she wanted nothing to do with a little brat like me, a sentiment he'd repeated to me apologetically a few weeks later when he explained why I wouldn't be hearing from him much in the future. He'd moved to Miami before I finished seventh grade, and for the next decade—as long as Monica was in the picture—I had almost no contact with him. It was like he'd forgotten he had a child in the first place.

He tried to reconcile with me after their divorce, but as far as I was concerned, it was too late. Walking away from your child like that was unforgivable. It was made worse by the fact that he hadn't come back in the wake of my mother's death. I'd just turned eighteen when she died, so there was no custody issue involved, but he must have realized how alone I felt. Evidently, it hadn't mattered. He'd called once, to tersely express his sympathy, and that had been it. Later, I'd felt like a fool for spending the next month hoping every time the doorbell rang that he'd be the one standing outside my house, waiting to make me his daughter again.

By the time he resurfaced, showing up outside the journalism building at the University of Florida during my senior year of college to beg for a second chance, my walls were already up. I'd learned by then that I couldn't rely on anyone but myself. I'd never forgiven him for teaching me that lesson at such a young age. And although he'd spent the last several years apologizing profusely on my voice mail, explaining that walking away had been the biggest mistake of his life, the damage couldn't be undone.

"I was so glad to get your call, Emily," my father said now, closing the front door gently behind him and following me down the hall. "I know I have a lot to explain to you and a lot to make up for, but—"

I cut him off. "This isn't a social visit," I told him. "I received something that I need to ask you about."

He looked crestfallen, but he nodded and ducked into the kitchen behind me. I gestured to the kitchen table, and when he saw the painting propped up there, he stopped short and stared. "Emily, what is this?"

"I think it's Grandma Margaret." I hesitated. "Isn't it?"

Silently, he reached for the painting the same way I had an hour earlier. He traced the lines of his mother's face, and when he looked up again, I was startled to see tears in his eyes. "Where did you get this?"

"It came from a gallery in Munich, Germany." I handed him the note. "There's no signature. I don't know who sent it."

His eyes widened as he scanned the small card. "'I read your column, and you're wrong,'" he read aloud. "'Your grandfather never stopped loving her. Margaret was the love of his life.'" He looked up to meet my eye. "This is about your column from a couple months ago, the one where you talked about damage that trickles down through the generations."

I turned away, suddenly guilty. "Yes." I cleared my throat. "I guess I owe you an apology. I didn't know you read my column."

"Of course I do." His tone was gentle and didn't carry any of the blame I expected. "Every single one. And no apology needed. You were right about everything. I behaved abominably."

"Right. Well, anyway." I bit my lip and turned back to the

painting, changing the subject. "How sure are you that this is actually Grandma Margaret?"

He looked at the painting for a moment. "I'm positive, actually. At the end of her life, she kept telling the same story over and over again. She kept saying that the day she met my father, she was wearing a red dress, and the sky was turning violet as the sun came up. Just like in this painting. It's the exact scene she was describing." He closed his eyes for a moment. "I always felt so sad that the person who'd hurt her the most was the person she was thinking about at the end, as her mind got foggier. It was the only time in my life I ever heard her voluntarily mention him."

"She missed him," I said softly, feeling a surge of guilt that I hadn't spent much time with my grandmother in those final months. I'd been so busy with my career that I hadn't made the time, and now I'd regret that forever. I looked back at the painting now, my eyes tracing the familiar lines of my grandmother's face. "But what about the person who sent the painting? Do you think they know who your father is?"

"I don't know how that could even be possible. My mother couldn't explain what happened to him, but some stranger in Germany mysteriously knows our family secrets? It just doesn't add up."

"I know. But what if it's true, though? What if Grandma Margaret really was the love of your father's life?"

My father looked away. "And he just vanished? Never looked back? And now someone's sending random, cryptic messages saying that he never stopped loving her?" He shook his head. "I'm afraid it's unlikely."

Something dark was simmering inside of me all of a sudden. "What's unlikely? That he loved her but still managed to leave her behind?"

"Well, yeah. You don't just walk away from the people you love like that." He glanced at me, and suddenly, he seemed to realize what he'd just said. "Emily, I didn't mean me and you. It's not the same situation."

I blinked a few times, any rapport between us gone in a flash. "Sure. Like father, like son, I guess."

He waited until I met his gaze. "Emily, I'm sorry. I'm so sorry. There's nothing I can ever say or do to change what I did."

"Then why do you keep trying?" I hated the coldness in my voice, but it's what I reverted to every time I talked with my father. It was just easier that way.

"Look, I left because of my own baggage, my own shortcomings. And I need to try to explain that to you. I need to make it up to you."

"Please stop." I felt suddenly exhausted. "I hear what you're saying. But it doesn't change anything." I paused and looked down at my grandmother's face.

"I know." After a moment of silence, my father cleared his throat. "So what do you plan to do about the painting, Emily? What are you thinking?"

I took a deep breath. "I need to find out who sent it and what they know. I want to understand what happened."

"I do too. And I'll help you in any way I can."

I turned away. "Thanks, but I can do this on my own."

"Then why did you call me?" My father's tone was gentle, but I felt defensive all the same.

"I don't know. I thought you might know something that could help. But I guess I was wrong."

My father turned to stare at the painting. "All I know," he said after a while, "is that I grew up without a father. And then I turned around and did the exact same thing to you." He looked

WHEN WE MEET AGAIN 17

up and gave me a sad smile, and then, after giving my arm a quick squeeze, he headed for the door. "Believe me, I want to get to the bottom of this too.

"Emily," he said, pausing at the threshold. "I'm glad you called."

The phone rang the next morning just past six, jarring me out of a nightmare about my father and Monica standing at my mother's grave, taunting me.

"This is Nicola Schubert of the Galerie Schubert-Balck in Munich," said the heavily accented voice on the other end as soon as I picked up. "I am returning a call from Emily Emerson. You are Miss Emerson?"

"Yes, that's right." I was instantly awake as I reached for a notepad and pen.

"I do hope I am not calling too early. But I wanted to get back to you as soon as possible."

"No problem," I said quickly. "I was trying to reach you because I received a painting from your gallery and I—"

"Yes, yes," Nicola interrupted. "I am aware. But I am afraid there is not much I can tell you. Of course *The Girl in the Field with the Violet Sky* is a beautiful painting."

"The painting has a name?"

"No, no, it is just what we are calling it. It arrived with very few details."

"But who sent it to you?" I asked. "And why?"

"That's what I am trying to tell you. I truly do not know. It arrived by courier with a typewritten note."

"Do you still have it?"

She snorted. "Surely not. I recycle. But I can tell you what it said. It said that money had already been wired to the gallery, and that it should be more than enough to pay for the restoration and the shipping—which it was. The letter said that the painting had been kept for many years in a room that was too damp, and the sender was concerned that before the painting was sent on, it should be restored to perfect condition. The sender also included a sealed envelope and asked me to include it with the painting. Perhaps the sender included some information there."

"No," I said with a sigh, thinking of the cryptic note. "Do you know where the painting was sent from? Another gallery in Munich?"

"To be honest, one of my assistants processed the paperwork. So I have no knowledge of the painting's origin."

"Could I speak with the assistant?"

"Bettina? I'm afraid she quit a month ago."

"Is there any way to get in touch with her?" I could hear the desperation in my own voice. "I'd just like to ask if she remembers anything about where the painting came from."

Nicola sighed. "I'm afraid that's not possible. She didn't leave us on good terms."

I could almost feel each possible lead slipping away, one by one. "Do you have any idea why the painting was sent to your gallery specifically?"

"Because I am one of the foremost restoration specialists in the world for this type of art, obviously." I could tell by her clipped tone that I'd offended her. "And clearly the sender was aware of my gallery's reputation."

"And you don't know who the painter is?"

She hesitated. "No. I do not." There was something in her voice that told me she knew more than she was saying, but before I could ask anything else, she continued, "Now, Miss Emerson, it is imperative that I return to my customers. I just wanted to give you the courtesy of a return call. I hope you enjoy the painting. It is very beautiful. I was struck by the skill of the artist's brushwork, and I must say, I enjoyed the restoration."

"Is there anything else you can tell me?"

"Do you know a lot about art?"

"No. Not really."

"Then I'm afraid my technical explanations would be wasted. Things can't really be explained properly over the phone anyhow. Please, enjoy the painting. Good day." She hung up without another word, and I was left holding the phone and feeling even more confused than I'd felt the night before.

CHAPTER THREE

It was just after 7 a.m., and Peter Dahler stood alone in the middle of an endless sea of rolling green. If he squinted, he could imagine he was in a boat in the middle of Hackensee Lake, Franz beside him, his father manning the oars, his mother with her head tilted to the sky, warming herself under the rays of the sun. But those days were long gone.

The sky that lived in Peter's childhood memories was a crisp, glacial blue, but here in the swampy farmland rolling toward Lake Okeechobee, the first light of morning would turn the sky a startling cobalt, then a velvety indigo, melting into a soft violet. During that first hour of dawn, the heavens would cast a shadow over the soaring sugarcane stalks, turning the infinite fields of cane water-blue as their long, gentle fingers rippled like waves in the breeze.

"You planning to work? Or you gonna gaze at the sky all morning, Dahler?" Harold's voice wafted across the stalks, jarring Peter back to reality. He glanced over his shoulder and forced a smile at his favorite guard, the one willing to break the rules once in a while to give Peter a glimpse of the beautiful sunrise. Most days, the prisoners started work at nine, and from their encampment south of Okeechobee, there wasn't much of a view. Their barracks were nestled in a tangle of trees on the edge of an over-grown swamp, a reminder, Peter supposed, that if they tried to run, there was nowhere to go. But Harold, who was the kind of person Peter might have been friends with under different circumstances, seemed to understand that some-times a person who's seen so much ugliness in the world needs a little beauty too.

"Sorry," Peter said, his English rolling off his tongue as naturally as if he'd been born with it, albeit with the tendrils of an accent. "I will work. I want to thank you again for bringing me out here this early."

"It's nothing." Harold turned his attention back to the horizon. Peter wondered if he was thinking about what lay east, across the ocean: the terrible war that neither of them were a part of. Peter had been captured on the battlefield; Harold, some ten years his senior, had been assigned to a military police unit and kept stateside to guard prisoners while his friends shipped off to defend the country. Now, they were both stuck here. "I like mornings like this too," Harold said after a moment. "Just don't let the foreman catch you slacking off, you hear?"

"Right, yes, of course." Peter smiled another apology and hoisted his cane knife over his shoulder, turning east again. He would work facing the sunrise so that he could watch the sky turning all its brilliant colors. As the sun as-cended, the day would get hotter, the mosquitoes would swarm with a constant, gentle buzz, and the humidity would grow thick enough to choke on. But for now, the world was perfect.

In Holzkirchen, the small Bavarian town where Peter had been raised, it had been the sunsets that sometimes looked like this, although the colors had presented themselves in reverse: first the milky blue, then the violet, then the deeper indigo, and finally cobalt, blackening like oil as they faded into the thin line where the earth met the heavens. It seemed strange to Peter that the colors that had heralded the end of a day in Germany were the same ones that announced the coming of a new one here, across the ocean. His ending had become his beginning.

Peter easily found the line of demarcation between yesterday's work and today's. In a few hours, he'd be elbow to elbow with a dozen other prisoners, so he treasured this time alone, and he appreciated that Harold wasn't hovering. He let himself imagine for a moment that it was because Harold trusted him, but of course that wasn't it. As much as Harold showed kindness, he knew well that Peter was still the enemy.

Peter lowered the cane knife, grasping its wooden handle and feeling the heft of it in his hands. He'd never seen one before arriving in Florida. It resembled a *Buschmesser,* a machete, but the blade was shorter and thinner, perfect for slashing through the towering sugarcane stalks. The knives had hooked tips, which helped the workers to pick up the felled crop, but still, the men had to bend time and time again to scoop up the cane, hauling it to wagons nearby. At the end of each day, they were all aching and coated in the sticky syrup that oozed all around them.

The dawn sky grew lighter as Peter fell into the rhythm

of his labor. As his knife slashed against the base of stalk after stalk, he began to play a familiar game: calling to mind a memory from home with each swipe of the blade.

Swoosh: His mother's hands as she kneaded bread.

Thwack: His father reading the paper in the morning, his knuckles white around a cup of coffee.

Swoosh: Franz, trying on Peter's field cap the day before he left for the front, laughing because it was still too big for his head.

Thwack: All three of them framed in the doorway, the sun setting behind their small cottage, waving as Peter walked away for the last time.

There were bad memories too: the way his parents used to scream at each other sometimes when they thought the boys were asleep; the nights when there wasn't enough food on the table; the way his father's face darkened when Peter dared speak out against his political beliefs; the morning the Kleinmanns, who ran the butcher shop down the street, were dragged out of their home by the SS and shoved into the back of a truck, never to be seen again.

But mostly, Peter felt nostalgia for the land he hadn't seen in four years. And on mornings like this one, with the sky awash in beauty, he felt particularly close to home.

Home. *Heimat.* That was the word on Peter's tongue when he first saw her.

She was walking from the east, the first in a line of four local laborers who emerged from the sugarcane sea onto the main path. She was wearing a red cotton dress, frayed and tattered at the edges, and the way she was bathed in the morning light, set against the purpling dawn, made her look like someone who didn't belong here: a film star, perhaps, or an angel. Her long, brown hair danced behind her on the morning breeze, and the way she moved was both gentle and strong at the same time. Peter was rendered immobile, his cane knife paused almost comically in the air.

Perhaps feeling attention upon her, she turned in Peter's direction, and their eyes met. She didn't blink, and neither did he. Instead, they held each other's gaze for a long moment, both of them motionless, as if life had simply frozen in place. Or maybe, Peter would think as he replayed it in his head later, it was his imagination. Maybe she hadn't stopped at all. Maybe she hadn't even noticed him.

But she had. He knew she had. She finally looked away and began walking again, leading the others, who seemed younger than she. He watched her as she paused to let them go ahead of her, into another maze of sugarcane. And then, just when he thought he would lose her forever, she turned, looking over her shoulder for just a moment. Their eyes met again, and it was enough to make Peter feel buoyant and hopeful as she walked on, vanishing into the field.

He dreamt of her that night, the girl in the red dress. It was strange, actually—not just the fact that he was seeing her in his dreams, but also the idea that for the first time in almost a year and a half, his slumber was sweet and peaceful rather than restless and troubled. Since that terrible night in the African desert, the night his best friend, Otto, had died in his arms, he hadn't slept without dreaming fitfully of blood and death.

Peter had been part of the *Afrika Korps*, and though he'd heard terrible things about the conditions for Hitler's armies marching across Europe, he couldn't imagine things being much worse than they were for him and his fellow soldiers. The sand was everywhere, endless, stinging, vicious, and there were some days when Peter couldn't remember the last time he'd taken a sip of water. They had followed General Rommel there, but then Rommel had returned abruptly to Germany in March of 1943, saying he needed to convince the führer of the severity of the situation on the African front. But he hadn't returned, and everything had deteriorated. General von Arnim and the Italian, General Messe, had taken over Rommel's command, and it hadn't taken long for Peter to understand that the men didn't know what they were doing.

Otto had died there, and Peter could never forgive the forces that had conspired to make such a tragedy occur. Otto had grown up just down the lane from Peter's family, and the two had been like brothers since they were three years old. They'd been just a month apart in age, and even with the German economy collapsing around them, they'd used their imaginations to conjure an embarrassment of riches when they were boys. They were always hunting treasure, imagining themselves to be great adventurers at sea, and they had made a pact when they were ten years old that one day, they would explore the world together. They'd only been eleven when Hitler had begun his rise to power, and they'd been alone in their dislike of the man, whom they both secretly agreed resembled a rodentlike pirate named Ratte from a chapter book they had read the previous summer. But it seemed that all Germany was in love with Hitler, especially the families of both boys, and so they had to escape to their tree house in the woods in order to whisper made-up tales of the dastardly Pirate Ratte who had fooled the country into believing he was their savior.

A decade later, no longer boys but men, Otto and Peter found themselves in a sandy, arid alternate universe, fighting for a cause they didn't believe in. "You know, Peter," Otto had said with a smile the night he died, "this isn't what I meant when we were children and I said we should explore the world."

Peter had laughed, despite his hunger, despite his thirst, despite the fact that death lurked everywhere in this endless desert. "You were not dreaming of fighting a war in Africa?"

"I rather think we should go to America when this thing is over," Otto replied.

Peter raised an eyebrow. "America, you say? But they hate us. They have come all the way across an ocean to wage a war against us."

"Can you blame them?" Otto grumbled. "No matter. After the war, you and I will be great ambassadors for Germany. We will show them that not all Germans are like the rat pirate."

Peter laughed, thinking that his friend's words were absurd. America! He couldn't imagine. "You have always been a big dreamer, my friend. Now get some sleep, or we will never be up to the march tomorrow."

Two hours later, something jarred Peter out of a deep slumber. He immediately sprang from his bedroll into a crouching position, ready to fight an invisible enemy. But the night was silent, and after a long moment of holding his breath, Peter looked up toward the sky and realized instantly what had awoken him. The blackness was alive with dozens of dancing pinpoints of brilliant light. *Mein Gott,* he murmured to himself, sinking back down into a squat. It was important to stay low to the ground here, for one never knew when the enemy was lurking. "A miracle."

And though the scientific side of his brain realized that the dazzling streaks across the darkness were the result of a meteor shower, the romantic in him knew it was much more than that. Here, in the middle of hell, he was seeing heaven.

"Otto!" he whispered, shaking his friend awake. "Quickly, come see!" He pointed upward, and Otto, still rubbing the sleep from his eyes, followed his friend's gaze and gasped.

"It's amazing, Peter," Otto replied, staring upward, his jaw slack. "Which way is north?"

Peter pointed to his left, ninety degrees from where the half-moon dangled in the sky. "I think it's that way."

Otto stood and peered into the blackness. All around him, stars continued to streak through the night. "I can almost see Germany, Peter," he said. "Look, the stars are showing us the way home."

"Sit down, friend," Peter said with a laugh, "before you make yourself a target."

No sooner were the words out of Peter's mouth than the world exploded, a hailstorm of bullets whizzing and careening through their encampment like a swarm of drunken bumblebees. "Otto!" Peter screamed. "Get down!"

But there was no answer from his friend, and while the encampment came alive around him, and the night filled with smoke that obscured the brilliant stars, Peter fell to his knees and groped around for Otto. He'd been only a foot away. Where had he gone? "Otto? Otto, where are you?"

Then, Peter's hand landed on something warm and wet, and in a split second, he realized it was Otto's shoulder. "Otto!" he cried.

He bent to his friend, and as bullets continued to slice through the air and the Germans returned fire, he struggled to find Otto's pulse. But he found only an oozing hole the size of a chestnut in his friend's neck, and when he pulled away in horror, he was covered in blood.

"Otto?" he whispered. But it was already too late. Otto's eyes were wide and motionless, staring up at the endless sky as if he could see through the haze of smoke and horror to the heavens above, to the beautiful streaking stars. "No, my friend! No."

But there was no answer.

"Come on, Dahler!" someone yelled in the chaos.

"I can't leave him!" Peter screamed, trying to lift Otto's limp body from the wet ground as bullets whizzed all around them.

"He's dead!" yelled another voice. "Put him down or you'll die too!"

Peter managed to carry Otto fifty yards across the camp before two soldiers materialized beside him, forcing him to release Otto and dragging Peter to safety against his will. He had never forgiven himself for leaving his friend alone in a bed of blood and sand. Nor had he forgiven the fact that he'd been the one to cause Otto's death. If he hadn't woken him to see the meteor shower, his friend would still be alive.

A mere two months later, the war ended for Peter.

The night he was captured, he had dozed off, raw from exhaustion and thirst, in a shallow ditch he'd dug with his bare hands. When he'd awoken, the Allies were upon them.

Their commander was speaking, telling the troops that it was time to surrender to the Americans. And as Peter put his hands in the air, he felt an overwhelming sense of shame. But the shame wasn't for the loss in battle, for the defeat inherent in surrender. It was for the relief he felt that his war was finally over.

———

For more than a year now, Peter had wondered what it all meant, what God's purpose was in delivering him from Africa to this endless expanse of sugarcane in the Florida heat. He had traded the arid desert for the humid swamplands, the continent of Africa for the continent of North America, both terribly far from the land of his birth. He'd felt homesick at first, but gradually, the good cheer of the American guards and the bounty of the land had grown on him. Otto had been right all along about this place.

Now, as Peter woke with the image of the girl in the red dress fresh in his mind, he wondered fleetingly if perhaps everything had been leading to this. The terror of war, the despair of capture, the exhaustion of labor: perhaps she was the reason.

But it was crazy to think like that. He didn't know her. They'd never spoken. He had no idea how old she was, or whether she was already married, or if she hated Germans on sight like so many Americans seemed to.

But in the dream, which he could still see on the back of his eyelids, she had been smiling at him. Smiling and beckoning. And even now, in the clear light of day, he wanted nothing more than to follow.

CHAPTER FOUR

"I've been thinking," my father said when he called the following Monday morning, "that I might have a lead for you."

The painting was still propped up on my kitchen table, and I'd spent the last four days alternately staring at it and searching the Internet for anything I could find about my grandmother. She'd died in February at the age of eighty-eight, and before that, she'd lived a relatively quiet, solitary life. The only mentions of her I could find in newspaper archives were her obituary and an article from 1964 in which she'd been interviewed by a reporter while dropping her son, Victor—my father—off for his first day of college at Yale. I had tried searching for her name along with the terms *Munich*, *Germany*, and *painting* too, just in case something popped, but the results were meaningless. I'd gotten sidetracked yesterday with a new freelance assignment from *Seventeen*, so I'd been busy, but the mystery of the painting's origin was still weighing on my mind.

"A lead?" I asked skeptically.

"Yes. I can't believe I didn't think of it sooner. When my assistant was organizing your grandmother's memorial service, she called everyone in your grandmother's address book. One of the people who came up for the service was a man your grandmother had grown up with. He introduced himself at the funeral, but I didn't get the chance to talk with him."

"I don't understand." I knew very little about my grandmother's past; she had been born in 1926 and raised on a farm somewhere in South Florida, but she'd cut ties with her family after leaving home, and she'd never spoken of the years before she gave birth to my father in early 1946. "I thought she had completely walked away from that part of her past."

"I thought so too. But this man, Jeremiah Beltrain, told my assistant they'd called each other over the years here and there. In fact, he said he was around a lot when I was a kid, although I don't remember him."

"Your middle name is Jeremiah. Did Grandma Margaret name you after him?"

"No idea. I'd never heard of him before." He paused. "I'm thinking now that he might know something about your grandmother's past. It's a place to start, anyhow. If I give you his information, will you tell me what you find out?"

"Okay." I jotted down the number my father gave me and thanked him, although I hung up wondering why he hadn't thought to call the man sooner, before the painting had arrived. Wouldn't he have wanted to know more about his mother's background? I certainly did. But that was the difference between my father and me. To me, family meant something.

Before calling, I searched for Jeremiah Beltrain on the Internet; I preferred to go into cold calls with as much prior knowledge as possible. But there was very little to be found. He was mentioned only in a 2006 article in the *Palm Beach Post* about independent sugarcane farming, and the newspaper identified him as a seventy-four-year-old longtime farmer in a town called Belle Creek. I did the math and realized he must be eighty-three now—six years younger than my grandmother would be if she were still alive. So if they'd grown up together, their age difference would have been significant. I wondered how they knew each other.

I picked up my phone, dialed the number my father had given me, and waited through three rings.

"Hello?" A man answered just as I was about to hang up. He sounded out of breath.

"Hi. I'm looking for Jeremiah Beltrain."

"This is he. May I ask who's calling?" His tone had taken on a suspicious edge.

"My name is Emily Emerson," I began. "I'm—"

"Margaret's granddaughter!" he interrupted. "Oh my. I was hoping I'd hear from you one day, dear. She was so proud of you."

I didn't say anything for a moment. I was startled that he'd known exactly who I was. "Thank you," I said finally. "The two of you were friends?"

He chuckled. "I can't remember a time before I knew your grandmother, Emily. She was a great woman."

"Thank you. I think so too." I took a deep breath. "The thing is, I'm calling today with a bit of a strange request. I just received a painting in the mail from an anonymous sender with a note saying that my grandfather never stopped loving my grandmother, that she was the love of his life."

He drew in a sharp breath. "What?"

"It's a painting of my grandmother. Or I think it is, anyhow. And I want to understand what the painting and the note mean, but I don't know anything about her past. She never told us who

my father's father was; she always refused to speak of him." I
paused. "But my dad said you grew up with my grandmother. So I
was wondering if maybe you know."

There was a long moment of silence. "Well, I think that's a
story to be told in person, don't you? Any chance you can make it
down to Belle Creek? It's a little postage stamp of a town on the
southern edge of Lake Okeechobee. Should only take you a few
hours to get here if you're still living in Orlando."

"How did you know I live in Orlando?"

"Your grandmother spoke of you often." I could hear the
smile in his voice. "Can you come to see me?"

I checked my watch. It was only ten in the morning. "How's
today? I can leave here in about an hour."

"That sounds perfect. I think your grandmother wanted you
to know the truth, my dear. But sometimes, when one is living
with a broken heart, it's too hard to give voice to the stories that
hurt the most."

He gave me his address and directions from the highway, and
we hung up with a promise to see each other in a few hours.

After showering quickly and throwing on a sundress and some
makeup, I took a few cell-phone pictures of the painting and
headed for Belle Creek, a town I'd never heard of until today.
The trip would snake me down the Florida Turnpike to U.S. 441,
then across the state on State Road 78, cutting west toward Lake
Okeechobee, a huge, shallow lake that looked on a map like a
jagged O cut out of the southern half of our state.

As I took the I-4 exit for the Turnpike and headed south,
the road opened up ahead of me, and my mind wandered. Was
Belle Creek really my grandmother's hometown? Why had she

never mentioned it? And what would this man be able to tell me about her?

She had always been, to me, a woman of mystery. I'd never had any doubt that she loved me, but she wasn't a person who told stories about her own life or wore her emotions on her sleeve. The secrets of her past were locked away so deep that I'd always assumed she never thought of them at all.

I'd spent a lot of time wishing I'd inherited that skill. To be able to lock the past away in a box, closing it off forever, sounded wonderful. There was nothing I wanted more than to forget everything that had taken place the year Catherine was born, but the more I tried to push it away, the more it haunted me. And now that she had just turned eighteen, I found myself thinking about that year and everything that had happened a lot more frequently. In fact, I'd been having trouble sleeping, because all the things I'd tried so hard to forget were suddenly invading my dreams.

My mother had been killed in a car accident that March, just two and a half months before I graduated from high school. My father had left seven years earlier, but his mother, my grandma Margaret, had stayed in touch with my mother and me. She was as appalled by my father's decisions as we were, and although she was still in contact with him, I knew that their relationship had gone cold. "I always thought I had instilled the right values in him," she said to me one day when I was sixteen. "But in the end, he left just like his own father did. I'm so sorry that I raised a person who would hurt you that way, my dear. I'll bear that guilt for the rest of my life."

When I was thirteen, Grandma Margaret had moved from Atlanta to an apartment overlooking the bay in St. Petersburg, Florida, and I'd visited her each summer. When my mother died,

Grandma Margaret came back to Atlanta to live with me while I completed school. She was the only person in the world who knew I was pregnant.

It had been a mistake, of course. When my mother was alive and life was good, I'd had a boyfriend named Nick. And I'd loved him. God, I'd loved him. We'd only been together for six months when my mother died and, devastated and reeling, I'd pulled back from everyone. My friends had faded after the first few weeks, but Nick stuck around. He was the only one who did, even when I pushed him away. I could see that now, but at the time, I hadn't been able to see past what I'd come to believe was the looming, central fact of my life: the people who are supposed to love you will inevitably leave.

You can't rely on anyone but yourself. That was my mantra, day after day, so when I discovered I was pregnant—exactly a month to the day after my mother died—I knew I couldn't tell him. What if it made him hate me? Or worse, what if it made him stick by me solely out of pity, only to abandon me once the baby came? I couldn't handle that.

And so I didn't tell anyone. Nick didn't notice the nausea, the growing swell in my belly, or the fact that I shot up a bra cup size in a month, because I was slowly backing away from him, wolfing down lunch by myself in an empty classroom, and dodging his calls in the evening. Still, the fact that he was still trying, still looking at me with what I knew deep down was love, meant something. But admitting it at the time would have been a chink in the armor I was working so hard to construct.

Graduation was June seventh, and on the morning of June eighth, Grandma Margaret and I set off for Florida without looking back. I'd already been accepted to the University of Florida, where I planned to major in journalism. But a visit to my doctor had confirmed that I was due at the end of October, and so I called the registrar's office to see if I could defer admission, citing the death of my mom. They agreed to let me begin in January, which left me the next seven months to myself.

So I moved into Grandma Margaret's spare bedroom and spent my days reading or driving out to the beach for long walks. I spent my evenings trying in vain to fall asleep without thinking about Nick. The first time I felt the baby move, I almost called and told him everything, but I hung up halfway through punching the numbers in. In the final three months of my pregnancy, I picked up the phone at least once a week and got halfway through dialing before slamming the receiver down, hating myself a bit more each time.

"You're doing the right thing," my grandmother told me over and over as my belly—and my doubts—swelled. "Boys don't stick around. You can't count on them. I'm so sorry, but Emily, it's better for you to do this without Nick." She brought me the name of an adoption agency, and we talked, night after night, about how she'd help me find the baby a good home. "You'll give your child a better life," she told me gently. "It's the greatest gift you could give. It's an option that didn't really exist for me when I was your age."

"You would have given my dad up?"

She was silent for a long time. "Maybe it would have been better for him if I had."

By the time I went into labor three weeks early, I was fully convinced that I was doing the right thing by giving my little girl up for adoption. She'd never have to worry about people leaving her. And by not telling Nick, I was doing him a service. There was no way that at eighteen he was prepared for a baby any more than I was. Becoming a father would have derailed his life. *I'm protecting him too,* I told myself. *One final act of love.*

But then I held Catherine in my arms for the first and only time. She had Nick's eyes, Nick's dark hair, and the beautiful shape of his lips; seeing his features so clearly reflected in her made me realize, in a flash of searing lucidity, that I'd made a huge mistake. Nick and Catherine were my family, even if that wasn't what I had planned. And even if Catherine would go on to have a good life with her adoptive parents—as I believed she would—my reasons for giving her up were all wrong.

But it was too late. Everything was already in motion.

I never saw my daughter—or talked to Nick—again. And for the rest of my grandmother's life, we never spoke of the child I gave away—or of the yawning hole in my heart that could never be filled.

———————————

I almost missed the turnoff for Belle Creek, a town so small that there was no road sign announcing its existence. But Jeremiah Beltrain's directions took me left at an intersection and right at a stop sign. Then, I turned once again, my Mazda CX-5 rumbling along a dirt road flanked by two fields of wispy, grassy stalks at least a dozen feet tall, like tropical, supersized versions of the cornfield in *Field of Dreams*.

The stalks eventually gave way to a much neater-looking field of short, dark, leafy bushes in militarily precise rows. Beyond them lay a small, wood-framed house that sat slightly crooked on its foundation. The pale blue paint on the exterior was worn and peeling, but the flower beds out front, sporting marigolds and petunias, looked well tended.

I parked in the small dirt driveway beside a rusted-out sedan from the late '70s or early '80s that was covered in a fine layer of dust. For a moment, I just sat there, trying to imagine my well-spoken, put-together grandmother growing up around here. It just didn't feel right, and I was temporarily paralyzed by the conviction that I was in the wrong place.

Still, I'd come all this way, so after a few minutes, I got out of the car and walked up to the front door. I took a deep breath and knocked. I could hear a television on inside, but no one came, so I knocked again, harder this time. I could hear the television volume being lowered, then footsteps moving toward me. The door opened a moment later, revealing a tall, slightly stooped man. His hair was snow white, his skin the color of espresso beans. Two jagged scars ran down the right side of his face. He looked me up and down and broke into a broad smile.

"Emily," he said. "By golly, you look just like your grandmother. It's so good to see you."

"Mr. Beltrain?" I asked, extending my hand.

His smile widened as he shook my hand firmly. "Please, call me Jeremiah. And come in, come in. I have so much to tell you."

I followed him down a dimly lit hallway into a sparse living room. There was nothing on the walls save for a plain white clock with thin black hands. In front of a small television with rabbit ears sat a beat-up brown leather recliner and a brown fabric sofa with faded blue throw pillows. "Have a seat," Jeremiah said, gesturing to the sofa as he settled on the leather chair.

"So," I said after sitting down, "how exactly did you know my grandmother?"

He smiled and looked out the window without saying anything for a moment. "You know what that is? That crop growing out there beyond my back fence?"

"Corn?" I guessed, following his gaze to the seemingly endless expanse of homogeneous farmland that rolled toward the horizon.

He chuckled and turned back to me. "That, my dear, is sugarcane, as far as the eye can see. And back in the day when your grandmother and I were young, it was the lifeblood of this here community. Now, most of the fields are part of bigger conglomerates, but when we were young, there was still work for locals like us." He paused. "Did you know your grandmother used to farm sugarcane?"

I stared at him. "I knew her father had been a farmer, but . . ." My voice trailed off.

Jeremiah frowned, and his expression was suddenly faraway. "Ah yes. Your grandmother's father. Sure, he was a farmer. A bean farmer, mostly, on the edge of the sugarcane fields. But your grandmother, she didn't have much to do with him. They didn't see eye to eye about many things. In fact, your grandmother didn't see eye to eye with many people around here. But she sure looked out for me. From a very young age, she was like my guardian angel. She must have been twelve or thirteen when I met her, and I was only six. I worked sometimes on her family farm."

"You worked when you were six years old?"

"Had to. My mother died in childbirth, and my daddy was a real hard drinker who couldn't hold down a job. The only way I could keep food on the table was to go out there and work. Never got to go to school, but Margaret, she taught me to read and write and to understand history. Sometimes, I harvested her family's green beans, but mostly I worked in the cane fields. Margaret harvested cane too, because her family's farm was failing and they needed the extra money. It wasn't exactly traditional in those days for a girl to do manual labor like that, but she wanted to help her family out, and her father, he didn't have much choice if he wanted to keep afloat.

"She always seemed to arrange it so that we wound up on the

same crew," he continued. "We'd be working, and she'd be quizzing me about who the president of the United States was in 1845, or how the First World War had started. Nearly everything I knew when I was a boy came from her. Back in the day, Emily, your grandmother was a vivacious young woman, so full of hope."

"She was?" The thought made me sad, because by the time I knew her, she had retreated into herself. "What happened to her? What changed?"

For a moment, I thought he wasn't going to answer, but then he said abruptly, "In the 1940s, one of the worst things to be in the South was a black boy. Did you know that?"

I wasn't sure what to say or what that had to do with my grandmother, so I merely nodded and waited for Jeremiah to continue.

"The second-worst thing to be in the South was a German prisoner of war," he said, looking me in the eye.

I shook my head, confused, although his mention of Germany suddenly had me thinking about the painting that had come from Munich. "A German POW? In the United States? What do you mean?"

He smiled, but he didn't answer. "And the third-worst thing to be, as far as I could see, was a person who sympathized with both little black boys and German prisoners. And that's what your grandmother was—someone who looked beneath the surface when the whole rest of the world wanted only to judge. It made life difficult for her."

"I'm sorry, I'm afraid I'm not understanding you. You're saying there were Germans here in Florida? During World War II?"

"It's amazing that your generation doesn't know that." He glanced at me and added, "It's strange how some stories get passed down and others don't. Truth is, there were German prisoners of war all over the United States. The U.S. government set them up in camps in places where there weren't enough laborers. You got to realize how many young American men were off fighting in Europe and the Pacific. There just weren't enough people left to keep the factories and farms running. Here in Belle Creek, we had a bunch of POWs from 1943 on who came to harvest the cane."

"Here in Florida," I repeated flatly, still trying to process what he was saying. "Right in the middle of the war? Germans?"

"Hundreds of them. And they were hard workers, too. Hardly ever complained, at least as far as I could see. Lots of people around town, the ones who didn't work in the fields, hated the Germans on sight. It was like that back then; the war made a lot of people angry. But those of us who worked with them, well, we came to realize that most of them were a lot like us. Just from a different part of the world."

"And my grandmother was friendly with them?" I asked, perplexed.

"She was just that kind of a person, polite to everyone. But she kept most people at arm's length too, at least until she got to know them. And as far as I saw, during those last years she lived here in Belle Creek, there were just two people she let into her heart. Me, a little boy who was supporting his family, and him, a German soldier trying to find his place in the world."

"*Him?*" I repeated. "Who do you mean?"

Jeremiah held my gaze. "Peter. The man you came to ask about. Your grandfather."

CHAPTER FIVE

Jeremiah excused himself to use the bathroom, and I sat paralyzed, staring out the window at the sugarcane fields my grandmother had apparently once farmed, trying to process what Jeremiah had told me.

My grandfather had been a Nazi soldier? How could my grandmother fall in love with a man like that? And how had she gotten close enough in the first place to know him? Wouldn't prisoners of war have been kept separate from local residents for safety reasons? And most pressingly, what had happened to him?

My mind was still spinning when Jeremiah returned, carrying two glasses of iced tea. He handed one to me. "I bet you have a lot of questions," he said, raising his eyebrows as he sat back down. "But let me start by telling you this. The fact that Peter was a German didn't mean a whole lot. Most of the German boys who wound up over here weren't even really Nazis."

"What makes you so sure?" I gave him a skeptical look.

"Most history books would agree with me," he said with a smile. "These young Germans didn't have a choice about joining the military. Truth is, most of them were relieved to be away from the battlefield. Here, they worked eight-hour days and got three square meals and a warm place to sleep. It was better than the lives many of them had come from."

I nodded slowly. What he was saying was plausible, at least. "Okay. But how did he and my grandmother even meet? Weren't the prisoners kept in, well, a prison camp?"

"Believe it or not, in many places around the country, including Belle Creek, it was common for the prisoners to work alongside the locals, with guards supervising them. There was still a separation, of course, but if you were viewing it from the outside, you might think we were all the same, the locals and the Germans." His gaze turned faraway again, as if he was looking into the past. "I was with her the first time they spoke. I'd cut my hand with a cane knife, a foolish accident, and I was bleeding." He held up his right hand to show me a jagged scar. "Margaret—your grandmother—was walking me to her house to clean it out, and out of nowhere, this tall, blond German soldier called out to us. I didn't understand at first—I wasn't exactly used to white people being kind to me, nor were any of us accustomed to being spoken to by the Germans—but he was actually offering to help us.

"Seemed to me he and your grandmother talked for a time," he continued. "And later on, when Margaret was dressing my wound, she looked like she was in a daze. I asked her what was wrong with her. I remember asking her, 'Did that no-good German say something to make you upset? I can tell the guard if you want.'" He paused and shook his head. "And you know what your grandmother said? She said, 'Jeremiah, you can't judge people before you know them. I think maybe that German soldier is a good man.'"

He stopped speaking and seemed lost in thought. After a while, to urge him back to the present, I asked, "And was he? A good man?"

Jeremiah sighed. "I don't know. I thought he was." He drew a ragged breath. "And your grandmother, well, she came to love him. She really did. I never knew that they'd—you know— consummated their relationship. I was just a boy; she wouldn't have told me that." He cleared his throat, and I could tell that even now, so many years later, he was embarrassed to be speaking of such a thing. "But then she was pregnant. Her family was threatening to disown her once the baby was born if she didn't just abandon it at the church like a piece of unwanted trash. Of course she wouldn't do that. In those days, there wasn't any guarantee your baby would wind up safe and sound. So she decided to keep the child, of course. And Peter, he was nowhere to be found."

"But what happened to him?"

"Eventually the war ended, and the prisoners were sent back to Europe. Margaret wrote and wrote to him, you see, but he never wrote back. Until the letter that changed everything." He turned his head to gaze out the window again, and when he looked back at me, I could swear there were tears in his eyes for a moment before he blinked them away. "He broke her heart. And I never saw it coming."

"What did the letter say?"

Instead of replying, Jeremiah stood and shuffled out of the room. In a moment, he returned clutching a yellowed envelope. He handed it to me and shook his head. "Your grandmother had just given birth to your father when she received this. At first, she didn't believe it. She thought someone must have forged it. But then she never heard from him again. What other explanation was there? He wasn't the man we thought he was, in the end. It wasn't long after that your grandmother decided to leave Belle Creek forever." He gestured to the envelope in my hands. "Go ahead. Read it."

I hesitated. "Why do you have it?"

"Your grandmother threw it out. I kept it, just in case she ever changed her mind. Just in case she tried to find him. I wanted to remind her that he'd left her and that she was better off."

I looked down at the envelope, noting a return address from someplace called Holzkirchen, Germany. Slowly, I removed the single yellowed sheet of paper and unfolded it. Sadness surged through me as I read the short note, which was dated December 1945 and written in elegant cursive.

Dear Margaret,

I have received your letters and would like to request that you stop writing. I am many miles away from you now. There is no future for a German boy and an American girl. I will always remember our days together, but this has to cease.

I am sorry to hear that you are with child. But there is nothing I can do. It was a mistake, all of it. I am sorry for any trouble I have caused you.

I will wed my old girlfriend, Gerda, in a month's time, and I wish not to trouble her with the reality of my life in your country. It is best that she does not know.

This will be my last letter to you. I wish you a good life.

Sincerely,
Peter A. Dahler
Holzkirchen, Germany

"That's horrible," I said, looking up after I'd finished reading it. "He knew she was pregnant, and he basically just told her to deal with it because he was marrying someone else?"

Jeremiah nodded slowly. "To this day, I do not understand. He seemed to be a very different kind of man."

"But who's to say that Peter Dahler actually wrote it?"

"That was Margaret's argument for a long time too, I think. But if he didn't write it, who could have forged his handwriting so accurately? Margaret grew sure it was his. And where was he? He had promised to return, and he never did. Years later, in the sixties, Margaret swore she saw him in a big crowd in Washington. But he looked right at her and turned away. I never believed that it was actually him, Emily. What would he have been doing in the United States? And at Dr. King's March on Washington, of all places? It just didn't make sense. But for your grandmother, it was the final straw. If there was any hope that the letter wasn't real, it was dashed entirely that day. She said he just looked at her like she was a ghost, like she meant nothing to him. She tried to make it across the crowd to the spot where he'd been, but he was gone, as if he had seen her and fled."

"But you don't think it was him?"

He shrugged. "Truthfully, I think Peter Dahler probably made a life for himself in Germany and never thought of Margaret again. I think that theirs was a wartime romance, something forbidden, and though the feelings might have seemed real to her at the time, it was never meant to last. And I also think we misjudged Peter Dahler, your grandmother and I. He may not have been a Nazi, but that didn't make him a good man either. Perhaps the two of us saw merely what we wanted to see."

I sat in silence for a moment. "She never spoke of him, you

know. Not to me, and not to my father. We only knew that the man she'd loved had left her behind."

"I always felt that keeping it a secret was a mistake."

"You knew she didn't tell us about him?"

He hesitated. "Yes."

"So why are you telling me now?" I stopped abruptly and shook my head. "I'm sorry. I don't mean to sound ungrateful. I'm so glad that you're sharing this with me. But if she didn't want us to know . . ."

He smiled. "In the end, she realized she'd been wrong, I think. I spoke with her about a month before she passed, and she told me that as she neared the end of her life—for of course she knew she was dying—she had come to terms with what had happened. She had forgiven him. And she had forgiven her family for disowning her. But she couldn't forgive herself for keeping the truth from you and your father. 'They have a right to know,' she told me. 'But I don't know how to tell them. Not after all this time. I can't bring myself to speak of him.' I asked if I could help in any way, and she thought about it for a long time. Finally, she said, 'Tell them if they ever come looking.' And here you are."

"Why didn't she just write us a letter or something?" I asked. "Something we could open after she died, if she wanted us to know?"

"Because she wasn't sure that telling you was the right thing," he replied. "Do you understand? You had to seek the truth out on your own. I imagine she had a bit of a sense that you'd do just that one day. She was always telling me that you were a girl full of questions and that you always searched for the answers."

I was silent for a moment as I imagined my grandmother in her final weeks, filled with regret but not knowing how to make

things right. I swallowed hard. "How come I've never met you before?" I asked. "If you were so close to my grandmother?" I regretted immediately how rude the words sounded, but the journalist
in me needed to know.

He looked surprised for a split second, but then he nodded,
as if he'd expected the question. "We lost track of each other for a
long time. When she left Belle Creek, I went with her, but only
for a few years. Your father had just been born. I was only fourteen, and she was nineteen, almost twenty. She was scared and
alone. We traveled separately until we got to the North—to
Philadelphia—where I got a job at the Italian market on Ninth
Street and she worked as a seamstress. I used to watch your
daddy sometimes when she worked. I owed her everything. But
then, just after your daddy turned four years old, I received a tele-
gram saying that my father had lost his arm in a farming accident.
I had to move home to care for him; there was no one else. I lost
touch with Margaret after that because she didn't want to be
found, and she certainly wanted no connection to Belle Creek.
She changed her name, totally reinvented herself."

"She changed her name? Why?"

"I think she just wanted to be someone else," he said. "Someone who didn't come from a family that had turned their back on
her, someone who hadn't been rejected by the man she had believed so strongly in. She used to be Margaret Mae Evans, you
know. But she was running from the past, and running is easier
when no one can find you. It wasn't until 1963 that I heard from
her again. She was living in Atlanta then, and her son, your daddy,
had just turned seventeen. She had just gotten back from the
March on Washington, and like I said, she was sure she'd seen
Peter there. She called me here in Belle Creek to ask if he'd come
back looking for her. Of course he hadn't. I hated to tell her that,

because I knew how much it would hurt. But it was the truth. He never returned."

"And after that? You stayed in touch?"

He shrugged. "Here and there, Christmas cards, the occasional call. I had children of my own by then, you understand, and my life was very busy. I owned my own farm, and we were struggling to stay afloat. And Margaret made me promise not to tell anyone that I knew where she was. She didn't want to have anything to do with her sister."

"She had a sister?"

"Yes. Louise. Her parents were dead by then, but I think that they'd been dead to Margaret long before that. After your father was born, they said they wouldn't have the son of a Nazi living in their house, never mind a Nazi lover. Her sister was in complete agreement; she had totally turned on Margaret too. It hurt Margaret deeply, and she never forgot it."

"What happened to all of them?"

"Her parents died in the late forties, and Louise inherited the family farm. I saw her many times over the years, but she never mentioned Margaret again. It was like she had never existed." He paused. "Until last month. Louise died last month, and I got the strangest visit from her about a week before she passed. She said she was sorry for everything she'd done to her sister, and she wanted to know if Margaret was okay, if I still heard from her. I told her Margaret had died in February, and Louise seemed devastated. After a while, she gathered herself and asked, 'Did the German come back before she died?' I told her no, of course not. It was clear that Louise was still holding on to a grievance that was seventy years old. She just closed her eyes, murmured, 'I'm so sorry,' and walked away from my front door. She was dead a week later." He looked up at me. "Her granddaughter still lives here in Belle Creek, you know. Maybe you should go see her."

"For what?" I asked. "After all, it sounds like Louise went out of her way to make my grandmother's life miserable."

"But she was still your family," he said. "Besides, maybe her granddaughter knows something I don't."

"Sounds like you were much closer to my grandmother than Louise ever was."

"Yes, of course that's true." He paused. "But I've always wondered if there was more to the story of Peter Dahler than Margaret and I understood. It's worth a try, isn't it?"

I nodded slowly. Of course he was right; as a journalist, I always followed up on every available lead, and this time shouldn't be any different. "Do you have contact information for the granddaughter?"

He nodded and jotted something down on a piece of paper. "Julie Candless. She's a little younger than you. She lives over on Harper Road, on the other side of this cane field. It's the same house your grandma grew up in, as a matter of fact. Might interest you to see it."

I took the address and number from Jeremiah and then stood to shake his hand. "I can't thank you enough for everything you've told me," I said.

"I owe Margaret far more than this, believe me. But may I ask a favor of you?"

"Of course."

"The painting you mentioned. The one that arrived with the note. May I see it sometime?"

I pulled out my phone. "I actually took a photo of it this morning. Will this do?" I scrolled through until I found the image.

I handed it to him and watched as his eyes widened and then filled with tears.

"It's her," he whispered. "It's exactly how she looked that day."

"What day?"

He looked up at me. "The day she first met Peter in the fields."

My heartbeat quickened. It was exactly what my father had said. "Is it possible that he painted this? Was Peter a painter?"

Jeremiah shook his head. "He wasn't artistic at all, as far as I know. But he had a friend who was always sketching things in the dirt." He smiled. "The man even used charcoal to draw on the sides of barns whenever the prisoners would be working on farmland. He was quite good."

"What was the friend's name? Do you remember?"

He was silent for a moment. "Maus, I think. Something Maus. I can't recall his first name. I realize it's not much to go on."

"Still, maybe I'll be able to find old POW records. Maybe I can find him."

"May be a dead end, but it's worth a try. If there's anything I can do to help, anything else I can answer for you, feel free to call, Emily."

I shook his hand again and he walked me to the door. "I really appreciate it, sir."

He surprised me by pulling me into a hug. "I wouldn't be here today without your grandmother. I owe her my life."

He stood in the doorway, waving, until I'd pulled out of his driveway and was headed back across the vast expanse of sugarcane fields.

CHAPTER SIX

The soft thwacks of the cane knives flowed together in an endless rhythm, reminding Peter of rushing water. He was ankle-deep in muck, sweat pouring from his brow, his deeply tanned skin turning even browner in the beating sun. It was blazingly hot, the same temperature one might find on a sunny July day in Germany. But here, it was October, the month when at home, leaves fell, temperatures dropped, and the people of Munich were just finishing up their Oktoberfest celebration. Would there be an Oktoberfest this year? Peter doubted it. The festival hadn't been held since 1938, and Peter wondered if it would ever happen again. Perhaps Germany would be defeated, wiped off the map, all its traditions erased. The thought made him sad. He didn't believe in Hitler's politics, but he believed in Germany. It was a beautiful country with a beautiful history, and to consider that it all might die because of greed and pride ripped Peter's heart in two.

Peter liked to think about Germany while he worked.

It kept his mind off the backbreaking labor, the blood of the men who'd been careless with their knives, the sunstroke that sometimes took one of them down in a dead faint. It kept him from thinking about the things he'd seen on the battlefield—blood, fear, terrible pain, the horror of young lives snuffed out in a senseless instant. And when he let his imagination wander, he could almost pretend that he was working alongside a babbling river—the Kirchseebach, perhaps—side by side with his friend Otto, close to his family, the Bavarian Alps looming in the background. But when a foreman's voice or the rumbling arrival of an empty pallet truck jarred him back into the present, he was always dejected to find himself here, in the endless, rolling sugarcane fields on the edge of Florida's Lake Okeechobee.

Every day, he and his fellow prisoners rose with the dawn, ate a hearty breakfast in the camp's mess hall, and climbed aboard transport trucks that would take them ten kilometers up the road to the fields of Belle Creek. Their camp was on the edge of the wild Everglades, far outside of town, presumably so the residents would feel protected from the intruders at night. Peter knew that many of the people in the nearby towns viewed the prisoners as enemies, and he couldn't blame them. But the locals who got to know them one on one—the foremen, the guards, the field hands, even the local doctor and priest—seemed to forget after a while that they were so different. And that was the truth of it, wasn't it? Take a man's weapons and put him to work, and he's just a man, regardless of where he comes from. There were a handful of American Negroes working the fields too, and Peter always thought it odd when the foreman spoke to the foreigners with more respect than to his own countrymen.

"It's your turn," Maus said in German, nudging Peter's shoulder and snapping him out of his reverie. Peter blinked at his new friend, whose nickname, German for *mouse,* had come from the amusingly white whiskers that sprouted above his top lip whenever he neglected to shave. They hadn't known each other in Africa, though they had both served there, but they'd found themselves bunkmates here in the wilds of Florida, and they'd discovered they had much in common. They were both from the outskirts of Munich, and they were both skeptical about Germany's chances of winning the war. While many of the other men in the prison camp were boisterous and sarcastic, Maus was, like Peter, quiet and pensive much of the time. At night, when the others played cards and told crude jokes, Maus liked to sketch on scraps of paper, and Peter liked to read books in English from the small camp library. They had become fast friends.

"Peter, are you listening?" Maus asked now, nudging him again.

"What?"

Maus laughed. "Daydreaming again, are you? It won't get you home any faster."

"I know," Peter muttered. He wasn't sure he even wanted to go home. Not while Germany was still in the midst of a war. Did that make him a coward? Or simply a realist who didn't want to fight for a cause he didn't support?

"It's your turn," Maus repeated, pointing to the ground and smiling. "I already got one this week."

Peter followed Maus's gaze to a curving, dark line at the

base of a pile of freshly cut sugarcane stalks. A water moccasin, more than a meter long, lay still in the grassy underbrush. Peter could feel himself tensing.

"Relax!" Maus said with a laugh, noting Peter's reaction. "He's harmless."

"Hardly," Peter said. Water moccasins, he knew, were more benign than the deadly eastern diamondbacks, which were also spotted in the fields sometimes. But the venom of one of these shorter, blacker snakes could still render a man helpless. There were snakes in the fields constantly, one of the things that made Peter so uneasy. Although his fellow prisoners often made a game out of killing and skinning them, salt-curing and saving their hides as trophies on the barracks walls, Peter knew the reptiles were no laughing matter.

"Aren't you going to kill it?" Maus asked.

"No," Peter said. "I think that if we do not hurt him, he will not hurt us."

The words were hardly out of his mouth when Dieter, a burly soldier who had served with Peter in Africa, slammed the heel of his work boot down on the head of the snake, killing it instantly. "Got it," Dieter said, his voice flat and emotionless. "Next time, you have to be quicker, Dahler."

Peter stared hard at Dieter, who smirked back. More than once, their arguments over politics had turned to fisticuffs, and Peter was tired of the man, who seemed to believe that they were always a hairsbreadth away from returning triumphant to Germany. Dieter didn't like it much when Peter pointed out that the American newspapers suggested the war was turning in a different direction. In fact, Peter was confident that fighting would be over within the year, and that Germany would not be the victor.

"Just because you can read English, that doesn't make you smart," Dieter had snapped at him. "You're too foolish to realize it's all just propaganda. The führer will be victorious. You wait and see. You're a traitor if you don't believe it."

As Dieter picked up the dead snake now, slinging it over his shoulders like a neckerchief, Peter turned away.

"You could have had it, you know," Maus said quietly. "It was your turn."

"I didn't want a turn," Peter replied. He breathed in deeply, though it was impossible to draw relief from the humid air. It was impossible to draw relief anywhere here.

He turned back to the crop and hefted his cane knife over his shoulder before the foreman or one of the guards accused him of *whistling Dixie,* a strange phrase he'd heard more than once. It meant wasting time, and although the slang sounded amusing, it came with unwelcome penalties — usually the most demanding assignment in the field the next day.

Maus began to sing quietly under his breath — Peter thought it was *"Schön ist die Nacht"* — as they sliced their way through the cane. Heft. Swing. Slice. Heft. Swing. Slice. Maus's lips moved in time to the rhythm he was creating with his cane knife, and without really meaning to, Peter matched his tempo. He could see, in his mind's eye, his mother sitting at the kitchen table, humming the familiar song along with their crackling radio while she peeled potatoes. He missed her voice, missed the way it felt when she touched his cheek with those warm, worn hands, missed the way she used to comfort him. He was twenty-three; was that too old to miss one's mother?

Sweat was pouring from Peter's brow twenty minutes later as he paused to gather an armful of cane stalks. He took them to the first of four wagons hitched to an enormous, faded yellow tractor with tanklike continuous tracks over the wheels to keep the vehicle from sinking in the muck. The workers would labor each day to load the wagons, and then they'd accompany the tractor to the train tracks, where they'd hoist the cane, armload by armload, into train cars bound for the sugar mill.

"I'd give anything for a cool dip in the water right now," Maus said as Peter returned to cutting. "Anything to escape this heat."

Peter followed Maus's eyes to the shallow ditch that bordered the field they were working in. The fields were separated by neat, even canals that weren't more than a meter and a half across or a meter deep. They were there for the times when the workers had to burn the wilted leaves from the cane; it was always done the day that particular field was to be harvested. The cane itself didn't burn, because the stalks were more than 70 percent water, so it was efficient to burn the dead brush first, leaving only a charred field of naked sugarcane behind. It was easier to fell the crop quickly after that without underbrush in the way. The canals were there to keep the fire from jumping to another field.

Unfortunately, the narrow waterways were also a ripe breeding ground for alligators, who lurked in the murky shallows. The huge, scaly beasts generally stayed out of the way, but Peter had heard stories of men who had tried to cool off in the water, only to find their limbs in the vise grip of enormous territorial lizards. "Do you want to get eaten, Maus?" Peter asked.

Maus shrugged. "Would it really be worse than having to work in this heat?"

"Yes," Peter answered immediately. "I am absolutely positive it would be worse."

Both men laughed and went back to cutting. Peter understood what Maus was saying, but for him, the sweat that poured from his brow was cathartic. When he was young, his mother used to tell him that sweat was your body's way of getting the bad out. A fever sweat, for example, was the illness seeping from your pores. *The bad things escape,* his mother used to say, *and then you can start over, good as new.*

Peter wondered now if the sweat that seeped from his brow each day was serving the same purpose: getting the bad things out. All those terrible things he'd seen on the battlefield, the guilt he carried for living while Otto had died, the shame he felt for firing into faceless masses of oncoming enemy soldiers, the disgrace of fighting for something he didn't believe in—they were all black stains on his soul. Maybe the grueling work was his atonement. Maybe he'd get to start over one day.

That's what he was thinking when he looked up, his eye caught by something red flashing in the next field over. It was *her,* he realized with a start, the beautiful girl he'd seen three weeks before. She was wearing the same red dress she'd worn in his dreams each night, and this time, she had her arm around the shoulders of a young Negro boy, maybe twelve or thirteen, who was cradling his right hand and crying.

Without considering the consequences, Peter hurried, cane knife in hand, toward the edge of the canal separating his field from hers. The girl and the boy were walking quickly through the stalks, and they weren't looking in his direction.

"We just need to clean the wound out," Peter could hear her explaining to the boy as he drew closer. "Then I'll bandage it for you, and you'll be good as new."

Peter was struck by both the musical lilt to her voice and her gentleness with the injured boy. "I can help!" Peter heard himself call in English. He clapped a hand over his mouth and spun around, afraid one of the guards or the foreman had heard, but they were nowhere to be seen. Maus, however, was staring at Peter. When Peter turned back, he saw that the girl and boy had stopped and were looking right at him. The boy looked scared, but the girl wore a different kind of expression. Her pink cheeks had paled, and her eyes were wide.

"It's you," she said, taking a step closer to the canal. Now, they were just three meters from each other, separated only by a shallow strip of water that Peter knew he could jump over easily. But he wouldn't. Not now. He might scare her. And that was the last thing he wanted to do. Instead, he held her gaze, simply because he couldn't force himself to look away. As her eyes seared into him in the charged silence, he felt a strange fluttering in his chest.

"Hello," Peter finally said, and he was disappointed when his single word seemed to snap the girl out of her trance.

She lowered her eyes. "I'm sorry. I must have thought you were someone else."

As her gaze returned to his, Peter could feel his own cheeks growing warm, warmer than the sun had already made them. "No, I'm only me," he said, but he immediately wanted to kick himself. What kind of fool would say such a thing? *I'm only me?*

But then the girl surprised him by laughing. "I suppose we all are," she said. "Only ourselves, that is."

Peter nodded, still flustered. "'To be yourself in a world that is constantly trying to make you something else is the greatest accomplishment,'" he blurted out, instantly convinced that reciting an obscure quote was even more foolish.

"You know Ralph Waldo Emerson?" she asked.

Peter could feel his eyes widen. "You know him too?"

"He's one of my favorites." She studied him more closely across the ribbon of murky water. "But you are German, aren't you? How do you know an American writer? How do you know English so well?"

"I've always admired your language. I love the way Emerson wrote, and as I learned English, I made it a point to study him." He didn't mention the fact that he'd kept a book of Emerson's poems hidden under his bed in Holzkirchen, refusing to take it to the town's book burning when Hitler had ordered all foreign books destroyed. At night, when he'd read it by candlelight, he'd felt a bit like he was standing up to the rat pirate.

"You learned English in school?" the girl asked.

"Yes," Peter replied. "But I also studied it at home. My best friend and I talked of coming to America one day." He thought of Otto and looked down at his work clothes, stamped with the unmistakable letters *POW*. He felt a wave of shame as he added, "Although I didn't imagine coming like this."

"He's a prisoner," the young boy spoke up. "You ain't supposed to talk to prisoners."

"Why don't you run along to my house?" the girl said to the injured boy. Peter followed her gaze to a wooden house in the near distance, just over the edge of a sugarcane field. He could spot vegetables of some sort growing in neat rows and a small barn toward the back of the property. It was, he realized, a family farm. "I'll be along in just a minute, Jeremiah. I'll fix up your hand then."

"I don't want to leave you alone with this German," the boy said, glaring at Peter. "He might try to hurt you."

"He won't hurt me," the girl said. "Please, Jeremiah. Go, and I'll be there in a moment."

The boy nodded reluctantly, and giving Peter one last pointed scowl, he turned away and headed to the house the girl had pointed to.

"What happened to him?" Peter asked after a moment.

"He cut his hand on a cane knife. He works on my family's farm from time to time when sugarcane isn't in season."

Peter nodded. "You should put some alcohol on that wound too. To disinfect it."

The girl smiled. "I know."

"Peter!" Maus called out from somewhere behind him. Peter jerked around, surprised. He'd nearly forgotten that he wasn't alone in the world with the girl in the red dress. "Peter, what are you doing? The guard will see you!"

Peter waved him off, and Maus shook his head, stared for a moment at the girl, and turned back around, hoisting his cane knife high.

"I should go," said the girl, and suddenly, Peter felt a sense of panic.

"Wait!" he cried as she began to walk away.

She stopped and turned expectantly.

"I —" he began, suddenly at a loss. He had no idea what to say or how to make her stay.

But the girl seemed to read his mind. "I'm Margaret," she said.

Margaret, he thought. It was the loveliest name he'd ever heard. "Peter," he managed. "I'm Peter."

"Peter," she repeated in her musical voice. No one had ever said Peter's name as beautifully, as perfectly, as that. But before he could say another word, she was already walking away. He stared after her until he could no longer hear her footfalls in the muck, and then slowly, he sank to his knees, the wind knocked out of him.

"Peter?" Maus was saying his name with concern somewhere in the distance, but Peter couldn't move. Something had just changed within him, something he couldn't quite put a finger on, but he had the strange feeling it had altered the course of everything.

"Peter!" Maus said again, this time much closer to Peter's ear. Peter turned around and was surprised to see Maus right behind him, his face tense with concern. "Come on! I can hear the guards coming back. What is wrong with you? You've never seen a pretty girl before?"

Peter didn't reply, but he let Maus drag him back to the field, where once again, he began to slice through the stalks of sugarcane. And even though he was surrounded by dozens of his countrymen, even though someone had begun singing the familiar *"Memelwacht"* in the next row of stalls, Peter suddenly felt more alone than ever, lost in a forest of cloying sweetness, a million miles from home.

CHAPTER SEVEN

B ack at home that evening, I heated up yet another Lean Cuisine, sat down with my laptop on the back porch, and googled *Peter A. Dahler*. Pages of search results appeared instantly, but they all seemed connected to a Danish professor who was obviously too young to be the Peter Dahler I was looking for. There were a few stray results for other Peter Dahlers, but they all led to unused Twitter accounts or family tree projects in which the Peter in question was the wrong age.

I checked the envelope Jeremiah had given me and entered in the barely legible Holzkirchen return address, but that didn't bring up anything other than a Google map indicating that it was located on a side street near the town center. I tried searching for the address with the last name Dahler, but that didn't bring up anything meaningful either.

Other than discovering that Holzkirchen was just thirty minutes from Munich, where the painting had been shipped from, I came up empty. Tomorrow morning, I would call my ex-boyfriend Scott at the *Orlando Sentinel* to ask if he could run a search for

Peter A. Dahler using the newspaper's research system; their software would scroll through driver's license databases across the country and a few registries in Europe too. In the meantime, though, I had hit a wall.

I gave up on looking for Peter for the time being and instead entered *German POWs in U.S. during WWII*. I still couldn't quite believe what Jeremiah had told me—that during the Second World War, German soldiers had been employed in civilian jobs all over our country. But as soon as I began scanning search results, I realized that the prison camp system across the United States was even more extensive than he had described. For the next hour, I read quickly, my surprise growing as I scanned page after page of information.

I was floored to learn that nearly four hundred thousand Germans had been imprisoned in the United States during the 1940s, but that newspaper coverage of the POW camps was limited, so many Americans didn't even know about them. Most of the prisoners had been captured in battle or on German U-boats and had been brought to the States to work. According to the Geneva Conventions, enlisted prisoners could be used for labor, but only if they were paid and worked reasonable hours, so most were on a roughly nine-to-five schedule and received eighty cents a day, equivalent to an American private's pay in the army at the time.

Apparently some seven hundred prison camps were dotted all across the country—in almost every state, although the majority of the prisoners were housed in the South. Many of the larger camps provided university-level courses, English instruction, libraries, church services, soccer fields, and great medical care. For soldiers who had come from an economically depressed Germany, this was, in some cases, the most comfortably they'd ever lived.

There were a handful of escape attempts and complaints from locals angry about having the enemy in their backyards, but most of the experiences I read about seemed positive. As many as five thousand Germans had enjoyed their lives in America so much that they decided to immigrate to the United States after the war. Yet two generations on, none of this was common knowledge. How could I have never known there were German prisoners here, when they'd clearly been such a vital part of the wartime economy?

My phone rang, and I sighed and snapped my laptop shut. My father's name came up on the caller ID, and I hesitated before answering.

"Hi, Emily. I'm calling to see if you managed to get in touch with Jeremiah Beltrain." His tone was all business, which made me feel surprisingly sad. There was a part of me—a foolish part, admittedly—that was hoping for more. Hadn't my father been trying to make amends for years? Hadn't I finally let him in the door a little bit? Perhaps his brusqueness should have been a relief—after all, I was the one determined to put up walls. Instead, I felt let down.

"Actually, I made a trip down to Belle Creek, where Grandma Margaret grew up, earlier today."

"Belle Creek? But that's hours away, isn't it?"

"Jeremiah said he wanted to meet in person, and I didn't see any reason not to. Anyhow, he had some answers for us." I took a deep breath. "From what he told me, it appears that your father might have been a German prisoner of war."

"You're saying my father was a Nazi?" He sounded horrified.

"No," I said quickly. "Or—I suppose it's possible, but I don't think that's a conclusion we can draw. According to what I've read so far, and what Jeremiah said, the majority of the enlisted men who were captured and brought to the States didn't identify with the Nazi Party. Most were just young men who had no choice but to fight for their country."

"But . . . I don't understand." His voice sounded hollow. "What were Germans doing over here during the war?"

I quickly recounted what Jeremiah had said, then I explained what I'd just learned about the prevalence of German POWs in the United States.

"You're telling me that there were four hundred *thousand* POWs here?" he interrupted.

"It was news to me too."

My father was silent for a moment. "So what on earth happened? How did my mother wind up getting involved with a German prisoner? Who was he?"

"His name was Peter Dahler. It sounds like they were in love. Jeremiah said that both he and Grandma Margaret thought that Peter was a good man."

My father choked on a laugh. "A good man? Good men don't wind up in prison camps, seducing local girls."

"I don't think it was like that." I didn't know why I was defending Peter Dahler; he obviously hadn't turned out to be such a great guy in the end. But something about the painting and the note that had come with it made me believe there was more to the story.

"So Jeremiah is positive that this Peter fellow is my father?" His voice cracked on the last word, and I realized for the first time how much this was bothering him. "How could he—?" My father trailed off in midsentence, and I closed my eyes, knowing exactly what he was going to say. *How could he vanish like that?* He cleared his throat, obviously aware of his near-stumble, and tried again. "So now what? Mystery solved?"

"Not at all. If Peter Dahler left your mother and never looked back, what explanation is there for the painting? I have the feeling we've only scratched the tip of the iceberg here."

"Maybe that's far enough," my father said softly. "Maybe there's a reason your grandmother didn't want us poking into this."

"Actually, I think she'd want us to know the truth," I said. "I'm just not sure she knew it herself."

———

Myra dropped by for a drink that night at nine thirty, after she'd put her daughter, Samantha, to bed. Her husband had been happy to stay home on their couch watching football, and Myra had practically begged me over the phone to give her an excuse to get out of the house. We lived four blocks from each other in the historic Colonialtown neighborhood just east of downtown Orlando, where the homes dated back to the 1920s and the streets were tree-lined and filled with joggers and dog walkers.

"Sometimes, the two of them just drive me crazy," she said, settling into an Adirondack chair on my front porch as I handed her a glass of chardonnay. She took a long sip as I sat down on the chair beside her. "I mean, if I have to hear Jay say one more word about how great the New England Patriots are, I might actually have to strangle him. And Samantha is in this phase now where she refuses to go to bed at her bedtime, because she's afraid she's missing whatever else is going on in our household. Apparently in her four-year-old brain, the moment the lights are out in her bedroom, the living room turns into a full-on disco filled with *Sesame Street* characters."

I laughed and clinked glasses with her. "Now I have a mental image of you doing the hustle with Big Bird."

"Nah, I only dance with Elmo." She smiled, and I felt a little stab of pain in my heart as I thought about all I'd missed out on with my own child.

I shook my head and forced a smile. "So you'll never believe where I was today."

"Somewhere more exciting than the *Sesame Street* disco?"

I laughed and recapped the arrival of the painting, my meeting with my dad, and my visit with Jeremiah. When I finished, Myra was staring at me, her eyes wide.

"I don't even know where to begin," she said. "I mean, you voluntarily reached out to your *dad*? That's huge. And you're finding out that sweet little Grandma Margaret had some kind of sordid love affair with a German prisoner?"

"I don't know that it was sordid, exactly."

She waved me off. "Don't rain on my parade, lady. This is splashier than a soap opera. Seriously, though, what are you going to do next? You have to find this Peter guy!"

"I know." I avoided her gaze as I added, "I'm going to call Scott in the morning to ask for his help."

"Scott," she said finally, her voice flat. "Scott Caruso, who dumped you last year because, according to him, you didn't have enough time to dedicate to him."

"Yes." I cringed.

"Scott, who had a new girlfriend within a week. After dating you for seven months."

"I was never really that serious about him anyhow." I avoided her gaze.

She sighed. "But when are you serious about anyone, Emily?"

"So now you're on Scott's side?"

She snorted. "Hardly. You know I never thought he was right for you. I wanted to throw a party when the two of you broke up.

But you have to admit, in the whole time I've known you, you've never really thrown yourself into any relationship. You just kind of coast along, waiting for it to end."

I shrugged and looked out at the darkness beyond my front porch. How could I tell her that the last time I'd really loved someone was eighteen years ago, when I was head over heels in love with Nick? I'd always thought I'd find someone else who I felt that way about, but half a lifetime later, I was still looking— and still thinking of the high school boyfriend I'd walked away from. Clearly there was something wrong with me. "Can we change the subject?" I muttered.

Myra gave me a look. "Why not? We always do."

I ignored the dig. "Okay, so I've been thinking about this supposed grandfather of mine all day. I just can't piece it together. My grandmother was such a cautious person, and she always seemed to know when someone wasn't a good person. The thing is, I can't figure out how she'd judge this Peter Dahler guy so incorrectly. If what Jeremiah said was accurate, she was completely in love with him, and then he just dropped off the face of the planet."

"First of all, you have to remember that your grandmother was basically just a kid at the time. What was she, eighteen or nineteen? Think of all the dumb decisions we made at that age."

I nodded and looked away. Did sleeping with Nick count as a dumb decision? Or was it just the leaving that was the stupidest thing I'd ever done? "I guess."

"And who's to say she was cautious back then?" Myra continued. "Maybe that experience changed her. Maybe this Peter guy was responsible for making her a different person."

"Do you really think one bad experience has the power to change a person's character that way?"

"I think that if you love someone enough and they hurt you deeply, it can change you forever."

I swallowed hard, thinking for the first time that Peter Dahler leaving my grandmother had a certain parallel to the way I'd left Nick. But maybe Peter Dahler had had his reasons, like I had. Maybe he'd never meant to hurt my grandmother. Maybe he'd been trying to do the right thing and had only realized later that he'd made the biggest mistake of his life. When I thought of it that way, the note with the painting made more sense. "I think I have to find out what happened," I said, glancing at Myra.

"I agree that it's worth trying to track down an explanation," Myra said slowly. "After all, the painting has to mean *something*, right? But you have a lot on your plate now. Don't you need to be going after some more freelance work? Figuring out your next move?"

"I have some money in savings, and I haven't taken a real vacation in years. Maybe this is worth taking a little time for. And who knows? Maybe at the end of it, I'll have learned something. Maybe I can write one of those first-person pieces for *Redbook* or something. Or one of those Modern Love essays for the *New York Times*. I've always wanted to write for them."

"I just don't want you getting hurt." She paused. "I mean, are you planning to involve your father in this?"

I looked away. "He *is* involved, isn't he? I mean, this is his history even more than it's mine."

"That doesn't mean you have to roll out the red carpet for him to hurt you like he did when you were a kid."

"You think I'm making a mistake," I said softly.

"Are you?"

I shrugged but didn't say anything. I didn't know the answer.

"No offense," she said after a moment, her tone a little gentler, "but your family is already a bit of a mess. Who knows what you'll find out? And talking to your dad right now, Emily? I just don't know. Maybe there's something to be said for the past remaining in the past."

I considered this for a moment. "But the thing is, the past never really stays in the past, does it? You can't bury it, because it influences everything."

"Are you quoting your column at me right now?"

"I just have the feeling that figuring out what happened will change my life somehow."

Myra looked at me for a long time before speaking. "Or maybe the best way to change your life is to look inside yourself. But that's harder to do, isn't it?"

"Emily? Geez, it's been a while," Scott said when he answered my call just before eleven that evening, after Myra had gone home.

"I hope I'm not calling too late."

"Nah, you know me. I'm a night owl."

"I remember." It was one of the problems that had plagued our short relationship. I liked to get up early to work, so on weeknights, I was usually in bed by ten thirty. Scott, on the other hand, loved to go out, and he often got frustrated when I told him I'd prefer to turn in. I was always a zombie the next day when I stayed out late, whereas Scott seemed to thrive on refueling with multiple cups of Starbucks in the morning.

"So what's up?" Scott asked. "I was just headed out to Casey's, actually. Dan is playing there tonight. You remember him?"

"Yeah. Tell him hi for me." Dan was a friend of Scott's and a talented local musician who often played acoustic guitar at Scott's favorite bar. "So . . . I was actually calling to ask you a favor."

"A favor, hmm?" Scott's tone had turned playful. "It's going to cost you."

"Are you flirting with me?"

He laughed. "So what if I am?"

"I thought you were dating Lila."

"We broke up a few months ago. I'm single again, in case that information interests you." Yes, he was definitely flirting. I wasn't sure how I felt about that. I was still attracted to him, but we had obviously crashed and burned the first time around. Wasn't that enough to warrant keeping my distance now?

"So what's this favor?" Scott asked after a pause.

"I need you to run a database search for me, if you don't mind."

"Ah, so you're calling about business."

"Well, it's actually more of a personal thing."

"Now I'm intrigued." I could hear the smile in his voice. "Want to meet me at Casey's in a few minutes? I'll buy you a drink, and you can tell me all about it."

"How about breakfast instead? My treat."

"Make it Dexter's tomorrow morning at nine, and you have a deal."

I smiled. It had been our favorite brunch spot when we were dating. "I'll see you there."

"Great. And Emily?"

"Yeah?"

"I miss you."

I paused, surprised. But did he mean it, or were they just empty words? "I miss you too," I said, not entirely sure whether I was telling the truth. "See you in the morning."

CHAPTER EIGHT

I woke up the next day thinking of Catherine, as I often did. I went for a run around Lake Eola, and as my feet pounded the pavement, I let my mind wander back to the night Nick and I had conceived her. The ridiculous irony of it was that we'd only slept together once; we were like one of those this-could-happen-to-you after-school specials. I'd told my mother two days later that I'd lost my virginity, because we'd had the kind of relationship where we shared everything, even the things you weren't supposed to tell a parent. "Just be careful," she'd said, and later, after she had died and I thought back on the conversation, I had the strange feeling she could see into the future. "The decisions you make now will impact you forever. And you're still so young, Emily. If he really loves you, he'll be there when you both grow up. No reason to rush things."

But it hadn't felt like a rush. It had felt inevitable. Nick was different from other guys our age; he was funny and a little nerdy and wore his heart on his sleeve. While other guys seemed to delight in pressuring girls to go to third base and then ignoring them, Nick wrote me endearingly corny poems and drew little cartoon pictures of us, which he slipped into my locker between classes. Every kiss with him felt magical, because he always took his time, cupping my cheek with one hand and resting the other gently on the back of my head, as if he was cradling something delicate and important. His mouth on mine was always tender, deliberate, and sometimes, although my body was responding and my heartbeat quickening, I forced myself to pause and savor the sweet slowness of the moment, the fact that Nick always seemed to treat each kiss like the very first one.

On the night we'd slept together—in his bedroom, when his parents were out at a work function for his dad's office—he'd asked me if I was sure I wanted to do this.

"I love you, Emily," he'd said, his pupils dilated and his voice husky as he looked into my eyes. "I don't want you to feel any pressure. We don't have to do this."

But I could tell that he wanted to as much as I did, and there wasn't a doubt in my mind that this was the right thing. "I know. I want to lose my virginity to you," I'd said firmly.

His response was a guttural moan as his lips fell on mine again. After that, he'd taken his time, slowly peeling my clothes away from my body. He'd run his fingers and then his lips over every inch of me until I was practically begging, although I was terrified of what it would feel like. He'd felt my fear, and he'd waited until it had melted away in a haze of anticipation and ecstasy before he finally slid between my legs.

I'd cried out, and his face had filled with concern for a second, but I'd pulled him toward me before he could say anything, and my body took over, rising and falling in rhythm with his. I'd never felt so close to someone before, so intertwined with another person, and when we were finished, lying sweaty and smiling and tangled in his sheets, I swore I would never forget the way I felt that day.

And I hadn't. I'd tried to, because it wasn't normal to be thinking all these years later of the night I'd lost my virginity. But that day had been a force that changed my life in more ways than one. And at the times I'd felt the loneliest over the last eighteen years, I'd sometimes retreated to those lost moments, to that feeling of total and utter belonging and connectedness I'd felt with him that night.

But my mother had died three weeks later, and after that, everything had changed. It had to. I didn't know how to believe in anything anymore. Even Nick.

After my run, I showered, changed, shook my thoughts of Nick off, and walked to Dexter's, about a half mile from my house. Unsurprisingly, Scott was twenty minutes late, but he hurried in full of apologies about how he'd closed the bar down last night and had slept through his alarm this morning. Instead of making me feel annoyed, his excuses—a reminder of the way things had been between us—just made me weary.

"Look, Emily, I'm really sorry," he said after he'd ordered a cup of coffee and looked at the menu.

I just looked at him.

"For everything," he elaborated when I didn't say anything. "For the way things ended between us. I was wrong, and I'm sorry. I was a crappy boyfriend. I see that now. I took you for granted, and I screwed everything up."

I took a deep breath. "I'm not very good at the girlfriend thing either," I admitted. "It wasn't all your fault."

He nodded, accepting this. "What do you think about trying again?"

I blinked at him a few times. "Why would it work this time around?"

He shrugged. "Maybe it would, and maybe it wouldn't. But I always felt like we were good together, Emily. We had fun, at least."

"But there's more to a relationship than having fun, isn't there?" I hated the way I sounded, but I knew I was right. "There's that feeling of really *getting* each other. And I don't think you ever really got me."

Scott shifted in his chair. "I could try harder. To get you, I mean. Maybe we should just see."

We were interrupted by the arrival of our waitress, who took our breakfast order: the restaurant's specialty eggs Benedict and a glass of orange juice for me, a breakfast BLT and Bloody Mary for Scott. When she walked away, I dove right into my request before Scott could return to the subject of us, because frankly, I didn't know what to say.

"I was hoping you could do me a favor," I began.

"Ah, the mysterious favor that summoned me here at the ungodly hour of nine a.m." He glanced at his watch and grinned. "Well, nine thirty. So what is it? What can I help with?"

"It's about my grandfather."

"I met him, right?"

I sighed. I knew I'd told him about my family, about how Grandma Margaret had raised my dad alone. I'd also told him that my mother's parents had died before I was born. If he'd given a shred of thought to it, he'd realize there was no way he could have met my grandfather—but that was Scott in a nutshell. "No," I said. "But I'd love your help in tracking him down."

As Scott leaned forward and listened intently, I told him the short version of Jeremiah's story, concluding with the fact that the man who was probably my grandfather was named Peter Dahler and had wound up back in Holzkirchen, Germany—close to where the painting had been mailed from.

"So what do you think?" I asked. "Could you track this Peter Dahler down?"

"I'll see what I can do," he said. "Of course our database does a much better job of finding people within the United States, but my friend Neil works for the London *Times,* and he might have access to some resources that I don't. Either way, write down the details, and I'll give it a try."

I dug in my purse for the notes I'd written earlier about Peter Dahler, including his name, his middle initial, his potential age range, and the address in Munich from which Grandma Margaret had received the last letter. I handed the paper over to Scott. "Here's everything I know."

Scott scanned the piece of paper and nodded. "Okay. I'm on it." He slipped the paper into his shirt breast pocket. "I'll get started when I get in to work today."

"You're the best. I owe you one."

He arched an eyebrow and leaned in conspiratorially. "I'll keep that in mind."

Our food arrived five minutes later, and as we ate, we caught up on each other's families and friends. I was happy to hear that Scott's little sister was getting married in the spring, and he seemed surprised but pleased to hear I'd spoken with my father a few times. "I always thought you should forgive him," he said.

The words rubbed me the wrong way. "Sure. Everyone should go around screwing me over, and it's just my job to let it go."

Scott's smile faltered. "That's not what I'm saying. Just that family means something." He patted the pocket where he'd put my Peter Dahler notes. "But you know that. After all, you're trying to track down your granddad, aren't you?"

Twenty minutes later, I insisted on paying since Scott was doing me a favor, and we walked together to the door, where Scott gave me a quick hug good-bye. "Think about what I said about me and you, okay? Life's short; you have to seize the opportunities and all that, right?"

"Right," I said, but I wasn't thinking of him. I was thinking of all the opportunities I'd squandered in the past and wondering if it was too late.

———————————

I was home by 11:15, and after studying the painting for a while more, as if it could tell me something, I dug out the information Jeremiah had given me for Julie Candless, Louise's granddaughter.

I dialed her number, and someone picked up after just two rings. "Hi," I said tentatively. "I'm looking for Julie Candless."

"You've reached her."

"My name is Emily Emerson." I was lousy at figuring out family trees, but I took a stab in the dark. "I think I'm your second cousin. Or your second cousin once removed or something like that."

"I don't have a cousin named Emily."

"I'm Margaret's granddaughter," I told her. "Margaret was your grandmother Louise's sister, I think."

"Oh, right." She sounded surprised. "But how'd you get my number? I don't think my grandmother talked to her sister in, like, sixty years."

"Do you know Jeremiah Beltrain? I met with him yesterday.

He thought you might know some things about my grandmother and her past."

Julie hesitated. "I doubt I know anything you don't, considering I never even met her."

"I'm specifically wondering about the years she lived in Belle Creek. Especially the end, when she apparently fell in love with a German prisoner of war. I think he might be my grandfather."

"Your grandmother never talked about it?"

"No." I glanced across the room at the painting. "I think he really hurt her. But now I'm wondering if there's more to the story."

Julie was silent for so long that I began to wonder if she'd hung up.

"Julie?" I ventured.

"Are you still here in Belle Creek? Do you have time to swing by my house?"

My heartbeat picked up, and I glanced at my watch. "I can be there by about two fifteen. Will that work?"

"Yeah, I guess. Let me give you my address. But I hate to get your hopes up. I'm not sure how much I'll be able to help you. I just have some letters and stuff."

"Letters?"

"I'll show you when you get here." She gave me her address and directions, and then we hung up with a promise to see each other soon.

Two and a half hours later, I was pulling off the main road into Belle Creek, noting once again what a different world it was here. As a longtime Floridian, I knew that most of the state's big cities, including Orlando, had cow pastures, orange groves, and farms on the outlying edges of their urban sprawl, but the setting in Belle Creek was somehow different from all that. The buildings on the town's tiny main square all looked like they were built in the 1920s or 1930s, and the rest of the town seemed to match. It was clean and well preserved, but it also felt trapped in time.

As I made my way out toward Julie's house, I passed field upon field of sugarcane, the stalks swaying in the breeze like giant blades of grass. I rolled down my windows to get a better look and was surprised to discover they smelled faintly like creamed corn. White egrets pecked at the dirt, and vultures circled lazily overhead. When the wind picked up, the rippling fields sounded like they were whispering. The featherlike plumes atop some of the stalks were so wispy and insubstantial that they appeared to float like fairies above the earth.

I slowed down to a crawl and tried to imagine my grandmother here. When she met Peter, she would have been roughly the same age my daughter was now, I realized with a start. It was as hard for me to imagine my grandmother at eighteen with her whole life before her as it was for me to imagine Catherine at eighteen with her whole childhood behind her. I had the overwhelming sense that in both cases, time had moved too quickly.

I continued down the dirt road until I was at the end of a huge expanse of sugarcane. I knew that Jeremiah's house was off to the right, behind a small thatch of palm trees, but at the fork in the road, I turned left instead to head toward Julie's. I pulled into the third driveway I came upon, about a mile down on the right, just as she'd directed.

The house was wooden and painted yellow, and although it looked old and ill-constructed, it also appeared well kept. There was an old, maroon Toyota Corolla out front and a child's bike tipped into a neat bed of marigolds. I parked behind the Toyota and walked up to the front door.

The woman who answered looked about a decade younger

than I was, but I could see the family resemblance. She had my grandmother's eyes, slightly almond shaped with long lashes, and the same narrow chin. "Julie?" I asked.

"You must be Emily." She looked me up and down. "Come in."

She ushered me into a brightly lit kitchen that looked like it hadn't been remodeled since the 1970s. "Can I get you a glass of lemonade or anything?" she asked as I sat down at the chipped kitchen table.

"That sounds great."

She was silent as she poured two drinks, then she sat down across from me, pushing one of the glasses across the table. I took a sip and smiled at her. "Thanks so much for having me over on such short notice," I said.

"You *are* family, I guess."

I nodded. "I heard your grandmother passed away last month. I'm sorry to hear that."

"Thanks." Julie looked away. "This was her house, you know. The house she and your grandmother were born in and grew up in. I was living with her these last few years. I've been trying to get my college degree."

"Good for you," I murmured, looking around and trying to imagine what the house must have been like seventy-five years ago, when my grandmother still lived here. It was strange to think I was sitting in the same kitchen where she'd likely had her very first meal, the kitchen where she'd probably sat daydreaming about Peter Dahler long ago.

"Palm Beach Atlantic," Julie went on. "They have a degree in organizational management. I'm taking it slow, because I work too, but I'm getting there. It helps to live here rent-free."

"That was nice of your grandmother."

"She was mostly a nice lady, you know." Her words sounded

almost combative, as if she was challenging me. "She didn't have very good things to say about your grandmother."

I refocused on Julie and frowned. It was a strange thing to tell a virtual stranger, and I felt instantly defensive. But I didn't want to risk offending her for fear that she wouldn't tell me about the letters she'd mentioned on the phone, so I bit my tongue and tried to think of something nonconfrontational to say.

"But then again, I think my grandmother had a very closed mind sometimes," Julie added before I had a chance to formulate a response. "And she held grudges. Boy, did she hold grudges!"

"You're saying she held a grudge against my grandmother?"

"Understatement of the year." She shook her head. "Imagine feeling like that most of your life. It's crazy when you think about it."

"Do you know why she was so angry at her?"

"Yeah, I do." Julie studied me for a moment and then abruptly pulled a small sheaf of papers from her back pocket.

"You know there was a man," she began, holding the papers up. "The German. He ruined everything in this family." She sighed. "Or maybe it wasn't him who ruined things. Maybe it was the fact that my grandmother's parents were just as pigheaded as she was."

"So you know something about Peter Dahler?"

"Only a few things. My grandmother didn't talk about the situation much. I didn't even know she had a sister until I was a teenager." She looked up at me. "But in the end, she talked about her a lot. I think she was sorry. I think that's why she gave me these letters." She held up the papers in her hand.

I followed her gaze, my heart thudding. "Are they from him? Peter Dahler?"

She didn't answer my question right away. Instead, she

turned to look out the window, where the sugarcane fields were visible beyond several shorter rows of what appeared to be some sort of vegetable crop. Green beans, I guessed from what Jeremiah had told me. "I think your grandmother really loved the German. But that made my grandma furious. She was older by two years, and she had a fiancé, Jimmy, who'd just been killed in the war. By a German." She paused. "So I guess you could say the timing was bad for a German POW camp to land practically in her backyard."

"Geez, I'm sorry," I murmured.

Julie shrugged. "Yeah, I'm sorry too. But if this Jimmy hadn't died, my grandma wouldn't have met my grandfather, and I wouldn't be here. So maybe things work out the way they're supposed to somehow, right? Anyhow, far as I know, what happened was that your grandmother fell in love with one of the prisoners, and my grandmother took it like a complete betrayal. Can you blame her? All she could see was that a German had shot her Jimmy in the head, and there her little sister was gallivanting with the enemy. When it turned out your grandmother was pregnant—and the father was obviously the German—I think my grandmother just snapped. She called her little sister a whore and told the whole town. Of course that mortified their parents. And it sounds like my grandmother's father had a temper, a bad one. They wanted your grandma to give the baby away, because of course the whole thing brought shame to the family. But your grandma, well, apparently she was in love with the German and was convinced he was coming back for her. As you know, she kept the baby, and her parents threw her out."

I shook my head. "But he never came back."

Julie chewed her lip. "But I think maybe he wanted to. For a while anyhow." She hesitated then handed me the envelopes in her hand. There were three of them, and they were yellowed at the edges.

I stared at them for a moment. All three were from a return address in Barnoldswick, England. All three listed Peter A. Dahler as the sender. "He wrote to her," I said softly. But what was he doing in England after the war?

"My grandma said there were more. She only kept three." She hesitated. "I think maybe there was a part of her that felt bad, that wanted your grandma to know he'd cared after all. But it was too late."

"So what about the letter my grandmother *did* receive?" I asked. "Jeremiah gave it to me. It was supposedly from Peter, and he said he was marrying someone else. He wasn't coming back for her. Did your grandmother forge that or something?"

"No. It was the only letter they gave to Margaret, for obvious reasons. But it really did come from Peter Dahler, far as I know. I'm sorry."

I nodded, my heart sinking again. Regardless of what promises he'd made in the letters I now held in my hands, he'd failed her in the end. Maybe it was better that my grandmother had never seen these, had never been allowed to hope.

"The thing is," Julie said after a minute, "unless he's just really good with words, I think he really loved your grandmother. It's hard to believe that he fell out of love with her so quickly. It just doesn't make sense."

"None of it does," I agreed, thinking of the note that had accompanied the painting last week. "Can I have these?" I held up the letters.

Julie nodded. "For what it's worth, I think my grandma was real sorry about what she'd done. I think that in the end, she realized she just might have ruined her little sister's life."

I stood up and tucked the letters into my back pocket. "Her life wasn't ruined," I said. "But I also think that maybe it wasn't complete. And I want to understand what happened."

Julie stood too and walked me to the door. "If there's anything else I can do to help, will you let me know? I owe you at least that. Considering what my grandma did."

I nodded, thanked her, and leaned in for a quick hug. I wasn't sure I'd ever consider Julie family, but she was a connection to a piece of my grandmother's past I'd never known about, and that was something.

I pulled the letters out of my pocket and set them on the passenger seat before starting my car. I was dying to read them, but I didn't want to do it in Julie's driveway, for although this might have been where my grandmother's story had begun, it was also the place where her heart had been broken. I wanted to put some distance between myself and this place before I opened that particular door to the past.

CHAPTER NINE

DECEMBER 1944

Love was a funny thing, Peter thought. You grow up thinking you'll have some control over it—when you'll fall in love, who you'll fall in love with. But then life surprises you out of nowhere, and you fall in love when the world is falling apart, with a person you never could have predicted, from the other side of the globe. Who would have thought Peter would be in America—falling in *love* with America—never mind falling in love with an American woman he was forbidden to talk to?

But it had happened. There was no denying it. Now Margaret was all he thought about, and he knew she thought of him too, which was all the more miraculous and unbelievable.

Margaret. Margaret Mae Evans. Peter wasn't sure if a more beautiful name had ever existed, a more perfect woman.

Suddenly, the days no longer felt endless and arduous. Yes, every one of Peter's limbs ached constantly, and sometimes he thought he'd simply collapse from dehydration in the middle of one of the vast fields of cane. But now, the beating sunlight was something to look forward to, for each day brought a new chance of glimpsing Margaret, a new opportunity to catch her eye or speak to her across the divide of a narrow canal. Exchanging even a few words with her made him feel normal, whole, like a man in charge of his destiny rather than a prisoner whose life was already dictated by forces beyond his control.

She was often with Jeremiah, the boy she'd been helping when Peter saw her for the first time. Jeremiah was twelve, Peter had learned, slight for his age with arms that were sinewy and strong. Peter knew the boy worked hard. He should have been in school, but instead, Jeremiah rose with the sun like the prisoners did and labored in the fields. Sometimes, he cut sugarcane. Other times, Peter saw him harvesting sweet potatoes or green beans at Margaret's or the other small farms that ringed the vast cane fields.

"His mother is dead," Margaret had whispered to Peter one day as he worked on the edge of a field. They were separated, as they often were, by a thin canal and a thousand invisible barriers, and he longed to touch her.

He had glanced at the boy, who was a hundred yards away, weeding a patch of overgrown potatoes. "And what of his father? He doesn't encourage Jeremiah to go to school?"

"He's a drunk," she told him. "Jeremiah has to support him, or they'll lose their home. They'll lose everything."

Peter had looked over to the boy in astonishment. "But he's just a child!"

"In a place like this," she said sadly, "one doesn't stay a child for long." There was something in her eyes that chilled

Peter. But then she blinked and glanced away. "It's why I try to work with him as often as I can," she added. "When I'm in the field with him, I try to continue his lessons. We talk about history and geography and politics. I think I have helped create a boy who wants to change the world."

"Good," Peter said. "We should all want to change the world."

"Yes." Margaret smiled shyly. "There are many things I wish were different, Peter."

He held her gaze. "As do I."

She had told him that she'd had to drop out of school at the age of sixteen to help out on her family farm and that there was no hope of attending university now, for her family was very poor. So she read voraciously, borrowing books from the library two towns over and trying her best to absorb as much poetry, history, and literature as she could. "I want to see the world one day," she had said, her expression suddenly fierce. "I've never even left Florida, but there's so much out there that I must see with my own eyes. Will you tell me, Peter? Will you tell me about the world?"

And so he told her stories of the food he'd eaten in Germany, the tribes he'd encountered in Africa. He sang her the songs that were traditional in Bavaria, and he told her about the time his grandparents took him to London for a month when he was six, and he'd had afternoon tea at the Ritz. He told her about the traditional Christmas tree in his town square and the legend of Christkind, the German equivalent of Santa Claus, and he talked of politics and poverty and Hitler's rise to power.

In turn, she told him of the hurricanes of 1926 and 1928 that nearly wiped out Belle Creek. She told him about the dike Herbert Hoover had ordered built and how it had taken away the lakeshore but would save the town from future disasters. And she told him about her family: her older sister, Louise; her quiet, reserved mother; her hardworking and hot-tempered father.

"I would like to meet them someday," Peter said wistfully late one afternoon, when Margaret had snuck to the edge of the field where he was working to bring him a glass of water. He gulped it down gratefully and looked up to see her wearing a somber expression.

"It isn't possible," she said, her voice dropping to a hushed whisper. "My father fought in the Great War, and he has no warmth toward Germans. And my sister, well, she lost her fiancé, Jimmy, last year, on a battlefield in France."

A knot formed in Peter's stomach. "I'm very sorry to hear that."

"As am I. He was a nice boy, and Louise loved him. But now, well—" Margaret paused. "Now she holds all Germans responsible."

Peter nodded. On some level, he understood this and grieved for Louise. "She hates us." He had seen Louise a handful of times and had already guessed she was Margaret's sister. They had the same brown waves, the same tall, slender frames. But where Margaret's green eyes twinkled and her full mouth always seemed a moment away from curving into a smile, Louise's eyes were cold and empty, and her mouth was set in a thin, hard line. On the days when the prisoners worked near the edge of their farm, Louise often came to the front porch with a shotgun and just stood there, staring. It made Peter uneasy.

"Yes," Margaret said simply. "But one day she will understand that Jimmy died in a war, and that the strings were being pulled by people in power. It was not you who shot him, nor any of the men here. And if Jimmy hadn't been shot, he would have shot others. There is death in war. It's part of the bargain.'"

Peter thought of Otto and how losing his friend was a bargain he never intended, a bargain he'd regret forever. "War is a terrible thing," he said softly. "It turns us all into something lesser, no matter which side we're on." He paused and added, "Even those who aren't on the battlefield are hardened by it, aren't they? Look at the way the town views us, just for being German."

Although the people of Belle Creek were warming slightly to the prisoners—who were, for the most part, polite and hardworking—Peter knew it was easier to see them as a hated class of people rather than as individuals who were just as trapped by circumstance as they were.

"It's a small town, and in small towns, one often finds small minds," Margaret said softly.

Peter smiled. "The same is true of large cities. Small minds aren't dictated by geography."

"I suppose not." She paused. "I've never been to a city, Peter. Will you take me to one someday?"

He stared at her. "I would love to take you anywhere, even to a restaurant for a simple meal. But it is impossible now."

She reached out to touch his arm, and he felt a surge of warmth through his whole body. "It won't always be this way."

"You are so hopeful, Margaret," Peter said. "It is one of the things I love about you." His eyes widened as he realized what he'd said, and he could feel his cheeks burning. But he wouldn't take it back, because it was the truth. He loved so many things about this girl from the other side of the world. He held his breath while he awaited her reply.

She, too, turned pink. "There are many things, Peter, that make you different from anyone I've ever known." She hesitated. "I feel more for you now than I ever have for anyone before. How is that possible? We hardly know each other, and yet, I feel like you're already a permanent piece of my soul."

"Sometimes, things are simply meant to be," Peter replied. He longed to kiss her, but the guards were too close, and he could be shot for such an offense. It was almost worth the risk, but instead, he held her gaze for a long while and imagined a life with her, a future with her. As she stared back, he wondered if she was picturing the same beautiful vision.

Some days, they talked of history and world affairs. Other days, Peter would make her laugh with a joke he'd rehearsed the night before or charm her with a tidbit about his hometown. He loved it when she gazed off to the eastern horizon, as if she could see the Germany he was describing. He knew she understood why he loved his homeland despite what was happening there at the moment.

"You don't have to love everything about a place to carry it in your heart," she said one day in early December. The humidity had dropped off, and though the sun still blazed hot overhead, work had become much more comfortable. "Belle Creek will always be my home, but there are many things wrong here."

"Yes," Peter said simply. He knew what she thinking,

because as she spoke, she glanced over her shoulder at Jeremiah with such sadness that it caused him pain too.

She turned back to Peter and asked softly, "Is it true? The things the newspapers are saying about the camps for Jewish people in Germany and Poland?"

Peter could feel the color drain from his face. He hadn't known of these camps during his time in the *Afrika Korps*, but at Camp Belle Creek, the guards distributed newspapers that told of Allied victories and German atrocities. *It's only propaganda,* many of the prisoners would murmur to each other after lights-out. *It must be. It is only the American government trying to get us to turn our backs on Germany.* But Peter knew better. The reports from the camps were the kinds of things he couldn't imagine a newspaper making up. And he'd seen with his own eyes the deportations of his neighbors, forced to wear yellow stars long before being stripped of their businesses, their homes, and their freedom. "I don't know," Peter finally answered Margaret honestly. "But I fear the worst." What he didn't say was that he didn't know how he'd forgive himself for wearing a German uniform if the stories turned out to be true.

Margaret nodded, her expression grim. "I wish I could say that it is hard to imagine humans treating each other in such a way. But then I witness things here every day that make me question all of humanity."

Her eyes went to Jeremiah again. "There's no reason everyone shouldn't be treated equally, Peter," she said. "No reason at all."

And then, early on the morning before Christmas Eve, Peter and Maus were working on the eastern edge of the sugarcane fields, about a quarter mile from Margaret's farm, when they heard screams. *Margaret's* screams. Peter didn't hesitate before taking off at a full run toward the sound, and Maus, cursing, ran after him. Behind them, Peter could hear the yells and the footfalls of the guards chasing them, but he was faster, far faster, because he was propelled by an icy, desperate fear.

Still, nothing prepared him for the scene that awaited in the trees just beyond Margaret's house.

Jeremiah was hanging from one of the branches of a huge slash pine, his neck twisted precariously, his feet jerking wildly, and his bare chest streaked with blood.

Margaret was still screaming when Peter arrived, her arms wrapped around Jeremiah's thighs as she tried to lift him up, taking the weight off his neck. She was wearing a white cotton dress, and it was drenched crimson in Jeremiah's blood.

Peter rushed to her side immediately and hoisted Jeremiah up from the waist. He was relieved to see that the boy was still breathing, albeit shallowly.

"Margaret, are you okay? Are you hurt?" Peter demanded as Maus ran up begin him, exclaimed in disbelief, and rushed over to help Peter to support the boy's weight.

Within a few seconds, Harold and another guard, a squat man named Carl, burst into the small clearing, guns drawn, yelling for Peter and Maus to get down on the ground. But they both stopped in their tracks when they saw the scene before them.

"What in God's name?" Harold breathed, holstering his gun. He hesitated only a second before ordering Carl to get up on his shoulders. In silence, Peter handed Carl his cane knife, and Carl hacked through the thick rope until Jeremiah, heavy and limp as a sack of flour, fell from the tree. Maus caught him and lowered him gently to the ground, and in an instant, Margaret was draped over him, sobbing as she tried to make sure that he was still breathing.

Peter, Maus, and the guards straightened up and stared at one another in silence. "I thought you were trying to escape," Harold finally said to Peter.

"No, sir," Peter replied. "I heard her screaming."

They all looked at Margaret, and Peter ached to go to her, to hold her, to comfort her, but he knew he couldn't do it in front of the guards. The things he felt for her, the things he hoped she felt for him, were forbidden.

"Miss, what happened here?" Harold asked. "Who's responsible for this?"

"I don't know," Margaret sobbed. From the way she avoided meeting his eye, Peter knew she was lying. "Please, can someone help me get him to my house? We must summon a doctor."

Harold and Carl exchanged looks, and Harold looked at Peter. "Dahler, you grab his arms. I'll take his legs. Maus, you support him in the middle. Gently now."

Without a word, the three men hoisted Jeremiah slowly from the ground. He moaned, and Peter could hear Harold murmur under his breath, "He's just a boy, for God's sake. How could someone do this to a *boy*?" Behind them, Carl was helping Margaret to her feet, and as she leaned into him for support, Peter felt a surge of jealousy, surprising in its power. He should be the one comforting her, the one letting her lean on him, the one drying her tears. Instead, Carl—a man his own age—was holding her close and murmuring to her. Peter swallowed back his anger and focused on Jeremiah, who, still and bloodied, looked far younger than his twelve years.

The men carried Jeremiah to Margaret's house in silence, and for the first time, Peter stepped over her threshold. As his eyes adjusted to the dim light and he helped the others lift Jeremiah to a worn-looking couch in the living room, he drank it all in. This was Margaret's life, the place she'd come from, the place she spent so many of her moments. He wanted to remember it all: the warped wooden floors, the sun-bleached yellow floral curtains framing the windows, the scent of fried fish clinging to the air, the dust particles dancing in the morning light. It was mundane, but it was also somehow magical.

Margaret was still crying as she came in the door with Carl, and Peter took a step toward her.

Maus reached out quickly and put a hand on his arm. "*Mach nicht,*" he said firmly, quietly. *Do not.* And instantly, Peter was reminded of where he was, *who* he was.

He watched helplessly as Margaret hurried down a small hall, emerging a moment later with a roll of bandage cloth and a bottle of grain alcohol. "Can you clean and bandage his wounds, please?" she asked, walking right up to Peter. "And keep him calm and comfortable? I'm going to call the doctor."

"Ma'am," Carl said, stepping forward and giving Peter a dark look. "This boy here's a prisoner. A *German*. We'll take care of things."

"No." Margaret's answer was immediate and fierce. "I saw the way he carried Jeremiah here. He was gentle with him, and kind." She glanced at Peter and held his gaze for a moment. He could read determination, sadness, and fury in her eyes, and he ached again to hold her, to comfort her. Maus's grip on his arm was the only thing holding him in place. "He will stay. I trust him. I need you to go get the sheriff."

Carl hesitated, but Harold answered for him. "He'll go. Carl?"

Carl gave him a dark look, but he hurried out the front door. Harold stood there for a moment, surveying the room, and then his eyes landed on Peter, who had finally pulled away from Maus and was bent down beside Jeremiah, applying alcohol to the boy's wounds. Jeremiah twitched but didn't awaken.

Peter looked up and caught Harold watching him. The guard stared at him for a moment, as if deciding something for himself, and then his expression softened. "You are comfortable caring for the boy, Dahler?" Harold asked.

"Yes, sir," Peter replied. "I know basic first aid. I can help him until the doctor arrives."

Harold nodded. "Well, then, we will leave you to it. Maus and I will keep watch outside until the sheriff comes, in case the boy's attacker comes back." He turned to Margaret. "That okay with you, ma'am?"

Margaret nodded. "Thank you."

Harold glanced once more at Peter, smiled sadly as if he understood everything, and gestured for Maus to follow him outside. When the door had closed behind them, Peter looked up at Margaret.

"He knows," she said simply. "He must know about us. Otherwise, he wouldn't have left me alone with a prisoner."

Peter nodded. "And he didn't try to separate us." The enormity of this was almost staggering, but Peter was too numb to absorb it. "Margaret, what happened to Jeremiah?"

The boy's breaths were coming in ragged spurts as Peter applied alcohol to every spot where his flesh had been ripped open. His chest, Peter realized now, was shredded with what looked like lashes from a whip. More than twenty lines crisscrossed his dark skin, and there was blood everywhere. His face was oozing blood too. "Dear God," Peter murmured.

"They were trying to kill him, Peter," Margaret said. "If I hadn't arrived and scared them away . . ."

Peter looked up at her in astonishment. "You came upon the attack?"

"Yes," she whispered. "I wish I could have killed those men myself. To do this to a boy . . ." She closed her eyes as her voice trailed off again.

He reached up and squeezed her hand. He wanted to embrace her, but he had to tend to Jeremiah first, and there was so much blood. "What happened?"

Margaret took a deep breath and looked at him. "A man named Raymond Chambers accused him of stealing chickens from his farm."

Peter shook his head. "Surely Jeremiah didn't commit this crime."

Margaret shook her head. "Of course not. He'd sooner starve than steal. But Chambers, well, he's a bad man. A bad, bad man."

"What did he have against Jeremiah?"

Margaret bit her lip. "Jeremiah did some work on the Chambers farm last week to earn some extra money, which he desperately needs, and Chambers refused to pay him afterward. Chambers called him names and said he and his people should still be slaves. Jeremiah went to the sheriff about his wages, and the sheriff laughed him right out of the office. But the sheriff must have gone to Chambers about it. It can't be a coincidence that a week later, Jeremiah is suddenly accused of something like this."

"And so they . . . lynched him?" Peter asked, looking back at Jeremiah in horrified disbelief. "You can't stay here, Margaret. You can't continue to live in a place like this."

"What choice do I have?" she asked. "I have no money to start a life somewhere else. But I have to figure out a way to send Jeremiah away. He'll be in danger now."

Peter was silent as he continued to clean Jeremiah's wounds. What they'd done to the boy was almost unthinkable. He would certainly have died if Margaret hadn't come along, and even now, there was a chance he wouldn't survive. He'd lost a lot of blood, and Peter had seen men die on the battlefield from wounds less substantial than these. War was one thing, but to string a man—no, a boy—up by a noose and whip him within an inch of his life was inhuman.

It was Margaret who broke the silence between them. "There were four men there with Raymond Chambers," she said, so softly that her words were almost inaudible. "One of them was my father."

Peter's head jerked up. "Your father?"

She was crying again now. "Peter, the way he looked at me when I burst into the clearing . . . There was such hatred in his eyes. How could he do something like this?"

Peter stood quickly and wrapped her in his arms. "You're not safe here, Margaret."

She looked up at him. "He won't hurt me. Not with my

mother here. I will be fine. I just—I can't imagine that I'm the daughter of a man who's capable of this kind of cruelty."

Peter thought of his own father, a cold, hard man. "We aren't fated to become our parents," he told her. "We can choose to be better."

"Thank God for that." She cried into his chest for a minute, and he held her tightly, his own eyes filling with tears. He was powerless to help her, and that destroyed him. As long as he was a prisoner, he couldn't be there to look out for Margaret. He wouldn't be there to save her if someone tried to hurt her.

Outside, they could hear a vehicle arriving, and then men's voices. Peter hoped it was the doctor, that he'd be able to hand Jeremiah over to someone capable of saving his life. "I hate that I cannot protect you," Peter murmured into Margaret's hair. "I hate that I cannot make things better for you."

She pulled away and looked at him. "Peter, you make everything better."

They stared at each other for a second, and then, before he could second-guess himself, he leaned in and kissed her. She responded immediately, her mouth soft, her tongue gentle, and in the kiss, he could taste the future. For the first time in this seemingly endless war, in a world turned upside down, he could truly imagine a life beyond this moment.

The voices outside were getting closer, and Margaret pulled away. "I love you, Peter Dahler," she whispered.

He stared at her in disbelief. How was it possible that she would love a man like him? "I love you too," he said. "And when this war is over, I will come back for you, Margaret. I know they will send me home to Germany, but I will come back and take you away from this place. I will protect you. I will build a life with you."

"And I will wait, Peter. As long as you are alive, I will wait for your return."

There was a knock on the door, and as she stepped away from him to answer it, Peter already felt like he was losing her. As he watched the doctor rush to Jeremiah's side, dread and love in equal measure flooded Peter's heart.

CHAPTER TEN

I drove back across the sprawling sugarcane fields and pulled into a small gas station, the first business I came upon along the main road leading out of town. I put my car in Park and gently extracted one of the letters from its yellowed envelope. It was dated July 1946.

Dearest Margaret, it read in neat script.

I am writing again from the camp in England in the fervent desire that this letter will reach you. I must admit, the long silence from you has frightened me. I am hoping there is merely a complication with the mail delivery, but I fear the worst, and I lie awake at night wondering if something terrible has happened.

The days here are bleak and dreary, even in the summer. Often, the sun shines for hours on end, but the earth is charred and broken, streaked with rubble from the bombs Germany dropped on the innocent countryside. I work each day until

WHEN WE MEET AGAIN 103

my fingers are raw and bloodied, atoning for the sins of my countrymen. How could we not have seen, when Hitler marched us into battle so long ago, that this would be the end result? Sometimes, I find shoes and spectacles and hats that no longer have owners, and I wonder what happened to the people who once inhabited them. I wonder if they are dead, and I feel that guilt too. The towns can be rebuilt, but there is no way to replace the lives that have been stolen.

I do not know when I will be sent home, and I dare not ask. There are too many people on this shattered isle who have lost sons and fathers and brothers in the war. The fact that I am alive is enough for now.

I dream of the day when I will see you again, and I pray that it will be soon. In the interim, you live in my heart always, and I find solace in my memories of you. I will love you forever, Margaret, and I pray I will hold you in my arms again soon.

Yours always in love, Peter

I read the letter twice before folding it and slipping it back into the envelope. My confusion had deepened. Where had Peter Dahler been writing from? Some sort of prison camp in England? It certainly sounded like he was being forced to stay there, but who was doing the forcing? It seemed as if prisoners of war would have been returned to their home countries after the fighting was over. But in July 1946, more than a year after hostilities had ceased in Europe, somehow Peter still hadn't made it home.

And yet he'd been thinking about Margaret. Unless he was lying, he still loved her deeply and was still planning to come back for her. So what had changed? Had he eventually gotten frustrated by her lack of response? But if that was the case, how had he not guessed that her family was keeping his letters from her?

The other two letters, dated October 1946 and January 1947, were shorter. The first one read:

> *Dearest Margaret,*
>
> *It has been more than a year now since I last held you in my arms, and I fear I am beginning to forget the feel of your body against mine. I try to hold on to those memories when I close my eyes, but as time passes and I do not hear from you, I begin to wonder if you were merely a dream. It would be fitting, would it not? After all, this war has been a nightmare, a terrible vision from which I cannot seem to find my way out. Perhaps you were the sweet interlude, the salvation in all that darkness. But I must believe that you are real, that our love is real, that one day I will hold you again. When that day comes, dear Margaret, I will never let you go.*
>
> *Yours always in love, Peter*

The final letter was even briefer, and I could feel myself tearing up as I read it. Peter had written:

> *Dearest Margaret,*
>
> *The new year has arrived in darkness, for you are not with me, and I have not heard from you in more than a year and a half. If you are gone from my world, I no longer believe that the spring will come, that the flowers will bloom, that the world will once again give birth to new life. For you, sweet Margaret, are my reason for existence. You are the light*

in the blackness, but each day, I can feel that light growing dimmer. I wait for you, dear Margaret, and I carry my love for you forever in my heart.

Yours always in love, Peter

I read the last letter a few times, savoring the almost poetic words, before slipping it back into its envelope and placing it back on the passenger seat with the other two notes. I felt strangely breathless as I stared at the envelopes, which had made their way across the Atlantic seventy years ago but had never reached their intended recipient.

Five minutes later, I was still sitting there in silence, studying the letters, when I realized something: Peter was still writing to Margaret in January 1947 from somewhere in England. And yet the letter Jeremiah had given me, the one that told Margaret that Peter wasn't coming back for her, had been sent in December 1945, more than a year earlier, from Germany. Although the handwriting seemed remarkably similar, there was no way that the rejection letter had come from Peter himself. Someone back in his homeland had written to Margaret to break her heart. In fact, especially given the words in these letters, it seemed he'd never meant to leave her at all.

My heart thudding, I turned the key in the ignition and pulled back onto the main road. Someone had set out to deliberately separate Margaret and Peter, and they'd both seemingly fallen for it. But who? And why? My grandmother's family had played that role here, hiding the love letters from Peter. Had there been someone similar across the ocean who was concealing Margaret's letters to him? I was increasingly sure that the answers to my questions lay in Germany, where the painting had originated. But most of the people involved in my grandmother's story here in the States were dead. Perhaps the same was the case in Germany; after all, these letters had been written seven decades ago.

As I drove away from Belle Creek, I felt further from the truth than I had been when I'd started searching. I had the uneasy feeling that I'd never really known my grandmother at all.

My cell rang just after I got back on the Turnpike at Yeehaw Junction, and I saw Scott's name on the caller ID.

"Hey," Scott said when I answered. "I think I found something on your Peter Dahler. Sort of."

My breath caught in my throat. "You did?"

"Well, a lead, anyhow. I could only find one Peter Dahler with the middle initial 'A' in any of the databases, and he's too old to be your guy. Peter August Dahler, born 1897."

"Oh." My heart sank.

"But he was born in Holzkirchen, where that letter was from. I think maybe he's the father of the guy you're looking for. This Peter Dahler is listed as the father of two sons. I can't find names for them, but they were born in 1921 and 1924. What do you want to bet that one of them is the Peter A. Dahler who ended up over here?"

"Well, the ages would fit." Both men would have been old enough to have fought for Germany during World War II. Old enough to have fallen in love with my grandmother in the mid-1940s. "Did you find anything else?"

"I have a death certificate for the Peter Dahler born in 1897. Looks like he died in the early seventies. And there's a Franz Dahler currently listed at the last-known address of the elder Peter Dahler, in Munich. I've found his license, and it appears he was born in 1924."

"Munich," I murmured. "So maybe he's the brother of the man I'm looking for. Is he still alive? He'd be in his nineties by now, wouldn't he?"

"I haven't found a death certificate. And it looks like the son born in 1921 has totally vanished."

"But that's a bad sign, isn't it? If he was in the military, there'd surely be a record of him."

"Not necessarily," Scott replied. "I talked to my contact at the London *Times,* and I guess a lot of the German military records from that time period were destroyed." I could hear keys clicking in the background, and then he added, "Anyhow, Em, I've got to go. I hope this helps. I'll e-mail the address to you, okay? There's also a phone number, but I tried it myself, and there was no answer. This might be the best we can do from over here. Maybe you can find someone in Germany to help you out."

"Thanks, Scott. I really appreciate it."

"You owe me a date."

I smiled, despite myself. "You bet. My treat."

He hung up, and I put my cell phone down on top of the letters on the passenger seat, my mind reeling.

All roads seemed to be leading to Munich. Somehow, I had to find a way to get there too.

I barely slept that night, and when I finally got out of bed the next morning at six, the first thing I did was to call the Munich telephone number Scott had given me for Franz Dahler. I let it ring eight times, but not even a machine picked up. I tried again at eight and eleven while I worked on my assignment for *Seventeen,* but by the time I called for the fourth time, at three, which would have been nine in the evening in Munich, I was feeling discouraged. What if Franz Dahler was screening my calls because he didn't recognize the number? Or what if he didn't live there anymore? I had no idea how I'd track him down from across an ocean armed only with an address and a phone number.

I clicked over to KAYAK.com, hoping to find a reasonable fare to Munich, but the cheapest option I could find for the next week was a $1,162 round-trip with two stops in each direction on Turkish Airlines, with a total travel time of more than thirty hours each way. Air Berlin offered flights for $1,520, but they were also time-consuming at sixteen hours each way. Both options were out of my price range too, considering that I'd just lost my source of stable income. I'd still need to pay for a hotel in Munich, and I couldn't afford to drop more than two thousand dollars on a single trip. I extended the search for the next month, but the prices were similar, and besides, I didn't want to wait much longer to go. Aer Lingus could get me there for $1,064 in a month, but by that time, the trail of the painting might have grown even colder. No, I needed to go now.

I opened my retirement account—the one thing I'd been responsible about as a freelancer—and evaluated my balance. I didn't want to do it, but if I needed to, I could borrow the money for the ticket from myself. Considering that my grandmother had taken me in during my darkest hour—when I was pregnant, alone, and scared—this felt like the least I could do to repay the favor. Still, it made me uneasy. Spending so much money now would leave me with virtually no cushion, and I had no idea how long I'd be between steady writing gigs.

Conflicted about what to do, I called my father an hour later to update him. He listened silently while I recapped my visit with Julie and what I'd learned from the letters and from Scott.

"So I think Peter Dahler never intended to leave Grandma Margaret," I concluded. "I think somehow, their letters never reached each other, and they both thought the other person had moved on. Maybe Peter came back, after all, but Grandma Margaret was already gone."

My father was silent for a moment. "So what do you think we should do next? What's our next move?"

"*Our* move?" I didn't mean to sound rude, but the idea that we were working together was almost laughable.

"I want to help," he said. "She was my mother, Emily. And this is an overwhelming thing for you to be working on alone."

"Dad, this is the kind of thing I do all the time for my job," I said stiffly, bristling at his words. "I'm not overwhelmed."

"I'm sorry. I didn't mean it that way." He took a deep breath. "I just meant that sometimes things are easier when you work as a team."

"And when, exactly, have you and I ever been a team?"

He hesitated, but only for a second. "When you were a little girl. You and your mom were the best team I ever had."

His response stunned me into silence for a moment. I didn't know how to reply, so I finally cleared my throat and said, "I think I need to go to Munich."

His answer was instant. "I agree. I'll go with you."

"What? No. I don't need you to go."

"Do you speak German?"

"No."

"Well, I do. A little, anyhow."

"Dad—" I began.

"I'll pay for the trip," he interrupted. I could hear clicking in the background; he was typing something, and for a second, I was convinced that he was so uninvested in the conversation that he was writing someone an e-mail while we talked. But then he added, "There's a flight tomorrow afternoon that arrives in Munich the next day. Say yes, and I'll book it now."

"No, Dad. I'll find a way there myself." I'd never asked my father for a dime, and my pride prevented me from doing so now.

"But you just lost your steady source of income." There was more clicking in the background, and I tried not to let the words sting. "And we may be running out of time. If Franz Dahler is still alive, who knows how much longer he'll be around? He's in his nineties, right? And even if we can't find him, isn't it a good idea to track down where the painting came from while it's still fresh in everyone's mind?"

"I guess," I said slowly. "But really, you don't have to—"

"It's already done." My father's tone as he interrupted my protests was firm. "I'm buying the tickets now. I just need your passport number, and I'll meet you at the airport tomorrow for a three o'clock flight."

I hung up five minutes later feeling unsettled—and like I'd lost a battle I hadn't been prepared to fight. I had the uneasy feeling that although I'd kept my retirement account safe for the time being, I'd just put everything else I'd worked so hard to protect on the line.

For the second night in a row, I couldn't sleep. I tossed and turned for hours, battling my apprehension about taking a trip with my father. We hadn't spent more than a few minutes in each other's presence in more than twenty years, and now we were setting off together on a transatlantic journey? The more I thought about it, the more insane it sounded.

I finally drifted off sometime after two in the morning, and I dreamt of being trapped in a deep pit filled with quicksand. I was trying to get out before I was pulled under, but everyone I knew was peering over the edge at me with blank expressions on their faces. My father was there, scrolling through his cell, while I screamed for help. "Dad!" I cried in the dream. "Save me!" He looked up only briefly, shrugged, and turned his attention back to the phone. It was then that I noticed Nick standing there at the top of the pit, staring down at me with a look of horror on his face. "Nick?" I cried, somehow not surprised at all to see him there. "Help!" Without a second of hesitation, he jumped in after me, wrapped his arms around me, and began to pull us both up the walls of the pit using his bare hands.

I awoke with a start, still feeling the solidity of Nick's chest and the comfort I'd felt in his arms. I'd known for a moment that everything was going to be completely okay. But it was just a dream, and lying in my bed, staring at the ceiling at four in the morning with a racing heart, I was just as alone as ever.

I got out of bed, booted up my laptop, and clicked over to the bookmarked site for NW Creative, the advertising agency I knew Nick owned in Atlanta. Scanning his website was a guilty, self-destructive pleasure, an urge I gave into now and then when I was at my lowest. Yawning, I skimmed the news column on the left of the main page—noting with a smile that Nick had just won a prestigious ADDY Award for a campaign he'd created for a local nonprofit—and then I clicked over to his bio, which I knew practically by heart. It was playful, revealing just enough tongue-in-cheek information about Nick for potential clients to feel like they already knew him. It appeared he still liked '80s movies, enjoyed golfing, and had appeared on *The Today Show* once to discuss advertising trends in America, a clip I had found and rewatched so many times that I knew every word. And according to the bio, he was married to a woman named Jessica. I knew it was bizarre that I kept checking that last sentence, waiting for it to disappear, but of course it never did.

Sighing, rubbing my temples, and feeling like a loser, I went back to Google, and for the next fifteen minutes, I scrolled through the threads of the most popular adoption search sites, looking—as I always did—for some trace of Catherine. But no one matching her description had posted anything about looking for her birth parents, and all of my search strings remained unanswered. I finally closed my laptop and climbed into bed feeling dejected. I was tired of being so lonely.

Before I could stop myself, I reached for my cell phone and dialed Scott's number, even though I knew he was certainly in bed already. "I can't sleep," I said when he picked up.

"Is that an invitation to come over?" he asked, his voice thick.

"If you want to."

"I'll be right there."

Twenty minutes later, Scott was at my front door. He leaned down to kiss me, and I silenced my internal objections and leaned in to the feeling of being wanted. I led him to my bedroom, where I let him clumsily peel off the T-shirt and boxer shorts I'd been sleeping in. As we fell into bed, I wasn't thinking about Munich or a path of destroyed relationships anymore. I was just thinking about Scott's hands on my body, the feel of his skin against mine, the way he filled me when he slid inside me with a groan.

But afterward, as he was snoring beside me, I closed my eyes, and all I could see was the painting. My mind spun with the details of the letters, the things I'd been told, and the blanks I was beginning to fill in about a past I didn't yet understand. Finally, I drifted off to sleep thinking of Catherine and the life we could have had together if I'd been stronger, wiser, better. No amount of distraction could change the regrets I'd always carry with me in my heart.

CHAPTER ELEVEN

The next evening, after a connection at Dulles International Airport, I was on a flight to Munich with my father.

"You didn't have to spring for business class," I said as we took off, the monuments of Washington, D.C., spreading out below us like miniature pieces on a Monopoly board.

My dad patted my knee and smiled. "Once you've gone business class, you never go back. I don't think I could have managed folding myself into an economy seat for a flight this long."

"Well, thank you." I paused and gave him a half smile. "Although I suspect you've now ruined economy flying for me."

He chuckled. "I think you'll be okay. Besides, it's a father's job to spoil his daughter, isn't it?"

The sentence hung awkwardly between us, the silence an indication of the wrongness of his words.

"Dad—" I began.

"I'm sorry," he said before I could complete my thought. "I keep sticking my foot in my mouth, but it isn't really about that, is it? It's the fact that I totally screwed up for all those years. I can't expect you to forgive that."

I pressed my lips together and shook my head. "Let's just not talk about this for now," I said. "Nothing will change the way you left, but I can't keep punishing you for it, can I?"

He looked surprised. "It would certainly be your right to."

"Honestly?" I looked out the window for a second before turning back to him. "I'm exhausted. I'm so tired of being angry at you."

He nodded. "I don't think you have to forgive me," he said after a moment, "in order for us to start over."

"I know. But the starting over scares me." I didn't elaborate, but from the look on his face, I knew he understood what I meant. What guarantee did I have that he wouldn't do the same kind of thing again? What if I let down my guard and began to re-establish a relationship with him and he decided to simply walk away again? I hated to admit it, but it would destroy me. The walls I'd built up were my only protection.

"I don't blame you for hesitating, but I give you my word that I'm not going to let you down this time."

I nodded and looked out the window again. I wasn't sure whether to believe him, and at the same time, starting over with him felt like a betrayal of my mother. He'd hurt her, and now she was gone. But my mother wasn't a person who held grudges, and maybe she wouldn't want me to be either. Maybe she'd encourage me to open my heart a little.

Your mom probably wouldn't want you to hate him, you know. The words floated back to me unbeckoned, startling me with their clarity. It was exactly what Nick had said to me when I first told him about my father, about a month after we'd started dating. It had also been the start of the only real fight we'd ever had.

"Oh, so you know exactly what my mom's thinking and feeling?" I had snapped defensively, turning away from him. We were heading to a movie in his little Honda Civic, and as I stared out the window, I tried hard to blink back my tears before he could see them.

"I didn't mean it that way," Nick said. "I just meant that, well, you seem really mad. And it's not like you're wrong or anything. But I think it's hard to be that mad at someone for such a long time."

His patient tone somehow made me feel even more combative. "It's actually pretty easy when the person you're talking about just completely vanished from your life."

"I know, Em. But I guess what I'm saying is that maybe your mom wouldn't want you walking around so pissed off just for her sake, you know? Like, she'd want you to be happy and not to worry about her."

"You don't know anything about it," I said flatly, trying not to let his words worm their way inside my brain. I knew on some level that he was right, but my anger toward my dad was like a badge of honor, something that united my mom and me. Letting it go would be like losing a piece of who I was.

"But I know you," he'd said after a long pause. His tone had turned careful, and I knew he was trying hard to say the right thing, but I'd been so annoyed at him for butting in that there wasn't anything he could have said that wouldn't make me angrier. "And I know you would do anything for the people you love. But I don't know, sometimes you kind of forget about doing things for yourself."

"Yeah, well, looking out for my mom makes me happy, okay?" I snapped. "And it's none of your business."

"Yeah, you're right," he said finally. "I guess you'll let go when you're ready."

"So have you been to Germany before?" my father asked, cutting into my thoughts and jolting me back to the present. I realized I'd been silent for a long time.

I cleared my throat. "It's actually the first time I've been anywhere outside the United States except for a cruise to the Bahamas," I admitted, and my dad looked so surprised that his mouth literally fell open.

"What about seeing the world? Experiencing life beyond our borders? Eating a baguette in Paris or drinking a cup of tea in China?"

"Last time I checked, the supermarket carried French bread and green tea." I didn't want to tell him that I'd always dreamed of traveling the world, but I'd never made the time. And somehow, I'd never lucked into the journalistic assignments that came with international travel.

We were interrupted by a flight attendant delivering us small bowls of snack mix and offering us flutes of champagne from a tray. My dad and I clinked glasses, and we both took long sips of bubbly.

"I could get used to this," I said.

He looked past me out the window. "You're going to love Germany, Emily," he said after a minute. "I'm glad I'm going to be there with you."

From the air, Munich looked like something out of a fairy tale. We landed just past eight in the morning, and by the time we got through customs and retrieved our luggage, it was nearly ten. I'd slept on and off during the eight-hour flight, but I still felt groggy and disoriented; Germany was six hours ahead of Orlando, which meant that as we climbed into a taxi at the curb, it was just past four in the morning at home.

"Need a nap at the hotel or anything?" my dad asked as our taxi driver accelerated onto the highway heading for Munich.

His concern rubbed me the wrong way, somehow, but I forced myself to take a deep breath before responding. "No, I'm good." As we drew closer to the city, the pine trees and apartment buildings of the suburbs gave way to the magical-looking outskirts of a Bavarian city with creamy Gothic architecture and brick-colored roofs set against an impossibly blue sky.

"That's the Frauenkirche," my dad said, pointing to a pair of twin clock towers topped by bulbous green domes. The towers seemed to dwarf the rest of the buildings. "The main cathedral of Munich. The church was built in the Gothic style during the 1400s, but the domes were added on later, in the 1520s, in a completely different architectural style."

"You sound like a travel show."

"I used to travel here occasionally on business. I've picked up some things here and there." He smiled at me.

"How nice for you," I said, but he didn't seem to register my sarcasm, and after silence fell over us, I wasn't even sure how I'd meant the words as a dig.

Our hotel was on a side street near the city center, and after we'd checked into rooms down the hall from each other and changed out of our travel clothes, we met in the lobby. My father was already deep in conversation with the concierge when I walked up.

He turned around holding a map. "I asked for a taxi to the address you have for Franz Dahler, but the concierge tells me we're only about fifteen minutes away on foot. Feel like walking?"

I nodded, and with the help of the tourist map and the GPS on my father's iPhone, we wound our way in silence down a few side streets until we emerged in the Marienplatz, Munich's central square. For a moment, we both simply stopped and stared.

It was gorgeous and unlike anything I'd ever seen. It was laid out in a rectangular shape, with cafés and shops spilling into the bustling central area. In the middle was a tall column with a gold statue of the Virgin Mary on top. The buildings around the square were a charming mix of historic and modern. The Gothic-looking building with the soaring clock tower that seemed to anchor the square was breathtaking.

"Look," my dad said, nudging me and pointing. There was a crowd gathered around, and as bells chimed the hour, the Glockenspiel beneath the clock tower began to move. First, on the top level, there was a procession of figurines carrying horns, swords, and flags. Then, two sword-toting figures on horseback appeared, rotating in opposite directions. "That was supposed to be the wedding of Duke Wilhelm the Fifth, complete with knights jousting," my dad whispered, just as the lower half of the Glockenspiel began to rotate. "The second part is a dance called the *Schäfflertanz*, which first took place during a plague in the 1500s to demonstrate loyalty to the duke despite hard times."

We stayed to watch as a bunch of male figurines danced and twirled around the bottom half of the tower. It was charming and magical and reminded me of an old-fashioned carousel. "That was kind of amazing," I said as the music ended. There was a smattering of applause from the tourists gathered in the square.

"I'm glad we got to see it," my dad said, and I felt a surge of guilt for enjoying myself with him. What would my mother think?

As the crowds began to disperse, he pointed off to the right and led me in a weaving zigzag through the crowd until we were in the midst of a sprawling, bustling farmers' market. We were surrounded by stalls that overflowed with everything I could imagine: fruits and vegetables in every color, meats, fish, cheeses, spices, flowers, and clothing. There was a beer garden, alive with people, in the center of the mass of booths, and the market's edges were dotted with more established-looking shops and restaurants.

"This is the *Viktualienmarkt*," my dad said as he gestured for me to follow him. "The city's main farmers' market. It's been here for a couple hundred years." I didn't say anything, and he consulted the map again as we wove through the maze of booths, the scents of yeast, sausage, and spices heavy in the air. My stomach rumbled, and I realized I'd been so intent on hitting the ground running that I hadn't eaten since the croissant and coffee we'd been served on the plane just before landing.

We turned down a side street, leaving the bustling market behind. A block later, my dad stopped in front of a seven-story apartment building. The windows were in neat rows across the painted beige exterior and the burnt-orange roof was punctuated by narrow chimneys and small, windowed alcoves.

"I think this is it," he said. We leaned in to look at the listing of names beside the front door's buzzer, and he whispered, "Yes," at the same time I spotted the last name *Dahler* beside apartment 5B. We exchanged looks, and he pushed the buzzer.

But no one answered. My father frowned and tried again, but once again, we were greeted with silence.

"I guess we should have known," I said. "This was too easy."

He shrugged. "Maybe he's just out. Hey, maybe we walked right by him in the market."

We agreed we'd head to the gallery that had mailed the painting to me. I was hopeful that the owner would be more forthcoming in person. After all, we'd flown thousands of miles to get here. Surely this would garner us at least a bit of sympathy.

After scrolling through his phone with a furrowed brow, my father pulled up his map app and punched in the address of the Galerie Schubert-Balck.

"It's a fifteen-minute walk sort of in the direction of our hotel," he said. "You still okay walking?"

I nodded, still unsettled by how comfortable I was feeling with him, and we made our way back through the *Viktualienmarkt* and off to the right—east, I thought. We took a wrong turn down a side street at the end of our walk, so it took us a few extra minutes to find the gallery, which was tucked into the basement of a large industrial building. A black sign with small white lettering marked the entrance to the Galerie Schubert-Balck, with an arrow pointing down. We followed the narrow staircase to a black wooden door, which was painted with stout white letters that said in English, ENTER PLEASE.

My father pushed the door open and held it for me. We walked together down a dim hallway, turned a corner, and emerged into a brightly lit room with stark white walls, each of which featured three small, evenly spaced paintings in frames. The space felt clean, airy, and modern.

A woman with flowing jet-black hair, dressed in a white linen blouse and white linen pants, emerged from a door to our left, saying something in rapid German. My father turned and replied with a few German sentences of his own, gesturing to me. The woman turned and studied me.

"Ah, you are the owner of *The Girl in the Field with the Violet Sky*? You did not need to come all this way. I told you what I knew on the telephone." She looked me up and down and extended her hand. "I am Nicola Schubert. I own the gallery with my partner, Torsten."

"Emily," I said, shaking her hand. "And this is Victor Emerson. My father. We think the woman in the painting is my grandmother." I paused and added, "My father's mother."

Nicola studied us for a moment before nodding and gesturing for us to follow her. "Come to my office, and I will explain what I know, but I'm afraid it is very little. I fear that your trip here is perhaps, how do I say it, wasted time."

"I hope not," I murmured as she led us down a long, narrow hall into a small office. There was a bookshelf on one side of the room and a huge painting of a naked, dark-haired woman surrounded by three white rabbits behind her desk.

"That one is a Lothar Faust," she said, following my gaze. "Well, in reality, it is a Faust print. An original would be destroyed by the sunlight, of course." She nodded to the window to the left of her desk that spilled a pool of light into the room from the street above. "We have been trying to obtain the original on loan for an exhibition this autumn about twentieth-century realism. But where are my manners? Please, have a seat."

We settled into the two chairs in front of her desk, and she sat down facing us. "Now, where was I? Oh yes, twentieth-century realism. You see, I'm very much a supporter of the style. In fact, I'm quite well known in art communities as an expert." She paused and smiled. "I believe this is why the painting you mention was sent to me for restoration. It's obviously a fine example of realism, and I am known as someone who has a specialty in the restoration of works like these.

"The brushwork in your painting was very skilled," Nicola continued, gesturing to the print behind her. "You see how, even though this is not an original, you can tell that Faust used broad, distinct strokes? It's what makes the painting feel so dynamic, so warm. Please, lean in closer to see."

My father and I both sat forward in our chairs to look more closely at the image behind her desk. I didn't know much about art, so I couldn't really make out what she was talking about. But I nodded wisely and sat back in my chair. My father caught my eye and shrugged as he leaned back too.

"So you see? But in the painting that I sent to you, *The Girl in the Field with the Violet Sky,* the brushwork was different. Very emotional. You could feel the artist's pain."

"His pain?"

"Ah, you doubt me. But when you develop an eye for art, you can see the emotion, the same way one develops an ear for music and can hear anguish or elation in a trumpet's song or a violin's wail." She sat back in her chair and seemed to be puzzling something over for a moment. My father and I exchanged looks as she added, "At first, the painting reminded me very much of an early Wyeth or maybe an early Gaertner."

"Who?" The names rang a bell, but I couldn't immediately place either one.

She didn't even bother to pretend she wasn't rolling her eyes. "Andrew Wyeth and Ralph Gaertner, of course. Two of the best-known artists of the twentieth century. Their paintings were simply transcendent."

"So you're saying the artist might be one of those two men?"

"No, no, of course not," she snapped. "Wyeth painted subjects in a much different kind of landscape, mostly in the northeast region of your country. And his use of shading was entirely different. As for Gaertner, he categorically refused to paint faces. He said once in an interview that to paint a face was too intimate; it was like baring a person's soul to the world without their permission. And of course the painting that arrived here, the painting that I restored, showed a woman's face in such detail that I could almost imagine I knew her myself." She tilted her head to the side and studied me for a moment. "In fact, she looked just like you, didn't she?"

"Emily always resembled her grandmother," my father said softly, and I smiled slightly, knowing he'd meant it as a compliment.

Nicola nodded. "In any case, the best suggestion I can make is that the painter of *The Girl in the Field with the Violet Sky* might have been a pupil of either Wyeth or Gaertner. I know that Gaertner in particular mentored several young artists over the years. But both men, you see, lived their entire professional lives in your country, so I'm afraid that perhaps the answers you seek are on your side of the ocean, not mine."

We sat in silence for a moment. I felt like I'd run out of steam, and I could read the same feelings on my father's face. We were talking to an art expert who'd worked on the painting at the heart of our mystery, but it felt like we'd come away with more questions than we'd arrived with. This was beginning to feel like an entirely wasted trip. I gave it one last shot. "You haven't heard of a man named Peter Dahler, have you?" I asked.

She shook her head. "No. He is an artist?"

"I don't know," I said. "Or any realist painter with our last name? Emerson?" It was an even bigger shot in the dark.

"No one who paints in this style."

We thanked her and stood to leave. "Wait," I said. "What about your assistant? The person you said received the painting? She might remember where it was from. Can I talk to her?"

Her expression tightened. "Bettina? As I mentioned on the phone, she left us a month ago."

"Can you tell me how to reach her?"

Nicola frowned and seemed to be thinking my request over. "Very well," she said after a long pause. "I do not see the harm. She defected to the Galerie Bergen three blocks from here. They seem to think she has some talent as a restoration artist, but in truth, she wasn't ready. I wanted to fully train her before promoting her, and they just wanted to put her subpar skills to work immediately. Good riddance to her, I say." She pursed her lips and scribbled something on a piece of paper. "The address of the gallery. Turn right out the door, walk two blocks, go left, and proceed one block. You'll see how inferior their gallery is to ours."

"Thank you," I said, clutching the address in my hand.

Nicola walked us to the door of the gallery. "On your next visit to Munich, you must return to see my collection in more detail. And if you find the artist who painted *The Violet Sky,* you will call me, yes?"

"Yes," I agreed.

"Well, then, I wish you luck." She smiled. "Or as we say in German, *Viel Glück.*"

CHAPTER TWELVE

The year 1945 arrived on a Monday morning cold, damp, and gray. There were rumors around the POW camp that the war would soon be over, that Hitler was close to surrendering, that Germany would soon fall.

The Red Army and the Allies were advancing, and within the first month of 1945, a five-week major German offensive into Ardennes had failed. "This is undoubtedly the greatest American battle of the war and will, I believe, be regarded as an ever-famous American victory," Winston Churchill had said to the British House of Commons upon Germany's defeat, a quote that was wafted across the airwaves and repeated again and again among the guards and the prisoners. The tide had turned, and everyone knew it.

For Peter, knowing that the end of the war was near was both exhilarating and terrifying. Of course he longed to be free, to build a life for himself. He yearned for a time when he would no longer have to toil in someone else's fields under the watchful eye of an armed guard. He missed his mother, his books, the streets of his hometown, the gentle familiarity of hearing German spoken all around him.

But going home would mean leaving Margaret, and that, to Peter, was almost impossible to fathom. He had fallen in love with her, and there was no going back. Sometimes, the earth simply shifts on its axis, and there's nothing one can do but move along with it. Peter knew that his life would never again be complete without her, and he would do everything in his power to make sure he spent the rest of his days by her side.

He knew that she, too, felt the same way. They had whispered promises to each other and dreamed about the future each time they were alone. Their stolen moments were few and far between, though. The guards were never far away, and although Peter was sure that Harold realized there was something between Peter and Margaret, it couldn't be spoken aloud. Nor could another guard be allowed to find out—they'd transfer Peter to another camp and away from Margaret forever.

But more than his own possible fate, Peter worried about what would become of Margaret if news of their budding relationship were to spread. Peter couldn't get the image of Jeremiah, beaten and bloodied, out of his mind. He couldn't stand to imagine what kind of retribution might be taken against Margaret if people in this town viewed her as a traitor to the American cause.

Since that day in Margaret's house—the day she had said she loved him—something seismic had shifted. Peter was no longer simply in love with her from afar, fearing she would never feel the same way. He knew now that he had a chance, a real chance. He just had to hold out until the end of the war. Then he could return to Belle Creek a free man. He could give her the life he dreamed of.

And so while he waited for that day to come, he courted her the best way he knew how. He walked as closely as he could to the edge of her family farm on the mornings when he was assigned to fields in her vicinity. On the other mornings, he kept an eye out for her, sometimes asking people whether they'd seen Jeremiah, because he knew Margaret was often with the boy; he was fully recovered from his ordeal, but she was still watching over him. When Peter was fortunate enough to encounter her, he'd wait until she was alone, so as not to get her in trouble, and then he'd tell her an anecdote he'd rehearsed all night. She was like a sponge, he thought, soaking in everything. He loved seeing her wide eyes and her easy smile as he shared stories of Germany, of the homeland he loved, of the days before the war, of a culture so different from anything she'd ever known.

And he loved hearing of her memories too. He loved her tales about childhood on the edge of Florida's wild Everglades, her stories of life on a bean farm. He liked hearing of the films she'd watched, the books she'd read, the meals she and her sister had learned to cook at their mother's knee. He loved hearing what her life was like, because the more he knew, the more he could imagine himself a part of it.

"I never thought I'd meet someone like you," she told him late one afternoon in early April, when she'd found an excuse to creep to the edge of the field the prisoners had been working that day. She'd worn her brown dress, the one that allowed her to blend into the terrain, and she'd squatted down in a cluster of overgrown cane just across the narrow canal. Maus knew she was there, but he moved away to give Peter the space to talk with her. "To think that my life could ever be bigger than this town used to seem so far-fetched to me."

The words made Peter's heart ache. "But your world has always been bigger, Margaret," he said. "You know the world because you have read about it in books, just like I always did."

"But you had the possibility of leaving where you'd come from, Peter. It's not the same for someone like me. I don't have any money of my own, and my parents would never allow me to go. They would disown me, and I would have nothing. I used to think I'd have no choice but to marry a local boy and to spend the rest of my life having babies and working the land. It's the only kind of future a girl's allowed to imagine in a place like this."

"And now?" He stopped and stared at her.

"Now you have shown me that more is possible." She paused and looked down at the ground. "As long as you're in my world, my life has no limits."

"Margaret, I do not know what to say." He wanted nothing more than to take her away from this town, to give her the life she could imagine, but his own future was uncertain. It was impossible to forget that they were in the midst of a war. "I want to be able to give you the world, but what if I cannot come back for you right away? And when I do, what if I'm poor? What if it takes me a long while to give you the life you're dreaming of?"

"But it won't," she said softly. "Because it doesn't matter how much money we have or where we will live. What will matter is that I'm with you. What I'm trying to say, Peter, is that *you're* my world. As long as we're together, I can dream.

And as long as I can dream, anything is possible. Don't you see? You've given me wings, and one day, I will use them to fly with you."

"I pray that we can be together again soon," he murmured. "I await the day when we meet again, my dear Margaret."

But he hadn't told her everything. He hadn't told her how frightened he'd been in combat, or how it had felt to find himself covered in the blood of his lifeless best friend. He hadn't told her what it was like to level your gun at another man on the battlefield for a cause you didn't believe in, or to wonder if your soul had been destroyed forever by war. She loved the Peter who arrived with stories and laughter and tidbits to lighten the day, the Peter who told her about the world beyond this country's borders. Would she love him still if she knew the heaviness in his heart?

And so, on the second day of May, just after he'd heard about the cowardly suicide of the führer, he told her everything. The guards had been up late drinking the night before, celebrating the impending end of the war, and so they'd been lax in their duties the next morning. Instead of accompanying the prisoners out into the hot sun, they had stayed in the shade of their vehicle.

The sugarcane harvest was nearly done for the year, and the prisoners were down to their final cluster of fields. That day, they were working two hundred yards from Margaret's property, and so Peter hurried along, slashing through more than his portion in record time, promising Maus his week's wages at the canteen if only Maus would carry his cane to the tractor for him. He watched until Margaret came up the path at the back of her farm, trailed by Jeremiah. Keeping low to the ground so that the guards wouldn't see him from their vantage point on the road, he hurried over to her.

It was Jeremiah who saw him first, waved, and then nudged Margaret. When she turned, her whole face lit up like a sunrise as she smiled at him. "Won't you get in trouble?" she asked.

"The guards are asleep in their truck," he told her as he took her hands in his. They were so warm, so smooth, and he never wanted to let go. "I need to tell you some things, while there is still time. I will be sent back to Germany soon, and I want to have an honest conversation with you before I go."

"Of course." She glanced back at Jeremiah, who nodded knowingly and turned toward the house. They both watched for a minute as the boy walked away. "Follow me, Peter."

She held tightly to his right hand as she led him into a cane field that hadn't been touched yet. The stalks were shorter than in the fields where Peter worked, and he knew enough by now to realize this crop wouldn't be harvested this season; it was still maturing and would be one of the first to be farmed in the fall. He looked back over his shoulder to make sure no one was watching. "I only have a few minutes, Margaret," he said with regret. "I must get back before the guards notice I'm missing."

"I know," she whispered, so close to his ear that he could feel her breath on his cheek. It caught him off guard, made him feel like someone had set him on fire. Every nerve ending tingled.

"Where are we going?"

"You'll see."

Peter was surprised a moment later when they emerged into a small clearing in the center of the field. The space wasn't visible from the outside, but someone had sliced down several of the stalks and leveled their roots to the ground to create a spot that felt a bit like a secret cave. The clearing was in the shape of a circle, eight or nine feet across, but the way the surrounding stalks arced gently over it, shielding it from the sun, made it feel smaller than that.

"What is this place?" Peter asked.

"I cleared it out," Margaret said proudly. "For Jeremiah. No one will notice the hole in the field until the next harvest season, and by then, he'll be gone from here. But for now, he knows that if anyone ever comes after him again, he can hide here. I will find him, and he will be okay. It is our secret."

Peter put a hand on her cheek. Her skin was soft, smooth, and warm. "You did this to protect him?"

"I couldn't stand by and do nothing. The law is against him. The culture is against him. But if I could do anything to give him a fighting chance, I had to. I know it's just a place, just a spot in the middle of a field, but—"

Peter cut her off with a kiss. He couldn't stop himself. It was only the second time he'd tasted her lips, but he hadn't been able to stop thinking about their first kiss, the one on the day of Jeremiah's attack. Her mouth was soft and supple, and she tasted like sugarcane and innocence. He drank her in, pulled her to him, held her against him like the world depended on it. When she finally pulled away, her lips pink and her eyes wide, he felt breathless.

"I shouldn't have been so forward," he said. "But Margaret, you are extraordinary."

She looked at the ground for a moment, and when she looked up again, there were tears in her eyes.

"I'm sorry," he said, horrified to have saddened her. "Margaret, did I hurt you in some way? Are you all right?"

"Peter, it's just that this is perfect. When I'm in your arms, I can forget the rest of the world. I can forget that you'll be leaving soon. But reality has to crash back in, does it not?"

Peter bowed his head. "I would kiss you forever if I could."

Margaret touched his chin and tilted his face toward hers. "I would kiss you forever too." She leaned into him, pressing her lips to his again. When she pulled away, she put a hand on his cheek and looked into his eyes. "You said you wanted to tell me something."

Peter took a deep breath. "I'm not a perfect man, Margaret. I have seen things I cannot unsee and have done things I cannot undo."

"We all have," she said gently.

"But, Margaret, you haven't been to war." He took a deep breath. "In the desert, I wanted to run. I wanted to die. Can you imagine the shame in that? I do not know if I killed another man, but I might have. I might have killed many. There were times we had to fire at the enemy, and there was nothing I could do but follow orders. I fear that you see me as the man I want to be, not as the man I truly am."

He was crying now, and he knew he should feel ashamed to be showing such emotion in front of Margaret, but her face held only compassion, not judgment.

"Worse, I let my dearest friend die," Peter continued, looking away. "It was my fault, Margaret. I was only trying to show him the stars. There was a meteor shower. It looked like heaven itself was rejoicing, and I wanted him to see it. But if I had not woken him . . ." He trailed off and drew a shuddering breath. "He was shot by the enemy standing there in the middle of our camp. His blood is on my hands to this day. It should have been me who died that night."

"Peter," she said gently, "I'm so sorry about your friend. But it's not your fault he's dead. How could you have known that someone was waiting there to shoot him?"

"I should have known," Peter whispered.

"You couldn't have." She reached for him and cupped his chin in her hands. "You couldn't have," she repeated firmly once he was looking at her.

"But it is my fault he was there in the first place." It was the first time he'd spoken the words aloud, and his heart ached for his lost friend as he said them. "Before the war, Otto wanted to leave Germany. We were still boys, a few months away from our compulsory military service. He had a friend whose cousin was spiriting people out of Germany for a price. He wanted to go, but I was the one who convinced him to stay, Margaret. I did not believe in what Germany was fighting for, but in those days, I believed that running away was cowardice. I told him that a real man would stay. A real man would fight, if that is what was asked of him. He listened to me, and he stayed. I was the one who persuaded him, and now he is dead."

"Peter," she said after a long moment. "I have read what the Germans do to deserters. You really think he would have survived by running?"

"Maybe." Peter choked on the word. "Maybe, Margaret. He would have had a chance, anyhow."

"There's nothing you could have done. Not in war, Peter. You were only trying to do what was right."

"Yes. But it was a mistake. All of it."

"Did you know that at the time you made those decisions?"

"No," he whispered.

She was silent for a moment, "Peter, 'Life is a succession of lessons which must be lived to be understood.'"

He raised his head. "More Emerson."

She smiled. "Yes, from *The Conduct of Life*."

"I know it well."

"Then you know how true the words are. Life is about learning, Peter. We're not meant to be perfect. We're only meant to strive for betterment. If each day you are a better person than you were the day before, you are one step closer to understanding life, don't you think?"

He nodded. "But how can you love a man like me, Margaret? A German? A man who has made mistakes that can never be taken back?"

This time, she put a hand on both of his cheeks and pulled him to her with force. She kissed him fiercely, and when she stepped away again, her eyes were blazing. "I *do* love you, Peter. From the depths of my heart. I understand all that you've told me, and I love you still. But now, you must work hard to forgive yourself. You are carrying around a weight that isn't yours to bear. It's time you laid it down."

———

Five days later, on the seventh of May, in a redbrick schoolhouse in the nearly destroyed town of Reims in the Champagne region of France, American General Walter Bedell Smith and Soviet General Ivan Susloparov accepted the unconditional surrender of the German armed forces. The war was over, and the next day, as the world celebrated, the final papers solidifying Germany's defeat were signed in Berlin.

In Camp Belle Creek, beautiful chaos reigned. The prisoners were given the day off, and the guards drank beer and celebrated with one another and with the local girls all day long. By nightfall, there wasn't a sober one among them, and they weren't enforcing the rules of the camp. The prisoners were unsettled and divided. Some were jubilant that their long imprisonment was drawing to an end. Others, the ones who still believed in Hitler's ideals, were stunned and devastated by Germany's defeat. And then there were men who saw the coming future with clear eyes, realizing that although the war was ended, their immediate journey home wasn't guaranteed. They didn't know where they'd end up after leaving Belle Creek, and the thought of returning to a Europe who hated them chilled them to the bone.

But for Peter, all those thoughts, all those fears, were very far away. All he could think of was Margaret and the way she had looked at him with eyes on fire, the way she had seen straight into the depths of his soul, the way she somehow loved him despite everything.

He hadn't seen her in six days, not since the day in the field when she had shown him the magical hiding spot among the soaring sugarcane stalks. And as twilight fell on Victory in Europe Day, Peter began to form an idea.

"It's too dangerous," Maus told him after Peter explained what he was thinking. "What if you're caught?

What if they think you're trying to escape now that we've lost the war?"

"Look at the guards, Maus," Peter said. "They're not paying attention tonight. And perhaps now that the war has ended, we are no longer the enemy anyhow."

They both looked toward the guards' barracks. The lights were on, and strains of "We'll Meet Again"—the popular Benny Goodman Orchestra version featuring Peggy Lee—wafted across the yard.

The lyrics—about two lovers meeting again someday—weren't lost on Peter, and he decided that perhaps the song was a sign. Tonight, with the guards distracted, he would go to Margaret. It might be the only chance he'd have to hold her in his arms before he was sent back across the Atlantic. God only knew how long it would take him to make it back to her.

"I'm going," he said to Maus as a burst of rough male laughter erupted from the guards' barracks, followed by the tinkling sound of several female giggles.

Maus's brow knit together. "You are sure it is worth the risk, Peter?"

"I am sure."

"And you are certain she loves you?" Maus didn't meet Peter's gaze as he asked the question.

There was something about Maus's reaction that made Peter think his friend was jealous, but he didn't have time to consider that now. "Yes, Maus, I am," Peter said.

Maus turned away. "Then Godspeed."

Peter waited until full dark, and then, his heart in his throat, he made his way to the edge of the camp. He knew that the fence was weak in places; he himself had repaired a section of it last week, and there was a strip along the north side that was scheduled for repair on Friday. In truth, there was no real hurry to complete the fence's restoration. A prisoner would have to be crazy to try to escape during the night. They were on the edge of the Everglades, teeming with alligators. Running into the swamps would be akin to signing one's own death warrant. Fleeing in the opposite direction would send a man straight into town, where he'd surely be discovered at first light.

And so Peter found the fence as he knew he would: unguarded and torn along a fence post by a storm-downed tree. He peeled the chain link back as far as he could manage and squeezed out, ripping the back of his shirt on one of the barbs.

It took him forty minutes at a slow run to reach her house. He had followed the road that the prisoner transport normally took, hugging the shadows for fear of being seen. By the time he made it across the cane fields to her backyard, he was damp with sweat. He wiped his brow and took a deep breath. There were two lights on in the house: one in the main room, and one in the room he believed to be Margaret's. He'd seen the inside of the house only once, the day Jeremiah was attacked, but he had memorized its layout.

Slowly, he crept from the shadows along the edge of the bean field, then in silence, he crossed the neat rows of crops until he was alongside the house. He found four pebbles on the ground, moved behind the old oak tree that shadowed the side yard, and aimed.

His first pebble missed its mark, but the second one he threw pinged off Margaret's window. He held his breath, but there was no reaction. He threw again, and this time, he could see a shadow moving inside the room, but still, no one came. He wound up once more, and he threw his last pebble. It clinked off the pane, and for a second, nothing happened. Then, to Peter's relief, the curtains rustled and Margaret appeared. She slid the window up and looked out.

"Who's there?" she said softly into the darkness.

Peter stepped from behind the tree without saying anything. The moon was barely a sliver, but the sky was clear and full of stars, so there was a wash of pearl light softening the darkness. He knew she would see him as her eyes adjusted, and a moment later, she did.

Peter watched as her eyes widened and her beautiful rose mouth parted in a smile. But just as quickly, concern fell over her features. "What are you doing here?" she whispered. "You'll get in trouble."

He took a few steps closer, being careful not to make any noise for fear of triggering the attention of her parents or sister. "I had to see you," he whispered. "Can you come out?"

She hesitated and looked over her shoulder. "Not until my parents and sister have gone to sleep. Can you wait?"

"I would wait forever to be with you," he responded solemnly.

She smiled again, and Peter's heart swelled. He was hers, and she was his, and that was all he needed.

"Meet me in the clearing," he said, "the one you made for Jeremiah."

She nodded and closed the window quietly, pulling the curtains closed against the night.

It was nearly two hours later when she finally appeared

in the sugarcane field. Peter had taken one of the sheets from the clothesline stretched across the edge of Margaret's backyard, and though it was still slightly damp, it made for the perfect ground cover. He'd picked wildflowers from along the edge of the road on his way here and used sugarcane blades to twist them into a beautiful bouquet of reds, oranges, and pinks, the colors of a Florida sunset.

He heard her footfall before she arrived, and though he knew in his heart that it was Margaret, he crouched, ready to run, just in case someone else happened upon their spot. But then she broke into the clearing, wearing her familiar faded red dress, her brown hair falling in loose waves over her tan, slender shoulders.

"Peter," she whispered, and that was all it took to undo him.

He stood slowly and pulled her into his arms. Her body was warm, soft, strong. "You're my home," he murmured and buried his face in her neck. Her hair smelled like strawberries.

They kissed, gently, slowly for a long time, for tonight, there was no hurry. Peter could tell from the moon that it wasn't quite midnight, and he knew the guards wouldn't stir until after dawn. He couldn't quite believe that he had hours with her, with Margaret, the woman he loved more than anything in the world. She was his hope, his salvation, his future.

"Peter," she murmured, her lips leaving his. He felt at once like a starving man. He wanted more of her touch, the softness of her lips on his. But then she put a slender hand on the flat plane of his stomach, just above his waist, and his whole body tingled. She looked him in the eye and then slowly knelt down on the blanket, beckoning for him to follow.

"Margaret?" he whispered as he knelt beside her. He didn't want to assume anything, didn't want to take advantage of her in any way. He yearned for her in a way he hadn't known was possible, but he was a gentleman.

"I'm yours," she said, interrupting his train of thought. And in case there was any doubt, she pulled her red dress over her head in one swift movement, and Peter stared in awe at her beautiful, perfect, naked body, which seemed to glow in the silver moonlight. "I'm all yours, Peter," she whispered.

"And I am yours." He laid her down gently, and then he took his time running first his hands and then his lips over every inch of Margaret's body. He wanted to know all of her. And when he finally gazed into her eyes and slid inside of her, he felt her tense around him as she cried out, and it was like heaven itself was embracing him.

When it was over, he wrapped her in his arms and pulled her against him. They stared into each other's eyes for a long time in silence.

"That was my first time," Margaret finally said shyly.

Peter smiled and pushed a tendril of her hair behind her ear. "Mine too."

"I never knew love could feel like this," Margaret murmured. "It is gentle and fierce, forgiving and demanding, and once it finds you, it lives in your heart forever."

"A quote from Emerson?" Peter guessed.

"No. My words, this time. You make me a poet."

Peter kissed her. "If only we could stay in this moment forever."

"But we can't," Margaret said, "so let's make the most of every second now."

In the darkness, they made love twice more, talking and laughing and holding each other until the first rays of the violet dawn began to pierce the sky along the eastern horizon. Never before had Peter been so sad to see morning come. "I must go, Margaret," he whispered, his heart heavy with regret.

"Just stay a moment more." She kissed him, long and hard, and although he knew that every second after daylight put him in danger, he didn't care. Nothing else mattered but her.

It was May 9, 1945, and the war was officially over. But for Peter, the journey had just begun.

CHAPTER THIRTEEN

"Do you think Peter Dahler himself could have been the artist behind the painting?" I asked my father as we headed out into the afternoon air to follow Nicola's directions to the competing gallery where Bettina worked.

"I don't know," my father said. "You said there was no indication that he was an artist in anything Jeremiah or the letters said. I tend to think that someone with that kind of talent doesn't just stumble upon it late in life. Surely he would have always been sketching."

I nodded. I had the same feeling. "So what about Wyeth and Gaertner? Do you think the artist who painted Grandma Margaret is somehow affiliated with them? Maybe Peter Dahler was friends with one of their pupils."

My father shrugged. "I don't know enough about art to make an educated guess, I'm afraid. After we visit with Bettina, maybe we can look them up and see if that gives us any ideas." He waved his iPhone in the air. "Although if both Gaertner and Wyeth were American painters, their pupils must have studied in the States, right? It makes me wonder how the painting found its way to a gallery in Munich."

"None of it makes any sense," I agreed.

We found the Galerie Bergen easily; it was marked by a huge white sign with purple lettering over a storefront with floor-to-ceiling windows. We headed inside, and my father asked the man who greeted us if Bettina was in. They exchanged a few words in German, and then the man strode away, returning a few minutes later with a small, slender woman in her twenties with a close-cropped dark pixie cut. She introduced herself in German as Bettina Schöffmann, and my father asked in German if she spoke English.

She glanced at me. "Only a little," she said with a thick accent. "Not well."

My father nodded and turned to me. "Mind if I speak to her in German and translate for you?"

"Sure, go ahead." The decision to travel with him suddenly seemed a little less foolish.

My father asked Bettina something in seemingly fluid German, and she smiled and looked briefly at me before replying.

"She says you look just like the woman in the painting," my father translated. "She says it's like the painting coming to life before her eyes."

"Please tell her thank you."

My father translated my words and then asked Bettina something else. They went back and forth in German for a few minutes, and I was just getting antsy when I heard Bettina clearly say, "Atlanta, Georgia." My father drew a sharp breath and looked at me before responding.

"What did she say?" I asked.

He said something else to Bettina in German, and then he

turned to me. "She says that the painting arrived from a gallery in Atlanta. The Ponce Gallery."

I blinked at him. "The Ponce? In *Atlanta*?"

He nodded. "She called the gallery to ask about it, since the instructions seemed so strange to her, but the curator there said he had received an anonymous typewritten note, along with the sealed one that was forwarded to you, asking for the painting to be restored specifically by the Galerie Schubert-Balck and sent on to you."

I shook my head in disbelief. "So it traveled all the way across the ocean and back? And it came from the city I grew up in?"

My father nodded solemnly.

"The plot thickens," I murmured as my father turned back to Bettina and resumed their conversation. After a few minutes, she turned to me.

"I wish you good luck," she said slowly and formally. "I hope you—" She stopped and trailed off, then she said something to my father in German.

"She hopes we find what we're looking for," my father translated, and Bettina nodded.

"Thank you for your help," I told her.

"You are welcome," she said. "The painting, it is very beautiful. Is painted with love."

My father and I thanked her again and left the gallery. My father's face was scrunched in concentration, and as soon as we rounded the corner, he pulled out his iPhone and began typing.

"What are you looking for?" I asked.

"I'm looking up Ralph Gaertner. If I'm remembering right, I'm pretty sure he was from Atlanta."

My heartbeat picked up. I kept pace with my father as he

hurried along, reading rapidly as we walked back toward the river.

"What does it say?" I finally asked eagerly.

"Well, Ralph Gaertner *did* spend most of his career in Atlanta." He turned the phone around and showed me an image of a painting. In it, a woman stood on a cliff beside a lighthouse, her hair wafting in the breeze beside her, her hand shielding her eyes as she looked out at the ocean. Over the deep blue water, the sky was purple at the edges—either sunrise or sunset, it appeared. The woman's face was in the shadows, though you could tell she was strong and beautiful.

"That's a Gaertner? It's pretty. But it doesn't really look like our painting, does it?"

"I don't know. I can see what Nicola Schubert was saying about the similarities."

I gave him a skeptical look. He held up his hands in mock surrender. "Look," he said, "I'm the first one to admit that I know next to nothing about art—I had one art history class in college, and that's about it. But you have to admit, the sky sort of looks similar to the painting you received, doesn't it? It's darker here, but it has the same purple shades, and the same sort of dreamy quality to it, don't you think? It adds a bit of credence to the idea that Gaertner taught our artist."

I took the phone from him and studied it more closely. The sky in the painting was deep and layered. The title of the painting was *East,* so I assumed the colors were supposed to be those of a sunrise from somewhere on the Atlantic coast of the United States. My father was right about the dreamy feel to the wispy, color-saturated sky.

I handed the phone back to my dad, who pocketed it. "It's a

long shot, but maybe there's a link between Gaertner and Peter Dahler," I said. "Want to try Franz Dahler again?"

"Sounds good to me."

As my father and I strolled back over the river, I marveled at how the late-afternoon sun cast the sky in a deep shade of blue as it dipped lower in the sky. The rooftops of Munich seemed to glow in the honeyed light.

We buzzed Franz Dahler's apartment, and again, there was no answer. We tried twice more before turning away. "What if he's out of town or something?" I asked as we emerged back into the *Viktualienmarkt*. "Or what if he's dead?"

"That's not very optimistic."

I could feel myself bristling. His words felt like a criticism. "If he's Peter Dahler's brother, he'd be in his nineties. People in their nineties die."

"Look, don't give up yet. If we're meant to find him, we will. I'm a big believer that in life, things happen the way they're supposed to."

I couldn't resist rolling my eyes. Since when was my father a philosopher? "Yeah, well, forgive me if I don't share the same opinion. In my life, it's more like if something can go wrong, it will."

My dad was silent for a moment. "Or maybe the tide is turning, Emily. I'd like to think that's true."

"I'm sure you would. But it's not that easy."

We were quiet as we wove our way back through the bustling farmers' market. My father consulted his iPhone again as we walked and led us down a side street to the right. "How's your appetite? I know it's only five thirty, but I could eat. There's a place a block or two away that's recommended on TripAdvisor."

"I'm starving," I replied. "Lead the way." I followed him down another small lane to a restaurant on the corner with a big sign outside that said GASTHOF MEYERHANS. To the left of the building, there was a tree-shaded area, dotted with tables and trimmed with tiny white lights. A sign bearing a blue Löwenbräu logo announced that it was the restaurant's *Biergarten*. The restaurant itself looked old-fashioned and charming, with window boxes overflowing with flowers, antique shutters, and a gabled arch over the front door.

Inside, a cheerful blond waitress chatted with my father in German and showed us to a small table in the nearly empty restaurant's back corner. The dark-paneled walls and the exposed wood beams of the ceiling reminded me a bit of a cellar, but the windows let in enough light that the room seemed to glow. Three gray-haired men, all wearing suspenders, were clustered around a table against the opposite wall, each of them clutching the handle of a giant beer stein.

My father followed my gaze and smiled. "When in Rome," he said. He scanned the beer list and asked if I felt like a drink. I nodded, and he helped me decipher the beer offerings, then he flagged our waitress down and ordered a Hacker-Pschorr Münchener Gold for himself and a Hofbräu München Original for me.

"You speak German really well," I said as she hurried away to get our order. It felt strange to compliment him; I was much more accustomed to carrying around a chip on my shoulder. "I never knew."

He shrugged. "I took it in college for a few years. My accent is terrible."

"But you're fluent?"

"Mostly. I brush up every now and again."

The waitress returned a moment later with two giant glass beer steins. She plunked one down in front of me and the other in front of my father, splashing a bit of beer on the table in the process. She asked him something in German, and he replied with a smile. She nodded and walked away.

"She wanted to know if we're ready to order," he explained. "I told her we needed a minute with the menu."

I looked at my huge beer and then at the unintelligible food descriptions, feeling suddenly overwhelmed.

"Don't worry, I'll translate," my father said, and though it felt strange to rely on him for anything, I knew I didn't have much of a choice. Ten minutes later, I had ordered a *Schlachtplatte*—a platter of Bavarian sausages, potatoes, and sauerkraut—and he had ordered *Nürnberger* sausages with a side of *Käsespätzle*, which he explained were German egg noodles with onions and cheese. We toasted, and we each took a giant sip of beer. I wasn't usually a beer drinker, but after traipsing around Munich for a few hours, the Hofbräu was incredibly refreshing.

While we waited for our food, my father called up the Wikipedia article on Ralph Gaertner again and began to read the brief biography of the artist aloud.

"Ralph Gaertner, born February 10, 1921, died just this February. He was a realist painter," he began. "He was one of the most well-known American artists of the 1960s and 1970s, helping to shape the resurgence of realism in the United States."

"He only died earlier this year?" I asked, feeling strangely crushed. After all, there was no real proof that he was in any way connected to my grandmother or to the painting we'd received. Still, it felt like another possible lead vanishing. What if we could have reached him, and he could have pointed us in the right direction? Now we'd never know.

My father nodded and looked back at his phone. "It says he was born in Germany, and that he moved to the United States in the 1950s, eventually settling in Atlanta." He read a bit more and added, "Gaertner was known for his vibrant skyscapes. Every one of his paintings featured a signature image: a woman in the shadows, with her back to the artist. Sometimes, the woman—known simply as the Gaertner Angel—was in the foreground. Sometimes, she was in the background, in the middle of a crowd. He refused to discuss the significance of the imagery, and art critics have long speculated that the familiar feminine silhouette was meant to represent the everywoman. Some say she's supposed to represent justice, and others say she's supposed to be a humanization of the Statue of Liberty, to honor his experience as an immigrant. But one thing always remained constant: Gaertner never painted her face. 'It's too intimate,' he told *Newsweek* in a 1995 interview. 'Painting a person's face and revealing it to the world is like a form of robbery.'"

My father looked up at me and frowned. "So that seems to support what Nicola Schubert told us. The painting you have definitely couldn't be a Gaertner, because it features the woman's face."

"But it also includes a beautiful sky," I argued. "And doesn't it say Gaertner's known for that?"

"Maybe that's why Nicola thought of Gaertner when she saw the painting." My father scanned the Wikipedia entry in silence for a moment. "There isn't much here about his background. It says he favored watercolor, drybrush, and egg tempera, much like Andrew Wyeth, who was a contemporary of his." He read some more and looked up. "Emily, I don't know. I can see the similarities between Gaertner's style and the style of whoever painted our painting. But would he encourage his pupils to paint faces if he didn't believe in it?"

"Maybe," I say slowly. But I had to admit that my father was right. We were almost back to square one.

"Penny for your thoughts," my father said, and I realized I'd been staring into space for the last few minutes.

"I was just wondering if we've run out of leads." I took a sip of my beer. "Maybe we shouldn't have come here."

"But we *do* have a lead. Bettina mentioned the Ponce Gallery in Atlanta."

"I guess."

"Besides, I'm glad we came," he said after a pause. "It's giving us a chance to reconnect a bit."

The words rubbed me the wrong way. "We're not really reconnecting, though, are we?" I said, hating myself a little when I saw hurt flicker across my father's face for a second. "I mean, I appreciate you being here with me, and I appreciate you springing for the tickets. But don't make this into more than it is."

"Emily," he said after a pause, "this is the most we've talked to each other in years. That has to mean something."

"I think you're reading too much into it." I clenched my hands into fists in my lap. "It's not like I'm going to give you the silent treatment while we work on something together. This is about Grandma Margaret, not you and me."

"I just want to believe that maybe there's a day in the future when you'll think about opening the door a crack. I can't begin to make things up to you until you start to let me in."

I opened my mouth to reply, but we were interrupted by the arrival of our food, delivered by our waitress and an equally cheerful-looking waiter with a thick mustache and beard. Our plates were heaped so high it was almost comical; I couldn't imagine eating that much sausage and sauerkraut in a lifetime. But my stomach growled, and I dug in.

The food was savory and incredible, and for a few minutes, we ate without talking. My dad was the one to break the silence between us.

"You know I love you, Emily," he said. "Always have, always will."

I didn't reply right away. There was a lump in my throat that had no business being there. I had to remind myself that the words meant nothing if he didn't have the strength of character to do right by me. And for so much of his life, he hadn't. "Yeah, well, forgive me if I have trouble believing you. You used to tell me you loved me when I was a kid too, but it was awfully easy for you to vanish when it became convenient for you, wasn't it?"

"Biggest mistake I ever made."

"I know you want me to believe that," I said finally. "But you can't erase the past."

"I know."

"So why are you trying to rewrite history? We're never going to be buddies, you and me."

"I hope you know that makes me profoundly sad."

"But it's your fault!" I could hear my voice rising an octave, and I knew my blood pressure was rising along with it. "You can't just sit there and act like this is some sort of unfortunate thing out of your control. You screwed up. Then you spent years and years pretending I didn't exist, because it was easier for you that way. And now, suddenly, you think you can just stroll back in and we'll be friends again? What, because you're a good German translator?"

My dad opened and closed his mouth without saying anything, and I tried not to be bothered by his wounded expression. I wasn't sure whether he was speechless because I'd hit the nail on the head or because he was appalled that I was such a terrible daughter. "I really hurt you," he finally said.

I blinked a few times. "Yes."

"I'm sorry."

When I looked up at him, he held my gaze.

"I'm sorry," he said again, more firmly this time. "And I'll keep telling you that for the rest of my life, because it's truer than you'll ever know. I've said it before, and I'll say it again. I left because I was a fool, and then I didn't know how to fix it. I know you think I rode off into the sunset and didn't think about you anymore, but the truth is, you were with me every day. I just didn't know how to undo what I had done. It was my own weakness, pure and simple. I have to live with those regrets every day, and I know I deserve every angry word you say to me. I just hope that someday, you'll understand, and you can forgive at least a little bit of what I've done."

I didn't reply, because I couldn't seem to summon words. It wasn't just that I'd never heard my father declare his emotions so plainly. It was that he was echoing some of my own sentiments about Nick and Catherine. *I just didn't know how to undo what I had done.* It made me uneasy to be reminded of how closely I had followed in his footsteps.

But I didn't know how to forgive him. And if I couldn't forgive him, how could I ever expect Nick and my daughter to forgive me for walking away? Was my father living with the same kind of guilt I was day in and day out? Maybe I owed it to him—and to myself, in a way—to try harder to understand where he was coming from, but the thought of letting down my walls was terrifying. It was my anger that kept me safe.

We ate in silence for a few more minutes before I pushed away my meal. My appetite was gone.

"I know you mean well," I said finally. "I'm just not ready to move forward with you, okay?"

"Understood." My father looked like he wanted to say something else, but then he shook his head and placed a hand on my arm. "Let's change the subject, then. Would you like to see a bit more of Munich this evening?"

I shook my head. I wasn't capable of switching tracks that easily. "I think I need to catch up on sleep. And I want to read a bit more about Ralph Gaertner and see if I can find any connection between him and Grandma Margaret. Maybe he was a POW in Belle Creek too."

"I'll walk you back to the hotel, then," my father said, pulling his credit card from his wallet and beckoning to the waitress. I reached for my wallet too, but he waved me away.

When we walked outside, twilight had already fallen over the city, and I was struck by the thought that the rich purple sky here looked a lot like the sky over Belle Creek in the painting. The city had come alive with twinkling lights, and the fading sun cast an ethereal glow over the rooftops as it sent its last rays over the horizon.

As my father held the door to the hotel lobby for me and walked with me to the elevator, I couldn't quite believe that we were here, together, on the other side of the world. What would my mother say?

"This is you," my father said, pausing at my doorway and waiting while I fumbled around in my purse for my room key.

"Thanks for walking me back." I felt suddenly awkward. "So are you heading out again?"

"I think I'll walk for a little while," he said. "But I should be back in an hour or two. And it looks like I'm getting e-mail access on my phone, so if you need anything in the meantime, just shoot me a message. I'll keep checking it."

"Thanks, but I'll be fine."

He leaned in for a hug, and I felt strange as I hugged back. I couldn't remember the last time we had done that.

When he pulled away, he cleared his throat, took a big step back and said, "Good night, Emily. I'll see you in the morning." He was walking away before I had a chance to reply.

CHAPTER FOURTEEN

I woke up just past six in the morning, disoriented and confused. It took me a few seconds to realize where I was—a hotel bed in Munich, Germany.

I turned on the small lamp on my night table and sat up. Had my father and I really connected a bit last night? For the first time in nearly twenty years? I didn't know quite what to make of it, and in my foggy state, it felt almost like a dream.

I spent the next two hours on the Internet, clicking through my usual roster of adoption search sites to see if there was anything new from an eighteen-year-old girl who could possibly be my daughter. It was, as usual, an exercise in futility, and I finally shut the computer down, frustrated.

I met my father in the lobby at nine, and we grabbed to-go coffees in the hotel's dining room before heading back out to Franz Dahler's apartment. The streets of Munich were quiet as we walked; the Marienplatz was uncrowded, the market not yet bustling.

"It feels like we have the city to ourselves," my father said with a smile.

I nodded my agreement, but I didn't reply. The fact that I understood him a little better meant that something had shifted between us, and now the ground beneath me felt unstable and foreign.

We buzzed Franz Dahler's apartment once again, and there was no answer. My father and I exchanged disappointed looks. "Let's try once more," he said.

I nodded and pushed the button beside the name Dahler again. We were greeted with silence, and dejected, I shrugged and began to walk away. But just then, a voice crackled from the speakers.

"*Hallo?*" It was a man's voice. "*Wer ist da?*"

I looked to my father, confused, but he was already responding in a string of rapid German. I heard my name and his, and then I heard him say *Franz Dahler*.

There was a pause, and then the man said over the speaker, "*Ja. Kommen Sie herein.*"

My father grinned at me as the door buzzed and he pulled it open. "He said to come up. It's Franz Dahler, Emily. We've found him."

We climbed three flights of stairs and found an old man waiting for us on the landing. He looked like he was in his eighties or nineties, with snow white hair, pale wrinkled skin, and cloudy blue eyes. "*Sie sind* Victor?" he asked, looking at us suspiciously. He asked something else, and my father replied in German, gesturing briefly to me.

"Ah, you are American," the man said in a thick German accent. "And your father says you don't speak German? I can speak some English, *ja*? I will try."

"Thank you, sir," I said. "You're Franz Dahler?"

"*Ja,*" he said. "Come." He beckoned for us to follow him into his apartment. Inside, the lighting was dim, and the place was austere, with no photographs or artwork on the walls. It looked like it was barely lived in, and yet the furniture and carpets were obviously old and worn. There was a small table with two stiff chairs pressed up against the wall beside the dated kitchen, and in the living room, I saw a single, worn sofa, a coffee table with a small pad of paper and a pen, and another hard-backed chair. That's where he led us now, gesturing to the sofa as he settled stiffly into the chair.

"So what can I do for you?" he asked as we sat, his speech pattern slow and deliberate.

"Mr. Dahler, we're looking for information about a man named Peter Dahler, and we believe he's your brother," I began. "Are we right?"

A shadow passed across Franz's face. "Peter?" He paused and looked at the ceiling for a minute, as if trying to gather himself. "Peter *was* my brother. He is long gone."

"He's dead?" I asked, my heart sinking. It was irrational to be holding out hope that a man in his nineties would still be out there when I knew the odds were against it. But still, I'd believed there was a chance.

"Dead?" Franz Dahler asked. "How would I know? I haven't spoken to him since 1947."

I took a deep breath. It meant that there was a chance Peter Dahler was still alive. But the way Franz Dahler was frowning at me made me feel uneasy. "Why?" I asked.

"He was imprisoned in America during the war," he replied. My father and I exchanged looks. "And he fell in love with an American girl."

"My mother," my father murmured.

"What?" Franz asked.

"Margaret. Was the girl's name Margaret? She lived in Florida?"

Franz blinked rapidly, and his face turned a little pink. "Yes. But how do you know that?"

My father gestured to me. "This is her granddaughter. And I'm her son."

Franz stared at my father first and then at me. "*Mein Gott*," he murmured. "I see it now. You have Peter's eyes, both of you. It is unmistakable. But how is this possible?"

"I don't know," I replied. "That's what we're trying to find out. We didn't even know he existed until last week."

Franz looked confused. "I do not understand. Surely he came back to America to find the girl he loved?"

"No. I don't think he did," I said.

"That is a tragedy." Franz looked tremendously sad. "And I believe it is perhaps a tragedy that began here."

"What do you mean?" I asked.

Instead of replying, Franz excused himself and walked into another room of the apartment. I glanced at my father, and he shrugged. A moment later, Franz returned carrying a yellowed photograph.

"I do not keep this out," he said. "There are many things I wish not to be reminded of. But you will see Peter here when he was young, before he went off to war."

I took the photograph and stared, my heart in my throat. It was a bit blurry and had clearly been taken in the late 1930s or early 1940s. A solemn-faced middle-aged man with a Clark Gable mustache and wispy dark hair stood in the middle of the image, his arm around a small, light-haired, middle-aged woman who was so pale and thin it looked as if she might disappear. To the woman's right was a boy of about fourteen or fifteen, with short, spiky brown hair; he was wearing shorts, suspenders, and kneesocks. The only person smiling in the photo was the blond young man to the left of the man with the mustache. He looked like he was seventeen or eighteen, and he was wearing an ill-fitting dark suit. I ran a finger over his foggy image.

"That is Peter," Franz said, watching me closely. "My brother. This was the day of his school graduation. Of course that's me in the suspenders. And those are our parents."

My great-grandparents, I thought, studying them and then looking long and hard at Peter. The man who was probably my grandfather. He was handsome and kind-looking, and Franz was right; the shape of his eyes looked a lot like mine. I handed the photo to my father, who examined it and gave it back to me.

"The photo was taken in 1939," Franz said after a moment. "The last year we were all together. You see, soon after, Peter went off to the RAD to do his compulsory time."

"The RAD?" I asked.

Franz nodded and seemed to be struggling to find the right words. "The *Reichsarbeitsdienst.* The compulsory labor force. Early in the war, young men were required to have six months in the RAD before they were drafted into the *Wehrmacht*—er, the armed forces. Peter did his six months and then he came home for a few days before he left on his military assignment. During that time, there was a large fight that changed everything."

"A fight?" my father asked. "Between whom?"

"Peter and my father." Franz gazed off into the distance for a long time, and I had the sense he was reliving whatever had taken place seventy-five years ago. "When Peter was younger, when he lived here still, he was sheltered from the news reports. Of course he heard things, saw things, but my father prohibited the discussion of politics at home. It made my mother very distressed, and she was often ill, often weak. It was to protect her, you see.

"But then, Peter returned from his RAD service, and he was angry," Franz continued. "My father, he was a Nazi. He was a strong political supporter of Hitler's regime. And Peter, he was not. When Peter came home, he insisted on discussing politics with my father before he left for the war." Franz paused and shook his head. "I can still remember him saying, '*Ich weigere mich zu kämpfen, ohne den Grund dafür zu verstehen.*' It means he refused to fight without understanding the cause. He disagreed with my father, and my father was outraged to have a son who didn't worship the führer."

"How did you feel?" my father interjected.

Franz sighed. "It was a long time ago, you understand. And Hitler was a magician, a storyteller. He cast many of us under his spell. I admit, I was one of those who were charmed by his words, his promises. I believed that Germany would rise and that somehow, we had the right to do what we were doing."

My stomach turned, but then Franz looked up and met my eye. "As I said, it was a long time ago. I have great shame over the way I felt then. But my father always believed that Hitler had been right, even long after Hitler was dead and Germany was defeated. He grew old and bitter, blaming everyone he could think of for Germany's defeat. Including Peter. *Especially* Peter."

"Peter?" I asked. "How was he responsible for Germany's defeat?"

"Of course he wasn't," Franz said. "But my father always believed that Peter was a coward. When we got word that Peter had been captured on the battlefield in Africa, my father was furious."

"What was he doing in Africa?"

"He was in the *Afrika Korps*," Franz explained. "You have heard of *Generalfeldmarschall* Erwin Rommel? The Desert Fox?"

"I think so," I said while my father nodded.

"General Rommel was the commander of the *Afrika Korps*. And the only time my father felt pride in Peter during the war, I think, was when Peter wrote in a letter to our mother that he actually respected Rommel, despite everything. You see, Peter wrote that Rommel refused orders to kill Jews and civilians. You must realize that elsewhere, the opposite was taking place, yes?"

I nodded.

"Yes, well, Rommel was different. He was humane, perhaps even a good man. Peter hated the war, but he did not mind fighting under Rommel, because he felt that at the least, he would not be asked to do things that went against his conscience. You understand? But by late 1942, Africa was lost to the Germans, and soon after, Rommel returned to Germany. It was not very many months later that Peter, along with many others, was captured by the Allies. When we received notification, my father was very angry, you see. To my father, the only thing worse than someone who didn't agree with him was someone who was weak enough to fall into enemy hands."

"Were you in the army too?" my father asked.

"I was three years younger than Peter, so I did my time in the RAD and then joined the *Wehrmacht* in 1943. It was the same year Peter was captured and the same year our mother died."

"Your mother died during the war?" I looked again at the photo, at the waif of a woman who looked like a ghost even when she was alive.

Franz nodded. "Our father always said that it was news of Peter's capture that killed her. Of course that wasn't true at all. She was miserable with my father, you see. He ruled with an iron fist, and she had a tendency toward illness anyhow. But my father lived on blame the way some people live on bread and water. It was his *Nahrung,* his sustenance. And he blamed Peter for our mother's death.

"I spent most of the war on the eastern front and was fortunate to survive," Franz continued. "When the war ended, I came home to a hero's welcome from my father, but he had become a different man by then. While Peter and I had gone to the battlefield, my father had been stuck in Holzkirchen, our hometown, growing more and more distressed at what he called the death of Germany. When I returned in 1945, I found my father cold, hardened, and bitter."

"When did Peter come home?" I asked.

"You see, the prisoners weren't released immediately. Peter was sent to a prison camp in Great Britain, where he was compelled to do nearly two years of hard labor before being released."

"Of course," I murmured, thinking of the three letters Julie had given me.

"He wrote to us from England, but my father never wrote back," Franz continued. "The letters from America had begun to arrive by then, and my father was furious."

"What letters?" my father asked.

Franz sighed. "The letters from the American girl. Your mother, I suppose. Before leaving America, Peter had apparently given her our family address so that she could reach him. But my father opened all the letters addressed to Peter. The first few—in which she talked of missing him and loving him—infuriated my father. He said Peter had no business falling in love with an American woman. He felt she was the enemy and that Peter had betrayed Germany by doing such a thing. But then there was a letter in which she said she had discovered she was with child . . ." Franz's voice trailed off as I leaned forward, eager to hear what he had to say. "Something changed in my father that day. His anger at Peter turned to cold hatred. It was irrational but complete."

I sat back in my chair. Beside me, my father gently placed his hand on my shoulder. So my grandmother had written to tell Peter she was pregnant, and instead of creating joy, the news had made my grandfather the target of his father's fury. "So Peter learned that he was going to be a father when he was in England, then?" I asked.

Franz hesitated. "No. My father burned most of the letters."

I stared at him. "He deliberately kept the news from Peter that my grandmother was pregnant?"

"Yes. And when Peter finally came home at the end of 1947, my father didn't tell him right away. No, instead, he began to yell at Peter, to call him a traitor. Imagine that. My brother had come from many years as a prisoner, a free man for the first time, and instead of coming home to a welcome, he came home to an avalanche of wrath. At some point before I arrived at our house, my father told Peter that the American girl he'd loved had been pregnant. I arrived in the middle of it. You could feel the hatred."

Franz paused, and for the first time, I noticed that his face had reddened and there was sweat on his brow.

"Are you okay?" I asked. "We can stop if you need to take a break."

"No, I must tell you this." He took a deep breath. "You see, I took the side of my father. I have regretted it in the years since, you understand. But at the time, I too was still smarting over Germany's defeat. And I felt the same as my father did. How could Peter have been the prisoner of an enemy nation and somehow fallen in love with a woman there? I thought it unconscionable."

I opened my mouth to defend him, but Franz waved me off. "I was young at the time. I have realized the error of my ways. You do not have to tell me how wrong I was. In any case, my father thrust the one letter he hadn't burned at Peter and told him to get out."

Franz sighed. "I never saw him again. Peter left that night. It was snowing, and I remember watching from the window. As he trudged down the street, it was as if the snowfall swallowed him whole. I always expected him to come back someday, but he never did." He looked up at me. "This is the first time I've spoken of him in seventy years, you see. After that day, my father didn't permit talk of Peter in the house. Peter was dead to him, he said. He was dead to our family. But he didn't die, did he?"

It took me a moment to realize he was looking to me for answers. "I'm sorry, but I don't know," I told him. "We have no idea what became of him."

He turned and looked out the window. "So many secrets and lies," he murmured. "They destroy everything, do they not?"

For an instant, my mind flashed to Nick. *Secrets and lies. They destroy everything.* I shook off the thought. "A few weeks ago, I received a painting in the mail," I told Franz. "It's what made us come here. The painting appeared to be of my grandmother standing in a field, maybe a sugarcane field in Florida, and it came with a note. It said, *Your grandfather never stopped loving her. Margaret was the love of his life.*"

Franz looked startled. "And who was the note from?"

"We don't know. It wasn't signed. But that's what's led us here. We thought maybe the painting was done by your brother."

"Peter?" Franz frowned. "No, he did not paint. My father discouraged artistic expression of any kind."

"Does the name Ralph Gaertner mean anything to you,

then?" I ask. "The owner of the gallery that restored the painting thought it resembled his work."

"Yes, of course. He's quite a famous American painter, isn't he?"

"Right. Is there any way Peter could have been friends with him? Maybe when they were young? Or could they have been in the army together? Gaertner is from Germany too."

Franz thought about this for a moment. "There was an Otto Gaertner in school with Peter. They were friends, I remember that. But I don't think he had any brothers. Gaertner isn't a terribly uncommon name, you see."

I exchanged looks with my father. "Do you have any idea where we could find this Otto Gaertner?"

"I believe Otto died during the war," he said. "Of course the parents are long gone too. I think perhaps you have arrived at a dead end, as you Americans say."

"Not if we go to Atlanta," my father said.

I turned to him, my stomach doing a little flip. I hadn't been back to Atlanta since I left at the age of eighteen, a secret daughter in my womb. "Atlanta?"

He nodded. "It's where the painting came from. And it's where Ralph Gaertner lived. I think it's our only logical move at this point. If he was tied to Peter, we might be able to find a family member there who can tell us something."

"And then you will tell me?" Franz asked. His tone was suddenly desperate, and I was surprised to see tears glistening in his eyes. "You see, I am an old man, and many of my memories have abandoned me. But you never forget that which you regret. And my greatest shame in life is the role I played in sending Peter out into the cold with no home, no family. It was a terrible thing to do. I have regretted it every day since." He paused and looked up at the two of us. "But if you are his son, and you are his granddaughter, some piece of my brother lived and returned to Germany. And that warms my heart."

The thought made me ache. "I'll let you know if we find anything," I promised.

"And the painting you mention," he said after a moment. "I would like to see it someday."

I dug my iPhone out and pulled up the photo I'd taken. Franz slipped on a pair of reading glasses and studied it for a long time before handing it back to me. "She was beautiful, your grandmother," he said softly. "I can see why Peter fell in love with her. But my dear, he could not have painted this himself. He just was not an artist."

I nodded and pocketed my phone, feeling dejected.

"Thank you for visiting," Franz said, reaching out to shake my father's hand and then mine. "And now, I must take my rest. Talking of the past makes me feel very tired."

"Of course," I said as my father and I stood. We followed Franz toward the door, which he opened for us.

He paused and put a hand on my shoulder. I looked up at him, and he held my gaze for a long time. "I'm sorry," he finally said. "I am very sorry for the role I played in separating you from your grandfather. He was a good man, and I wish you could have known him."

"Maybe it's not too late," I said. I gave Franz a quick peck on the cheek, and then my father and I headed down the stairs and out into the morning sunlight.

CHAPTER FIFTEEN

For a month after the end of the war, Peter thought—with an absurd kind of hope—that perhaps he wouldn't be sent back. There would be a record-keeping error, or Camp Belle Creek would somehow be passed over, its prisoners released by default.

But of course that was foolish, and he knew it. Still, as the days ticked by—and as Peter was moved to a work detail making repairs to the dike around Lake Okeechobee—he allowed himself to dream. He would find a plot of land here! He would build a farmhouse with his own hands! Perhaps he would find a job teaching literature to children in a school!

"*Tagträumer*," Maus muttered more and more frequently. *Daydreamer*. It was like throwing bricks from a glass house, though. Maus was the biggest daydreamer of all, spending his days doodling pictures of his hometown with a stick in the sand and sketching shapely women on the sides of their barracks with discarded pieces of coal. His head was always in the clouds.

"I am the daydreamer?" Peter asked one day.

"You forget that we are the enemy," Maus replied tersely. "And now we are the *defeated* enemy. Why would they want us here?"

"Because we have worked hard," Peter replied firmly. "We have been kind and respectful, and we have fallen in love with their country."

"Yes, but their country hasn't fallen in love with us, you see," Maus grunted.

And though Peter knew that Maus was right, that he was living on borrowed time, he was still hit with a wave of shock when Harold came into the prisoner barracks early one Tuesday at the end of June and gave them the news.

"You will be sent three days from now to a camp in Great Britain," the guard said, reading from a piece of paper. He looked up. "Pack your things, boys. You're going home."

Peter saw Margaret just once more, on the eve of his departure, and it was only because Harold had taken pity on him. "I know you love her, Dahler," the older man had said gruffly without meeting Peter's eye. "But for God's sake, don't get caught, or I'll be on the hook for it." He paused and looked Peter in the eye. "Your intentions are honorable?"

"Oh, yes sir."

"And she loves you too?"

Peter hesitated. He didn't want to create any problems for Margaret.

"Son," Harold said, his voice softening, "I don't disapprove. And your secret's safe with me."

Peter looked up. "Yes, sir. I cannot believe it, but she loves me too."

Harold nodded. "Then go. Just be back by eleven. My shift ends then, and I can't protect you after that."

Peter glanced at the clock on the wall. It was already 8:30 in the evening. The other prisoners were packing, laughing, joking around, sure that they were about to be reunited with the people they loved. They would never notice him gone, except perhaps for Maus. But Maus would keep his secret.

"Thank you, sir," Peter said. Harold nodded, and without a word, he pointed Peter toward his car. They climbed in and drove in silence to just outside the camp gate. "Go," Harold said. "And when you return, I suspect you know where the torn corner of fence is located."

Peter looked at him in surprise, but Harold just smiled. "I was young once too." He handed Peter his wristwatch, gave him a serious look, and said, "Remember, eleven. Not a moment later."

"Yes, sir." Peter got out of the car and shut the door. He leaned in to thank Harold again, but the guard was already pulling away, heading toward town.

Peter slipped into the shadows at the side of the road and hugged them all the way to Margaret's house, running as fast as his legs would take him. His hours were limited today, and he didn't know how long it would be until he saw her again. He had to seize every possible moment.

It wasn't until he was nearly at her house that it occurred to him that her family would still be awake, that it would perhaps be impossible for her to sneak away. He emerged from the sugarcane at the edge of her property, and his heart sank immediately. Of course the windows of her house were ablaze with light. Peter stared from the shadows for a moment, his mind whirling. He couldn't just walk up to her front door and ask her parents if she could come out, now could he? Nor could he throw pebbles at her window again and risk exposing their relationship. Plus, he had Harold to think about. If Peter was caught roaming through Belle Creek alone, it would be Harold who would answer for it.

No, he would have to think of something else. But he was due back to the camp before eleven, which didn't give him much time.

While he thought, his feet carried him toward Margaret's clearing, the one in which he'd held her, kissed her, made love to her. If he could live somewhere for the rest of his life, he decided, it would be there, in the memory of her. Perhaps when he returned to Belle Creek one day, they would buy the land the field sat on, raze the center section, and build a house. It was a dream to hold on to.

He was so deep in thought when he reached the clearing that it didn't occur to him he wouldn't be alone. But no sooner had he emerged from the cane than something hit him in the midsection. "Oof!" he grunted, the breath knocked out of him as he doubled over. He was suddenly on high alert. A townsperson had found him out! A police officer was here to arrest him! But when his vision cleared, he saw that there was not a waiting mob in the clearing. It was just Jeremiah, breathing hard, his eyes wide, looking as surprised to see Peter as Peter was to see him.

"What are you doing here?" Jeremiah demanded. He set down the knapsack that he'd slung at Peter and reached out a hand. "I'm sorry. Did I hurt you?"

Peter shook his head. "No, Jeremiah. I did not mean to startle you."

"Shouldn't you be at the prison camp?"

"They're shipping me to England tomorrow. I had to see Margaret again."

Jeremiah looked confused. "But she ain't here."

"I know. I don't have much time, and the lights in her house are still on. I don't know how to get her attention without her family realizing I am here."

Jeremiah chewed his lip for a moment. "You really love her?"

"I do."

"You won't hurt her, will you?"

"Never." He hesitated. "You really care about her, don't you, Jeremiah?"

Jeremiah nodded. "Yeah."

Peter understood then that while Margaret had been light and salvation to him, she had been mother and protector to Jeremiah. The boy wanted the best for her too. "Jeremiah —" he began.

"I will go get her," Jeremiah interrupted. "I will bring her to you. You make her happy, Peter."

"Thank you," Peter said. The boy turned to go, but Peter reached out for his arm. "Wait. Will you look out for Margaret while I'm gone as best you can?"

Jeremiah nodded. "Of course. But I'm fixing to leave soon. Margaret's going to get me out. It ain't safe for me here. She found a children's home in Georgia that'll take me. She's going to help me get the bus fare."

"Is she?" Peter wasn't sure he'd ever loved Margaret more than he did in that moment.

"Of course. Don't you know by now that she's the one looking out for all of us? Including you?" And then Jeremiah was gone, slipping silently through the dark fields toward Margaret's house.

Nearly an hour passed before Margaret arrived. Peter was getting antsy; it was already ten minutes after ten, and he'd need to leave in another ten minutes—twenty if he ran all the way—in order to make it back to camp on time. He was so relieved to see her suddenly standing before him in the moonlight that as he stood up, his legs shook under him for a moment. "Margaret," he whispered. "My sweet Margaret."

She was breathless from running, and there were tears in her eyes. "You're going?"

He nodded. "Tomorrow morning. First thing. They're shipping us to England."

She blinked a few times, as if the news was too much to bear. "I knew the day would come. So I suppose you'll go back to Germany from there?"

Peter nodded. "I wanted to give you my address in Holzkirchen so that you'll have a way to reach me." He handed her the piece of paper he'd been carrying in his pocket all evening. "And I will write to you here, as often as I am able."

She nodded, slipping the paper into the pocket of her dress. "And you will return one day?" Her tone was shy, worried.

"As soon as I can." He waited until she looked up and met his gaze. "I promise, Margaret. My life is with you. I will come for you."

"I know," she whispered. She melted into his arms, and they stayed like that, holding each other, until Peter finally pulled away, his heart heavy with regret and fear. Her face was lit by the moon, and she seemed to glow like a spirit in the darkness. Like she was already disappearing.

He touched her cheek, trailing his fingers gently down her jawline to her collarbone. "I will love you forever, Margaret. I will see you again soon." He kissed her long and hard, and then he pulled away, his eyes already filling with tears he didn't want her to see. "Good-bye, my Margaret. Until we meet again."

And then, with the greatest regret he'd ever felt, he slipped back into the shadows of the sugarcane field. He didn't look back, because if he had, he would have stayed forever.

———

Peter, Maus, and the rest of the prisoners from Camp Belle Creek found themselves, some three weeks later, in rural Lancashire, England, where they were thrown in with hundreds of other prisoners who had been held in America throughout the latter years of the war. Peter was shocked from the moment he stepped off the transport. England had been leveled, parts of it obliterated, in a way that was horrifying. Peter had served in Africa, where the battles were mostly man against man. Here, it appeared that the German army had attacked the land itself. Cities had been bombed, fires had spread, and what must have once been beautiful was now a charred ruin.

And so when the guards were unkind to the prisoners, or when they forced them to work much longer hours than they'd worked in the United States, Peter bore it without a word of complaint. He looked around and felt a vast burden of guilt and sadness. It was his countrymen who had done this, and that meant it was his responsibility to fix it as best he could. Some days, he was called to work in the cotton mill in Barnoldswick. Other days, he was sent into the small towns throughout the county to begin the lengthy process of repair and restoration. But although the buildings were being mended and reconstructed, though the churches were rising once again toward the sky, though the physical traces of the war were being slowly washed away, Peter knew that their physical labor couldn't begin to fix everything. Everywhere he went, there were mothers who had lost sons to battle, wives who had lost husbands, children who had lost fathers. The war had hit hard here, and though structures can be rebuilt, souls remain forever damaged.

Peter accepted the tough conditions, the long hours, the backbreaking labor without complaint, because working his fingers to the bone also allowed him to fall deeply asleep each night, exhaustion his lullaby, despite the fact that he hadn't heard from Margaret. He had given her his home address in Germany, of course, and while he had received occasional short missives from his father, he had received nothing from her. Surely his father would have forwarded her mail if she'd sent any. Peter had written many times to ask if any letters from America had arrived, but his father always wrote back in the negative if he replied at all.

So during his waking hours, as his body toiled, Peter's mind whirled, imagining the worst. Had she died? Or fallen in love with someone else? He couldn't imagine it, but war did strange things to people. Surely if she was gone from this earth, he would have felt it in his bones. But would he have sensed it if she had simply moved on, decided to stop loving him? Could he even blame her? As the months wore on, and Peter and the other prisoners realized that their re-patriation to Germany wasn't going to happen anytime soon, Peter sunk deeper into a depression. Why would Margaret want to be with a German prisoner trapped a continent away, anyhow? She deserved an easier life than that.

He wrote to her every day at the beginning, and then, when he never heard back, he began writing every other day, and then every third day. It wasn't that he was losing interest. No, he loved her more with each passing moment. But he was beginning to worry that he was merely a burden to her, a mistake to be forgotten.

"Don't worry," Maus would say to him on the nights when Peter's world felt particularly dark. "You will find her again someday."

"But what if I find her," Peter often replied, "and her love for me is gone?"

"Then you will go on." It was Maus's reply each time, his tone firm and gentle.

But Peter knew that wasn't possible. It was Margaret who sustained him.

It was a snowy December day, a week before Christmas 1947, that Peter was finally sent home to Germany. His heart was in his throat as he climbed off the train in Holzkirchen. There was no welcome party, no fanfare, despite the fact that he'd written ahead to say he was coming. He hadn't heard from his parents or his brother for the last year, and his in-creasingly worried letters home had all gone unanswered. What if they had all died? What would he find when he knocked on the door to his childhood home?

But when Peter arrived on the doorstep of Auwald-straße 18, carried there by feet made heavy with dread, it was his father who answered the door. A million things tumbled through Peter's mind. Relief that his father was alive, confusion over why he hadn't written in so long, hurt at the sneer that crossed his father's face as he stood there on the doorstep.

"You have brought great shame to this family," were his father's first words to him. "You were too weak to survive in battle. You were captured as a coward. You disgraced us."

Peter stared at him, taking in the fury in his father's eyes. The man had aged to an almost shocking degree since Peter had last seen him. His dark hair was all gone, replaced with patches of white on a bald pate. His face was creased like a raisin, his eyes sunken. He was barely the same man, and Peter couldn't make sense of what he was saying.

"But, Father," Peter said, "I fought for Germany, just like you wanted." In an instant, he was ten years old again, desperate for his father's approval, desperate enough to ignore the clanging bells of his young conscience for just a little longer. He shook his head, reminding himself that he was, in fact, an adult now. An adult who loved his homeland but who regretted fighting for things that weren't right. An adult who was sickened by the news reports that seemed to get worse by the day, reports of the atrocities committed in the concentration camps. An adult who wondered how his nation would ever atone for the murders of millions of innocent men, women, and children.

"You did not fight," his father growled. "You surrendered."

Peter felt bile rising in his throat as his father glowered at him. "We had no choice!"

His father's expression twisted. "There is always a choice, Peter. Always. A bullet in your head would have been more honorable. Just look at how Otto died. His parents, at least, got to bury a hero."

He backed away from the doorway and disappeared inside the house as Peter blinked back sudden tears for his lost friend. After a moment, Peter followed, shutting the winter out behind him, but he couldn't shake off the deep chill that had settled in his bones. He brushed a few snowflakes from his collar as he moved into the kitchen, where a fire roared in the old stone fireplace. But something was off. The counters were too neat, as if no one had cooked there in a long time. His mother's knitting needles were nowhere to be seen, nor were there scraps of yarn and fabric lying about, as there had been for Peter's whole life.

"Father?" he asked, a pit forming in his stomach as his father shoved past him and filled a kettle with water. "Where's Mother?"

His father stopped what he was doing and stood motionless for a second before whirling to face Peter. "Dead," he spat. "Four years ago."

"Dead?"

"That's what I said, you fool."

Peter felt like he was in a terrible dream. "But . . . . You never told me."

"Why would I?"

Peter stared in disbelief. "Because she's my *mother*."

His father's eyes narrowed. "She died of a broken heart

in November of 1943. *You* broke her heart, Peter. Your capture, your defeat, your cowardice. The shame overwhelmed her."

"No," Peter whispered. "It's not possible. She's been dead for four years and I never knew?" He had never wondered why she didn't write, because she was illiterate. The writing of letters was always his father's job. And yes, his father's letters had been curt and cold before they had stopped coming altogether. But never had Peter suspected that his father would keep something like this from him. It was unconscionable.

"I don't know why you bothered to come home at all," his father said at last.

"And what about Franz?"

His father turned slowly. "Franz is a hero, Peter. Franz fought for Germany and wasn't weak enough to be captured."

"So he is alive?"

"Of course."

Peter exhaled his relief. But when his father didn't say anything else, he didn't either. He could feel his tears coming, and he knew his father's disdain for him would only grow if he showed that sort of emotion. So he nodded, picked up his knapsack from where he'd set it down on a kitchen chair, and headed for the bedroom that he had once shared with Franz.

His bed was gone, Peter realized immediately. There was just one mattress there, one that clearly belonged to Franz, whose clothes were strewn casually across the top of the quilt. Franz's things marched across the bureau; his pinup photos of Ilse Werner and Marika Rökk were tacked to the walls. All traces of Peter had been erased. Still, suddenly exhausted, Peter collapsed onto the bed, breathing hard, and finally succumbed to tears.

Not only was he devastated by the loss of his mother, but now, fear was nibbling at his heart. He hadn't known she was dead for four years. *Four years*. He'd always guessed that when you loved someone deeply enough, you kept a part of their spirit with you. When their light was snuffed out, a piece of your own soul went dark too. But that hadn't happened when his mother died—was there a possibility that Margaret was gone too, and he simply couldn't tell?

Night was falling by the time his father appeared in the bedroom doorway. He looked down at his son with disgust, and Peter knew his father could see the evidence of the tears he'd shed for his mother, for the past, and for the woman he'd left behind in America two and a half years earlier. "This came for you," his father grunted, tossing him a crumpled envelope.

Peter reached for it, and he could feel his eyes widen as he glimpsed the postmark. It had come from the United States! *Margaret!*

As his father walked away, Peter pulled the letter from the envelope, which had already been torn open. His hands were shaking so violently that he had to steady himself with a few deep breaths before he began to read. The letter was indeed from Margaret, dated October 1945, four months after he'd seen her last. His eyes flew over the first two paragraphs, where she told him that she loved him and missed him, and alighted on the third, where she had written words that changed everything.

I am carrying your child, Peter. I cannot hide it any longer, and I fear my father's reaction when he learns what we've done, but I haven't a single regret. For however wrong the world might believe our love to be, I know it is right. It is the only true thing, and as this life inside of me grows, I can feel you here with me. I know you will return and that I will see you again. I know I will feel your gentle embrace and feel the light of your love on our child. But for now, I know I must wait. I know I must carry on. And I will do whatever it takes to protect the life we made together.

Forever yours,
Margaret

Peter stared at the words, and then he read them again and again. It was impossible, wasn't it? He had lain with her only once. May 8, 1945. Victory in Europe Day. He did the math quickly, realizing that if Margaret had carried the baby to term, his child would have been born in late January or early February of 1946. That meant that somewhere out there, he had a son or daughter who was nearly two years old now. Margaret had been raising that child alone, perhaps believing that Peter had turned his back on her, that he had betrayed her. *But what if something happened to her? Or to the baby?* Peter shook his head, banishing the ghosts of terrible thoughts. No, Margaret was out there, waiting for him, just like she said. He had to believe that.

In that moment, something shifted within Peter. He

hadn't thought it possible to hate his own father, despite everything. His father was a Nazi, a terrible man, a punishing man, a cold man. Still, Peter had loved him in the way that only blood can make you see past evil. But now, everything was different. Peter had a child of his own out there somewhere, and his father had stolen that from him.

He stormed out of the bedroom and into the kitchen, where his father was sitting at the kitchen table, his hands folded around a steaming mug. He looked up with a smirk when Peter entered the room, and Peter realized he'd been waiting, preparing for a fight.

"When did the letter arrive, Father?" Peter demanded. "How could you keep something like this from me?"

His father shrugged, his expression cold. "It came a couple years ago. And there were more. I burned the rest without reading them, and eventually, they stopped."

Peter's entire body went cold. "How could you do such a thing?"

His father stepped closer, his face suddenly twisted with rage, a vein throbbing in his sagging neck. "How could *I*? How could *you*? You are a traitor! You fornicated with the enemy!"

"The war is behind us, Father! We lost! Germany *lost*."

When his father looked up at him, Peter had the sense that the man's eyes were burning a hole right through him. "You had a baby with an American whore," his father said, his voice flat. "How can I ever forgive that?"

Peter could feel the anger pumping through him, energizing him, turning him into something he wasn't. For a few terrifying seconds, he imagined what it would feel like to put his hands around his father's neck and to choke the life out of the man. But he forced himself to calm down, to remember himself. If he let his fury turn him violent, he was no better than the man in front of him. So instead, Peter strode into the room he no longer shared with his brother and grabbed his knapsack from the bed. There was barely anything in it, but it contained every material possession he had. It would have to be enough. He returned to the kitchen and studied his father's face for a moment. "I do not want your forgiveness," Peter said. "For I have done nothing wrong."

His father laughed cruelly, and Peter could hear the front door opening and closing. A moment later, Franz walked into the kitchen, taller, sturdier, and older than Peter could have imagined. It had been six years since Peter had seen his younger brother, and for a moment, he was overcome.

"Franz!" he exclaimed.

Franz started to smile, but then he glanced at his father, whose face was purple with rage, and something in his expression darkened. "What is happening here?" Franz asked, his voice clipped. "What have you done, Peter?"

"Your brother is defending his decision to impregnate a whore," their father said.

Peter swallowed hard. "Franz, you do not agree with the things Father is saying, do you?"

Franz looked from his brother to his father, and then he looked at the floor. "You have brought our family great shame, Peter," he said.

Peter stared at him for a moment, his own heart singing a quiet swan song of grief. So that was that. His father had turned against him, and now his brother had too. He took a deep breath. "From this moment forward, I am no longer a Dahler," he said.

His father's jaw flexed and tightened, and Franz looked up, startled.

"I am ashamed to be your son," Peter continued, looking his father in the eye for what he knew would be the last time. He turned to his brother. "And from you, Franz, I would have expected more."

Neither man replied. They merely looked away, and after a moment, Peter nodded to himself, hoisted his pack on his shoulder, and walked out the front door, into the snowy, frozen night. He didn't know where he would go, but he knew he couldn't go back.

Now, the only thing that was certain was that Peter would find his way back to America, whatever it took. Somewhere out there, he had a woman who loved him and a child. And that was all that mattered.

CHAPTER SIXTEEN

By early afternoon, my father had booked us tickets on a nonstop Delta flight to Atlanta that was scheduled to take off just past ten the next morning. That left us the rest of the day to sightsee, and so we strolled through the English Garden, looked at the science and technology exhibits at the Deutsches Museum, and had beers in the Hofbräuhaus. We ended our day with a climb up the south tower of the Frauenkirche, where we could see Munich spreading out below us, all the way to the edge of the Alps. Peter's hometown of Holzkirchen lay somewhere to the south.

"Breathtaking," my father said as we began our long descent from the Frauenkirche's tower. "This city is breathtaking."

"I wish we didn't have to leave so soon," I replied, startling myself a bit with the words. I hadn't expected to be comfortable with my father, and I was grateful to him for not taking the opportunity to push harder on the boundaries of our relationship. But my reluctance to leave ran deeper than that: I just couldn't quite imagine being in Atlanta again. The longer I'd been gone, the more the city had begun to feel like kryptonite to me. "Mom's buried there, you know. In Atlanta," I said.

My father stopped and turned to me. We were alone in a dark stairwell leading back to the ground. "I know, honey. I've been to her grave."

I felt a lump in my throat. "You have?"

"Several times."

"But—" I paused, struggling to understand. "But I thought you hated her."

"I didn't hate her, Emily," my father said softly. "I hated myself, and I thought Monica was the way out. It was too late by the time I realized what a mistake I was making. I owe your mom a million apologies."

I didn't know what to say. "I haven't been back since the year she died, you know. I just finished high school and left." I felt like an idiot as I blinked back tears. "I don't know why I'm telling you this."

My father put a hand on my shoulder and kept it there. "I'm sorry, Emily. I didn't know you hadn't returned. This must be very difficult for you."

For a split second, I almost told him about the pregnancy. I almost told him that the real reason I left was to have my baby far away from the eyes of those who knew me, far away from Nick, far away from the memories that haunted me. But my father spoke before I had a chance to.

"Is that why you don't want to go to Atlanta?" he asked. "Does it have to do with your mom?"

"How do you know I don't want to go to Atlanta?"

"I could see it in your eyes at Franz Dahler's place." He hesitated. "And I can see it now."

I regarded him warily for a moment. "It's not because of Mom," I finally said.

"Okay," he said after a while, when I didn't elaborate. He took his hand off my shoulder, and suddenly, I felt exhausted. When he began walking down the stairs again, I followed, feeling strangely incomplete.

That night, after dinner at our hotel bar, my father and I had ordered after-dinner drinks—Laphroaig fifteen-year scotch on the rocks for me, and Rémy Martin cognac for him—and were talking about what time we'd meet in the lobby the next morning for our ride to the airport when my father stopped midsentence and put a hand on my forearm. "No pressure, Emily, but do you want to tell me about Atlanta before we're there?"

"No." But that wasn't true. I wanted to share the story of Catherine with him, if only to lessen the weight on my own shoulders. Myra was the only one who knew, which left me carrying the burden alone most of the time. The search for my own grandfather—who had missed my father's childhood in the same way I had missed my daughter's—was bringing it all to the surface.

"Okay." There was something about the look in my father's eyes that told me he wouldn't judge me. "But whatever it is, I'm here if you ever want to talk."

Was I being foolishly optimistic? Maybe. But the words were already rolling off my tongue before I could stop them. "I had a child once," I said.

"A child?" Time seemed to freeze for a moment. I watched his face, tensing for a sign that my words had shocked him enough to make him retreat. But his hand stayed on my arm, and his expression didn't grow judgmental. It grew sad. "Oh, honey. What happened?" he asked after a long silence.

I looked down at his hand, thinking for a minute that it felt like a tether to reality. "Not long after Mom died, I . . . I moved to Florida with Grandma Margaret and gave the baby up for adoption." I paused and added, "I just walked away from her like she didn't matter at all."

"Oh, Emily." His eyes filled with tears. "I'm so, so sorry."

"It's not like *you* made me give her away," I said.

"But I wasn't there for you, and I can never change that."

"No. You can't."

He was silent for a moment. "The baby was a girl?"

I nodded.

"Do you know what happened to her?"

"No." I took a deep breath. "She just turned eighteen, and I've been posting on all the adoption sites and looking for posts that might be from her. But maybe she doesn't want anything to do with her birth mother. Why would she, right? Maybe she feels like I didn't want her. Maybe she thinks I never thought of her again."

"I'm sure she's not thinking that, Emily."

"I thought it of you," I said before I could stop myself.

He stared at me for a moment before looking away. "Emily, I've told you that you were on my mind every day."

"Yeah, well, you had a funny way of showing it." I sighed. "I built up all these stories in my head about you. I was convinced you hated me. What if my daughter feels like that about me?"

"No," he said firmly. "You felt that way because I knowingly hurt you. What you did was different from what I did. You had the courage to do what you felt was right for your child. I, on the other hand, only had the weakness to do what felt right for me. You made the choice to give your child a better life. I'm sure she can see that." He paused. "You shouldn't be carrying around this kind of burden. I can see it in your eyes. But you made a responsible choice. You made a choice out of love. You can't feel guilty about that."

"Yes, I can. I can feel guilty because I did it for the wrong reasons. I did it because I was lost and scared and alone."

"I'm so sorry. I'm so sorry you were alone, Emily. If I'd known . . ."

"What, you would have miraculously rematerialized? When you couldn't be bothered to come back for me after Mom died?"

"I was having a lot of problems with Monica by then," my father said haltingly. "She—she wouldn't let me come back for you. She said if I did, she'd leave me. And instead of fighting her on that, instead of standing up for you, I just caved. It was easier that way."

"Well, gee," I said, my voice dripping with sarcasm. "It makes total sense now that you've explained."

"I can never expect you to forgive me for that. And I'm sorrier than you'll ever know. In the end, all you have are the people you love, and I . . ." He trailed off and bowed his head. Neither of us said anything for a few minutes, until he broke the silence. "Have you tried hiring a private agency to find your daughter?"

I sighed and shook my head. "I can't afford it, but even if I could, it's not my place. I gave up the right to know her when I let her go, didn't I? And what if her life is going perfectly, and I throw her off balance by intruding in it? No, I'm dying to know that she's okay, but I can't risk disrupting her life. So I'm waiting. If she wants to find me, I'm here. I'm findable."

"Do you think that maybe it might help to let her know you love her and still think about her?" my dad asked after a pause. "But in a way that leaves the ball in her court and lets her come to you if she wants to?"

I shrugged. "I don't think I'd know how to do that. I gave her up, Dad. I don't want to hurt her any more than I already have."

"The records are sealed?"

"Yeah. It was a closed adoption."

"Have you tried the agency that facilitated the adoption?"

"They went out of business years ago. And the owner died. I've tried every way I can think of to access the records, but they're just not there."

"And you're on all those adoption search sites?"

"Every one of them."

"Then when your daughter is ready someday, she'll come looking for you. And in the meantime, all you can do is to be the best person you can be, to make the best choices you can make, and to try hard to fix the things that are broken." He paused. "We make mistakes along the way. We all do. That's life. You have to do your best to correct any damage you've done. But then, you have to forgive yourself."

I surprised myself by bursting into tears, and then I shocked myself even more by letting my father pull me into his chest and hold me tightly until I stopped crying. "I don't think I'll ever feel at peace until I know that my daughter is okay," I murmured. "Is that crazy?"

"No," my father said softly. "That's what being a parent is: loving someone so much that they'll be a part of you forever, no matter what. Knowing that your happiness is forever tied to theirs."

"But *you* don't feel that way," I said. I didn't mean it as an accusation, and I felt a little guilty when my father's eyes filled again.

"Of course I do, Emily. I've just screwed everything up so badly that it's hard for you to see it."

I nodded, looking away. When I turned back to him, he

looked like he was struggling to say something, but finally, he sighed heavily and said, "I don't know about you, but I'm pretty exhausted. Should we head to bed so that we're fresh in the morning for our flight?"

"Sure." But there was a part of me that was disappointed. I hadn't felt this kind of connection with my father in years, and I was afraid that in the morning, it would be like it never happened. I stood and gave him an awkward smile. "Good night, Dad."

I couldn't sleep that night, whether because of the time change, my conversation with my dad, or my anxiety over our trip to Atlanta the next day. I got up around four in the morning to log in to the adoption sites I frequented, thinking how poetic it would be if my daughter had finally responded while I was across the ocean, searching for her great-grandfather. But my search strings continued to dangle unanswered, and so I refreshed most of them and reposted on some of the boards.

I turned off the light around five and tried to will myself back to sleep, but I couldn't close my eyes without seeing the face of my daughter.

———————

Because we'd booked our travel so late, my father and I were separated on the plane the next morning. I dozed a bit during the ten-hour flight, but when I was awake, I was thinking about what he had said about forgiving myself. Still, by the time we touched down in Atlanta just before three in the afternoon, I felt unsettled to be back. We rented a car and set out on I-85, but as we passed familiar exit after familiar exit and saw the skyline that I knew so well, I felt myself coming quickly undone. It was one thing to try to find peace over the decision to give up Catherine.

It was another to find closure over the way I'd dealt with Nick. He still lived here; it's where his advertising agency was located. With every mile I drove, I felt like I was getting closer to my past.

My mother was here too, in every sight and sound. I remembered going to Turner Field with her for Braves games a few times a season. The last time she took me to the Coca-Cola museum, when I was twelve, felt like just yesterday. There was Centennial Olympic Park, where we'd both volunteered during the 1996 Olympics, and the Georgia Tech campus, which we'd visited my junior year of high school while I was trying to decide on colleges. The world passing by outside was so familiar, but it all belonged to a previous life.

"You okay?" my father asked as we got off the highway at exit 251A and took a right.

"Mostly." We turned right on Peachtree, passing the High Museum of Art, where Nick had once taken me for what he jokingly dubbed a "grown-up date." I swallowed hard as I tried not to remember the way it had felt when he kissed me that Saturday afternoon in front of my favorite Monet. It was all still vivid in my mind, perhaps because I'd made such a conscious effort to lock it away.

We turned right again a quarter mile later onto a side street, and a half block down, we drew to a stop in front of a squat, gray building with a metal statue of a ballerina out front. "This is it," my father said as he put the car in Park. "The Ponce Gallery. We should have a half hour before it closes. Let's go."

Inside, the lighting in the entryway was dim, and there was no one at the reception desk. While my father went off in search of the owner, I gazed around at the art on the walls.

I'd only been here once—at a Christmas party for my mother's office, back when I was sixteen—but it looked the same.

Tall, white walls. Black-framed monochromatic photographs. White-framed modern art with bold pops of color. It felt more like a wealthy person's apartment than an art space, but that was the gallery's charm. It apparently survived—and thrived—on donations from some of Atlanta's wealthiest families, who considered it more exclusive and personal than the High Museum. As my father returned, I looked behind him at the dapper, middle-aged man in a perfectly cut navy suit and silver bow tie following him and did my best to pretend that I wasn't as uncultured as I was.

"Greetings," the man said in an accent I couldn't quite place. "This gentleman here tells me you were the recipient of the lovely painting I sent to Munich."

My eyes widened, and I glanced at my father, who smiled. We had found the painting's source.

"*You* sent the painting?" I studied his face, trying to figure out who he was.

He nodded. "Well, I was the one who shipped it, in any case. I'm Walter Pace. I own the Ponce. Would you like to come with me to my office? Perhaps we'll be more comfortable there."

My father and I followed Walter down a narrow hallway to a sprawling office in the back of the building. The walls featured floor-to-ceiling windows that overlooked a small, meticulously kept garden in the back. "Please, sit," Walter said, gesturing to two stiff upholstered chairs that faced his desk. "Now where were we? Ah yes, the painting." Walter rifled through a few papers. "Now, you see, we don't do restoration work here at the Ponce. And though the painting was in beautiful shape, the owner was insistent on having it restored to perfection. Admittedly, it did appear that it had been damaged slightly by long-term exposure to moisture in the air."

I leaned forward. "But who was the owner? Who gave you the painting?"

"Oh, I'm really meant to keep that piece of information confidential." He laced his fingers together and propped his elbows on his desk. "Yes, she was most insistent on discretion."

"She?" I repeated. I realized I'd been assuming that the sender was a man.

He nodded. "She wanted this done in total anonymity. Then again, you *are* the one she had the painting sent to, aren't you?"

"Yes." My heart was pounding wildly. "She must have been reaching out, right? Why else would she send the painting?"

Walter studied me for a moment. "The problem is, I have no way to contact her. She wrote that she would check in with me to ensure that the painting had been properly delivered, but I haven't heard from her since I received it."

"But who is she?" I asked, trying to keep the desperation out of my voice.

He hesitated. "Ingrid Gaertner. The widow of the famed realist painter Ralph Gaertner."

My father and I exchanged looks. "So the painting *is* a Gaertner?" I asked.

"Oh, no, no, of course not. The painting we're speaking of is obviously quite different from his work." He frowned, and I had the feeling he thought my question was foolish. But then he added, "That said, the technique is very similar to Gaertner's. My guess is that the work is by one of his students. He occasionally mentored other artists early in his own career."

I leaned forward. "Could a man named Peter Dahler have been one of the artists he worked with? Have you heard of him?" What if somehow, all these years later, Gaertner's widow had discovered my grandparents' love story and was trying to tell me something?

"No," Walter said after a pause. "The name doesn't ring a bell. But I'm sure there were many artists he took under his wing who never received the acclaim that Gaertner did."

"And you don't have any contact information for Ingrid Gaertner?"

He chuckled. "No one does. She's very private. In fact, I'm fairly certain I'm one of the only ones in the art world who has heard from her since her husband's death." He puffed up his chest proudly as my heart sank.

"Well, if she calls, can you give her my number?" I asked, scribbling it on a piece of paper and handing it to him. "Can you explain that both I and my father, Victor, are here because we want to know what happened to my grandfather?"

"Certainly." He took the piece of paper from me and slipped it into one of his desk drawers. "In the meantime, you might be interested to know that there's a Gaertner exhibit currently on at the Schwab Gallery in Savannah, which is only three and a half hours from here. Perhaps you might find the curator there, a woman named Bette Handler, more helpful. Bette's a bit of an expert on Gaertner; I believe a few of the paintings in the exhibit are on loan from Mrs. Gaertner's private collection, so she may have some contact information for her. Would you like me to make a call and set up a visit for you for tomorrow?"

"Yes, please." I glanced at my father while Walter dialed a number and spoke briefly with Bette Handler's assistant.

"Is one in the afternoon acceptable?" Walter asked, covering the mouthpiece. My father and I nodded, and Walter confirmed the appointment time before hanging up. "Well, if there isn't anything else . . ."

We took the cue to stand up and head toward the exit. He showed us out the front entrance, locking the door behind him.

"I feel like we're getting closer," my father said as we walked back to the rental car. "But the question is, why would Ingrid Gaertner send you the painting anonymously? Why wouldn't she just explain the whole thing? It's all so strange."

"I know. But maybe it's because she keeps to herself, like Walter Pace said. Maybe she doesn't want anyone to contact her." My dad pulled out of the museum and back onto Peachtree. A few minutes later, we were snagged in rush hour traffic on I-85 headed back toward our hotel at the CNN Center downtown. For the first portion of the drive, we were both silent, lost in our own thoughts.

"Dad?" I asked after a while as we inched forward on the highway, barely making any progress.

He turned to me. "Yes?"

I took a deep breath. "What are you supposed to do when it's too late to fix something that's happened in the past?" I couldn't believe I was asking him for advice, but being here in Atlanta, I couldn't stop thinking about Nick and the terrible thing I'd done by walking away and denying him the chance to know his child. "I just have the feeling that time is running out."

He stared at me for a long time. "How did you know?"

It wasn't the answer I expected. "How did I know what?"

His face had gone white. "It's not too late, honey," he said after a moment. "You're wrong about that. There's still time to fix things between us. And the doctors are optimistic."

"Wait, wait." I held up my hands. "I wasn't talking about me and you."

"Oh." He looked embarrassed. "I'm sorry. What were you asking about?"

"No. You can't change the subject now. What do you mean about the doctors being optimistic? Is something wrong?"

He clenched the steering wheel and stared straight ahead, although we were hardly moving. "I have cancer, Emily," he finally said quietly. "But I should be okay. I'm seeing a very good oncologist at Shands in Gainesville, and he has me in a trial that we both feel very positive about."

"Cancer?" I repeated, stunned. I shouldn't be feeling this devastated; after all, I had already lost my father in all the ways that were important. But he'd been working his way back into my life for a while now, and I had finally opened the door a crack. I'd thought we had all the time in the world to fix things. "What kind?"

"It's in my liver."

"*Liver* cancer?"

"I'm going to be fine," he said firmly. "I'm responding well to the chemotherapy. My doctor is very optimistic."

"Why didn't you tell me?"

He paused. "I didn't think you'd care."

The words wounded me. "I'm sorry. I'm sorry you felt that way. But I do care. Of course I care." I stared out the window and tried not to cry. "You're really going to be okay?"

"Emily, right now, I feel fine." He nudged me. "Now what were you trying to ask me about?"

"It doesn't matter," I murmured, still reeling.

"Of course it matters." Traffic was moving again, and we moved toward our exit at a crawl. "And in answer to your question, it's never too late to try to fix something you've done wrong, whatever it is. It's what I'm trying to do now."

I hesitated. "Are you sure it wouldn't be better to just let the other person live in peace without burdening them with your guilt?"

"Is that what you want from me? To be left in peace?"

I hesitated. "No."

"Good." My father glanced at me. "Do you want to tell me who you're talking about?"

"No."

"Okay." He thought for a minute. "And you hurt this person?"

"Yes. A long time ago." I hesitated. "And it wasn't just that I hurt him. It was that I made some choices that impacted his life too, and he doesn't even know about some of them. I—I have a lot to apologize for."

"Then it's something you should try to fix, if you can. That's what I think, anyhow. Hurt never really goes away, does it?"

We rode in silence the remainder of the way back to the hotel, and when we got there, my father pulled into the valet line and turned to me. "I'm pretty tired, but if you want to grab some dinner, I could meet you after I freshen up."

"No, you should get some rest." I took a deep breath. "There's actually something I need to do."

"Are you sure?"

I hesitated. Nick's office was less than a mile from here. I knew I wouldn't have time before we left town tomorrow to catch him. If I wanted to reach out in person, I'd have to do it now. My father was right; I needed to try to fix what I'd broken, even if it was impossible. Even if it terrified me. "Yes. It's time."

My father smiled. "Good luck, then." He handed me the keys, and I walked around the car to the driver's seat. He leaned in and squeezed my arm. "I'll leave your room key for you at the front desk. Give me a call when you're back, and maybe we can meet for a bite."

"You'll be okay?"

"I'm fine, Emily. Go do what you need to do."

I nodded, and as I pulled out of the lot and back onto Marietta Street, I looked back to see him staring after me. He raised one hand in a small wave, and then I turned the corner and he was gone. I was all alone, and I was finally about to do what I should have done a long time ago.

CHAPTER SEVENTEEN

NW Creative, the advertising agency Nick owned, was located on Poplar Street, just nine blocks from the hotel. It was pathetic that I knew that, but between his website and his company's Twitter feed, I always knew far more than I should. He had designed ads for charities, and he had several regular clients whose campaigns were always award winning. I imagined him as a real-life Don Draper, building an empire. I was proud of him, although I had no right to be.

It was strange that I still cared, but I couldn't turn those feelings off. He was like a guilty addiction, something I knew I should be quitting but that I had found impossible to put behind me. And so, nearly nineteen years after I'd last seen him, I was standing on the sidewalk outside his building, looking up at the fourth floor, wondering whether he hated me.

"You going in?" asked a delivery driver who had somehow materialized in front of me, a package tucked under his arm. "Or are you just going to stand there?"

He was holding the door open and looking at me with mild

annoyance. I cleared my throat and made the only decision I could possibly make. "I'm going in," I said. I could practically feel his eye roll as I hurried past him and pressed the button for the elevator. He followed me into the building and disappeared down a hallway, muttering to himself, just as the elevator doors slid open. I took a deep breath, stepped in, and hit the button for floor four.

When the elevator dinged and the doors opened several seconds later, I found myself staring straight at Nick's company logo—an *N* overlapping a *W*—and I realized that his office wasn't just located on the fourth floor, it *was* the fourth floor. I swallowed hard, blinking back the tears that had sprung to my eyes. He was okay. His life had worked out. I was thankful for that.

"Can I help you?" asked the dark-haired, twentysomething receptionist sitting under the giant logo. She was pretty, and for a moment, that made me hate her in a terribly irrational sort of way.

"Um, yes," I managed. "Is Nick Walker in?"

"Do you have an appointment?"

"No." I hesitated. How could I explain why I was here? *You see, I once gave birth to your boss's baby, but the thing is, I never told him, and I'm here to finally face up to it.* "I'm an old friend." *He was the love of my life, but I threw him away, because I was terrified.* "I was in town, and I thought I might drop by to say hi."

She gave me a strange look, as if she'd heard the words in my head instead of the words I'd said aloud. "It's your lucky day," she said. "He's still in. Who should I tell him is here?"

"Emily." It was all I could manage. And somehow, I knew he would know.

She nodded and stood up. I watched her walk to the back of the building, where she knocked and entered an office. I ner-

vously smoothed my skirt as I waited. A moment later, the receptionist emerged, looking flushed. But I barely saw her, because
there was another figure emerging from the doorway behind her,
his eyes fixed on me.

Nick.

He was two decades older than the Nick I remembered, graying around the temples, laugh lines and crow's-feet spidering
gently across a face that had been smooth and youthful the last
time I'd seen it in person. His shoulders were broader, his frame
bigger. I had left a boy behind, and he'd become a man—a dark-
haired, solid, gorgeous man.

He was staring at me, his gray eyes flickering like the sky before a storm. I stared back, and for a moment, every single word
I'd rehearsed, everything I thought I'd say, was lost to me. If
someone had asked me my own name in that moment, I'm not
sure I would have known it. All the pieces of my life were tum-
bling around in my brain, finally settling into an alignment that
left me only one crystal-clear thought: leaving Nick Walker was
the stupidest thing I'd ever done.

"Miss?" I could hear the receptionist's concerned voice, but
she sounded very far away. "Miss?" she asked again, more loudly
this time. She was probably wondering why the air was crackling
between us, why her boss was staring at me like he'd seen a ghost,
why neither of us had said a word yet. "Miss, would you like to
step in to Mr. Walker's office?"

"Yes." It was the only word I could muster, and silently, Nick
moved aside as I drifted toward him. As I passed, my arm brushed
against the cool gray of his crisp shirt, and I breathed in deeply,
taking comfort in the fact that all these years later, he still smelled
faintly of Ivory soap. I felt a powerful surge of attraction and did
my best to quell it.

"Have a seat." They were Nick's first words to me in nearly nineteen years, and I was struck both by the way his voice had deepened and the icy edge to it. I took another deep breath to steel myself and sat down in the chair he had gestured to. A moment later, he was sitting behind his desk, and I wondered if he was aware, as I was, that it felt like a tangible barrier between us.

Silence descended. I knew he was waiting for me to say something, to explain why I was here, but I couldn't. So instead, I gazed around his office, soaking everything in. There were splashy, retro drawings on the wall, and I realized they were early mock-ups of some of the ad campaigns he had done. There was also a framed diploma from the University of Georgia and a framed award from the Atlanta Ad Club. On his desk were several photos, and as I leaned forward, I could see just one of them, which was facing slightly outward. Nick was in the middle of the frame with a gorgeous blond child on each side—a little girl and a little boy. I felt a sudden crushing weight on my sternum as I managed to choke out, "They're beautiful, Nick."

He followed my eyes to the photo, and his eyes lingered there for a moment. "They're Abby's kids," he said, and suddenly, I could breathe again. Abby was his little sister. The kids weren't his. Did the great sense of relief I felt make me a terrible person? But then he added, "My wife and I . . ." before trailing off. My heart sank, and I looked away, blinking furiously to dry my eyes. "I don't have any children," he concluded firmly. I looked back at him, and he held my gaze for a beat. "What are you doing here, Emily?"

I took a deep breath. The could-have-beens didn't matter. He had a wife. He had a life that didn't include me. And I had no one to blame for that but myself. "I owe you an apology."

"Go on." The storm in his eyes had turned icy, and I imagined sleet and hail.

"I should never have left like that." The words were woefully inadequate. "I was young, and I was stupid, and I was scared, and . . ." I left it at that because my brain suddenly felt fuzzy.

He stared at me, clearly waiting for me to go on. When I didn't, he leaned forward, his jaw set stiffly. "That's it?" he asked. "Almost nineteen years have passed—*nineteen years,* Emily—and that's all you have to say for yourself?"

I was startled by his anger. I could feel it rolling off him in waves. "Nick—" I began, but he cut me off.

"No, I need you to listen to me now," he said, and it was the first time I recognized something else in his tone. Hurt. "Do you have any idea what it felt like to have no idea whether you were dead or alive? To have loved someone the way I loved you and to just have that person vanish one day without looking back? Do you know how scared I was that something had happened to you?"

"I'm so sorry," I whispered.

"I was in my second semester at UGA when Wendy Toliver—remember her from our trig class?—called me and said she'd seen you at UF. In the student union. Do you know I drove down there that night? I had to see for myself that you were still out there. Do you know I wandered around that campus for almost a week, looking at every single face?"

I stared at him. "You came to UF?"

He barely paused. "I saw you. On the fifth day I was there. You were walking across campus, laughing with another girl. And I thought, 'Well, that's it, then. She just didn't want to be with me anymore.' You were happy. You left me, you let me worry about you so much that I couldn't sleep half the time, and meanwhile, you were out there *happy*."

"I wasn't happy," I whispered.

"You were happy," he repeated firmly. "You just didn't want to have anything to do with me." Some of the anger faded from his voice as he added more softly, "After that, I could finally let you go. You weren't lying dead in a gutter somewhere. You'd just made a choice, and it didn't include me."

"I'm so sorry." I'd never meant the words more. "Nick, I'm so, so sorry. I don't deserve your forgiveness, but I owe you an explanation. And I've come here because I need to explain."

"Emily, I'm not trying to be cold, but whatever it is you've come to say is too little, too late."

"Nick—"

"I loved you, Emily. Do you know that? I really, really loved you." He paused, and I tried not to visibly flinch. "I didn't love you in the way that a normal teenage kid loves the first girl he falls for. I *loved* you. Damn it, Emily, I saw a future and a life with you. I thought you felt that way too!"

"I did. You have to understand that. I felt exactly like that."

He laughed, but the sound that came out was sharp and strangely choked. "Give me a break. You don't get to come here and rewrite the past."

"I'm not." I paused and looked at my hands. *Say it. Just say it.* "Nick, I had a baby," I blurted out.

Time seemed to slow. Nick's face froze and he stared at me. "You . . . . what?"

"*We* had a baby," I amended, my voice shaking.

He looked like I'd punched him in the face. "We had a baby," he repeated, his tone flat and disbelieving. "You and me. That's what you're telling me?"

"Y-yes."

"What the—?" He looked dazed, shocked.

"I gave her up for adoption."

He blinked a few times. "It was a girl? We have a daughter?"

I nodded.

"And you gave her up? Without consulting me? Without even telling me that I was a father?"

I hung my head. "It was the worst thing I've ever done to anyone. Ever. I was so screwed up after my mother died, and I was terrified that if I stayed, you'd leave me, and I'd be all alone. It was stupid, Nick, but I was scared and . . ." I stopped, midsentence, because the expression on his face was breaking my heart.

"What happened to her?" His tone was suddenly deadly calm. "Where is she?"

"I don't know. Nick, I don't know. I've wondered about her every day, and I've been looking for her since before she turned eighteen, in case she was looking for me too, but I haven't found her." I paused. "I know that what I did was terrible. I talked myself into believing that it was for the best—for you, anyhow—that you wouldn't have wanted to raise a baby with me, that it would have ruined your life."

"Emily—" His voice had softened, but I didn't let him finish.

"I was wrong. A thousand times over, I was wrong, Nick. I hurt you. I took away your chance to be a father, and that wasn't my decision to make. But please believe me when I tell you that I've suffered every day. I made the wrong decision, and I've had to live with that. It's become a part of who I am, something that's woven into me. I'm broken, Nick, and I have no one to blame for that but myself. I just don't want you thinking that I rode off into the sunset and lived happily ever after, because I didn't."

He just stared at me. Finally, he shook his head. "I can't . . ." he began, but he couldn't seem to finish the sentence. He looked down for a long time, and when he looked back up again, his eyes meeting mine, he appeared so sad that my heart nearly shattered under the weight of his gaze. "Please go, Emily," he said at last.

A lump rose in my throat. I hadn't expected forgiveness, but I'd come prepared for his anger. I wanted him to tell me I was terrible, to tell me he hated me. I would have taken it, all of it, because maybe it would have been a first step to forgiveness. But instead, he just wanted me to leave, and that hurt more.

"Of course," I whispered. I turned when I got to the doorway and saw that Nick had stood up, his back hunched, his hands on his desk. I cleared my throat, and Nick looked up slowly. "Her name was Catherine," I said.

"After your mother." His voice was so quiet that I could barely hear him.

"Yes." I showed myself out, slinking by the pretty young receptionist with her whole life in front of her. I scribbled down my name and number and left them with her in case Nick ever wanted to reach me. She accepted them without a word, and I could feel her eyes on my back as I walked away. I waited for the elevator to arrive, and I didn't begin to cry until the doors slid closed behind me.

———

I was sitting in the armchair in my hotel room, staring at the wall, when there was a knock on my door later that night. I ignored it at first, but then it was repeated, more loudly and insistently.

"Who is it?" I called out, my words slurred by sorrow.

"It's your father. Are you okay?"

I closed my eyes and then opened them again to look at the digital clock beside by bed. It was just past eleven. "What are you doing here so late? You should be asleep."

"I was worried about you."

I laughed at that, thinking of what Nick had said earlier. He'd been so worried that he'd driven three hundred fifty miles from Athens to Gainesville and lingered on campus for four days until he saw me. I hadn't deserved his concern then, and I didn't deserve my father's concern now. "I'm fine."

"Emily?" He paused, waiting for a reply that I couldn't manage. "Can I come in?"

"Please, just go away."

He hesitated. "Not until I see that you're all right."

I waited a moment before hauling myself to my feet and shuffling to the door. I was in pajama pants and a T-shirt, and I'd cried off every ounce of makeup. My eyes were red and puffy. But I'd already hit my emotional limit for the day, and I felt like I was sleepwalking. I opened the door.

My father stared at me for a moment. He was in jeans and a gray T-shirt, his thinning hair rumpled. Without a stiff button-down shirt and perfectly creased slacks, he looked older, smaller, more fragile, and for a moment, I was fixated on that. He looked like a man with cancer. How hadn't I seen it?

"Emily?" He interrupted my blurred thought process.

"Hmm?"

"You don't look okay."

I could feel my shoulders sagging. "Yeah, well."

He took a step closer, until he was filling my doorway. "What happened?"

I stepped aside to let him in. "Nothing. Everything's fine."

He came in and closed the door behind him. "I might be sick, but I'm not blind. What is it, Emily?"

I gestured to the chair I'd been sitting in, and I perched on the corner of my bed. "So remember how I told you about Catherine? My daughter?"

"You named her after your mom," he said softly.

"Yes."

"She would have liked that."

I let the words sit there for a moment. "I didn't tell you about Catherine's father." I closed my eyes and rubbed my temples. "He was a good guy, Dad. He *is* a good guy. He was my high school boyfriend, and I was head over heels in love with him. The thing is, I had his baby and I didn't tell him."

"Oh." My father's expression wasn't judgmental. It was just sad. And that made me feel worse.

"Until tonight. I told him tonight."

"*Oh.*" He hesitated for only a second before coming to sit beside me on the bed. He put a hand on my back and rubbed gently, just like he used to when I was a little girl. "That's where you went after you dropped me off?"

"Yeah."

"And I'm assuming he didn't take it too well?"

I looked up. "Would you?"

He hesitated. "No. Probably not."

I shook my head. "I don't know what I expected. I wanted him to yell at me, to tell me he hated me. But instead, he just wanted me to leave."

"I'm sorry. But you did the right thing."

"Nineteen years too late."

"But you still did it," he said. "That's the first step. Now, you have to try to look forward, not backward. You've done what you can."

"What if he can't forgive me?"

My father's hand paused on my back. "Then you have to live with that. The same way I have to live with your feelings toward me. It's your penance."

I wanted to tell him that I was trying to forgive him, that I could feel myself thawing. But I wasn't sure I was ready for that yet. So instead, I asked, "Is your cancer the reason why you've been calling me more often lately?"

He didn't answer right away. "Being sick has shown me that life can be short," he said. "Too short. And you have to try to right the wrongs before your time is up."

"So I'm just a wrong to be righted? Something to check off your conscience list?"

"No." His answer was firm and immediate. "I'm very afraid that the ways I've hurt you have echoed again and again in the decisions you've made in your own life. And I want that to stop. I want you to understand that the things I did had nothing to do with you. And I want you to be able to live the rest of your life without being held back by me."

I sniffled. "You haven't held me back."

"Of course I have," he said sadly. "Every time someone hurts you, you carry a little piece of that with you. When it's one of the people who's supposed to love you most in the world, well, I'd imagine that takes a whole chunk out of your faith in humanity. Maybe my father's absence did that to me a little bit too. I'm here because I don't want that to be my legacy to you."

I stared at the floor and thought about the decisions I'd made and the way that, yes, some of them could be traced back to him. But ultimately, I'd made my own choices, and I had to accept responsibility for that. "You can't blame yourself for who I've become."

"Emily." He paused and waited for me to look at him. "I want you to know that I think you've become someone extraordinary. And even if I can't claim responsibility for raising you, I want you to know I'm very proud of you. And I'm proud of what you did tonight by talking to your old boyfriend."

"Nick," I said softly.

"Nick." He repeated. "Well, you did the right thing, and it's never too late for that." He stood and yawned. "Now what do you say we both try to get some sleep? Who knows; tomorrow in Savannah, we may just crack this case wide open."

I laughed through my tears. "You sound like Nancy Drew."

"I was hoping for the Hardy Boys, but I'll take it." He smiled and kissed me on the cheek. "Good night, Emily. I'll see you in the morning."

CHAPTER EIGHTEEN

After leaving his father's house for the last time on that
snowy evening in 1947, Peter stopped at Otto's house and
spent two hours with his best friend's parents, apologizing
for the role he'd played in their son's death and trying in vain
to accept their promises that they didn't blame him. "You
were the best friend he ever had," Otto's mother said, kissing
Peter on the cheek as he left their house just past eight. "You
will always be like a second son to us. We are glad you were
there with Otto when he breathed his last breath. You must
forgive yourself, dear. We don't blame you at all." That night,
Peter slept fitfully at the station and took a train to Munich
the next morning. He would disappear into the crowds and
become a part of rebuilding his beloved Bavaria, all the while
working to return to Margaret and to the child he longed to
meet.

He wrote to her every day, always including the address
to the apartment he shared in Munich with four other dis-
placed former soldiers, three of whom had been POWs like

him. They'd fought a different war than those who had survived until 1945 on the battlefields, and they bore a different type of guilt. Their lives had been comparatively easy. Though they were prisoners, they had been treated relatively well and had been an ocean away from danger. Their friends and brothers had risked death each day. Many had been lost. Others bore the eternal scar of fighting for the Nazis until the bitter end, many of them realizing only later—far too late—that part of what they'd been fighting for was unconscionable atrocity. How does a man live with that?

Peter's letters to Margaret spoke of love, of hope, of his belief that one day, he would see her again. He explained everything—about how his letters to her had gone unanswered, how he feared she was dead, how his father had never forwarded her mail to him. He told her that he hadn't known of their child until recently, and that now, he lived each day in the fervent belief that God would reunite them. *I have to keep believing that despite everything, you're still out there. I have to believe that you and our child are alive. If I stop believing, I will stop living. And if I stop living, how will I find my way back to you, my dearest Margaret?*

Peter took odd jobs here and there, scraping by with the rest of Germany. His wages from America helped; he had earned eighty cents a day as a POW, and the money had been saved for him and forwarded on when he arrived home. Yet the funds would only stretch so far, and as the months ticked on, his savings were quickly becoming depleted. He went to every government office he could think of to try to expedite his American immigration papers. Once a month, he traveled by train to Bonn, where he visited the

American embassy in the vain hope of finding someone who could help him locate Margaret and his child.

Day by day, his hope waned and Belle Creek felt farther and farther away, as if the continents themselves were drifting apart just to defeat him.

And then one day in late 1948, he stopped in to a beer hall near his apartment for a quick meal after work. He had just found a seat at a crowded table when he looked up to see someone familiar.

"Maus?" Peter asked, hardly daring to believe that he was once again in the same room with the man who'd been his dearest friend in Camp Belle Creek, the only other prisoner who'd known about Margaret. They'd been released from their camp in England at different times, and Peter hadn't been able to track him down.

Maus turned, his face lighting up. "Peter Dahler? It can't be!"

They embraced, pounding each other on the back.

"Where have you been?" Peter asked.

"I thought you would be living in America by now!" Maus said at the same time.

They pulled away from each other. "I've tried everything I can think of to get back there," Peter said. "But it's been impossible, Maus. The paperwork is so slow."

"And Margaret? She is waiting for you?"

Peter felt a familiar hole opening up in the pit of his stomach. "I don't know. I haven't received a letter from her since 1946." He told Maus the whole story, watching his friend's eyes grow wider and wider as he mentioned the letter, the child he had out there somewhere, and the way he had walked away from his father once and for all.

"And so now what?" Maus asked. "What if you don't find her?"

"I will find her," Peter said. "I must."

Maus looked away. "What if she's not alive anymore, Peter?"

"She is." Peter's answer was firm and unequivocal. He'd thought a lot about it. "She is alive, or I would know. Do you understand that?"

"No, I don't. But I believe you."

Peter put a hand on Maus's arm. "Thank you, my friend."

"And what are you doing for work?"

"Whatever I can find. You know how difficult things are."

Maus's eyes lit up. "Peter! You must come work with me. I paint now. All the new buildings. We're making Germany beautiful again. I'm on a painting crew, and we're always looking for reliable workers. I will recommend you."

"Really?"

Maus nodded. "The best part of the job? They don't mind if we take the remainders home. I've purchased some brushes, Peter, and I've discovered a new passion."

Peter just looked at him.

Maus laughed. "Come with me. I will show you."

They left together and wove through the area near the market until they were deeper into the city center. Maus stopped in front of a building on Sebastiansplatz, used his key to open the front door, and led Peter up four flights of stairs. He opened the door to an apartment at the end of the hall, flipped on the light, and gestured inside. "See for yourself, my friend."

Peter could feel his heart thudding more quickly as he stepped over the threshold. Inside, the walls were covered with painted images. He recognized a footbridge over the Isar and the twin towers of the Frauenkirche. He saw the sandy expanse of an African battlefield and the exterior of one of America's Victory ships, the vessels that had carried German POWs to their temporary homes in the States.

"These are quite good!" Peter exclaimed. "You painted them yourself?"

Maus shrugged. "It is a hobby of mine. But I can't afford canvas or watercolor paper. The walls make a fine surface to paint on. When I get bored, I just paint over the images and start again." Smiling, Maus led Peter into the kitchen, where all the walls were painted to look like a vast sugarcane field. For a moment, Peter stopped breathing, for he recognized on one wall the barracks of Camp Belle Creek and on the opposite wall, three familiar houses on the horizon. One was Margaret's.

"Maus," he whispered, turning to his friend in awe. "You have brought back the past."

Maus smiled. "It is the magic of a paintbrush, Peter. Anything you can remember, you can re-create. You're limited only by your imagination."

"Will you teach me how?"

"I'll certainly try."

Peter stared at the walls again. "You know, you are very talented. I think you will be famous someday."

Maus chuckled. "Famous? Wouldn't that be nice? Right now, I am just concerned about having money for my next meal."

By the beginning of 1949, Peter was living with Maus, paying a percentage of the rent and sleeping on the sofa. Each
day, they painted the interiors of the new buildings going up
around town; at night, they worked by lamplight, painting
and repainting the walls of their apartment with landscapes,
still lifes, and anything else they could imagine. Peter had
discovered that he, too, had a talent for bringing the world
alive with a paintbrush. *Imagine that*, Peter thought. *Two
friends with a similar skill, finding themselves together again on the
other side of the world. It could only be fate.*

The living room was Peter's canvas, the bedroom was
Maus's, and together, they collaborated time and time again
on the kitchen, making each other laugh with the fantastical
ideas they would come up with. One day, it might be the inside of a volcano—or what they imagined the inside of a
volcano would look like, anyhow. Another day, they might
paint the walls with a cityscape of Munich, as seen from the
clouds. Or the contrasting whites and grays at the top of
one of the peaks of the Alps. Or a garden meadow full of
flowers. They critiqued each other's work, discussed ways
that they might become better, and even began to craft their
own paintbrushes when the ones they found at the store
were too broad and rough.

"You are very talented, Dahler. Perhaps we will both
be famous one day, yes?" Maus said one spring evening as
twilight filtered through the kitchen window and they
worked side by side on a painting of the *Viktualienmarkt*, a
challenge issued by Peter because he wanted Maus's help

in developing his own techniques for painting people. Peter's figures often came out looking stiff and unnatural, while Maus's seemed to spring whole and lifelike from the walls.

"I don't want to be famous," Peter murmured. "I just want to find Margaret."

Maus nodded, his jaw twitching. "Then come. I will paint her for you."

Peter followed Maus into the living room, where Peter had, the day before, filled the walls with a clumsy street scene from the Marienplatz. Maus looked around for a moment before selecting a spot on the wall just in front of the Gothic-looking Neues Rathaus, with its Glockenspiel open to chime the hour. He began to paint swiftly, his fingers flying, the paint shades gradually coming together to form the hue of Margaret's skin, the rich sheen of her brown hair. When he was done, he turned to Peter. "What do you think?"

Peter stared, transfixed. It was as if Maus had transported Margaret from across the Atlantic to the central square of Munich. It was beautiful and impossible, and it brought tears to Peter's eyes.

But there was something else. Peter leaned in and looked closely at the brushwork, at the intricate way that Maus had crafted her mouth, at the way he had so perfectly captured the exact angle that Margaret always held her head when she was deep in thought, at the twinkle he had somehow created in her eye. It was Margaret through and through, but it was Margaret the way Peter himself saw her, and that could only mean one thing. "You cared about her too," Peter said softly, realization dawning.

Maus looked away. "She is yours, Peter. She only ever had eyes for you."

"But you have feelings for her."

Maus was silent for a long time. "And yet she never looked at me the way she looked at you. I would never try to win her from you, Peter. You must know that."

"But how? You hardly ever talked to her."

Maus thought about this. "Sometimes you can tell, even from afar, when someone is extraordinary. But I will only ever care for her in the confines of my own heart. I'm sorry, but I cannot change my feelings."

Peter closed his eyes for a moment. A strange kind of sadness overwhelmed him. He loved Margaret, but his love had been returned in equal measure—at least for a little while. Maus would never have that. "No, I'm the one who's sorry," he finally said.

"That she cares for you and not me?" When Maus laughed, the sound was bitter. "That isn't something to apologize for, Peter. One day, I will meet someone else, and perhaps I will find with her what you found with Margaret."

Peter felt uneasy. "Maus, I—"

"I don't paint her, Peter," he said. "Not often, anyhow. When I see her face like this, she haunts me. In time, it will fade. All right, my friend?"

Peter nodded. "Life is terribly unfair sometimes, is it not?"

Maus smiled, but Peter could see the sadness in his eyes. "Or maybe it's all part of some greater plan we don't yet understand."

It was Maus who had the idea in the fall of 1949. "Perhaps we can contact Harold, and he will sponsor our applications for citizenship."

"The guard from Camp Belle Creek?" Peter asked.

"Yes! He liked us, didn't he? He wasn't like the rest of the guards. He saw us as people, not prisoners. Perhaps he could help us."

"Yes, it's worth a try."

They didn't have an address for Harold, but they remembered his last name, so they sent their letter simply to Belle Creek, Florida, hoping that the postmaster there would know how to find the Decker household.

Two months later, just before Christmas, they received a reply from Harold's wife, who wrote:

> Harold told me so much about the two of you. He really valued the time you spent together. He said it was unfortunate that war had to put you on separate sides of the line, because in other circumstances, he would have counted the two of you as friends. I'm sorry to tell you that Harold died of a heart attack last year, but I know he would have wanted to help you. So I have contacted my local congressman—I live in Georgia now—and I am doing all I can to sponsor your immigration to America. I wish you the very best.

"I can't believe he's dead," Peter said after they'd read the letter. "He was only in his forties."

Maus nodded. "But tough times do strange things to people, do they not? His country was at war, and he had to bear the weight of being left at home. Perhaps it was the guilt that ate at him."

Peter sighed. "All of us have lost so much."

With Maus's input, Peter wrote a letter back to Jackie, Harold's wife, sending their condolences and thanking her for any effort she was making on their behalf. He also asked if she knew anything about Margaret and her child. After they sealed and sent the envelope, they went to church to light candles for Harold—and for Margaret and the baby.

And then, they waited. There was little else to do. Peter continued to visit the same government offices again and again, and he made his journey to Bonn each month just in case, but he was frustrated at every turn. He wrote letters to Margaret's parents and sister, and he also tried to send letters to Jeremiah through the Belle Creek postmaster. No response ever came, and as the days slid by, Peter became more and more obsessed with the canvas of the living room wall. If he could learn to paint Margaret, he could bring her to him.

So while Maus continued to stretch the boundaries of what he could do with a paintbrush, Peter's focus changed. He no longer cared about the backgrounds, the flowers, the skies, the buildings. He only wanted to bring Margaret back, to make her come alive on his walls, to imagine her by his side once more.

But try as he might, he couldn't quite capture her. There was always something off about her eyes, about the curve of her brow, about the way her hair fell. Peter feared it meant he was forgetting her, so each night, he desperately tried again and again.

"It is not so much the seeing her that matters," Maus told him one night. "It is the feeling. You have to feel the things you paint in your soul, or they won't come through to your paintbrush. You are worrying so much about the lines and the shapes, but those aren't the things that make Margaret. The things that make her are the things you loved about her heart. Think of that, and she will come alive."

And within a month, she did. Peter had to learn to see with his heart instead of his eyes. Then, and only then, did everything change. His brushes seemed to have minds of their own, and he was merely the conduit as they captured Margaret's expression lines, her eyes, the tilt of her head, the perfect sheen of her hair. He felt like a conductor directing a symphony orchestra, harnessing all the notes into something that was beyond beautiful. But once he was able to paint Margaret, he found that it hurt to look at her, so each night, he would render her face, and each morning, in the harsh light of dawn, he would paint over it, trying not to sob as he did so.

In June of 1950, their immigration papers finally came through, and Peter and Maus set off for a new life of freedom in the land where they had once been prisoners.

CHAPTER NINETEEN

Savannah was one of the most beautiful places I'd ever seen.

I couldn't believe that in all the years I'd lived in Orlando, just a four-and-a-half-hour drive away, I'd never ventured to the moss-draped historic city. But as we got off I-16 and wove our way through the downtown area, I caught glimpses of the river, the soaring mansions, and the beautiful, shady squares, many of which were anchored by grand fountains.

"The city's supposed to be haunted, you know," my father said as we turned off Bay Street onto Abercorn and wove our way around what my father identified as Reynolds Square. He'd been making easy, lighthearted conversation all morning, and I appreciated the obvious attempt to distract me. And since if I thought about Nick, I'd probably burst into tears, I played along.

"Think that means the spirit of Ralph Gaertner is hanging out here, waiting to point us in the right direction?"

My father laughed. "Maybe. I'll keep an eye out for ghosts with paintbrushes."

The sign for the Schwab Gallery loomed ahead of us a moment later, and I pointed out a parking spot on the side of the road.

I would have liked to see the neighborhood a bit, but we were already fifteen minutes late. We hurried inside, where three twentysomethings dressed all in black were admiring a huge painting on the wall across from the entrance. It was, I realized with a start, a painting of what appeared to be a sugarcane field, with a beautiful sunset sky overhead. On the far right of the painting, you could just make out a small farmhouse. Perhaps I was connecting the wrong dots, but to me, it looked a lot like the home I'd visited last week, the home where Louise and my grandmother had been raised. In front of the house, barely visible, was a woman, her back to us, walking through the yard.

"I think that's Belle Creek," I whispered to my father, nodding toward the painting. "I think Ralph Gaertner was there. Outside Grandma Margaret's house."

He looked surprised. "What? You're kidding."

We checked in at the front desk, and a young man who had several ear piercings and a purple Mohawk told us that the gallery director, Bette, was expecting us. He stood and gestured for us to follow him down a narrow hallway. "Bette," he said, coming up behind a small woman with short-cropped black hair and deep brown skin. "Your guests are here."

"Ah," the woman said, turning to us. "Welcome to Savannah. You must be Victor and Emily."

She was older than I expected her to be—at least in her sixties, with black-rimmed cat-eye glasses and lines framing her mouth like parentheses. She indicated that we should follow her back into the gallery, where she led us into a smaller, more private room lined with paintings. "I thought it appropriate that we talk among the Gaertners," she said with a smile. "Now what can I help you with?"

I gazed around for a moment while my father explained our interest in Gaertner, our new suspicion that he may have been a German POW imprisoned in Florida during World War II, and our guess that he might, in some way, be connected to my long-lost grandfather. I could tell that he had Bette's attention, and I heard her ask a few questions, but as I looked closely at painting after painting, my heart began to pound, drowning out the conversation behind me.

Every single image in this room reminded me of something I'd seen in Belle Creek. I couldn't swear that every scene was from there, but they all looked familiar. There was a beautiful portrait of an old oak tree, sagging with moss, and in the background, Gaertner's signature female silhouette walking toward the horizon. There was a painting of two alligators baking in the sun, their scales so intricately rendered that it looked more like a photograph than something created with a talented hand. Again, in the background, there was just the shadow of Gaertner's trademark girl, slipping away behind a far-off tuft of palm trees.

In another image, there was a close-up of an old-fashioned tractor that I could have sworn was in the middle of a sugarcane field, and in one particularly searing painting, there was a young African American boy crumpled to the ground, his face turned away, his back stripped raw with peeling, red gashes that had left his dark skin chillingly shredded. Even that image felt somehow familiar to me, and it wasn't until I stared hard at the horizon of the painting that I noticed a house that resembled the one next door to Louise's farm. In this image, Gaertner's signature female form was a mere dot in the distance, running toward the foreground, her face obscured by shadow.

"He was there," I said, turning to my father and Bette. I could see from the surprised look on their faces that I had cut in mid-sentence, but I didn't care. "Gaertner was in Belle Creek. I'm almost positive."

Bette looked mildly annoyed at the interruption as I pointed out the familiar-looking farmhouse and explained how everything else I was seeing looked just like the town I'd visited.

"But you have to admit," Bette said, "there are probably dozens, if not hundreds, of sugarcane-growing towns in the country, right? And there's nothing particularly remarkable about the farmhouse you've pointed out. Perhaps it is this Belle Creek you're referencing, or perhaps you only have part of the story. Maybe Gaertner was indeed a prisoner of war, like you suggest, but he could have been stationed anywhere. Or this could be the place he moved to after the war." She must have noticed my dejected expression, because she held up her hands and added, "I'm just playing devil's advocate."

"But this can't just be a coincidence," I protested. "This could be the link we're looking for."

She gave my father a look. "Emily, I was just saying to your father here that Ralph Gaertner had many students, especially in the seventies. He was a generous man, and he always said that art had opened a lot of doors for him and he wanted to do the same for others. Perhaps your grandfather was one of his students. And maybe they did indeed meet during your grandfather's prisoner of war days. Anything is possible, is it not?"

I nodded. "Do you know whether Gaertner was even a POW?"

She shook her head. "I've made it my business to become an expert on Gaertner, since I've long wanted to host an exhibit of his work. But unfortunately, he was a very private man. There's very little known about his life prior to 1964, when he sold his first major piece. In fact, we have it here. Would you like to see it?"

She beckoned for my father and me to follow her. In the main room of the gallery, the three twentysomethings were gone, and the sun was peeking through the front window, which was made of frosted glass that filtered and diffused the light. It made the room look almost magical. "Here's the painting that made him famous," Bette said, walking us over to the largest image in the room, a huge painting that was at least seven or eight feet tall. "It is believed among art scholars that this painting's incredible success is one of the reasons why Gaertner chose to include his signature female silhouette in all of his future work. It was sort of like intentional branding, a way of creating a trademark that would earn him recognition." She paused. "I've always thought it was an ingenious strategy. It gave him that extra *something*, and it really kick-started his career. As you can see, he dabbled in tempera, though he was better known for his watercolors."

I stared at the image, feeling more and more certain that Gaertner had indeed worked with whomever had painted the picture of Grandma Margaret, because the sky—rendered in the pink and purple hues of a southern sunrise—looked very similar to the sky in the painting I had received. In the foreground of the painting stood a woman, her back to the artist. She was the painting's central image, the focus of the image rather than just an ornament in the background. Every brushstroke felt intimate and perfectly executed, and although the woman was turned away, her features obscured by shadow, she almost seemed to ripple from the painting, tangible and real. She was standing in a field, but it was impossible to tell whether it was a sugarcane field or simply a field of grain. The background seemed less developed in this one—Gaertner had clearly grown as an artist as his career progressed—but it seemed he had nailed the female image from day one. No wonder he had decided to make it his signature; he obviously had a gift.

"Did he use some sort of special paint?" I asked, leaning forward to inspect the painting more carefully. The woman seemed to shimmer and catch the light in a way I'd never seen before in another painting.

Bette smiled. "No, it's simple tempera—one of Gaertner's favorite mediums—but I believe that the reaction you're having now is exactly what catapulted Ralph Gaertner to stardom. The image looks so dynamic because he used a series of tiny—almost minuscule—brushstrokes. In fact, he crafted his own paintbrushes, because he couldn't find any on the market that were small enough. If you look more closely, you'll see that his almost microscopic strokes move in a way that hadn't been done before. He once said in an interview that painting this woman took him almost a full year. It's a piece of art that is studied extensively in art schools now, which makes me even more honored to have the opportunity to have it here for a time."

"How did you manage that?" my father asked.

"I wrote for years to Mr. Gaertner, explaining why I think Savannah is a perfect place for a retrospective show on his life and career," she replied. "He never wrote back—by the time I began writing in the late nineties, he had already become very secluded and private—but after his death, his widow reached out to me and said that I was the only gallery owner who had tried so hard to get a Gaertner show. She wanted to loan me several pieces from her private collection, including this most famous piece, which she bought back from an art collector the week after his death. Sadly, we only have it for a few more weeks, and then I have to send it back to her."

"So you have her address?"

She smiled. "No. She's sending a courier who will take care of returning the painting to her."

"Maybe we could speak to the courier. Do you have any contact information?"

"No. We're apparently to be notified forty-eight hours in advance of his arrival. We haven't heard a thing yet."

"Oh." My heart sank. Another lead out the window.

After spending a few more minutes pointing out various Gaertner paintings in the main room, Bette led us back to her office and asked us to tell her a bit more about what we were after.

"We think my grandfather—my father's father—is a former German POW named Peter Dahler, who was imprisoned in the States during World War II," I explained. "It's a long story, but we've only uncovered his identity recently, and we don't know what happened to him. My father never knew him at all." I told her briefly about the painting that had been sent to me and the way we had traced it back to the Ponce Gallery in Atlanta, where we'd been told it had come from Ingrid Gaertner.

Bette's eyebrows shot up in surprise. "Ingrid Gaertner? That seems highly unlikely. She's as reclusive as her husband was in his later years. I've only spoken to her myself through letters mailed to a post office box."

"That's how the instructions with the painting arrived—by letter," I said. "But there was no explanation. But why would Ralph Gaertner's wife have a painting by my grandfather or someone who knew him? It must be that the artist was a student of Gaertner's, right?"

"That makes sense," Bette said.

I pulled out my phone to show her the picture of the painting, and her brow furrowed as she studied it. "Definitely not a

Gaertner," she murmured, almost to herself. "Not with the woman's face so visible. But yet . . ." Her voice trailed off. "What did you say your grandfather's name is?"

"Peter Dahler."

She thought for a moment. "The name rings a bell . . ."

My heart was in my throat as she turned and rifled through some papers in a filing cabinet. I exchanged looks with my father. Could this be it? Could we have finally found him? But a few moments later, Bette turned back with a frown. "I thought I had some paperwork from a Gaertner event I'd attended in Miami Beach in the early eighties. But I don't have the program anymore. However, I do recall that a few German contemporaries of his spoke at the dinner. Perhaps that's where I remember the name from. Yes, I'm almost certain of it. There was a man named Dahler who was one of Gaertner's protégés."

I took a deep breath. "You're sure?"

"Ninety percent. It was a long time ago, but the name certainly sounds familiar." She thought for a moment and then swiveled to her computer, where she typed in a few things. Her face fell. "The gallery that hosted the event closed many years ago, and I've just found an obituary for the gallery owner. I'm not sure how you'd track down anyone with information about who spoke at the gala."

My heart sank. I'd worked as a journalist for long enough that I knew a dead-end trail when I saw it. I'd dutifully follow up on whatever information she had, but finding the featured speakers at an art event in Miami Beach in the early 1980s might be impossible. "Any idea what year the event was? Or the name of the gallery that hosted it?"

She told me that she believed it was in 1982 or 1983, and that it was the Thomas J. Trouba Gallery, which had long since closed. The dinner was at the Hotel Carbonell, which had been torn down a year later. I jotted down the information, just in case. I would do a newspaper search, and perhaps we'd get lucky.

"Honestly, I think your best bet of finding this Peter Dahler might be to hope that Ingrid Gaertner will speak with you," Bette said.

"I thought you said she was a recluse and didn't talk to anyone."

"But if she was indeed the one to send you the painting, she was reaching out, wasn't she? Perhaps your grandfather asked her to do it. The only address I have for her is a post office box, but I'll give it to you. It's a long shot, I suppose, but it's all I have."

"Thank you," I said as she clicked around on her computer and printed out the address.

She stood to walk us out and shook our hands at the door. "I'm sorry I wasn't able to be more helpful. But I do feel confident that if your Peter Dahler is out there somewhere, you'll find him."

———————

We had arranged to drop off our rental car at the Savannah/Hilton Head International Airport, and after a tight connection in Charlotte, we were back in Orlando just after 7:30.

"I'm exhausted," I admitted to my father as we walked to the parking garage together. We'd only been gone for a few days, but it somehow felt like weeks. The oppressive humidity of the evening was almost comforting, a familiar embrace that felt like home.

"Well, jetting to Europe and back, confronting your past, and almost finding a long-lost family member will do that to a person," he said with a smile. "Are you going to be okay?"

"I'll be fine. How about you? Are *you* okay?" I noted with concern that he looked more exhausted than I did, and I wondered for the first time if he was being honest about the seriousness of his illness.

"I'm fine, Emily. Don't worry." He smiled slightly. "Travel takes a toll on you when you're almost seventy."

"Okay," I said uncertainly. "Is there anything I can do? In terms of your cancer?"

"You can stop worrying."

"I don't think I can do that. Get some rest, okay?" We agreed to talk on Monday and gave each other an awkward hug good-bye as we headed in separate directions to claim our cars.

At home, I went through my stack of mail, dashed off a quick note to Ingrid Gaertner's P.O. box address, watered the herb garden out back, and called Myra. She had left two messages on my cell, the first inviting me to dinner, the second asking where I'd disappeared to.

"Wait, I'm sorry, you went to Germany without telling me?" she asked after I'd briefly explained the story. "With *your father*? Otherwise known as Satan's spawn?"

The words rubbed me the wrong way, even though she'd obviously gotten the sentiment from me. "He's actually not so bad."

"Wait, wait, wait. You *like* your long-lost dad now?"

I hesitated. "It doesn't change anything that happened, of course. But he keeps apologizing. I think he genuinely realizes that he made some serious mistakes, and he's sorry for them."

Myra snorted. "Too little, too late. Am I right?"

"I don't know. It would be easier that way, that's for sure. But maybe he deserves another chance." I paused and added, "He's sick. Cancer."

"Oh." Myra sighed. "Geez, I'm sorry. That's sad. It isn't terminal, is it?"

"He said no. But it's liver cancer."

She whistled, low and slow. "That's not good."

"I know."

We were silent for a minute. "So is that it, then? You forgive him?"

"No. But I'm trying."

"Well. I guess that's a good thing," Myra said.

"Is it?" I paused, trying to find the words for what I was feeling. "You don't think I'm betraying my mom?"

"Your mom?"

"He left her, Myra. Regardless of why or how it happened, he hurt her badly. And even if he can somehow make it up to me now, he can never make it up to her. Am I letting her down by even considering forgiving him?"

She was silent for a moment. "Do you think she'd be happy to know you're walking around with all this anger toward him?"

"I don't know," I mumbled.

"Well, I'll tell you this. If Jay ever left me, I'd be worried about him hurting Samantha one day too," she said slowly. "But I wouldn't ever, ever feel like Samantha owed it to me to be as pissed at her dad as I was."

"Why?"

"Because it would be a burden she wouldn't deserve," Myra replied. "It's fine if she wants to be mad at him for her own reasons. But a child should never have to fight a parent's battle. I don't think your mom would have wanted that for you either. Besides, you were just a kid when they split, right? How do you know your mom didn't already find a way to forgive him and move on?"

"I don't know." I wasn't convinced.

"My advice? Worry about how you feel, not about how

your mom may or may not have felt. My guess is that if recon-
ciling with your dad feels right to you, then maybe it's what
she would have wanted." She hesitated, and then she changed
the subject. "So tell me what you found out about your grandfather."

I gratefully shifted along with her and recapped our visits to
Munich, Atlanta, and Savannah. I didn't tell her about Nick, because she'd never heard a thing about him before, and I didn't
have the energy to explain it now.

"So what next?" she asked.

"Next, I sleep," I told her with a yawn. "Then, tomorrow, if
you have time, I meet you for a drink, and you help me make
sense of this."

"Oh, sweetie, I can't," she said. "I have a barbecue I have to
go to with Jay, and we have a thing with his parents on Sunday.
Maybe sometime this week?"

"Sure." We promised to see each other soon, but after we
hung up, I felt lonelier than usual. I'd gotten accustomed to living
in my own little world, which was fine most of the time. Not just
fine, but safe. Yet after spending the past few days with my
father—and after finally facing Nick after all these years—my
bubble of solitude had been punctured.

———

Four hours later, it was just past one in the morning, and I'd been
tossing and turning for an hour. It might have been the time difference from Germany, or it might have been the emotional storm
that had been kicked up inside me, but either way, I couldn't sleep.
Silencing the voice of logic in the back of my mind, I picked up
the phone and called Scott.

"Hey, beautiful!" He answered on the first ring. I could hear music in the background and a subtle slur to his voice. He was out drinking.

"Hey."

"You back from your trip?"

"Yeah. I just got in tonight."

I could hear someone shouting behind him, then laughter. "You feel like some company? I'm just down the street at Casey's."

I took a deep breath. It was why I had called, wasn't it? I wanted to spend the night with someone who wanted me. I wanted to feel that sense of belonging. So why was it suddenly so hard to get the words out? "Sure, if you want to come over, that'd be great," I said finally.

"Cool. I'll be there in fifteen."

Nearly an hour later, my doorbell rang. I hadn't even bothered to fix my hair or put makeup on, which I usually did before Scott arrived, even in the middle of the night. I was glad to realize, as he strolled in with too-loose limbs, that he was too inebriated to notice my appearance anyhow.

"I missed you, baby," he said, pulling me into his arms and nuzzling my neck.

When he let me go, I closed the door behind him. "Someone had a good night."

"Just a few drinks with the guys, babe," he said. "Dan was playing all these great hits from the nineties. I couldn't leave when 'Crazy for This Girl' was on."

"Evan and Jaron. Indeed, a classic." I felt stilted and awkward, like I usually did when he came over drunk and I was sober.

"You know," Scott said, dramatically waggling an eyebrow, "I think you'd be much more comfortable in fewer clothes."

"Is that right?" I managed a smile.

He tugged at the hem of the oversized T-shirt I was wearing. "So what do you say we get this off you?"

I smiled, took his hand, and let him lead me toward the bedroom.

But five minutes later, as his hands were snaking under my shirt, and I could feel him breathing hard as he pressed against me, I abruptly stopped.

"I can't," I said, pulling away and sitting up.

"What?" He raked a hand through his hair and stared at me with a foggy expression.

"I can't do this."

"Baby, you're going to have to give me a little more than that." I didn't say anything.

"You drag me out of a bar when I'm having a good time, and now you stop me once you get me all excited?"

"I'm sorry."

"I didn't think you were such a tease." He gave me a dark look as he grabbed his T-shirt from the foot of my bed.

"I'm sorry," I said again. "I'm not trying to be a tease. I just . . . I can't do this. You don't care about me, Scott. I'm just a convenient booty call."

"*You're* the one who called *me*," he muttered to himself as he pulled his shirt back on. It was inside out, but I didn't bother telling him, since he didn't bother telling me that I wasn't a booty call.

"This is a bad idea, you and me," I said finally. "It's not going to work."

He shook his head and stood up. "You took the words right out of my mouth." He walked out of my room without looking back, and a moment later, I heard the front door slam. I waited until he was long gone, and then I got up and locked it behind him.

As I crawled back into bed alone, I couldn't quite believe I'd just done that. Scott was safe, convenient, someone who would never want too much from me but could be counted on from time to time to make me feel attractive.

But that wasn't enough anymore.

I wanted what I'd once had with Nick. When you're young, you think you'll have a hundred opportunities to find the kind of love that fills you up, the kind of love that sustains you. But the reality is, you're lucky to find it even once in a lifetime. It's easy to turn a blind eye to reality, to make up a fairy tale in your head. But once you've felt real love, you know deep down when you're faking it. You know when you're lying to yourself.

The walls around me were crumbling, and it was time for the lies to end. I deserved better.

CHAPTER TWENTY

After spending the next morning working on my assignment for *Seventeen* and crafting a pitch for an essay about the search for my long-lost grandfather, I left for a visit to Camp Blanding, which was now a National Guard base located between Gainesville and Jacksonville. Seventy years ago, it had housed one of Florida's two main POW encampments, and it would have been the administrative center for Camp Belle Creek. My grandfather would have made a stop there—possibly for a few months—before being sent farther south to work in the sugarcane fields.

I'd made a midafternoon appointment with Geoff Brock, the man who ran the base's small museum. They had a small exhibit on the POW experience and he'd said he might be able to fill in a few blanks for me, but that he didn't have access to prisoner records. "It may not be worth the drive," he'd added.

"No, it'll be worth it," I'd said firmly. "I want to understand everything I can about what it was like to be a German POW during World War II."

I had two hours in the car to think about things, and as I

drove, I kept mentally replaying my conversation with my father. I knew he was making an effort. I knew I was supposed to forgive him. And if I couldn't find it in my heart to forgive, if not forget, the things he had done to me, how could I ever expect it of Nick?

Before I could second-guess myself, I picked up my phone to call my father's cell.

"Emily?" He answered on the third ring. "Hang on, I'm in a meeting. Let me just step out for a second."

"Oh, you went in to work today?" I had expected, especially with his illness, that he'd take at least a day off to recuperate after our whirlwind trip. I had to admit, I'd been worrying that I'd overtaxed him.

I could hear a door opening and closing, and then my father cleared his throat. "I'm out in the hall now. Yes, I had an important meeting today. I couldn't miss it."

"You should have said something. I could have handled Atlanta and Savannah on my own."

"Honey, I'm sure you could have managed just fine, but I'm glad I was there with you. I wanted to be."

I felt a rush of warm emotions. "I'm glad you were there too. But how are you feeling? I don't think you should be pushing yourself like this."

My father chuckled. "Thanks, Dr. Emerson. But I'm feeling okay. Don't worry." I could hear someone talking in the background, and my father asked me to hold on. When he returned, he sounded less warm than he had a moment before. "I'm sorry, Emily, but I'm going to have to let you go. Something came up that I need to handle immediately. Was there something you needed?"

"Oh. No. I'm just headed up to Jacksonville to talk to someone about German POWs, and I figured I'd tell you." I felt strangely let down.

"Well, that sounds good." He already sounded distracted. "Good luck. I'll talk to you later, then." And with that, he was gone, leaving me with the reminder that work would always come before me. It was pathetic that it still stung after all these years.

At just past three thirty, I pulled through the guard gate and into the parking lot of the Camp Blanding Museum. The long brick building was surrounded by a handful of mid-twentieth-century tanks and small airplanes, all of which were set up for display. Inside, I found Geoff, a middle-aged man with a buzz cut and deep-set green eyes, waiting for me in the entryway. "Ah, you must be Emily," he said. "Right on time. Come in!"

He ushered me into the museum, where there was a large collection of old weapons as well as a model of what the barracks at the camp would have looked like in the 1940s. Most of the museum, I realized, was dedicated to telling the story of what life was like at Camp Blanding during World War II. And most of the camp had been geared toward the training of young military recruits; the POW camp was just a small portion of what had gone on here.

"Feel free to look around as much as you'd like," Geoff said as we walked toward the back of the building. I glimpsed black-and-white photos of soldiers training in fields flanked by palm trees. "But I know you're here specifically to inquire about our German guests in the 1940s. Would you prefer I just jump into a bit of that history, in the interest of time?"

"Sure," I said, secretly grateful that I wouldn't have to feign interest in a bunch of seventy-year-old guns.

"Well, I suppose I should begin by telling you that before the bulk of the German soldiers got here, Camp Blanding served as a holding camp for a small number of German nationals who had been living in Latin America."

I gave him a confused look. "They were part of the military?"

"No. Just normal German civilians who had immigrated to Latin America. It's a sort of strange part of our history here, but the truth is, the first prisoners at Camp Blanding really shouldn't have been in prison at all. They were brought here without being convicted of anything, simply for being German. The government was afraid that there could be Nazi spies among them."

I stared in disbelief. "Our government interned German civilians?"

"Of course everyone was treated very humanely—eventually, in fact, they were moved to special facilities in other states that were exclusively for civilians—but yes, it was a crazy time, and there were some crazy things happening.

"In any case, the first military prisoners arrived in the fall of 1942," he continued. "They were naval boys from German U-boats at first, but by mid-1943, Camp Blanding was taking in German soldiers too. Actually, we were one of the only camps in the country to house men from the German navy, and when the army boys started coming, they were housed in completely separate barracks. You can see what the camp looked like here."

He gestured to a black-and-white photo on the wall, and I leaned in to look. Wooden barracks stood in neat rows, surrounded by raised sidewalks and grassy fields. Another photo showed soldiers marching down a wide road between rows of barracks. "Of course many of the soldiers who passed through were sent out to satellite camps," Geoff continued. "There was a huge labor shortage during World War II, because so many of our young men were off fighting in Europe and in the Pacific theater. So these young Germans who were suddenly in our country turned out to be very useful. There were more than a dozen locations in Florida that took prisoners from Blanding into smaller camps in the area."

"Like Camp Belle Creek, down by Lake Okeechobee."

Geoff nodded. "Exactly. There were camps nearby in Clewiston and Belle Glade too. Between the sugarcane industry, the citrus industry, and the upkeep of the dike that had just been built around Lake Okeechobee, there was plenty down there to keep them busy. But they were in metro areas too. For example, where do you live?"

"Orlando."

He smiled. "Well, if you'd been here in the 1940s, you could have seen small prison camps right in your city, as well as nearby in Winter Haven and Leesburg. Most of the prisoners in your area worked in the citrus industry."

I shook my head. "How did I never know about any of this?"

"Many people don't nowadays. Back in the forties, people in the communities near the camps were aware that there were Germans here, of course. But there wasn't a ton of newspaper coverage, which I think had something to do with the government not wanting people to panic about having enemy soldiers on our soil. Plus, most of the camps were in largely rural areas, so lots of people in big cities probably had no idea any of this was going on because their daily lives weren't affected."

"So what was life like for the prisoners?" I asked. "And would it have been the same here as it was in the satellite camps?"

"The population of the satellite camps was much smaller, of course, so everything would have operated on a much smaller scale. But you might be interested to know that most of the camps operated like small, self-contained societies. Yes, there were guards, but for the most part, the prisoners largely governed themselves. People with higher ranks in the German army were still in charge, in many cases, and there was a lot of pride that came with behaving right."

I shook my head. It all sounded so strange. "And were many of them Nazis?"

"Frankly, most of the prisoners were just young men who got caught up in something they didn't really believe in. You didn't have a choice about whether or not you went to war if you were a young male in Germany. A lot of the prisoners here were actually relieved to not be fighting anymore. Many of them even became so enamored with American life that they applied for visas after the war and eventually immigrated here."

My heartbeat picked up, and I thought of Peter Dahler. "I know you said you don't have prisoner records, but would you happen to know if Ralph Gaertner was ever imprisoned in one of Camp Blanding's satellite camps?"

Geoff's eyebrows rose. "Ralph Gaertner? The painter?"

I nodded.

"Oh, no, I'm sure I would have heard of it if we'd had a prisoner who went on to become so well known."

"Oh." My heart sank a little. "And I'm guessing that the name Peter Dahler doesn't ring a bell either? Or a prisoner with the last name Maus?"

"No, but again, I don't have access to most of the records. That said, I might be able to give you something better. There's a man named Werner Vogt who lives in a retirement home down in Boca Raton. He's a great supporter of the museum; he was a prisoner at Camp Blanding during the war, and if my memory is correct, I believe he was also in Belle Creek for a brief time. If you're right about this Peter Dahler being imprisoned there, he might remember him. Would you like his address?"

I nodded, smiling. This could be the best lead I'd had so far. "Do you have a number for him too?"

He shook his head. "He's in his nineties, and his hearing loss is pretty severe. He doesn't speak on the phone anymore, but you can either write him a letter, or you can just take a chance and show up at his door. He loves having visitors, and since he doesn't drive and he doesn't have any family nearby, you're practically guaranteed to find him at home."

I took the address he'd jotted down. "Thank you so much. I'll try him tomorrow."

Geoff nodded. "Great. Good luck, then. Tell him I sent you."

As I walked back out into the sunshine, a strange sense of peace settled over me. It was possible that my grandfather had once been in this very same place, had once looked up and seen these same trees, this same view of the Florida sky. Was he still out there somewhere? It was impossible to know, but for the first time since my search had begun, I really believed I might be on a path that would lead to him. Werner Vogt must have known him. And if that was the case, then perhaps I was only a day away from finally understanding the mysteries of my family's past.

I had just gotten home from Camp Blanding that night and was loading the dishwasher when my cell phone rang. I dried my hands and glanced at the caller ID, my heart skipping a little as I noticed the unfamiliar number with a 404 area code. *Atlanta.* I held my breath for a ring, but as I exhaled, I forced myself to stay calm. It was most likely a telemarketer, or perhaps a call from the gallery we'd visited in Atlanta a couple days earlier.

When I answered, I was greeted with silence at first. "Hello?" I said again.

I heard a masculine throat clearing, followed by a voice I knew well. "Hey, Emily," Nick said, just the way he used to. It was enough to bring tears to my eyes.

I dropped the dish towel I'd been holding and leaned hard against the kitchen counter. "Nick?"

"Yeah." He was quiet for a second, and I closed my eyes, trying to soak it all in. I couldn't believe he was on the other end of the line, after all these years. "Look, Emily, I'm sorry I asked you to leave," he finally said. "I needed some time to digest what you'd said."

"Nick, you don't owe me an apology. Not at all. I'm the one who should be apologizing, a million times over."

"I know. But I also have the feeling that you've been beating yourself up about this for years." He still sounded distant and detached, but there was a warmth to his voice that hadn't been there a few days ago.

"Yeah," I said. "But that doesn't make it okay."

"No, it doesn't." Nick took a deep breath. "I want to know everything, Emily. Will you tell me about her? About Catherine?"

And so I did. I told him about how she'd been a healthy seven pounds and three ounces, despite arriving three weeks early. How her eyes and the shape of her mouth had made her look just like Nick, how her narrow nose had reminded me of my mother, how she had even looked a little like my dad in her facial expressions when she tried to look around. I told him about those first few minutes of holding her, how her skin was so soft and pale, her fingers and toes so tiny. And I told him about the emptiness I'd felt, the complete certainty that I'd made a mistake, after the nurse came to take her away. "Every day since then, Nick, I've wondered about her and worried about her. She's in every moment of my life. I never knew I could love someone like that."

He didn't say anything for a long time, but I could still hear him breathing. He was still there, still with me. I knew he was processing my words. "She really looked like me?"

"So much," I whispered.

"Why didn't you tell me, Em?"

"I was so scared that you'd hate me. I thought you'd leave me."

He exhaled. "I never would have left you, Em."

"I know that now." And I realized as I said the words that I meant them. Nick *wouldn't* have left. He wasn't that type of guy. I had made a choice and it had changed the entire way our lives would have turned out. "I thought I was doing what was best for her and for you," I said finally. "I know that sounds stupid to say now. But having a baby at eighteen would have changed your life, Nick. And maybe we wouldn't have been good parents to her. I know I was a complete disaster. I wasn't equipped to handle a baby. I . . . . I wasn't sure if you were either, and I didn't want to put that weight on your shoulders. I didn't want us to be like my parents. I had watched them grow to hate each other, and I couldn't stand thinking of that happening to me and you."

"And you didn't believe that men stayed," he added softly.

My eyes filled with tears as I thought of how my father had hurt me so deeply by vanishing and how I'd grown up hearing Grandma Margaret's stories of being abandoned too. "I didn't believe men stayed," I repeated, my voice hollow.

Nick sighed. "Maybe she never belonged with us. Maybe you were right to give her up for adoption. But I deserved a say in that decision."

"I know. Of course I know. What I did to you, Nick . . . It is and probably always will be the greatest regret of my life."

He didn't say anything, but the strangled noise he made sounded like a muffled sob. It made me feel even worse than I already did. "Everything was so hazy when the nurse gave her to me," I continued after a moment. "I'd had all those pain medications during delivery, and I was out of it. But, Nick, when I looked at her, at our daughter, it was like you were right there with me. I could see you in her. I don't think I'd ever loved anyone as much as I did in that moment. I loved Catherine so powerfully that it hurt, but I loved you too. Seeing you in her eyes—" I paused, my voice trailing off. I took a deep breath. "The thing is, Nick, I loved you more in that moment than I ever could have fathomed."

"Emily," Nick said, his voice heavy. I waited, but he didn't say anything else.

"I loved you," I whispered into the silence. "No matter how angry you are at me, please believe that."

He didn't say anything for a moment, and I felt like a fool.

"How can I believe that, Emily?" he asked finally, his voice breaking. "How can you love someone and just walk away the way you did?"

I was crying now, tears rolling down my cheeks. "Because I was ashamed. And I thought that by carrying all the weight on my shoulders, I was saving you some pain."

I missed him terribly. Seeing him in Atlanta had awoken something dormant in me. But I had to remind myself that for him, I was in the past, not the present. He had a whole life that didn't include me.

"You didn't save me any pain," he said. "I had to deal with losing *you*, Emily. You have no idea what that was like."

"Yes, I do. I had to deal with losing you too."

"But that was your choice. Not mine." He cleared his throat, and when he spoke again, his tone was stiffer, more formal. "Anyhow, I'm sorry. I didn't call to get angry with you."

"Why *did* you call?"

"I don't know." Nick sighed. "I don't know. But . . . but I have to go. I'm sorry, but I have to go."

I nodded, although I knew he couldn't see me, but I was crying too hard to say anything in reply. After a moment, the line went dead. He was gone, and as I put down the phone, I felt suddenly exhausted.

Three hours later, I was staring at the ceiling, trying not to think about Nick and Catherine and all the mistakes I'd made when my phone dinged with a text message. It was from the same 404 number Nick had called from before. *I forgive you*, it said.

Thank you, I wrote back, but he didn't reply again. Perhaps there was nothing else to say at all. We had completed our arc. I had told him everything, and he had granted the forgiveness I knew I didn't deserve.

I put the phone down and closed my eyes. It was time to move on.

CHAPTER TWENTY-ONE

1950–1963

The Statue of Liberty appeared on the distant horizon, and Maus pulled Peter up to the top deck of the ship so that they could both see her beautiful face as they sailed into New York Harbor. "We have finally arrived, my friend!" Maus exclaimed, hugging Peter.

"We're home," Peter murmured, unable to tear his eyes away from the copper woman towering more than ninety meters above the water, welcoming them to the United States. He thought fleetingly of Otto, of how this had been his dream too. *After the war, you and I will be great ambassadors for Germany.* Otto's voice echoed in his head.

This journey was different from the last one they'd taken across the ocean, for this time, both men had their freedom. When they landed on American soil, they could go anywhere they pleased—north to Boston, west to Los Angeles, south to the Carolinas. But Peter only had one goal in mind. *Belle Creek.* Was it really possible that in a matter of days, he might reunite with Margaret and finally look upon the face of his own child?

"You have to prepare yourself for the worst, my friend," Maus reminded Peter, watching his face closely as they approached the dock. "Margaret may not be here anymore. You have to be ready to live a life in America without her, if it comes to that."

"Of course," Peter said, turning away. He didn't want Maus to see his expression, for he knew that the truth was written all over his face—he would never stop searching for Margaret as long as there was a chance she was alive.

Five days later, after taking the bus with Maus to Atlanta, where they met with Harold's widow to thank her profusely for her efforts on their behalf, Peter departed alone for Belle Creek. He promised to return to Atlanta when he could, but Maus had no interest in moving farther south, and Peter knew that if he found Margaret, he would stay wherever she was.

It was a Tuesday afternoon when Peter finally arrived back in the town where he'd once been a prisoner, after switching buses to get to Clewiston, hitching a ride to the edge of town, and walking the rest of the way to Margaret's home on foot. His heart pounded as he made his way up the dirt lane to the house he'd seen a thousand times in his dreams. The walls and roof looked more weathered and faded than he remembered, and the garden out back looked overgrown, as if farming there had ceased. The fear that had been nibbling at Peter's heart for years swelled huge and ominous. He couldn't imagine Margaret letting the farm fail like this unless something was terribly wrong.

And suddenly, without intending to, he was running. He had walked all this way with his suitcase in hand, but he dropped it in the dirt and dashed to Margaret's door, as if every second counted. There was no answer at first, but after Peter pounded more and more insistently, the panic threatening to overtake him, the door swung open.

"What?" It was Margaret's sister, Louise, who looked much older than the last time he'd seen her. Her once youthful face was weathered, and her eyes looked flat and faded, like a photograph that had been exposed to the light for too long. It took her a few seconds to recognize Peter, and he could tell the moment that she realized who he was, because her look of annoyance twisted into a full-fledged scowl. "What do you want?"

"Louise," he said. "I'm Margaret's friend, Peter."

"I know exactly who you are," she spat. "But her *friend*? Is that what they call a rapist these days?"

Peter took a step back, his eyes widening. "A rapist? Louise, I never—"

She cut him off. "She ain't here, anyways. Margaret's gone."

"Can you tell me where she is?"

Louise smiled coldly at him. "Sure thing." She leaned in closer. "She's dead. So I guess maybe she's in heaven if you believe in that sort of thing."

Peter took a step back. "No," he whispered. "It is not possible. I would have known."

"What, because you were so connected to her? Bullshit." Louise shook her head. "Besides, you know it's your fault, right?"

"What?" Peter felt like he couldn't breathe. How could Margaret be gone? How could he have not felt it when her soul left the earth?

"She died in childbirth. It was your baby, wasn't it? You might as well have killed her with your own two hands."

"Oh, God." Peter could feel himself falling, but he couldn't stop it. He crumpled on the doorstep of the house that had once been Margaret's, breathing hard. "And the baby? What happened to the baby?"

"He died too."

"He?" Peter asked. "I have a son?"

"You *did*."

"Oh, God," Peter said again. In his mind's eye, he had seen a little girl or boy out there somewhere, reveling in Margaret's love, maybe even hearing stories about a faraway father who had promised to come back someday. But none of it had been real. Peter began to sob, his shoulders heaving. He glanced up at Louise, his vision blurry with tears, and was surprised to see something in her eyes that looked like pity, or maybe regret, but then it was gone. "Tell me, did he have a name? My boy?"

"Wasn't alive long enough. And his mother wasn't around no more to name him."

"Where are they buried?" Peter finally managed to ask.

"They were cremated," Louise said, her voice clipped. "We scattered their ashes in the wind. There ain't no headstone for them either, if that's what you're asking."

"Why?" Peter whispered.

"Everyone in town knew you were the father," Louise said coldly. "You know why? My stupid sister was proud of it. *Proud*. She was an outcast. Don't you understand? She ruined everything for our family, brought all kinds of shame upon us. When she died, honestly, it was a relief."

For the first time since Louise had delivered the terrible news, Peter felt something else other than overwhelming sadness. He felt anger—hot, blazing anger. "How dare you?" he asked.

Louise blinked at him. "How dare *I*?"

"Your sister was an amazing woman. She did nothing wrong."

"She fell in love with a damned Nazi!" Louise spat.

"I'm not a Nazi!" Peter shot back. "I'm German, and I'm a human being, just like you. I'm sorry you don't see it that way, but that won't change what I feel. It won't change the way I loved your sister."

"Whole hell of a lot of good it does you now," Louise muttered. "She's long gone."

"So why do I still feel her here?" Peter asked softly. But the question was to himself, not to Louise, and after a moment, still glaring at him, she shut the door.

Peter stood there for a long time, unable to move. As soon as he began the long walk back toward town, he'd have to begin digesting the loss. But here, in this moment, with the scent of orange blossoms and sugarcane wafting through the air, he could believe it was 1945 and that he was waiting for Margaret, believing he'd have her in his arms again.

———

Peter couldn't go back to Atlanta. Not yet. It would have made the most sense to have rejoined Maus, to have started a new life, to have left Belle Creek behind forever. But if the ashes of Margaret and his son had been scattered on this earth, they were still here, in a way. They were in the wind and in the dirt beneath his feet. Perhaps that was why Peter didn't feel like they were gone. He would stay for a little while, he decided. He would stay to say good-bye.

He rented a room by the week in the town's only boardinghouse, owned and run by a woman named Meli Wilkes, and in the first few days, he set out to discover what had happened to the rest of the people he'd known in Belle Creek. He learned soon enough that Margaret's parents had died—her father in 1947 and her mother in 1948—which meant that Louise was all alone now. He visited the cemetery and knelt by their headstones, breathing hard.

"I'm sorry," he said after a long silence. Around him, the wind sang through the willows. "I'm sorry if I caused you any heartache. And I'm so sorry that you lost Margaret and your grandchild. It fills me with grief and despair, and I can only imagine that as her parents, you would have been heartbroken too. May you rest in peace."

He tried to locate Jeremiah, but he learned only that he had left town in 1946, gone in the middle of the night. No one knew what had become of him, and Peter hoped that he had made it up north the way he'd always planned to.

He hired an investigator to look into Margaret's death on the small chance that Louise was lying, but he knew it was a fool's errand. There was no death certificate for Margaret or the child, but the investigator assured him that this was normal for a small town in the South. "Especially when a woman dies while bringing shame to her family," the man had added pointedly, avoiding Peter's eyes.

Peter never considered going home to Germany. After

all, he had promised Margaret that he'd return for her. Even if she wasn't here, he would live a life in her honor. He would live a life in honor of his son too. In his mind, he named the child Victor, for he had been conceived on Victory in Europe Day. The boy should have been a symbol of triumph, of victory, of the end of the war. Instead, he had barely had a chance to live at all. It felt desperately unfair.

Finding work in Belle Creek proved difficult, as people still reacted badly to Peter's accent. Many still bore a grudge against the Germans, and those who hadn't gotten to know the prisoners one-on-one tended to assume that the POWs had been criminals convicted of wrongdoing. Plus, while Peter had intended to stay so that he could be surrounded by memories of Margaret each day, he instead found it very difficult to work the fields where he'd first caught sight of her, where he'd first spoken with her, where he'd first held her in his arms. Being there didn't bring the memories back; it only made them foggier somehow.

Peter moved several miles east in the fall of 1950, settling near a huge strawberry farm in unincorporated Palm Beach County. The skies and the land reminded him of Belle Creek, but they were different enough that he could live without being paralyzed by memory. He made money working in the strawberry fields and helping out around the barns and stables as more and more equestrians moved to the area. It turned out Peter had a knack with the horses. As he withdrew into himself more and more, he found it soothing to talk to them. It was easier than talking to other people and being reminded of just how alone he was.

That Christmas, he visited Maus in Atlanta, and though his friend tried to convince him to move to the city, Peter couldn't do it yet. He wasn't ready to leave Florida behind. And so Maus—who was beginning to establish a reputation as a talented artist—gave Peter a gift: a set of paints and brushes. "You have a great talent, my friend," Maus told Peter, clapping him on the back. "Don't waste your life shoveling horse manure just because you're sad."

Peter took one of the paintbrushes in his hand and twirled it thoughtfully. "I don't know what I would paint."

"Of course you do," Maus said, rolling his eyes.

Back in Palm Beach County a few weeks later, Peter picked up a brush, dipped it in some paint, and touched it to paper for the first time in almost a year. By the fading light of evening, he began to create again, and the first work he completed was the most beautiful and lifelike he'd ever done. He used his imagination to evoke what he wished fervently could have been reality: Margaret standing in the midst of a sugarcane field at dawn, holding the hand of a beautiful little boy of five—for that's how old his son would have been now. They were both staring right at Peter, their eyes full of love.

Once he finished, it was as if the floodgates had been opened. His brush seemed filled with magic, and whereas in Munich he had struggled with rendering things correctly, now he was able to capture the exact shade of the sky, the exact pitch of the shadows, and the exact shape of Margaret's lovely eyes. At first, the paintings were just for him. He filled his small apartment with them, painting on every available surface when he ran out of paper. And for a couple of years, the images were like a bandage on his heart. He was greeted each morning with Margaret's soft smile, and he watched his son grow up, getting taller and lankier every month. It was like they were still with him, and so Peter didn't bother living a life outside of work. Each day, he would whisper to the horses or pick strawberries in silence, then he would return home and spend the evenings painting.

In 1954, the strawberry farm closed so that developers could come in and make the land into a housing community. The stable where he'd worked folded six months later, and Peter wasn't able to find another job. People thought he was strange, a foreigner who operated in near silence. Maus surprised him with a visit that fall, just as the last of Peter's savings were drying up, and when his old friend stepped into Peter's apartment, his jaw dropped.

"You have gotten much better, Peter," Maus said, looking around at all the paintings. "You must try to sell some of these. You could be rich."

"Sell them?" Peter asked. "Never. It's how I keep Margaret with me."

"Maybe it's time to let her go," Maus said gently. "Come on. I'm part of an exhibit in New York next month. Why don't you join me? I can talk to the gallery owner, tell him how good you are. I'm sure he'll add you."

Peter considered this. "All right. I will come to New York. But not with these paintings. I'll paint something new."

"Whatever you wish. You have money for new supplies? And a bus ticket to New York?"

"I have a little. I will find a way."

"Very well. I'll send you the address of the gallery. And you can stay with me. I have a room near the Empire State Building."

In November of 1954, Peter met Maus in New York. Maus had a series of ten still lifes to sell, and they were all spoken for by the end of the exhibit's first day. Peter had brought only three images—all of them scenes from Belle Creek—but he, too, had sold out by the end of the weeklong show. He knew he wasn't as talented as Maus, but he could make money from his art. And now he realized that he could take Margaret and his son anywhere. He didn't need to be near Belle Creek, because they were with him all the time, wherever he went.

It was nearly nine years later that Peter saw her. Or he could have sworn he did, but that was impossible, wasn't it? It was 1963, which meant that Margaret had been dead for seventeen years. He still painted her in the privacy of his own home—which was now a high-rise apartment in New York—but he never made the mistake of seeing her in crowds. He knew she wasn't there.

Until she was.

It was August, and Peter had taken the train down to Washington with his sketchpad and pencils to see the Reverend Dr. Martin Luther King Jr.'s speech at the Washington Monument. The world was changing, and Peter wanted to capture it with his paintbrush. He imagined himself doing a series of paintings on the civil rights movement, leaving the imagery of Belle Creek behind once and for all. It was time he moved on.

Maus was there too. They had ridden down together, although Maus seemed to be struggling to understand why

Peter was so drawn to the subject matter. "Won't it just be a crush of people?" he asked. "Won't it be chaos?"

"I'm sure it will," Peter replied. "But they'll be fighting for something important. They'll be fighting for everyone to be seen as equals."

Maus raised an eyebrow. "I had no idea you were such a civil rights crusader."

Peter was silent for a long time. "My father kept Margaret's letters from me simply because she was American. He didn't know her at all, but he hated her. Because of that, she perhaps went to her grave thinking I didn't love her, and I will never forgive him for that. The people coming to Washington today are fighting for the same thing I was fighting for back in Belle Creek: a chance to be seen for the people they are on the inside. This has to be my fight too, Maus, because if my father hadn't had a heart filled with prejudice and hatred, maybe things could have been different."

"You couldn't have saved her, my friend," Maus reminded him.

"But we would have had more time. I could have made her happy."

They had parted ways in the surging crowd, each of them agreeing to work alone but to meet back at their hotel bar in Georgetown later that night. They would have a drink together and talk about what they'd seen, what they'd sketched, what they planned to do with their paintbrushes once they returned home. Today would be about gathering images and ideas; next week would be about creating something unique and special.

Peter found a spot toward the back where he could get a

decent view. He could see the podium where Dr. King would speak later in the day, and he had the perfect vantage point over the gleaming Reflecting Pool. Sketchpad in his left hand and pencil in his right, he was looking around the crowd, hoping to catch a glimpse of one of the celebrities rumored to be there — Marlon Brando or Sidney Poitier, perhaps, or Charlton Heston — when his eyes came to rest on the back of a woman's head some hundred yards away. He stared for a moment, not sure what had captured his interest, exactly. Was it the shade of her hair? Her posture? The way her head was tilted in conversation just so? It only took a few seconds for his brain to compute what his eyes were seeing. *It looked just like Margaret.*

And that's when she turned to the man next to her and laughed. Although Peter was a good distance away, he could see that in profile, her face looked exactly like the woman he'd been painting for a decade and a half. He had imagined her older, a woman in her late thirties now, and this is exactly what she would have looked like.

"Margaret!" he called out, startling the people near him, some of whom looked at him suspiciously and moved away. "Margaret?" But his cry was lost in the vacuum of two hundred thousand voices. The only choice was to leave his perch and find her. But to move would mean losing sight of her. What if she was swallowed by the crowd by the time he got to the spot where she'd been? Still, he had no choice. He had to try.

This is crazy, he told himself as he swam upstream against a rising tide of bodies, all flowing toward the podium. *Margaret is dead.* He knew it wasn't logical and that he was grasping at straws, but what if Louise had lied? What if Margaret had been banished from Belle Creek and her family had told the townspeople that she had died in childbirth in order to protect their own reputation? What if by the time Peter had arrived in 1950, the lie was so ingrained that it had become like truth?

He moved through the crowd as quickly as he could, abandoning his sketchpad when it became too unwieldy. It took him twenty minutes to reach the general area where he'd seen her, and though he looked wildly around, pushing his way through people, scanning every face, and calling her name, she was gone.

He spent the rest of the day walking in circles, calling for her, searching. Instead of sketching scenes that he would later paint, instead of watching the faces of people as they nodded and cheered, instead of capturing the angles of Dr. King's movements, Peter simply let himself get lost. By the end of the day, he was in a daze of despair. It felt like he'd had Margaret again for a moment but that he'd somehow lost her. He couldn't stop turning the image of her over and over and over again in his mind.

When he finally met Maus at their hotel bar late that night, Peter knew he looked as disheveled and dismayed as he felt. Maus reached for him in concern. "Peter, what on earth happened to you? Where's your sketchpad?"

"I lost it," Peter said vaguely. "I saw her, Maus. I saw Margaret. I tried to find her, but she was gone."

Maus found Peter a seat and ordered him a scotch. "Peter, you know very well that Margaret is dead," he said after Peter had downed the first glass of liquor in a single, long sip. Maus ordered another drink for his friend and put a hand on his shoulder. "She's been gone a long time, Peter."

"But she was there. I saw her. She was with a young man, or perhaps he was an older boy. Do you think it could have been my son? Victor?"

"Peter, there *is* no Victor. You know that! Your child died seventeen years ago."

"What if he didn't? What if they're both still alive?"

"Think about what you're saying. Not only have they risen from the dead, but they've chosen to come to Washington at the exact same time you're here? It makes no sense."

Peter opened his mouth to protest, but then he felt his shoulders sag. Maus was right, of course. "It wasn't her," he said softly. He stared into his refilled glass of scotch before looking up. "It wasn't her, was it?"

"No, Peter. It couldn't have been."

"I know," Peter admitted. "But it was such a glorious fantasy."

"You have to let her go, my friend."

Peter closed his eyes. "I need to find a way to move on, Maus."

That was the day that Peter decided to change his name. After all, he was no longer his father's son, no longer his brother's brother. He hadn't been for a very long time. Maybe it was time that he had a new identity to reflect his new life. He wasn't successful like Maus was, so there was no harm in becoming someone new. It was the only way to start over.

CHAPTER TWENTY-TWO

Werner Vogt lived in an assisted living facility three blocks from the ocean in Boca Raton. After downing three cups of coffee the next morning, I drove the three hours south, stopping to use the bathroom twice along the way, and checked in at the front desk. The receptionist directed me to Vogt's apartment on the eighth floor. "He'll be so pleased to have a visitor," she said, smiling at me. "You'll love him. He's a charmer."

I took the elevator up and had to knock three times on Vogt's door before I finally heard shuffling inside. A moment later, the door opened, and I found myself face-to-face with an old man with gray hair, watery blue eyes, a bulbous nose, and huge plastic hearing aids poking out of his ears. His skin was patchy and pale, but when he smiled at me, his whole face seemed to glow. "A guest!" he exclaimed. "And not just a guest, but a pretty girl! To what do I owe the pleasure?"

His voice was cloaked in a thick, German accent, and as he smiled at me, I couldn't help but smile back. His enthusiasm was infectious, and I could see what the receptionist downstairs had meant. "Hi, Mr. Vogt," I said loudly, remembering what Geoff had said about his deafness. "My name is Emily Emerson. Geoff Brock from the Camp Blanding Museum sent me."

"Geoff Brock! Why didn't you say so? Come on in!" He ushered me inside, where I passed a room full of cuckoo clocks covering every inch of available wall space. "I restore them," he said in answer to my questioning look. "An old hobby of mine, dear. Come, come, let's sit out on the porch."

I followed him to a screened balcony with a beautiful view of the Atlantic Ocean. "This is a lovely place you have here, Mr. Vogt," I said.

"Thank you. And please, please, call me Werner, or you'll make me feel old." He chuckled as we sat down. "So why did Geoff send you to me? Not that I'm complaining."

"I'm looking for some information about a man I think might have been my grandfather, and Geoff thought you might know something."

"Your grandfather, you say?" He leaned forward and adjusted the hearing aid in his right ear. "Who is your grandfather?"

"I think his name is Peter Dahler," I said. I watched something change in his face. "He might have been a prisoner of war with you at Camp Belle Creek."

"Dahler," he whispered. "My goodness, I haven't heard that name in seventy years."

My breath caught in my throat. "You knew him?"

He nodded slowly. "Not very well. I was only at Belle Creek for a month or two. They needed some extra help with the sugarcane harvest, and I was one of the men they sent. Dahler was there already. He'd been there awhile, I think."

"What was he like?"

He considered this for a moment. "Quiet. Nice, but quiet.

There was a group of us, used to get together at night to play cards, but Dahler stuck to himself. Always had his nose buried in a book, and he was always quoting an author he liked. He was always with another guy we called Maus, but I don't think that was his real name. It means *mouse* in German, and I believe it was a nickname. I don't think I ever knew his real name, but the two of them, they were tight."

"Do you remember anything else about him? About Peter Dahler?"

He frowned. "No. I'm afraid I don't. Maybe your parents can tell you some stories about him, young lady."

"That's the thing. I think he's my father's father, but my father never knew him. Something happened, and he never made it back to my grandmother."

"Oh, well, I'm sorry to hear that. So many stories like that during wartime. Your grandmother was German too, I assume?"

"No. She grew up on a farm in Belle Creek."

Werner sat up straighter and stared at me. "Your grandmother was a local girl? And she had a baby with a POW?"

"I think so. She never talked about my grandfather, and we all assumed he had just left her. But something happened recently that made us realize there was more to the story." I told him about the painting, about the trips to Germany and Atlanta, and about how we still hadn't been able to locate Peter Dahler.

"How extraordinary," he said when I was finished. "In those days, prisoners didn't just get involved with locals, you realize. Dahler was risking a lot to be with your grandmother. She was too."

I nodded. "I'd like to ask you something. The painting I mentioned was apparently sent by the widow of Ralph Gaertner. Is there any chance he was at Camp Belle Creek with you too?"

"The famous painter? Oh, no, I certainly would have remembered that." He paused and looked off into the distance. "But then again, I didn't know all the names of the other guys. So many of them just went by nicknames. One guy was called *der Fuss,* which means *the foot,* because he was so good at football. There was *Muttersöhnchen,* which sort of means *mama's boy.* Poor kid, he would cry in his bunk every night. And there was *die Zwiebel, the onion,* who used to smell like onions all the time, no matter what we were served for dinner."

"And Maus," I said.

"Yes. The mouse." He shrugged. "I suppose he could be Gaertner. But seems like I would have recognized the name years ago. Gaertner's been big since what, the fifties?"

"The sixties, I think."

"Well, I was a much younger man then. Seems I would have remembered if a famous artist had the name of a man I'd once known. But then again, I wasn't in Belle Creek long." He paused. "Do you have one of those smartphones? Maybe if you show me a picture of Ralph Gaertner, I'll recognize him as a fellow POW."

"Great idea." I pulled out my phone and googled Gaertner. I pulled up the image on his Wikipedia page, enlarged it, and handed it to Werner. He squinted at it for a few minutes then frowned. "Doesn't look familiar. But he's an old man here, isn't he? Can you find one of him when he was younger?"

I took the phone back and scanned through the images that appeared on Google until I came up with one where Gaertner's face was still youthful, though it was taken in the 1960s, long after Werner Vogt had been imprisoned in Belle Creek. He was a handsome man who looked a bit like a fair-haired Errol Flynn.

"No," Werner said after I'd handed him the phone and he'd studied the photo. "No, I don't think I know the man. But perhaps if Ralph Gaertner knew Dahler, they knew each other from Germany. We were all sent back there after the war, you know."

I tried to ignore the sinking feeling in my heart. Werner wasn't going to be able to help me find Peter Dahler or tie him to Ralph Gaertner. Still, he had known my grandfather at one time, which was something. "So if you were sent home to Germany, what made you come back to the States?" I asked.

He looked out at the ocean. "You know, from the moment I first arrived on American soil, I felt very welcome. Isn't that a strange thing to say? A prisoner isn't supposed to feel welcome in an enemy nation, is he? When I was captured in Italy and brought to America, I was expecting to be dropped into a country that hated me for being German, the same way we were taught to hate everyone who wasn't just like us. But it was different here. People didn't hate us. People were *nice*. And for the most part, it was okay one-on-one. People talked to us, took the time to get to know us. And there were three meals a day, Emily. I'd never had that. There was as much as we wanted. There was food to eat, so we didn't have to swallow hatred instead of meat and bread.

"The work in the camps was tough sometimes," Werner continued. "I worked in a cannery for a while, and I did some citrus picking. Belle Creek was probably the toughest assignment, just because the conditions were bad. It was blazingly hot every day, and the humidity was through the roof. Up here"—he gestured toward the ocean—"you get the sea breeze and the views. But when you're in the middle of the muck in a sugarcane field, sometimes it's like you can't breathe. There were snakes and gators and all sorts of wild creatures out there, and we were always a little afraid that we'd get eaten alive. I was glad to be out of there, I'll tell you. We really pitied the boys who were in Belle Creek year-round.

"But," he said immediately, "it wasn't like it was all bad. The camaraderie in the camps was nice. I think most of the boys were relieved not to be getting shot at anymore. The food was good, and would you believe we were paid eighty cents a day? We could buy cigarettes, newspapers, all sorts of things—even beer. Well, what the Americans called beer anyhow; it wasn't what we were used to, coming from Germany, but it was something. And most of us went home to Germany after the war with some money, thanks to those wages. Helped us to start over. It was pretty decent of the government, if you ask me."

"What was it like to go home after being a prisoner for so long?" I asked.

"First of all, you know we didn't go straight home. We had to do hard labor in Britain for a while first. I guess it was to make up for everything the Germans had done to their country. I didn't make it home until 1946, and I barely recognized the place. I was from Cologne, you see, and it had been bombed straight to hell during the war. It was in ruins, and so were people's lives for a while. I wanted to stay and help them rebuild, I really did, but my father had died before the war, my brother had died on a battlefield in France, and my mother died in '49. There just wasn't anything there for me after that. I was in the middle of all this rubble, and even when we were cleaning it up and starting over, all I could think about was the wide-open expanse of America, all the fields and farms and opportunities. I wanted to come back because it felt more like home than Cologne did. And so I applied for my papers, and I returned in '51."

"I think my grandfather may have come back too," I told him. "I've been wondering what that must have been like, to leave his homeland behind and start over. What was it like for you? Did you miss Germany?"

"Sure, all the time. And later in my life, when I had some

more money, I started traveling back there once a year or so. It'll always be a piece of me. But in life, Emily, for every path you decide to walk down, there's a path you've decided to turn away from. Each fork in the road leads us further from where we began. And one cannot look back. Only forward. Otherwise, you'll get stuck standing in place. It sounds to me like maybe your grandfather knew that. He couldn't stay in Germany. He had to move forward in life. And yet," he added, "it is only human to wonder about the road not taken."

"But what if the road we choose is a mistake?" I asked softly. I was no longer talking about his decision to leave Germany or my grandfather's life, and from the look of sympathy that crossed Werner Vogt's face, I had the feeling he knew it.

"Emily," he said slowly, "I would tell you that the things we do in life can be mistakes, but the road we find ourselves on never is. The road brought you here." He thought for a moment and then his face lit up. "I remember something Dahler used to say. A quote from one of the books he was reading, I believe. I might get the words slightly wrong, but it went something like this: 'Our greatest accomplishment is not in never failing, but in getting up each time we fail.' I'm certain I've misquoted it, but you get the idea. And if he were standing here with you today, Emily, I think he'd tell you the same thing. In life, we all fail, all the time. But the victory is in getting up and continuing on."

I could feel tears in my eyes as Werner got up to walk me to the door, telling me that he needed to rest for a while but that I could write anytime if I had more questions for him.

"Your grandfather would be proud of you," he said, placing a hand on my cheek in the hallway.

I sniffled. "You don't even know me. I've done a lot of things that weren't so great."

"But you're a kind person. You don't make it to ninety-five years of age without being able to tell whether people are fundamentally good or not. So you've made some mistakes, kid. We all have. But don't let those mistakes ruin your life. It's not worth it."

Werner's words were still ringing in my head long after I had gotten back on the Turnpike. *The road not taken.* I had spent so much of my life wondering what would have happened if I'd kept Catherine. What if I'd told Nick nineteen years ago? What if my father hadn't left? What if my mother hadn't died?

Yes, things would be different. But I wouldn't be me. *One cannot look back,* Werner had said. *Only forward.* And so I decided that I would do just that. But first, I had to put the past to rest.

That night, I sat down at my computer and began to draft the most important thing I'd ever written: a letter to Nick explaining everything once and for all. It wasn't enough to tell him about Catherine and the shame I'd felt from leaving. I also had to tell him the rest.

I've never stopped loving you. Not for one second. Life is too short not to be honest, Nick, and I need you to know that. Sometimes, all we have is now. I don't ever want to regret not telling you exactly how I feel. I know you're married, and maybe that's why I feel comfortable in telling you this. I know nothing can or will ever happen between us again, and I know that's entirely my fault, but I just wanted you to know. I wish you the very best in life, Nick, because there's no one who deserves it more.

It was just past midnight by the time I drove to the post office, in my slippers and pajamas, to mail the letter to Nick's office. If I didn't do it tonight, I might talk myself out of it in the
morning, and I didn't want to change my mind. Letting it go,
hearing the fluttering sound as I dropped it into the mailbox, I
felt like a weight had been lifted. *You can't look back. Only forward.*

I spent the next week searching in vain for more information
about Peter Dahler, but I continued to come up empty. He had
seemingly vanished off the face of the earth. I tried calling galleries all around the Southeast, tracking down people Gaertner
had mentioned in interviews and searching the Internet endlessly
for back issues of magazines and newspapers that had profiled
Gaertner and other German artists, but the man who was likely
my grandfather was nowhere to be found, and I was running out
of options.

I had dinner with my dad a few days after my meeting with
Vogt. Things were still awkward between us, and it seemed that
we'd slid backward a bit since our time together in Savannah.
Our conversation felt stilted, and I couldn't quite seem to ade-
quately express my concern over his health. "I'm fine," he said before abruptly changing the subject each time I questioned how
he was feeling or whether he would be having any chemo or radi-
ation treatments soon. "The last thing you need to be doing is
worrying about me."

But I was worried, and as we danced around other topics—
politely inquiring how work was going and commenting on memories of our trip to Germany—it felt like the elephant in the room

just as much as our long estrangement did. The only moment I felt like we really connected was when he asked me if I'd heard from Nick.

"As a matter of fact, I did," I said, quickly recapping the phone call I'd received from him.

My father smiled. "He sounds like a good man, Emily."

I looked away so that he couldn't see the tears in my eyes. "He is," I said softly, and the conversation had ended there.

That night, after my father and I parted ways, I sat in my kitchen and stared at the mysterious painting, trying to read the expression in my young grandmother's eyes. What was she thinking? What would she tell me if she were here?

A few days later, I finally got together with Myra for drinks, and immediately she could tell that something was going on.

"You're like a completely different person. You just seem . . . balanced, in a way I've never seen you," she said, staring at me across the table at the Bösendorfer Lounge downtown. Her eyes grew wide as I recounted everything that had happened since we'd last talked, ending with my letter to Nick and my decision to try to forgive my father. "But I can't believe you've never told me about the guy in Atlanta before!"

"I thought you'd judge me."

"Then you don't know me at all, sweetie." She reached across the table and squeezed my hand. "You went through something very difficult when you were a kid, and now you're taking control of the situation. I'm proud of you."

That Wednesday, I got a phone call out of the blue early in the evening as I was sitting out on my front porch, sipping a glass of wine. Myra was supposed to meet me in an hour for dinner at Maxine's, a little neighborhood bistro just down the street, and I was taking advantage of the beautiful spring weather and trying to clear my head.

"Emily Emerson?" the gravelly voice on the other end asked immediately when I answered my cell.

"Speaking." I sat up a little straighter in my chair. The caller had an accent that sounded German.

"I understand you have been inquiring about Ralph Gaertner's personal life."

I resisted the urge to explain myself and instead asked, "Who is this, please?"

There was silence on the other end of the line for a moment. "My name is Arno Fromm."

It sounded vaguely familiar, and I racked my brain for a second before settling on a possible answer. I was pretty sure I'd read his name sometime in the last week in one of the articles about German artists. "You're a painter too," I said firmly, though it was just a guess.

"Yes, I am," he said after a pause. "But what is your interest in Ralph Gaertner? I got a call from Bette Handler in Savannah. I understand that you're a journalist. My friend has been dead for several months now, and I don't want anyone poking around and stirring things up."

My reporter's instinct should have told me to play along a little longer, to trade information for information. But I wasn't thinking like a reporter. I was thinking like a granddaughter. "I think Ralph Gaertner knew my grandfather," I said. "I'm trying to track him down."

"Your grandfather? Who is your grandfather?" Fromm's voice had become even more suspicious.

"His name was Peter Dahler."

The sharp intake of breath on the other end of the line told me I'd struck a nerve.

"Do you know him?" I asked when Fromm didn't say anything. When there was still no reply, I added, "My grandmother was a woman named Margaret—Margaret Mae Evans at the time—who lived near a prisoner of war camp in Florida during World War II."

"No, that is impossible," Fromm said immediately. "Margaret died many years ago, in childbirth. So did her child."

"You knew her?" I asked, surprised. When he didn't say anything, I said into the suspicious silence, "She didn't die in childbirth, Mr. Fromm. She died earlier this year. Her son—my father—lived, and he desperately wants to find out what happened to his own father, as do I."

"This can't be true," Fromm said, but his voice sounded suddenly hollow.

"I swear it is."

"No," he said quietly before clearing his throat and adding, "If you're truly Margaret's granddaughter, I must see you in person to know if you're telling the truth."

"How did you know my grandmother?" I asked. "Were you there in Belle Creek too?"

He hesitated. "Yes."

My heart skipped. I was getting closer to an answer. I could feel it.

"If you want to speak with me," Fromm said after a pause, "you'll need to come to Atlanta."

Atlanta. There it was again. The magnet pulling me back. "When?" I asked.

"As soon as possible."

"You think this Fromm fellow could be telling the truth?" my father asked the next morning when I called him from the airport in Atlanta. I'd taken the first flight I could get, and I hadn't invited my father along because I was still concerned about pushing him too hard if he was sick. Still, I thought he deserved to know about the potential lead.

"I looked him up last night. It would make sense that he would have known Gaertner. He's also a painter who hails from Germany, and if what he's saying is true, he was a POW in Belle Creek during World War II also."

"Which makes me feel even more strongly that Ralph Gaertner was imprisoned there as well," my father said. "It makes sense, right?"

"Maybe. But doesn't it seem way too coincidental that somehow, two talented artists were locked up together? Fromm and Gaertner? Wouldn't someone—like Werner Vogt, for example—have remembered that there was some sort of contingent of incredibly skilled painters in a single tiny POW camp?"

"Perhaps they weren't painting in Belle Creek," my father pointed out. "Maybe they became friends there and picked up painting together later. Besides, it was only Gaertner who became really successful. Maybe he was just a great teacher and helped Fromm along. If you think of it that way, it actually makes sense."

"Maybe Fromm will have some answers."

"Why do you think he wanted to see you in person?"

"I don't think he believed me about Grandma Margaret. I think he wanted to see for himself whether or not I look like her."

"He must have known her fairly well, then."

I hesitated. "Listen, maybe this is crazy, but do you think there's any possibility Arno Fromm *is* Peter Dahler?"

"What?"

"I mean, what if he changed his name when he moved to the United States? If he knew Gaertner and knew Grandma Margaret . . . Isn't it possible?"

My father was silent for a minute. "Perhaps. But it seems sort of unlikely, doesn't it? After all, if we're to believe that someone who knew my father sent you the painting, then it stands to reason my father knows you're out there, right? And Arno Fromm sounded like he'd never heard of you."

"Oh. I guess you're right." My heart sank and I nodded, though I knew he couldn't see me. I sighed and changed the subject. "How are you feeling, anyhow? Have you seen your doctor this week?"

"Yes, Emily, and there's no reason for you to worry. I'm feeling fine. But thank you for your concern."

"You don't have to thank me. You're my father."

He cleared his throat. "I'm glad you called, Emily. I really am. I've failed you so many times. I don't deserve this chance to know you now, but I'm so glad you're giving it to me."

I was silent for a moment. Maybe I wasn't doing the right thing. Maybe my father belonged in the past. But I knew what it felt like to screw up and to feel that you'd lost your chance with someone you really cared about. I thought about the quote Werner had mentioned from my grandfather, and I smiled. "Dad, I think that maybe it isn't the failing that matters. It's the getting up and trying again."

CHAPTER TWENTY-THREE

After hanging up with my dad, I went straight from the airport to the diner where Arno Fromm had asked me to meet him, in the Castleberry Hill district west of downtown. The building, on a side street in a gritty-looking industrial area, looked like an old train car.

The place was bustling as I walked in, and the scents of grease and coffee were heavy in the air. I had no idea what Arno Fromm looked like; I couldn't find a clear photo of him on the Internet anywhere. And I hadn't expected that he'd recognize me either, but within twenty seconds of walking in the door, I noticed an old man sitting in a corner booth, waving to me. His hair was silver, and his pale skin was heavily lined.

I headed down the narrow aisle toward him. He stood with difficulty and stared at me as I approached. "Arno Fromm?" I asked.

"It's you," he said, taking my hands in his. "My God, you really are Margaret's granddaughter."

There were tears in his eyes, and suddenly, I was sure that

my father was wrong, that despite his reaction on the phone, it was possible that Fromm was, in fact, Peter Dahler. "Are you my grandfather?" I blurted out. "Are you Peter Dahler?"

He blinked a few times, seemingly startled by the question. "No," he said. "No, no. I am not Peter, nor am I your grandfather."

"Oh." I felt foolish and disappointed. "I'm sorry."

"Please don't apologize. Of course you must have many questions for me. I have many for you as well." He reached out for my face, hesitating when his hand was just a millimeter from me. "May I?"

I nodded, and he touched my cheek gently as he stared into my eyes. "You look just like her. You must understand, this seems so impossible. But you have her mouth, her nose. A painter can always tell by the features, you know. But tell me, what happened to her? How is it that she lived after all?"

"I don't even know where to begin."

"Of course." He took a step back and gestured to the table. "Please. Have a seat. I will order us some coffee, and we will discuss what we each know."

Fromm beckoned to a waitress, who hurried over. He asked if I wanted anything to eat or drink, but I declined, because my stomach was full of butterflies. I just wanted to hear what he had to say. He ordered himself a cup of coffee and a glass of water for me, and she nodded and hurried away.

"And how have you come to be here today?" Fromm asked when we were alone again. "Why, after all this time, are you searching for Peter?"

"We never knew anything about my grandfather," I began. "And then, a few months ago, I received a painting."

I explained the arrival of the painting, my trips to Munich

and Atlanta with my father, and my drive down to Belle Creek. When I mentioned Louise's name, Fromm's expression turned cold.

"She was very determined to keep Peter apart from Margaret," he said. "She was very angry. Her fiancé had died, and I think she resented not only the fact that Peter was a German, but also that he loved her sister. It was jealousy, plain and simple." He paused. "You know, Peter returned to Belle Creek, of course. And Louise told Peter that Margaret was dead."

I stared at him. "And Peter didn't question it?" I asked. "Knowing that Louise didn't like him?"

"Of course he did. He stayed in Florida for years, hoping beyond hope that Margaret was still out there. He even used the last of his savings to hire an investigator. But she was gone, my dear Emily. Completely gone. My guess is that your grandmother also thought Peter was lost forever and left to begin a new life for herself and their child. But where did she go?"

"Philadelphia and then Atlanta," I told him, and his eyes widened.

"But Peter settled here in Atlanta too! How is it possible that their paths never crossed?"

I shook my head. "Maybe by the time they moved here, they had both finally accepted that the other was gone forever and therefore stopped looking."

"What a waste." Fromm sighed deeply. "A tragic waste."

"Please, you have to help me understand what happened," I said. "I don't know anything about my grandfather. I didn't even know his name until just a few weeks ago."

"Your grandmother never spoke of him?"

"Maybe it was too painful." I hesitated. "She used to sing to me in German, though. I was too young to question it at the time, but now I wonder if she was trying to make Peter a part of our lives after all, in her own small way."

He smiled slightly. "I suppose that sounds like Margaret."

"You said you were in Belle Creek too?"

"Oh yes. There were many of us from the *Afrika Korps* who wound up there. It was said that Belle Creek was one of the worst POW camps in America because of the working conditions—the heat, the arduous labor, the blazing sun—but I always figured that the people who said that had never spent any time in the war. Belle Creek was a cakewalk compared with the conditions in Africa."

"Werner Vogt mentioned that too."

He stared at me. "Vogt? My goodness, I haven't heard that name in years. You've spoken with him?"

"Just last week."

"And was he able to tell you anything about Peter?"

"He had no idea where he'd gone. He also wasn't sure whether the artist Ralph Gaertner was in Belle Creek with you."

"Ralph Gaertner?" Fromm chuckled, a faraway look in his eyes. "Oh yes. He was there."

I leaned forward. "He was? Is that how my grandfather knew him?"

He sat back in his seat and stared at me for a moment. "And what makes you think that your grandfather knew Ralph Gaertner?"

"The painting I received was apparently sent by Gaertner's widow. And when my father and I spoke with people at galleries in Munich and Atlanta, they agreed that the work was very similar to Gaertner's but that it couldn't actually be a Gaertner, because the painting featured a woman in the foreground with her face clearly visible. Gaertner never painted faces."

"Ah."

"But it sounds like Gaertner mentored a handful of artists in the sixties and seventies. We thought my grandfather was perhaps one of Gaertner's students. Or maybe he knew one of Gaertner's students."

"I see."

"Did Gaertner mentor you too?"

Fromm smiled. "I suppose you could say we all mentored each other. There were several of us from Germany who moved to the States in the 1950s, and we formed a sort of community. Of course there's no doubt that he—Gaertner—was the most talented among us. And yes, he was very generous in helping others hone their craft early on. But as the years went by, he withdrew more and more into himself."

"Is that why his output of paintings declined so sharply in his later years?"

"I see you've done your research," Fromm replied. "And yes, I suppose that's why he created fewer and fewer things for public consumption. But he always painted. Once you discover that you can make magic with a brush, painting becomes like breathing. You can't live without it. Ralph continued to paint well into his nineties."

"So you were close friends with him?"

Fromm sighed. "We had a falling-out toward the end. I'll always regret that. There was a distance between us in that final year, and I'm afraid it was my fault."

I wanted to ask Fromm more, just out of curiosity, but I wasn't here about Ralph Gaertner. I was here about my grandfather. "Can you tell me more about Peter Dahler?"

"Yes, of course." He signaled to the waitress, who hurried over with our check. "But as you know, I am a painter. I believe images tell a story better than words. And that's why I would like to show you the story of your grandfather rather than tell you. Will you come with me?"

Fifteen minutes later, I was parking behind Arno Fromm's vintage Cadillac in front of a squat, brick warehouse that looked like it dated back to the nineteenth century. It looked like the kind of place where bodies were dumped. There was something about Arno Fromm that seemed trustworthy, though, so although this visit made little sense, I had to believe that there was a purpose in bringing me here.

Fromm got out of his car, slammed the door, and turned to me with raised eyebrows, obviously wondering why I hadn't made a move to follow him yet. I got out of my rental car, locked it behind me, and followed Fromm toward the front of the warehouse building. When we reached the door, Fromm stopped and stared at it for a long time.

"It's been quite a while since I've been here," he said, putting a hand on the door and sighing.

"Are you okay?" I asked when he didn't move.

"Just awash in the memories." He took a deep breath. "Emily, dear, would you mind entering the code?" He gestured to the keypad to the right of the entrance. "My hands are shaking."

I nodded and stepped forward.

"The code is oh-seven-oh-five-two-six," he said.

It wasn't until I punched in the numbers that I realized why they seemed familiar. "My grandmother's birthdate," I murmured. "July fifth, 1926."

"Yes." Fromm smiled sadly as he pushed the door open and gestured for me to enter.

The building was musty and stuffy inside, as if no proper air circulation had taken place in months. The atmosphere made it feel like we were walking into a place that had somehow been frozen in time. "Can you tell me where we are and why we're here?" I asked as our footsteps echoed through the long corridor. We seemed to be heading for a room at the end of the hall.

"You'll see in a moment," Fromm said without turning. "Then, it will all be clear."

He stopped in front of the last door in the hallway and entered another series of numbers on a keypad. I could hear something click into place, and then Fromm turned the knob and stepped into the room, flicking a switch on the right to turn the lights on.

I followed him in, my eyes adjusting to the sudden burst of illumination, and when I realized where we were, I stopped dead in my tracks. All I could process were the hundreds of paintings in the enormous room—some hung on the walls, some on easels, some simply tacked to the sides of cardboard boxes. The ceiling itself was even painted to look like a beautiful sunrise sky, with more graduated shades of purple than I'd ever seen in my life. The windows were all covered with blackout shades, keeping the sunlight out and the paintings preserved.

"What is this place?" I whispered, transfixed by the barrage of images. But I already knew the answer to my own question, and I think Fromm knew that as he turned to me with a sad smile.

"Your grandfather's private studio."

"My God," I murmured as I finally stepped fully into the room and began to take in each painting, one by one. There were rows and rows of them, in clusters and alcoves, and as far as I could tell, they were all of the same woman. My grandmother. In almost all of them, she was wearing the same red, wispy cotton dress that she was wearing in the painting that had been mailed to me. And in most, she was standing in the middle of sugarcane fields, or on the edge of backdrops that reminded me of the Everglades. I was positive now that the paintings were of Belle Creek. "My grandfather *was* a painter too."

"Oh yes. And Margaret was the love of his life," Fromm said quietly. "He couldn't stop painting her, no matter how hard he tried. So he did it here, where he could keep every one of the paintings. It was his own private place, a place where she always surrounded him."

As I walked around the room, dazed by the sheer volume of images dedicated to a woman I loved and missed so much, I realized that small pockets of the studio were dedicated to different settings. One corner, for example, included paintings of my grandmother walking through the streets of what appeared to be a Bavarian town. It might even have been Munich. "I think this was during a time when he was imagining what life would have been like if he'd been able to simply take her home with him," Fromm said from behind me. "You see, there are even some where your grandmother is holding a baby."

"He was thinking about what life could have been like if he'd known his son," I murmured. "Do you mind if I take a few pictures with my phone?"

"Snap away," Fromm said.

I knew I'd have to show my father these paintings, to let him know that he'd been loved, even if his father had wrongly believed him dead. Loving someone from afar was a powerful thing too. It was the way I'd felt about Nick for the last nineteen years, although I'd never had the courage to reach out across the divide. It was the way I'd always felt about Catherine, although there was

WHEN WE MEET AGAIN 285

no way to find her. But the lack of physical contact hadn't made me love them any less, and I realized that perhaps it had been the same for my grandfather. He had never stopped loving the woman and child he thought he'd lost.

I found more paintings of my grandmother as a young woman in Belle Creek, and another cluster where she was painted as an older woman. I knew my grandfather had imagined how she might have looked if she had aged, and he had been almost completely right in his depictions of her. There were crow's-feet exactly where they'd been in real life, and the tilt of her head and the shape of her smile were so accurate that it was like he had painted her in person. But he'd gotten one thing wrong; her eyes were missing the constant sadness that they'd always carried in the time I'd known her. It took me a split second to realize why. Here, she was painted by a man who loved her, who would have filled her life with happiness. If they had truly found their way back to each other, the sadness that defined her would never have been there. She had grieved for him, I now believed, and if things had been different, she wouldn't have had to carry that weight.

I was so absorbed in the paintings, and in the way that they took me down my own memory lane, that I lost track of where Fromm was until he walked up beside me. "Emily? I'd like to show you something else. Can you follow me?"

I nodded and let him pull me away from the series that included my father as a baby. I followed him down a row that featured paintings of my grandmother as he imagined her in the 1950s, and then in the 1960s. I could discern the era from the fashions and the backgrounds, but also from the way she aged gradually and gracefully as the years went by.

"So he *was* the one to paint the image Ingrid Gaertner mailed to me," I said softly as we walked.

"Oh, almost certainly." We stopped in front of a cluster of paintings in the back right corner of the enormous warehouse room. "Here," Fromm said. The entire space was filled with paintings that were different from the rest. None of them featured my grandmother in the foreground, and although a few of the paintings seemed to include a woman in a red dress far away in the crowd, the work didn't match the others. But clearly, the artist had been obsessed by the scene. The paintings seemed to depict the 1963 March on Washington. Sunlight gleamed from the Reflecting Pool, and in some of the paintings, I could make out the figure of Dr. Martin Luther King Jr. at a podium in the background. But what made the paintings so extraordinary was the sea of life spreading all across the image. The artist had taken care with each figure, though none of the faces were clear; they were all obscured by the light or turned away.

"These weren't done by my grandfather, were they?" I asked, turning to Fromm. There was something familiar about the images.

"Emily," Fromm said slowly, "do you know what these are?"

They were paintings of the March on Washington, and suddenly, I remembered what I'd read about how Gaertner got his start. "They're Ralph Gaertner paintings, aren't they? These are drafts of his famous March on Washington series."

Fromm nodded. "The series that established him once and for all as an artist to be watched."

"But what are they doing here in my grandfather's warehouse?" I asked, leaning forward in awe. To think that such a famous painter's works would be sitting in a darkened warehouse on the outskirts of the city was strange. "They must be worth a fortune."

Fromm didn't speak for a moment. "This was the day that changed him."

"Ralph Gaertner?" I asked.

Fromm nodded slowly. "He saw her in the crowd. He was sure he did. But he couldn't find her after that, so he wondered if he had imagined it, or if he had seen an angel. He had gone to the March on Washington because he felt it was his duty to capture and advocate for social change. I think he still felt a lot of guilt about fighting for Germany at a time when Hitler was trying to eliminate all but the Aryan race. I think this was his atonement, this sort of work that advocated for civil rights."

I stared at Fromm, stuck on the first few words he'd said. "Gaertner saw someone in the crowd?" I asked. I glanced at one of the paintings and saw the telltale girl in the red dress, her face turned away, the one who appeared in silhouette in so many of his images. The pieces clicked suddenly into place. "He thought he saw my grandmother," I whispered.

Fromm looked me in the eye. "Yes."

"And he loved her too."

Fromm hesitated. "Yes."

I could see something strange in Fromm's eyes, something that looked like guilt and sadness. Was it because Gaertner had betrayed my grandfather in some way by pursuing my grandmother? What had happened between these three men? I stared at the painting for another moment. "But she *was* there," I said.

Fromm's eyes widened. "Margaret? She was at the March on Washington?"

I nodded. "With my father."

Fromm's eyes filled. "So he was right. My God, he always said he'd seen an older boy with her." He leaned closer to one of the images and pointed to a gangly young man who stood partially behind the woman in the red dress, his face in the shadows. "Here," Fromm said. "And here." He pointed to another one of the series in which a man in his late teens was clearly visible. I had to admit, he bore a resemblance to my father.

"But why?" I asked. "Why was Gaertner painting my grandmother all these years later, if Peter Dahler was the one she had loved?"

"Because, dear Emily," Fromm said, reaching gently for the painting in front of him, as if he could pull the scene back from the mists of time, "Peter Dahler and Ralph Gaertner are the same man."

CHAPTER TWENTY-FOUR

Ralph. Ralph, are you awake?"

"What?" Peter stirred and struggled to grasp the present. It had been more than twenty years since he had left his old name behind to take on a new one, and still, there were days that he forgot he'd become someone else. The reinvention was never complete, because there was still a part of him living in a past that was long dead. The world had changed—everything had changed—but for Peter, one thing would always stay the same: he would never be as happy as he had been on that warm June evening when he'd last held Margaret in his arms. So the transformation to a new life as Ralph Gaertner was forever unfinished, and there were days he simply forgot to respond to the name.

This morning, it was Ingrid Beck who was whispering his borrowed name, and despite the fact that Peter had been seeing her for a little over a year now, he was having a hard time bridging the gap between the old and the new. In his heart, he was Peter Dahler, forever committed to Margaret.

But now, in this bed, he was Ralph Gaertner, the esteemed artist, who was waking up beside a woman his friends had wholeheartedly encouraged him to date.

Dating. What a strange thought, at his age! He was sixty-three, for goodness' sake! But Maus had insisted. Maus, who had been with him all these years. Maus was trying to take care of him, to give him someone to help him move on once and for all. And Ingrid—tall, cultured, beautiful, German-born Ingrid—was supposed to be his window to change. *You only get one life,* Maus had said sternly. *And you are wasting yours, my friend. What good will your paintings do if your heart is forever closed?*

Peter hadn't been a saint in the intervening years. There had been times—years after Margaret's death, of course—that a pretty woman had caught his eye at an art exhibit or at a party thrown by a gallery owner. He knew that when a woman wanted him because he was Ralph Gaertner, she would never see beyond the artist to the man he was inside, so it felt safe to spend a night here or there with one of them. He was always gentle and kind with them, but he made sure they had no illusions about a future together.

Yet Ingrid was different. At fifty, she was thirteen years younger than he, and she too came from Germany, though her childhood there had differed vastly from his. She'd been merely a child when war had ravaged the country, and she'd come of age just as Germany began to rebuild. She loved the country of their birth in a different way than Peter did, and he had to admit, her passion for their homeland was rekindling a long-lost flame in his own heart. She was an art dealer who traveled to Munich and West Berlin frequently for work, and already, Peter had surprised himself by agreeing to go with her on her next trip.

She made him feel less lonely, and she didn't seem as impressed by his credentials as many other gallery women did. In fact, right from the start, she had asked him different sorts of questions than he was accustomed to. She didn't want to know why he painted sugarcane fields and feminine silhouettes in the distance; she wanted to know things like whether he believed in God, how he had dealt with the death of his mother, and how he liked his steak cooked. In other words, she wanted to get to know the *real* him. But he could never show her everything. He would always be Ralph Gaertner with her, never Peter Dahler. Peter Dahler was dead.

"Ralph?" Ingrid asked again, running her manicured nails along his spine, making him shiver. She pressed herself into him. "Darling?"

"Good morning, Ingrid," he murmured, turning to her, taking her in. She was beautiful; that much was undeniable. In his experience, this wasn't what women in their fifties were supposed to look like. He remembered his grandmother, round at the edges and graying, and he thought of his own mother, who had only lived to forty-five. She had looked like an old woman even then, ravaged by starvation and the anguish of wartime. But Ingrid—blond, beautiful Ingrid—was different. She was a vision, and Peter had to admit, he liked the way it felt waking up beside her. But it was his body responding to her, not his heart. He liked the feel of her in his arms. He liked the way people looked at him when she was by his side.

And he knew she loved him. It was in her eyes each

time she looked at him. He wondered what Ingrid saw in his eyes. Shame? Sadness? Regret? He hoped there was love there too, but he was no longer sure what that meant.

For him, love had become almost like an illness. *You have to stop*, Maus had told him again and again, gazing at him with worry. *Keeping Margaret with you all the time like this, it's not healthy.* He knew that Maus was concerned about the fact that Peter had converted his attic into a shrine to his lost love. He painted Margaret again and again and again — he couldn't stop — and then he filled his attic with the images, so that whenever he needed to see her, she was always there. Maus thought Peter was doing something destructive, but what he didn't understand was that it was the only thing keeping Peter sane. When he was painting Margaret, he was able to go somewhere else in his mind, a world in which he could create the rules, in which he could color in the twists and turns and rewrite the story. The real world, Peter knew, dealt out tragedy, unblinking. But the world he created was something to hold on to, to keep him from drowning.

But he could never tell anyone else that. So when Maus finally threatened an intervention, Peter bought an old warehouse building in Castleberry Hill and moved the paintings there, intending to slowly distance himself from them. Instead, the obsession grew, and he began to spend more and more time hidden and alone in the warehouse, imagining the life he could have lived with Margaret.

Since he had begun painting he had always inserted her into his images. He never showed her face in his public work, because he felt that to reveal her to the world would be to give a piece of her away. But she was everywhere, in his every thought, and so he couldn't help himself. A painting wasn't complete unless she was somewhere in it. Over the years, art experts had speculated about the shadowy woman whose face was always turned away, and it had become Peter's trademark as an artist. *The Gaertner Angel*, the critics called her. Some thought she represented goodness; others said she was the symbol of the solidarity of mankind, and that's why her face was never shown; she was supposed to be an everywoman. Some even suggested that she represented the devil, for why else would she often be wearing a red dress? But nothing could be further from the truth. Peter was simply painting her as he'd first seen her — as a vision in faded red, floating against a perfect dawn.

The violet sky frequently made an appearance in his paintings too, for to him, it represented the meeting of heaven and earth. The world had been an almost unbelievable shade of purple at the moment he first saw her, and since then he had come to believe that it had been God himself opening up the horizon to let all the light in, and that Margaret, his angel, had somehow slipped through. He wondered sometimes if he could still feel her presence because she was always close by, just above him in a violet heaven, looking down.

Then something had changed. Last month, the night before Thanksgiving, he'd had a wrenching dream. Margaret was floating above him, just out of reach, trying to tell him something. But he couldn't hear her, and she smiled sadly and ascended toward the purpling sky. The clouds wrapped themselves around her like a perfect embrace, and then she was gone.

There was something strange left in the dream's wake.

Over the years, he had managed to mostly let go of the image of the son he'd never had, the baby who had been stillborn and cremated with Margaret. But after that night, he had begun dreaming something else. He'd begun dreaming of the face of his son, what the boy would have looked like if he'd grown into a man, and if that man had gone on to have children of his own. Now, when he awoke in the mornings, sometimes his paintbrush pulled those imaginary creatures from thin air. A man who'd be nearly forty now. A child—a granddaughter who looked like Margaret, Peter decided—who would be young and light, without a care in the world. He began to paint them, and because Maus rejoiced and complimented him for finally moving on, he didn't tell Maus who the figures were. He knew it was unhealthy. He knew it was wrong. He knew it was a betrayal of Ingrid, who had no idea that he kept a warehouse full of the life he wished he had lived.

In fact, Ingrid had her own idea of what the Gaertner Angel of his paintings represented. *Perhaps you were just waiting for me,* she said. *Perhaps now the woman in your paintings can have a face, for you have fallen in love.*

And because he wanted very much to love her, because he wanted his world to be centered in reality rather than fantasy, he made a decision. After that dream of Margaret, he decided to try to let her go. He knew he could never stop painting her, but he had to force himself to move on. Maybe the dream was somehow her good-bye. So on this morning, waking up beside this beautiful woman, he intended to finally make the change that he probably should have made years ago. Maus would be proud.

"Merry Christmas, Ingrid," he said, giving the woman in

his bed a sweet kiss on the lips. He waited, as he always did, for the kind of firework sensation he'd had each time he'd kissed Margaret, but it eluded him. "I will bring you breakfast, my dear. Just wait here."

She smiled at him, seduction in her eyes. "You won't come back to bed?"

He blinked. He wanted to. Of course he wanted to. But he had made himself a promise. He had to do this. Perhaps it was the way to become whole again. "Please, I will be right back."

He prepared a tray for her in the kitchen. Scrambled eggs. Strawberries. Freshly squeezed orange juice. Strong coffee. And a jewelry box. He carried it upstairs, arms shaking, and set it down beside her. He could tell that she'd gotten up and applied a bit of makeup before he'd returned, and there was something about it that twisted his insides. She should know he already found her beautiful. Why did she have to put on layers of artifice? But there was no time to think about it, for she had already spotted the little blue box, was already tearing the white ribbon off, cracking it open. "Oh, Ralph!" she exclaimed, looking up at him with wide eyes.

"Will you marry me?" he asked, swallowing the mysterious lump that had suddenly lodged itself in his throat.

"Oh yes! Yes, my darling, yes!" She pulled the Tiffany solitaire from its perch and slipped it onto her own finger before Peter had the chance to do it for her. "Oh, we will have such a wonderful life together!" she exclaimed, diving toward him on the bed to wrap her arms around his neck. The coffee spilled a little, sloshing onto the bedsheets, and they both laughed. But as she pulled back, already making plans about who she would call first and when they might marry and what kind of dress she would wear, Peter had to look away, because his eyes were wet and cold.

———

He wanted it to work. He wanted to love her. He wanted to put his thoughts of Margaret to rest at long last. It had truly been his intention.

And yet as the years swept by, he began to realize it was impossible.

He grew to care deeply for Ingrid, but it was a different kind of love than he'd had for Margaret. He felt an enormous sense of affection, and when Ingrid was happy, he was happy. When something good happened to her, he rejoiced with her. And on the nights when she was traveling for business, he missed her.

But was that love? Was that how it was supposed to feel? He tried to discuss it with Maus once, but his friend would have none of it. *You have a perfect, beautiful woman who loves you deeply,* Maus had said. *Why can't that be enough? Why can't you see how lucky you are?*

Why indeed? It was the question constantly ringing in Peter's head too. Why couldn't he close his eyes without seeing Margaret? Why couldn't he pick up his paintbrush without wanting to bring her alive in watercolor once again? Why couldn't he make love to Ingrid without having to hold Margaret's name back from his tongue?

He knew Ingrid could feel it too. She flinched, sometimes, when he looked at her, and he knew it was because the things reflected in his eyes were wrong. She could read emotions that shouldn't be there. In bed, there was a growing gulf between them too. Sometimes, at the beginning, she tried to hold him, as if the cradle of her arms would let him be reborn. But with the passage of time, she moved further and further away, retreating into herself. He knew she loved him, and he knew that with each refusal, he wounded her a little more. There was an emptiness inside of him that she could never fill, and after a while, it was a gulf too wide to cross.

CHAPTER TWENTY-FIVE

I don't understand." I was staring at Arno Fromm, my throat suddenly dry. How could Ralph Gaertner, one of the twentieth century's most celebrated artists, be Peter Dahler? *My grandfather?*

"Peter's father was a cruel man," Fromm said, "and after Peter learned that his mother had died and that his father had kept Margaret's letters from him deliberately, he left Germany. He wanted nothing to do with his family again. But it wasn't until 1963—after he thought he saw Margaret at the March on Washington—that Peter made the decision to leave the past behind forever, to become someone else entirely. He didn't know how else to let his grief over losing Margaret go, and he feared that if he didn't, he wouldn't survive. Gaertner was in honor of his childhood best friend, Otto Gaertner, who had died in his arms on the battlefield in Africa. And Ralph was for Ralph Waldo Emerson, his favorite poet. The first conversation Peter ever had with your grandmother was about Emerson, and the two of them spent much time quoting Emerson to each other. He said the name would always connect him to Margaret in a way only she would understand."

I could feel tears in my eyes. "Do you think that's why my grandmother chose Emerson as a last name too?"

Fromm sucked in a breath. "Emerson is not your married name? I just assumed."

"No, I'm not married. It's the name my grandmother took when she left Belle Creek behind."

"My goodness," Fromm murmured. "They were connected after all, their whole lives through."

"But what if it was the false names that kept them apart?" I asked after a moment. "What if they had been able to find each other otherwise?" They had both ultimately believed the lies they'd been told, but the most heartbreaking part of the story was that they had inadvertently created the final, insurmountable obstacle themselves.

"I had a nickname too," Fromm said. "And I think Peter saw that it was a way to separate from the past. I was a scrawny little man, but the nickname allowed me to sort of reinvent myself as the funny guy. I think that appealed to him, the way that a name allows you to become someone else."

Something that Werner Vogt had said suddenly clicked. "Are you the one they called Mouse? Or, um, Maus?"

Fromm looked surprised, and then he laughed. "Why, yes. No one but Peter has called me that in many years. Peter found it very funny. I think the name made me disarming. No one is intimidated by a man named Maus."

"Mr. Fromm, did you and my grandfather know each other in Germany, before Belle Creek?" I asked.

"No. In much the same way Belle Creek brought your grandparents together, it brought me and Peter together. He was my dearest friend, and my journey through life would have been far grayer without him. He brought color to my days, both literally and figuratively. He was a wonderful man, and I wish that you'd known him."

"Did the two of you paint in Belle Creek?" I ventured. "Is that where you got your start?"

Fromm chuckled. "No, in fact. The two of us never even thought of it. We'd both been raised in homes where boys were allowed only to speak of guns and politics, not of something as insignificant as art. The irony is that in the end, the lives we were both able to lead were supported by the talent we both stumbled upon, almost by accident. Although admittedly, Peter possessed much more talent than I did, in the end. My skills were learned, but his came naturally, as if he'd been born to paint. Then again, I was the one who first handed him a paintbrush, I suppose."

He explained how he and Peter had run into each other in Munich after the war, how he was working for a construction company, and how Peter was out of work and desperate to return to Margaret. It was Fromm who first began taking home brushes and paint samples, and soon, Peter followed suit.

"The rest, as they say, is history," Fromm concluded. "For a time, I think the painting saved him. He realized first that he could paint Belle Creek, and then that he could paint Margaret. So for me, painting was a way to make a living, something to be proud of, but for Peter, it became an obsession, a way to remind himself of a world he swore he'd return to."

"And then he finally made it to America," I said softly. "And Louise lied to him."

"She told him Margaret was dead," Fromm said with a frown. "Eventually, Peter moved away. I don't think he ever quite stopped believing, though."

"But then he married someone else," I pointed out.

Fromm frowned. "That was my fault, I'm afraid. I believed that Margaret was gone, you see, and yet Peter spent more than thirty years looking for her around every corner. He painted her constantly, and it made me worry. When Ingrid came along, well, it felt like she could save him from himself." He bowed his head. "I sometimes think I was wrong to encourage him so strongly."

"Didn't she make him happy?"

"The only thing that made your grandfather truly happy was painting your grandmother. Look around you. This was his world, and I think eventually, Ingrid realized that too. She didn't know about this place—neither did I, for a while—but we could both feel that he was never with us. Not entirely. His mind was always somewhere else." He glanced around at the thousand images of my grandmother, all of which were staring at us. "His mind was with her."

"Why did he marry Ingrid then?"

"He *wanted* to love her. But wanting and doing are not the same thing, are they? We all thought that she was what he needed: a beautiful, kind woman who truly loved him. Surely she would bring him back to life." He paused. "I thought he would never take our advice. But I pushed and pushed, and finally, he saw what I was saying. He saw that he couldn't hang on to Margaret forever without destroying himself. Ingrid was his attempt to move on."

I shook my head as Fromm began to speak again. "I know now that it was wrong to encourage him to marry Ingrid. Peter broke Ingrid's heart, you see. She loved him in a way that he could never love her. And that's why, ultimately, when I discovered this warehouse, I told him he must never tell her. It would hurt too much. And so he spent many of his hours here, painting

Margaret day in and day out without fear of hurting Ingrid any further. It was like an affair. Each day, with his paintbrush, he cheated on the woman he had married. But I was wrong, too, to encourage him to keep this place a secret. It became like a drug for him, an addiction, and after a while, Ingrid followed him and found out about it. She discovered that he was living in a world of make-believe instead of living in a world with her.

"He asked me to reason with her," Fromm went on. "But I wouldn't. I thought he was wrong. I told him that the only way to salvage his marriage was to get rid of this place—these paintings—once and for all. And that made him furious. He accused me of being jealous of the love he shared with Margaret, and although I denied it, he wasn't entirely wrong. I had loved her too, you see."

"You loved my grandmother?"

He smiled sadly. "She never loved me back, Emily. Really, she barely knew me. And she truly only had eyes for Peter. But yes, from the day I first saw her, she was in my heart too. Peter knew that and understood it. He forgave it, because after all, I couldn't be blamed for the way I felt. I never acted on it. But when I told him he needed to get rid of these paintings and close the warehouse down, well, he wrongly assumed that it had to do with my long-buried feelings. We had a huge argument—the only one we really had in our many years as friends—and I assumed that he'd eventually come around. My pride kept me from apologizing to him, you see."

"When was this?" I asked, though I already had the feeling it was toward the end.

"Three months before he died. I never spoke to him again." Fromm sighed. "In any case, I've set up a trust that will pay the real estate taxes and insurance for this warehouse from now on.

It's my final gift to Peter—I will preserve this warehouse in his memory, because I can still feel his presence here. The mistake wasn't in keeping his secret. The mistake was in thinking that I could force him to follow a path other than the one his heart was showing him. I realize now that some of us fall in love just once, and then nothing quite compares to that ever again."

Neither of us said anything for a full minute. I gazed at the painting of my grandmother to my right, one in which she was standing in a small clearing, surrounded on all sides by sugarcane, looking at the viewer with eyes that were wide and full of love. It made me miss her terribly. In the painting beside it, a hand reached out for my grandmother—my grandfather's hand, I imagined—and she was reaching back, her face radiant and hopeful. I thought suddenly of Nick, and my heart ached even more. Maybe I was destined to follow in my grandfather's footsteps, haunted forever by something I could never have.

"None of it feels fair," I said after a while. "How can two people love each other that much, wind up in the same city, and somehow never see each other? It's so cruel and senseless. Why do any of us fall in love like that if we aren't given the chance to find each other again?"

Fromm didn't say anything for a moment. When I looked up, he was studying the portrait of my grandmother standing in the clearing. "I think they both ran from their pasts rather than running toward each other," he said slowly. "Yes, they both believed the other was gone, and that was tragic. But if they hadn't shut down—if they hadn't reinvented themselves and run—maybe things would have been different. Maybe in the end you can't run from who you are without destroying your life."

I digested the words for a minute. "Do you keep in touch with Ingrid?"

Fromm nodded. "Here and there. I think she has never quite forgiven me for keeping Peter's secret, even when I disagreed with it." He turned to me. "But she loved him, and you are his grand-daughter."

"And yet she never told you about me. I don't know when she realized the truth, but she had to know in order to send me that painting."

He smiled sadly. "Ingrid is a lovely woman. But she's also a woman who lives in denial. How else could she have stayed with Peter for so long? Still, I think she'll want to see you. If I'm right, can you stay in Atlanta for another day?"

"Yes, of course."

"Well, then, if you'll excuse me, I'll go call her now." He nodded to me and slipped out a side door, leaving me alone with my thoughts. I felt stunned and winded, slapped in the face by a past that had been both so rich and so unfortunate. As I gazed at the paintings surrounding me, I felt a strange blend of sadness and hope. I pulled out my iPhone and snapped a few more pictures of the paintings, because I didn't want to forget them. I wanted to be able to show my father too.

Fromm returned a moment later. "Ingrid would like to see you tomorrow morning at eight. If that's agreeable, I can give you her address."

I nodded, and he said he'd call to confirm the arrangements. On our way out of the warehouse, he added, "You are welcome back here anytime, Emily. This is your history. And please, bring your father as well. But I'm afraid that for now, I must go. I have things to attend to."

"Of course. Thank you so much for showing me all of this."

Fromm nodded solemnly. He pulled a notepad from his pocket, scribbled down Ingrid's address, and handed it to me.

Then, he grasped both of my shoulders and looked into my eyes. "My dear Emily, I knew your grandfather for more than seventy years. So I hope you'll believe me when I tell you that he would have been glad to know you. He always dreamed of having a family."

"Thank you. For everything, Mr. Fromm."

"My pleasure, my dear." He smiled, gave my shoulders one last squeeze, and headed for his car.

As I walked back to my own car, I was thinking about my grandparents, but I was also thinking about Nick. My story wasn't like my grandparents'. Nick wasn't lost. I had driven him away myself, and I had to accept that. But in order to move on— to pick myself up and try again, like Arno Fromm said—there was one more thing I needed to do.

———

Forty minutes later, with the help of Google Maps, I was pulling off the highway in Decatur, a town I hadn't seen in nearly nineteen years. Coming back to Atlanta had been difficult, because it had forced me to confront my childhood, but Decatur was where all my ghosts resided. It was the town I'd lived in when my father left and my mother died. It was where I'd met Nick, and where we'd conceived Catherine. It was home, and it was also a place that I knew I had to face sooner or later, because it was a piece of the past I'd been trying to run from. I had to make a change now, or I never would.

I drove first down Hemlock Lane, the side street where I used to live, and I was surprised and somewhat jarred to see my old house repainted from blue to white. There was a tricycle propped on its side out front and a rope swing hanging from the old oak tree I used to climb. It wasn't my home anymore, though, and I forced myself to turn right at the street's end without looking back.

I drove next to my old high school, Ernest Evans High. It had changed a lot in the last two decades—a new sign out front, a completely rebuilt entryway, metal detectors at some of the entrances—but it was familiar enough to put a lump in my throat. The moss-draped oak outside the cafeteria, whose shade I had often used while gazing into Nick's eyes, was still there, but it seemed taller and wider. Had it grown that much in nineteen years, or was I remembering incorrectly? Memories, I knew, couldn't be entirely trusted.

I headed away from the school, passing Nick's childhood house, but I didn't slow down. It, too, was in the past. It was where Nick had first told me he loved me—in his bedroom, the third window from the right upstairs—and where we'd made Catherine. It was the beginning and the end. And now I had to put it to rest.

Finally, I arrived at Decatur Cemetery, on the edge of town. I cut the ignition and took a deep breath, but I didn't move. Finally, I pulled myself together and got out of the car. And then, as if I'd been coming here all the time, I made a beeline for my mother's grave.

I hadn't been here since the day I fled town all those years ago. I'd come then to tell her the bittersweet news that she would be a grandmother—but that I'd have to say good-bye. I'd felt a tugging at my heart then, a whisper in the wind telling me to stay, but I thought it was just my conscience speaking. I had to get out. I had to save myself.

But now, as I knelt beside her headstone in the shadow of a huge sugar maple, I knew I was wrong, and that's what I had come here to say.

"You never would have wanted this for me. My life, what I've become," I said. "I'm lonely, Mom, and I don't know how to find my way back to who I used to be." I waited for a moment, hoping that I would feel an answer of some sort, but there was only the sound of a gentle breeze rustling the trees.

"I'd tell you everything, except I feel like you probably already know it," I continued after a while. "I can feel you with me all the time. I miss you every day of my life, Mom." I paused and rocked back on my knees. "The thing is, there's something I have to let go of. I've been so angry at Dad for years for leaving. He left you. He left *us*. And I don't think I'll ever understand it. But I've realized now that I can't keep carrying that anger around with me, because it's too heavy. I'm worried that if I don't learn to let go of the past—all of it—I'll never really be able to move into the future.

"So I came here today to tell you, Mom, that I'm putting it down. I have to put down the weight of blaming Dad, but I also have to put down the weight of blaming myself. I don't want you to think I'm betraying you. I'll never feel about Dad the way I felt about you. You're the one who stayed, the one who raised me, and there will never be another relationship in my world that compares with that." I sighed and stood up. "But I've realized lately that letting the past define your life is like tying yourself to a version of the world that doesn't exist anymore. And I can't keep doing that. I hope you understand."

I stayed there for a minute, listening to the wind through the trees, watching the sunlight filter down in patches. "I found my grandfather," I added. "The love of Grandma Margaret's life. But it's too late. He's gone. If you're up there, Mom, if heaven is really a thing, can you help me find Catherine? If I just know she's okay, I think I'll be able to find some peace." I paused and added, "I love you, Mom. I'll love you forever."

There was no answer, and so I began to walk back to the car. I wasn't sure if my visit had really had a purpose. But the weight on my heart felt a little lighter, and that was something. I smiled as I turned the key in the ignition, backed the car out of its spot, and got back on the road to my future.

CHAPTER TWENTY-SIX

I called my father that night from my hotel room in Atlanta, but I didn't tell him much. I wanted to see the look on his face when I explained everything, and I knew I'd be home tomorrow afternoon; I'd already booked my flight.

"Let's just say I think you'll be surprised by what I have to tell you," I said.

"You're going to keep me in suspense?" I could hear the smile in his voice.

"For less than twenty-four hours. Can I drop by your office when I get back?"

"Of course."

"I'm going to send you a photo now, though. Consider it a clue."

"I'm intrigued."

We said our good-byes, and I hit Send on one of the pictures I'd taken in the warehouse earlier. He called back almost immediately.

"Wait, are those all paintings of your grandmother?" he asked when I picked up.

"Yep. And there are hundreds."

"You're kidding me." I could hear him breathing on the other end. "And you can't tell me anything now?"

"I want to wait until I have the whole story. I'll see you tomorrow, okay?"

"Good luck, Emily."

Ingrid Gaertner's house was a gorgeous, immaculately maintained brick bungalow in the swanky Ansley Park neighborhood just east of downtown Atlanta. It sat up on a small hill at the end of a cul-de-sac, which made it hard to find but also gave it a sense of privacy. The many live oaks dotting the property only added to the house's seclusion.

I parked, checked the address to confirm I was in the right place, and made my way up the winding brick steps toward the front door at just past 8 a.m. My heart thudded as I rang the bell. Fromm had said that my grandfather had lived here since the late 1980s, and it was strange for me to think that he'd stood in this very spot countless times. It was sad to realize I'd missed meeting him by less than a year.

There were footsteps inside, and then the door was opened by a tall, slender woman whose gray hair was swept up into a chignon. She was wearing a black silk blouse and flowy black linen pants, and even at this early morning hour, her makeup was flawless. "You must be Emily," she said, staring at me as if she'd seen a ghost. Her voice carried the hint of an accent, and I recalled that Fromm had said she was German. She didn't smile, but she didn't look unfriendly either.

"Mrs. Gaertner?" I asked, extending my hand.

She looked at my outstretched hand but didn't shake it. "Please. Call me Ingrid. After all, we are family, aren't we?" She turned without another word, and I withdrew my hand and followed her, closing the door behind me. I assumed that her disappearance into the house was an invitation for me to come in.

Inside, the home was dimly lit and richly furnished. My grandfather's paintings—all of them landscapes—lined the walls of the front hall, and as I entered the formal living room behind Ingrid, I was struck by the opulence. The sofa was high-backed, tufted, and upholstered in a rich red velvet, and the chairs facing it had gold legs that made them look like they belonged in a European palace. There was a white grand piano in the corner and a rich oriental rug beneath our feet. Sunlight poured in from floor-to-ceiling windows that overlooked an immaculate garden overflowing with roses. "What a lovely home," I said.

Ingrid shrugged. "It was my taste. Not Ralph's. He preferred to spend his time elsewhere." She sounded wounded rather than angry, and it made me sad to realize that months after his death, she was still hurting so much. I also noted the fact that she had referred to him as Ralph, his assumed name, whereas Fromm, his oldest friend, had still called him Peter.

She gestured for me to sit on the velvet sofa, and she settled gracefully onto one of the chairs. "Would you like some coffee or tea? I can ring for Alice, our housekeeper."

"No, thank you. I'm fine." I felt a bit like a bug under a microscope as she continued to stare at me.

"You look just like her, you know," she said abruptly after a moment. "Margaret. Your grandmother."

"I'm so sorry, Ingrid, about everything," I said, meaning it. No matter how tragic my grandparents' love story was, Ingrid's was almost as sad. To be married to a man you love only to realize he was still somehow beyond your reach must have been devastating.

"You're sorry?" She made a *tsk*ing sound and looked away. "Oh, Emily, you have no idea."

I didn't say anything, because I wasn't sure how to answer that.

"It's not your fault, of course," she said after a moment. "It's just, I don't suppose you know what it feels like to love someone who will never love you in return. To realize you missed your chance, all because your timing was wrong."

I thought of Nick, of the love I'd let go, of the way I still felt. "As a matter of fact, I do."

She studied me for a moment and nodded. "Well, I'm sorry, then. It's a terribly inconvenient way to feel, isn't it?"

The word choice was strange, but I nodded, because she was right. It *was* inconvenient to love someone who would never love you the same way, because it held you back in life. It tied you to something you could never have. "I'm sorry," I repeated, because I wasn't sure what else to say.

She sighed. "I'm sorry too, Emily. Despite everything, I would have liked it if you had found your way here while Ralph was still alive. He would have been so delighted to meet you. Timing is a strange thing, isn't it?" Her mind seemed to wander somewhere else for a moment. "In any case, dear Arno Fromm says you came looking for Ralph. Is that correct?"

I nodded. "Did you send me the painting?"

She regarded me thoughtfully. "Yes, I did. Did you show it to your father too?"

"Yes. In fact, we went to Germany together to try to trace where it had come from. We were here in Atlanta just last week."

"And yet he's not here now."

I looked down. "That's my fault. This was something I needed to do on my own. I know he'd like to meet you, though."

"The two of you are not close." It was a statement, not a question. "I have read your columns. You have a lot of anger toward him."

I took a deep breath. "Yes. I'm trying to let go of some of those feelings. I think I've carried them with me for too long."

"But your father, he is emotionless, yes?"

I squirmed a little under her penetrating gaze. "Not exactly. I think he just had trouble tapping into his feelings for a long time. When I was a kid, I never really felt like he loved me. But things are a little different now."

Ingrid looked at me for a long time. "So I see Margaret suffered too, then."

"What?"

"We are a result of what our parents make us, unless we stop the progression, aren't we?" Ingrid asked. "Knowing that your father hasn't coped well with feelings, well, it leads me to guess that he was raised by someone who shut her emotions away."

"Yes, maybe," I whispered, thinking of the way that although I knew my grandmother loved me, she would often drift away midsentence, her face going blank. I had often wondered where she was vanishing to, but now I knew. I wondered if my father's childhood had been filled with moments where he was right on the cusp of receiving his mother's love, and then she simply drifted. It would explain a lot.

"And do you do that too? Shut your feelings away?" Ingrid asked. She didn't wait for an answer before adding, "Your grandfather was that way, you know. Ralph. Easier to feel nothing than to feel the pain of loss each day."

"But I think he *did* feel, didn't he? There's such emotion in his paintings."

Ingrid's face fell, and I realized too late what I'd said. "That's because *she* is in all of them," she said through gritted teeth. "But just because he felt with his paintbrush did not mean he felt in the real world. They are different things."

"Of course," I murmured.

"You know I loved him," she said abruptly, looking me in the eye. "There were skeptics at first, people in the art world who thought I was just drawn to his talent. But that wasn't it. I *felt* something with him that I'd never felt before. Do you understand?"

"Yes. And I'm sorry."

"Stop apologizing. The story that led us here was written long before you were born." She sighed. "I believed he loved me too, at first. Maybe he did. There are different kinds of love in the world, aren't there?"

I thought of the all-consuming love I had for Catherine and the love I had for Nick, which wouldn't go away. I thought of the way I loved my father, despite the fact that it hurt, and the way my love for my mother was a constant, grounding ache of loneliness. "Yes, there are," I agreed.

"But when you fall in love with someone, when you promise your life to that person, you want to receive love the same way you give it. Freely. Openly. Without reservation. But in time, I realized I would never have that. It was only when I learned of Margaret that I understood why."

"How did you find out? Did he tell you?"

"No. He couldn't even speak her name aloud. Until the end, of course." Her mouth twisted with anguish for a moment, and then she pulled herself together, clearing her throat and smooth-

ing her face back into an expressionless palette. "I never knew
Margaret existed, you see. Not until I began to suspect him of
cheating, and I followed him to the warehouse. I'm sure you
know by now what I found. The place is an enormous shrine to
her." She laughed bitterly. "And would you believe that all along, I
thought the woman in the background of his paintings was a
symbol? I saw her as hope, as love." She looked out the window
for a long time before turning back to me. "Do you know he never
painted me? Not once?"

"I'm sorry. I didn't know that."

Silence descended, and I could hear the ticking of a grandfather clock somewhere in the house. Ingrid sniffled, and I looked
back in surprise as I realized she was crying.

"Ingrid . . ." I said, starting to get up.

She waved me away, and I sat back down. "Please, don't look
at me now. My emotions sometimes get the best of me. I know
better." She took a deep breath and went on. "After I discovered
the warehouse, I demanded that he stop. And I believe he
wanted to. He tried to. But it was an obsession."

"I'm so sorry."

"And your life?" she asked abruptly. "How has it been? Have
you been happy?"

"Um, sure," I said, startled by the rapid change in topic.

"I understand that your mother died," she said, her voice
softening as she leaned forward. I saw real sympathy in her eyes.
"I'm very sorry to hear that. And your father left when you were
young?"

I looked down. "You really have read my columns."

"Many of them. You were only a teenager, weren't you? When
your mother passed?"

"Eighteen."

"And your father didn't return?"

"No."

Ingrid looked at her lap for a long time. "I'm very sorry. I've been talking all about my loss, but you have suffered too. You have also waited for the kind of love that it is only natural to wish for."

My eyes were suddenly wet. "But he's trying now. I think he regrets what he has done."

"So did my Ralph." She paused. "But your father, he still has time left to change things, doesn't he? If he's strong enough."

I nodded slowly.

"And you will forgive him?"

"I want to."

"You are wise to keep trying."

"But didn't you keep trying?" I couldn't resist asking. "Didn't you keep getting hurt?"

She smiled. "Yes. And I would do it all over again in a heartbeat. That's terrible, isn't it? But the outcome didn't make me love Ralph any less. It just made me regret my lack of control. But given another chance, I think I would continue to forgive endlessly."

"Why?"

"Because it is the only way to find peace, don't you think?"

The words sat there for a moment as I realized how right she was.

"Can you tell me how you found me?" I asked after a moment. "How did you know to send me the painting? Didn't my grandfather believe my grandmother had died long ago?"

"Yes," she said simply. I waited, but she didn't say anything else.

"Did you want me to find you? Is that why you sent the painting?"

She considered this for a moment. "I'm not sure. I think I wanted you to know that your grandmother had been loved deeply. I'm not sure that I was prepared for such a meeting—*this* meeting—but I do feel it's the right thing."

"How did you know we even existed?" I asked. "Did you see my grandmother's picture in my column a few months ago?"

She smiled slightly. "That was startling, I admit. But I knew who you were before that, Emily."

"How?"

She got up and crossed the room, sitting beside me on the couch. She touched my face gently and looked into my eyes, and I wondered what she was thinking, what she was trying to see. "You know, I hated your grandmother." The words were weighted, bogged down in something inescapable. "I hated how, even in death, she had stolen Ralph from me and continued to steal him every day. I thought she was to blame for making him the sad, withdrawn man he was. But in fact, as it turned out, the opposite was true."

"What do you mean?"

"Something changed," she said, her voice suddenly hollow. "He knew he was dying, and it was in all the papers, of course. There was a very indiscreet doctor at the hospital, who spoke with a reporter, and suddenly, the art world was abuzz with the story." She pressed her lips together. "In any case, Emily, the day before he died, the light came on within him. He was happy—beyond happy, in fact—in a way I'd never seen before. And I suppose, well, I suppose I have your grandmother to thank for that."

I stared at her in confusion. "But he thought my grandmother died years ago. How could she have played a role in bringing him any happiness in the end?"

Ingrid rose and walked to the window. She gazed out at the rose garden for a long time before turning around. I could see tears glimmering in her eyes as she spoke. "Because the day before Ralph died," she said, looking me right in the eye, "he talked to your grandmother for the first time in seventy years."

CHAPTER TWENTY-SEVEN

Peter knew it was the end, and yet somehow, he thought it would be different. How could a man live to be ninety-four, endure everything that he had endured, and not expect that death would somehow be dignified?

But it wasn't. Of course it wasn't. The cancer eating away at his pancreas was making its way to the other organs of his body, rendering them useless one by one. It seemed almost absurd to have survived World War II only to lose his final battle to an army of invading cells so small he couldn't even see them.

And yet they were advancing. The doctor had halfheartedly suggested chemotherapy, but Peter had laughed aloud. He was in his nineties. He had been lucky to have this many years. No, he would go gently and peacefully into the night, he decided. But he hadn't expected the waves of nausea, the cascades of pain as the cancer spread. He hadn't anticipated the way that sometimes, reality would feel fuzzy, and he wouldn't quite be able to hang on.

He worried most about Ingrid, about leaving her alone. But he had already done so, hadn't he? By refusing to let her into his heart, he had left her long ago, and the remaining days were too few now to atone for that mistake. So he had to live with it, and sometimes, he wondered if the cancer was feeding on his guilt. If so, it would encounter a veritable feast, he thought. He was filled with regret over so very many things. But he knew without a doubt that it was Ingrid he had hurt not only the most, but the most deliberately.

He blamed himself sometimes for Margaret's death, too. If he hadn't gotten her pregnant, she wouldn't have died in childbirth. But over time, some of that guilt had slipped away, because he hadn't meant to hurt her—just the opposite, in fact. It didn't bring her back, but it absolved him slightly of the regret borne of conscious responsibility. He had done what he had done because he loved her. He hadn't taken advantage in any way. And if God had chosen this path for them, then so be it.

As he began to feel his body shutting down in those final weeks, capitulating to the enemy cells, he began to think seriously about heaven. It had been a long time since he'd considered it, in fact. At first, all those years ago, when a stone-faced Louise had told him that Margaret was dead, he hadn't believed her. He refused to ask himself if his love was in heaven, looking down at him, because he so desperately wanted to believe that she was still out there. The years passed, and his hope faded, but still, he wasn't sure about the afterlife. After all, if Margaret was up there in some sort of celestial kingdom, wouldn't he have felt her presence sometimes? Wouldn't he have sensed her with him in his darkest hours? But he never did.

And now, the end was coming, and Peter felt a strange sense of hesitant elation. Would he see Margaret on the other side? Would she know him? Would she love him? And what if she didn't? The thought terrified Peter more than the cancer itself did.

Then one afternoon in mid-December, Peter had gotten a call from a *New Yorker* writer named Lauren Golgoski who had interviewed him over the years during some of his major New York exhibits. "I understand you're ill, Mr. Gaertner," she said. "I'm so very sorry to hear that."

"Who told you?"

"A doctor mentioned it at a cocktail party. Very unprofessional, if you ask me, but word got back to me nonetheless. I'm so sorry."

He felt betrayed, but in the grand scheme of things, this betrayal was a small one, wasn't it? "I suppose the cat would have been out of the bag eventually."

"The perils of celebrity, I suppose," she said. "I wanted to check with you before writing anything, Mr. Gaertner. I'm afraid the news will indeed get out there, but I'd love to do it the right way. Would you be up for a brief interview?"

Peter thought about it for a moment. He had never minded the media when they were ethical. Even when art critics were taking aim at him, he respected that they had opinions—and a right to express them. This writer in particular had always struck him as kind and honest in her dealings. "Yes, Lauren," he said. "I'm not feeling well, but I could speak with you for a few minutes."

He was surprised that she didn't pry more. He would have told her everything, if only she'd asked. He might have told her his real name. He might even have revealed the identity of the shadowy woman in his paintings, which had long been a source of speculation within the art community. But her questions were softballs about his legacy and his life, and so he answered them succinctly and hung up the phone respecting Lauren all the more for not digging too deeply.

The article ran after the first of the year, and the news was picked up in newspapers across the country. He was even a ticker headline on CNN. It was astonishing. And then, on Valentine's Day, not long after the story hit, Peter got a call that changed everything.

"There's a woman named Louise trying to reach you," Ingrid had said, pressing her lips together tightly as she handed him the phone. "She says it's urgent and personal."

Louise? It couldn't be. "Hello?" he asked tentatively.

"Peter Dahler?" the woman said in a slow southern drawl, the vowels lengthened by age.

"No, this is Ralph Gaertner," he said, his heart suddenly racing.

"Right. And I'm the queen of England. Shall we just dispense with all the bullshit? We're too old for it, wouldn't you say?"

"Perhaps so," Peter replied after a moment.

"This is Louise Evans Candless. But you might know me as Louise Evans. Do you know who I am?"

"Margaret's sister," he said, and Ingrid, who had been lingering as she feigned a reorganization of the dresser, whipped around to stare at him in disbelief.

"Good. I was afraid you were one of those sad-sack cases with memory loss," Louise said. "I have some things to say to you, and I'd prefer to do it in person. Can we arrange that?"

Peter met Ingrid's eye, knowing that she would hate it, but he had to hear what Louise had to say. "Yes. But can you come to my home? I'm not well enough to travel."

"I'm calling you from the Atlanta airport," she replied immediately. "I can be there in an hour."

By the time Louise arrived at the door, Peter had had time to fight with Ingrid, who had stormed out of the house in a huff. Alice, their housekeeper, was kind enough to let Louise in.

"Well, you look even worse than I expected," Louise said as she plunked down in the chair Alice had set up beside Peter's bed. Alice raised an eyebrow and left the room. "You look like crap, actually."

"Nice to see you too, Louise," Peter said, oddly relieved that even his deteriorating body hadn't made Louise retract her claws. Consistency was comforting. And oddly, despite the gray hair and the deep wrinkles, she didn't look that different than she had the last time he'd seen her, in 1950.

"So what's all this Ralph Gaertner crap?" she asked. "You running from something, Peter Dahler?"

He coughed, a long, hacking cough, but she didn't move. She didn't even flinch. Finally, he managed to say, "How long have you known?"

"Oh, since the sixties or so. I'm not a big art lover, but I saw you on Johnny Carson. I would have recognized you anywhere. I couldn't imagine why you were going by some fake name, though."

"I had to leave the past behind," he said. "I had to start over."

"Well, that makes two of you," she said.

"What?"

She shook her head. "You're a fool, you know."

"I don't follow, Louise." Another hacking cough rattled his body, and Louise waited until he was done to continue.

"You should have just left her in the past, along with your name. Instead, you went and painted her in every single one of your goddamn pictures, didn't you?"

Peter knew she was talking about Margaret. "I couldn't forget her, Louise. You have to understand, I couldn't let her go."

"What'd she have that was so special, anyways?" Louise asked.

"Everything, Louise. She had everything. She was the love of my life."

Louise muttered something under her breath. Then she looked down, and after a moment, Peter could see her shoulders heaving.

"Louise? Are you all right? Are you crying?"

Her head snapped up, and although she was glaring at him, something in her expression had softened. "I ain't crying."

Peter coughed again, tasting blood. He felt his head spinning, and he grabbed on to the bed rail to steady himself. When he could breathe again, he said, "Why did you come here, Louise? I don't mean to be rude, but I'm not really up to socializing, I'm afraid."

Louise opened and closed her mouth a few times, as if she was trying to force the words out, but they wouldn't come.

"Louise?" Peter prompted. "What is it?"

"She didn't die," Louise said flatly.

Everything within Peter went cold. "What?"

"Margaret. She didn't die in childbirth, like I said she did."

Peter stared at her, his lungs constricting. "Is she still—?"

Louise didn't say anything.

"Is she alive?" Peter demanded after the silence seemed to stretch on forever. "Tell me, Louise."

"Yes. Or at least she was a couple months ago. I got a letter from her two days before Christmas. First I'd heard from her in seventy years."

Peter's heart seized, and he clutched his chest. He felt like he was having a heart attack, but when Louise got up and called for Alice, Peter silenced her by grabbing her arm with a death grip. "No!" he rasped. "Don't you dare! You stay right here and tell me everything."

"Not until you breathe. I ain't gonna be responsible for killing you."

Peter finally got himself under control, but still he was gasping for air. "Where is she?" he demanded sharply. "What did you do, Louise?"

She bit her lip for a moment before continuing. "You gotta understand, Margaret having the bastard child of a Nazi was real embarrassing for all of us. My daddy disowned her, and there wasn't much my mother and I could do. He was furious, and well, it was just best for everyone that they get out of town."

"*They?*" Peter whispered. "The baby lived too?"

"Yes." Louise cleared her throat. "Yes, he did."

Peter stared at her in disbelief. "*You lied and kept me from Margaret?*"

"I said I apologize."

"And you denied me the chance to know my own son?"

"Yes," Louise answered a bit more softly now. "Look, I'm real sorry."

That didn't matter to Peter. Not at all. Her apology meant nothing, for the things she had taken from him could never be replaced. But the ache in his chest over missing a lifetime with his family was replaced suddenly by a different kind of ache. He looked up at her in horror. "But how could Margaret leave without trying to find me? I promised I would return for her!"

"A letter arrived from someone claiming to be you in January of '46, the day before the baby was born," Louise said. "It said your fling with Margaret was a mistake and you were marrying your old girlfriend. You wanted Margaret to move on." She looked him in the eye, and Peter knew she wasn't lying. Someone close to him—probably his father—had destroyed everything. His stomach heaved, and he thought he might throw up as she continued. "I don't think Margaret believed it at first. But of course she never heard from you, and well, eventually, she realized she had to let you go. It was what was best for the baby."

"But I wrote to her so many times," Peter whispered.

Louise looked down again. "I—I never gave her the letters. I thought it would be better for everyone if she just moved on."

"Louise! Why?"

"Because she didn't deserve you!" Louise said, suddenly fierce. "And if she had gone off to be with you, it would have ruined all of us. Is that what you wanted? To ruin our family?"

"No," Peter murmured. "I wanted to build a family of

my own. With the woman I loved more than life itself. But you took that from me."

"Yeah, well, I'm sorry," Louise said, bowing her head.

"And you say she's still alive? Where is she? What happened to her?"

"I don't know, exactly. She said in her letter that she was in a nursing home in Orlando. She said she forgave me; she didn't know how much time she had left, and something her granddaughter said made her realize that she didn't want to leave this earth with a burden of anger on her heart."

"Her granddaughter?" Peter whispered. "My son's daughter?"

"I assume so."

"I have a granddaughter too?" He felt like he'd been punched in the gut. "Are they okay? What became of my son?"

"I honestly don't know. Margaret didn't give me any details. I guess she felt it wasn't my right to know about her life. And she said she didn't want me to call her. She just wanted me to know she wasn't taking her anger to the grave." Her eyes filled, and she looked away.

"So why are you here, Louise?" Peter demanded, suddenly furious at this woman who was calmly recounting all she'd stolen from him. "To kick me while I'm down? To ruin what's left of my life?"

She looked horrified. "Of course not."

"Then why?"

"Because I saw on the news that you were dying. And I don't know, I thought maybe it wasn't too late to set things right."

"To set things *right*?" He could feel his heart pounding too hard. He hadn't been this furious in years. He tried to breathe. "What could you possibly do to fix things now?"

"I got the name of the nursing home. It's in Orlando," she said quietly, handing over a piece of paper with the information jotted down. "Maybe you can call her there. Margaret changed her name too. Just like you. You were both running from the past, but the past was there all along, wasn't it?"

"You took it from us! You took away the past and any chance of a future! You and your parents and my father. There's nothing that can make up for that."

"I said I'm sorry."

"What name did she take?" He wanted to ask if she had taken his name, but to be honest, he had considered that before. Back in the '50s, when he didn't want to believe she was dead, he had also had the investigator he hired search for a Margaret Dahler, just in case.

"Emerson," Louise said. "Margaret Emerson. After some writer she liked."

Peter's eyes filled. "Ralph Waldo Emerson."

"Yeah, that's right." Louise squinted at him. "Hey. Ralph, like your fake name."

"Yes, Louise," Peter murmured. "Ralph, like my fake name."

Louise stared at him for a moment before understanding crossed her face. "Oh." She cleared her throat. "Well, the boy is named Victor. Victor Jeremiah Emerson."

Victor. Exactly what Peter had named the boy in his mind when he thought he was merely a figment of his imagination. "The middle name is for the boy Margaret used to care for?"

Louise frowned. "I suppose so. He was the only one who

stood by her when the whole town turned against her. Whole lotta good it did her, having a little black boy stand up for her. He left the same night she did. Boy, that would have started some rumors if we didn't tell people she died in childbirth."

"Good for them," Peter murmured. "And the girl? Our granddaughter? Do you know her name?"

"Margaret said in her letter it was Emily."

"Emily," he whispered. "Where are they now? Victor and Emily?"

Louise shook her head. "No idea."

"But they're your family, Louise. Don't you care?"

"It's too late, Peter. They'd hate me."

Peter coughed again, but this time, it wasn't his lungs betraying him. It was the lump in his throat. "Does Margaret know I'm still alive?"

"I got no idea. Probably not. You think she could have forgiven me if she knew that?" She paused and stood. "I wish I'd told her years ago, but it's too late for that. And like I said, I'm sorry. You ain't gonna hold a grudge, are you?"

Peter didn't know how to answer that. He couldn't possibly absolve her, but like Margaret had said in her letter, he didn't want to carry such anger to his grave. So he stared at her for a long time and finally said, "What's done is done."

From the way her face cleared, he knew she'd taken it as absolution. That wasn't what it was, but Peter was too weary to make the point. She stood to go, mumbling that she hoped he would get better. They both knew the words were useless.

"One more thing, Louise," Peter called as she made her way to the door. She turned and he took a deep breath, which led to another coughing fit. She waited, and finally, he managed to ask, "Did she marry? Did Margaret marry someone else?"

"No. I thought she would have, but she didn't. Said so in the letter. I figured it would only take her a little while to get over you. After all, you'd both been so young. No offense, but it sounds to me like you both wasted your lives." And then she was gone.

Peter stared after her for a moment before whispering, "No. None of it was a waste. Without us, Victor and Emily wouldn't be here."

But there was no one left to hear him.

"Alice?" he called out. "Alice?" A moment later, his housekeeper appeared in the doorway of his bedroom.

"I let the woman out, Mr. Gaertner," she said.

"Thank you. But Alice, I need you to do something for me, quickly. Can you bring me my laptop?"

"Of course, Mr. Gaertner." A moment later, she reappeared holding his MacBook. "Will there be anything else, sir?" she asked as she handed it to him.

"No, Alice, thank you." Hands trembling, he opened the computer and entered the name of Margaret's nursing home in Orlando. A search brought up a phone number with a 407 area code. He grabbed the phone from his bedside table and dialed quickly.

"Hello, Sunnyside," said the cheerful voice on the other end.

"I'm looking for . . ." Peter trailed off as his voice gave out. He took a deep shuddering breath. "I'm sorry. Hello. I'm looking for Margaret Emerson, please."

"One moment, and I'll connect you."

"Wait!" Peter sat up a little straighter. "She's still alive? She's okay?"

"Yes, sir." The woman on the other end sounded a little wary. "Of course, sir."

"Thank you. Thank you so much." Peter closed his eyes and waited while the woman transferred his call and the line began to ring.

But no one picked up. Peter let the line ring twelve times before hanging up and calling back.

"Hello, Sunnyside." It was the same woman.

"Hello. I just called looking for Margaret Emerson. But there was no answer."

"Hmm," the woman said. Peter could hear papers shuffling in the background. "You know what? She may have had a visit with her doctor today. Maybe try again in another hour or so?"

"Yes, yes, of course. But you're sure she's okay?"

"Yes, sir. She's fine. Have a nice day."

Peter put the phone down, breathless. Suddenly, he was exhausted. "Margaret," he whispered, sinking against the pillows. The cancer was stealing so many of his moments. "Victor, Emily." He said the names again and again until he fell into a deep, dreamless sleep.

When Peter awoke, he was sure at first that he had imagined Louise's visit, but just beside his bedside, Margaret's name was there, along with an address, written in Louise's unfamiliar hand. It had been real. *Margaret was alive.*

It was past ten in the evening, and Ingrid hadn't come to bed yet. He knew she was angry at him, angry that Margaret couldn't simply be erased. But of course she couldn't. She was forever stamped on his heart. He knew it was late, but he had to try reaching her again. He had the sudden sense that time was running out. He redialed the number of her nursing home, and when a man answered, he asked quickly for Margaret.

"Sir, it's past ten. She's likely asleep."

"Please, it's an emergency," Peter said. "I wouldn't ask you otherwise."

The man paused, and then Peter could hear ringing on the other end.

"Hello?" The female voice on the line was drowsy, but Peter would have recognized it anywhere.

"Margaret," he said simply, his heart thudding. He couldn't quite believe this was happening.

There was silence on the other end of the line for what felt like an eternity. "Peter?" she finally asked.

He closed his eyes. She had recognized his voice all these years later. That had to mean something. He was still in her heart too; he was almost certain of it. "Yes. Yes, Margaret, it's me."

"But you left me."

Her words were so raw and full of pain that they brought tears to Peter's eyes. "No, Margaret. No. I came back for you. Your sister told me you were dead."

"But you never wrote."

"I wrote all the time, my dear. I wrote love letters that told you how much I longed for you, how I was counting the days until I could return for you. She took them all. She explained it all today."

"You saw Louise?" Margaret's tone was confused,

cloudy. He could also hear a wariness there, and he didn't blame her.

"She heard I was sick, and she came to see me today for the first time in almost seventy years. She admitted everything—and told me where I could find you."

"It's impossible," Margaret whispered. "What about the letter? The one that said you were marrying your old girlfriend?"

"It was fabricated. Probably by my father. Or maybe by my brother. He was the one who was better with English. The truth is, I never loved anyone but you." He felt a surge of guilt about Ingrid, but the words were true. What he felt for Ingrid didn't hold a candle to the feelings he'd always had for Margaret.

"You were the love of my life," Margaret said after a long pause. "I didn't want to believe you had changed your mind about me. But you never came back. It was like you had vanished. I tried to convince myself I had imagined the love between us. It was the only way to move on. I had to tell myself over and over that it wasn't real, that it had never been real."

"But it *was* real, Margaret. All of it." He paused and blinked back tears. "I was stuck in a prison camp in England for two years after the war, and then it took me until 1950 to return to the States. I came right to Belle Creek. I couldn't wait to see you and our baby. I showed up at your doorstep, and your sister told me you'd both died in childbirth. I stayed in Florida for years, trying to find you."

"I didn't want to be found," she whispered. "Once I came to believe that you didn't want me anymore, I only wanted to start over, to become someone new. Being Margaret Evans meant I was always going to have a broken heart. I thought I could change that by reinventing myself. But my heart never healed, Peter. Never."

"I'm so sorry. Mine never healed either, Margaret. I never stopped loving you."

"And I never stopped loving you." Margaret drew a shaky breath.

Peter knew she was close to her nineties now, but he could imagine her on the other end of the phone just as she'd been the last time he'd seen her: eighteen years old with rosy cheeks, shiny dark hair, and eyes full of hope. He wondered if she'd lost that hope the same way he had. "Margaret," he began.

"You have a son and a granddaughter," Margaret blurted out. "Victor. And Emily. They're good people, Peter. I wasn't perfect, and I brought so much of the pain from losing you into the way I raised our child. I tried to be a good mother, but I know I failed Victor sometimes. I wish I'd been stronger. You'd be so proud. Of both of them. Victor runs his own business. And Emily is a wonderful writer. She writes about family, Peter. She understands love, even if she doesn't realize it yet."

"I can't wait to meet them." The words made Peter sad, because he didn't know if he'd have the time. His body had given out, and he was confined to bed now, but he'd find a way. He'd find some way to see his son and his granddaughter. He had to.

"Peter, you said you are sick?"

He took a deep breath. "Cancer. I'm afraid I'm dying. I should be grateful that I've had ninety-four years, I suppose, but all I can think, Margaret, is that I haven't had enough time. In that lifetime, I only spent a year of it with you."

"I'm dying too," she said softly. "I'm hooked up to machines, and my body is failing me. Do you think we will ever see each other again, Peter?"

He thought about the question for a moment. He knew she was more than three hundred miles away, and neither of them was in any condition to travel. Was it possible they'd come all this way, traveled through all of their lives without meeting again, only to miss each other at the very end? "Do you remember the way the sky looked the morning we first saw each other?" Peter asked after a while.

"It was violet," she said immediately. "It was the most beautiful dawn I'd ever seen."

Peter closed his eyes and imagined that day, the way Margaret had looked silhouetted against the sky, the way he'd known before he even talked to her that she would change his life forever. "I've always believed that the sky is just the edge of heaven," he said finally. "And that the most beautiful sunrises and sunsets are just a glimpse of a better world beyond this one. I know I'll see you again beyond that violet sky."

He could hear her crying on the other end of the line. "Is that all we get at the end of our long lives? A promise to see each other after we die? It hardly seems fair."

"None of it's fair," Peter replied, choking up. "But maybe the world that lies beyond the sky is everything. Maybe life is just a beautiful prelude."

She cried quietly for a moment, and then she drew a ragged breath. "So what happened to you, Peter? Where are you now? How did you live your life?"

"I go by Ralph now. For Ralph Waldo Emerson." He said it with a smile, and he could hear her gasp. "I live in Atlanta, and as a matter of fact, I'm a painter. I've made a whole career of painting my memories of you."

For the next four hours, they told each other everything. Peter told her about reconnecting with Maus, finding his talent, coming to America, searching for her, and settling into a life where his paintbrush was like a window to the past. She told him about how Jeremiah helped her with Victor during his early years, what Victor was like as a boy, how he'd grown into a man, and how he'd had a wonderful child of his own. They talked about the places they'd been, the things they'd done, and the dreams they'd had of each other. Margaret even gave Peter numbers to reach Victor and Emily. And finally, at two in the morning, they agreed to hang up, for their throats were dry and they could barely keep their eyes open.

"Promise me we'll talk again, Peter," Margaret said softly. "Promise me this isn't the end."

"Margaret, my love," Peter said, "I plan to spend eternity with you. This is only the beginning."

The next morning, Ingrid woke Peter at just past ten. "I slept in the guest room," she said curtly. "I figured you'd want to be alone with your thoughts of Margaret." She spat the name out.

"I spoke with her last night," Peter said softly. "I spoke with Margaret."

Ingrid's jaw dropped. "But she's dead."

"No. No, she isn't. She lived, and so did her son. *Our*

son. I have a child and a grandchild, Ingrid. Victor and Emily Emerson."

Her face was white. "That's impossible."

"It's true. And I must find them, Ingrid. I know I'm at the end of my life, but I must tell them that I love them."

"You don't even *know* them."

"They are my blood," he said. "And they are Margaret's blood."

Ingrid stared at him. "So that's it, then? I've been by your side for the last thirty years, but in your final days, Margaret comes back and I'm forgotten?"

"I could never forget you, Ingrid. You've meant so much to me."

"But you don't love me. Not the way you love her."

He longed to comfort her, but he didn't know how. "Ingrid, you and I have spent a life together. I missed a life with her. You can't envy her."

"What nonsense, Peter. Your life wasn't with me. It was with her. It was always with her."

He was silent for a long time. "If I die before I reach them, Victor and Emily, will you find them for me? Will you tell them about me? Will you explain what happened?"

He held out the slip of paper on which he'd written their names and numbers, and Ingrid nodded, but she didn't take it. After a while, he set the paper back down on his nightstand.

"Do you promise me?" he asked.

"I promise."

"Thank you. You're very good to me. I never deserved you, Ingrid."

"No," she agreed. "Perhaps you didn't." She bent to kiss him and walked out of the room.

He picked up the phone and tried Victor's number first and then Emily's. There was no answer on either line, and he didn't leave a message. What would he say? No, he would talk to them and tell them everything as soon as they answered his call. But in the meantime, he wanted to know everything about them. So he spent the next forty minutes searching their names on the Internet. He found Emily's columns and Victor's business website, and there were photos of both of them, enough to show him that Victor looked just like a younger version of himself, and Emily looked just like Margaret, just as he'd always imagined a grandchild of theirs would.

Slowly, with great effort, he rose from his bed, surprised at how weak his legs had become beneath him. In fact, once he was on the floor, he found that he could no longer walk, so he lowered himself to the ground and crawled toward the closet. He knew that in the back corner, he had stored blank watercolor paper and some old paint, along with a selection of brushes, and he needed them now. It took him twenty minutes on his hands and knees to pull them out and drag them into the center of the room, where he positioned them beneath the wash of sunlight from the window. He rested for a moment on his haunches, catching his breath, and then, he picked up his brush and began.

Tears burning his eyes, he painted. He painted the world as it could have been, the world he would never know. He painted the faces of the son and granddaughter he loved, and of the woman he had created life with after all. He worked until his hand ached, until the room throbbed, until he could no longer keep his eyes open. And then, he lowered himself onto the floor, prone on his back, and he stared up at the faces smiling back at him. *He had made them. They were his.*

Later that day, he would call them again. And he would call Margaret to hear her sweet voice. He knew that the great violet sky, the one that would bring him home, was closing in. But until it came for him, he had this. He had hope.

CHAPTER TWENTY-EIGHT

"Wait, go back," I said, staring at Ingrid in disbelief. "You're saying he actually talked to my grandmother?"

"The night before his death." As she turned toward me again, I could see that the tears had overflowed and were streaming down her face in silent rivers. "The day before he died, *Louise* came to visit," she said, spitting the name out like it was a dirty word. "She'd heard about his illness on CNN, and she came to tell him the truth."

"My grandmother's sister? She came here?"

Ingrid nodded. "She told him that Margaret had lived and that she'd had a child—*his* child—and a granddaughter. You."

"But my grandmother never said anything." I stared at her as a potential explanation dawned on me. "Wait. When did he die? What date?"

She shook her head and looked down. "February fifteenth. Just after Valentine's Day, in the afternoon."

I swallowed hard. "My grandmother died that day too. Several hours earlier. She passed away sometime during the night."

Ingrid's mouth fell open. "They even *died* together?"

I shrugged, suddenly uneasy. "I'm sure it was coincidence." But the truth was, it didn't sound coincidental to me. It sounded like two people who had always hoped against hope that the ones they loved were still out there. When it turned out they were right, they were ready to let go. Or perhaps once my grandmother died, Peter Dahler had felt it in some corner of his soul, and he'd followed her at long last. As Ingrid's face twisted tighter in despair, I hurried to change the subject. "But I had the impression that Louise hated my grandmother. As far as I know, my grandmother never talked to her sister again after leaving Belle Creek in the late 1940s. Why would Louise come here all these years later to reveal that Margaret was alive?"

"I don't know. To clear her conscience? To torture my husband once more? To make the last hours of his life miserable for me?" She looked at the floor. "Ralph asked me to call you if something happened to him."

The words were so quiet I barely heard them. "What?"

"He spoke to me that morning—just a little while before he died—and told me everything," she said. She took a deep, shuddering breath and looked up to meet my gaze. "He wasn't well. He said he was planning to call you and your father after ten, in case you were sleeping in. That day was a Sunday. But he asked me to call you myself if he wasn't able to do it. It was like he knew that he only had a few hours left." She paused. "He died just past four that afternoon."

"And you didn't call," I said softly.

"No."

Silence lay heavy between us. "Why?"

"Because *I* was his family." Her voice sounded almost like a whimper, a plea. "I'd been the one to stand by him for thirty years. To love him for thirty years. And it was never enough. He was dying, Emily, and at the end, that woman swept in to reignite the torch he had carried all these years. It wasn't fair. Don't you see that?"

"Yes." And somehow, I did, despite everything.

"It's why I sent the painting. I didn't want to be involved, but after I read your column, I wanted you to know that you were wrong about him. I'm sorry I didn't reach out to you sooner, Emily." She blinked back tears. "It was too little, too late, I know. But I wanted you and your father to know that Margaret had been loved."

"But why didn't you just explain it?" I asked. "Why send me just a painting and a cryptic note?"

"Because I didn't really want you to find me. You being here, it's the right thing. But do you know how much this is hurting me?" She sighed. "There's a part of me that wishes you hadn't come. That you didn't exist in the first place. I'm sorry. That must be hard to hear." She drew a ragged breath. "He was always hers."

"I'm sure he loved you too."

"But it wasn't the same. It was never the same." She took a step back and nodded toward a doorway on the left. "There is something I must show you. Will you follow me?"

I walked behind her down a long hallway to a closed door. Ingrid stopped in front of it, murmured something to herself, and turned the knob. As I stepped into the room and she flicked the light switch on, I could feel my eyes widen.

The room was the size of a bedroom, which is probably what it was intended to be, but there was no furniture. Instead, there was a single, small painting hanging on the far wall—the only object in the entire room. And in the center of the image were four figures: my grandmother, my father, me, and an older man, who I could only assume was my grandfather. We had our arms around each other, and my grandfather was gazing adoringly at the three of us under the same violet sky that had graced the painting that had arrived at my doorstep from Munich.

"What the—?" I murmured, staring at it in wonder.

"After Margaret told Ralph about you," Ingrid said flatly, "he looked you both up and found a handful of pictures online. While he tried to reach you, he imagined what his life would have been like with the two of you in it. With *Margaret* in it. This was the last painting he ever did. He painted it the morning he died."

I gazed at it in wonder. He had perfectly captured the shape of my eyes, my father's chin, my nose, my father's laugh lines. And somehow, he had conjured exactly how my grandma had looked at the end. When I finally turned back to Ingrid, I was crying, and she was too.

"He got all of it right, didn't he?" she asked.

"Yes. It seems impossible, but yes."

She sniffled. "That was Ralph. He was special that way. Art critics have speculated for years and years about his technique, but I've always believed that he painted with no specific process at all. He just let his heart pour into the work."

"I don't even know what to say."

Ingrid looked around the room. "Then just say this: that you'll take the painting."

"What?"

"It was for you. You and your father. It was his way of telling you he loved you. He wanted you to know that you were in his heart. He would have wanted you to have it."

"I couldn't possibly—"

"Please," she interrupted firmly. "It is yours. He always loved your grandmother, and once he knew about you, I know he loved you with every ounce of his heart. The proof is here. This is among the best work he ever created, and he did it in only hours. You and your father restored something in him that had always been missing, Emily." She paused and wiped a tear away. "In the end, he was happy—happier than I'd ever seen him, happier than I was ever able to make him."

I left an hour later with the beautiful painting carefully wrapped and packed into a small, flat gallery box.

"Are you sure?" I asked her once more before we parted. "It feels wrong to take it from you."

"Emily," she said, touching my cheek, "I spent all my years with Ralph trying to pretend that his life before me, his life with Margaret, didn't exist. But it *did* exist. It defined him. It was the basis for the man he was. *You* were the basis for everything he was, even if he didn't know it until the end. Family's like that, isn't it? The ones we love are always in our blood, in our hearts, even if they're not in our lives."

I arrived back in Orlando just past three in the afternoon. I hadn't told my dad yet about my visit with Ingrid because I wanted to explain things in person, so I called him as I was leaving the airport to let him know I was on my way. He was waiting for me when I walked through his office door twenty-five minutes later.

"What is this?" my father asked. He embraced me awkwardly and stared at the flat cardboard box in my hand.

"See for yourself," I said, handing it over.

My father slid the painting out, gasping as he saw the image. "This was done by my father?"

I nodded.

"He painted *us*," he said softly.

I smiled as he gazed at the image of all four of us together. "Yes."

"But . . . I don't understand. How? Where was he all these years?"

And so I explained everything. The lies that had kept Margaret and Peter apart. The way they'd both always carried a torch for the other, even when the flame should logically have gone out. The way that Peter never gave up, even when he changed his name, even when he tried to become someone else.

"You're telling me my father was Ralph Gaertner?" my father repeated in disbelief.

"That's how the world knew him," I said. "But I think in his heart, he was always Peter Dahler, a German boy waiting for the love of his life to come back."

My father's eyes were wide and filled with tears. "But . . . how did my mother never realize it was him?"

I had asked Ingrid the same general question. "He did one big TV appearance in the sixties, but after that, he became more and more withdrawn. He agreed to very few interviews, and even fewer cameras. Unless you were a huge art buff, or you'd happened to catch that one episode of the *Tonight Show*, there's no reason you would have seen his face."

"My mother almost never watched TV," my father said. "But all those years . . . They were both here . . ."

"They both thought the other was gone."

"But then how did he know about us?"

I told him about Louise's visit on Valentine's Day and the phone call he'd placed to my grandmother that night. My father simply stared at me as I explained that they'd died within hours of each other the next day.

"He was out there all this time," my father whispered. "He didn't abandon me. He didn't abandon my mother."

"No."

He sat down slowly in one of the chairs facing his desk. "It's all my fault."

"What do you mean? You had nothing to do with your father leaving."

"No. Not that." He paused and seemed to be gathering himself together. "You. What I did to you and your mother."

I didn't know what to say. "Dad—" I began.

"No. Please let me say this. Emily, I thought that when things got tough, it was okay to leave. I thought that's what my father had done. And you knew my mother: when life became too much for her, she just shut down. It was hard for me when I was growing up, when it was just the two of us, me and her. She'd disappear, even though she was physically there. Do you understand?"

I nodded.

"It doesn't excuse what I did," my father went on. "God, it's the opposite. It makes me an even worse person, because I knew how much it hurt to feel as if you weren't important enough to stay for. But I thought they both left because when life got hard, disappearing was the only option."

I thought of Nick, Catherine. "I've done that too."

"And that's my fault too. For teaching you that it's okay to run."

"No, that's not on you. It's on me."

"I was wrong about all of it, Emily. I became unreliable, because I thought that's just what people did. I didn't have the backbone to be better, to stick it out. I guess I felt like I'd been abandoned, so maybe it was okay to abandon you."

"Dad—"

"But he never abandoned me at all, did he?" he continued. His voice cracked. "My dad was there all along, loving my mom. Loving us. And my mom, she wasn't really disappearing from me. She was going to him—or to his memory, at least." He drew a shaky breath. "God, Emily, I'm so sorry. I was wrong about everything, and I completely screwed up your life because of it. I hurt you, and I hurt your mom, and there's no changing that."

I reached for his hand. "But we can try to do better, okay? We can't change the past. But we can change the way we deal with each other now."

Tears glistened in his eyes. "Emily, there's something I need to tell you."

Somehow, I knew from the way he was looking at me what he was about to say. "No," I whispered.

He sighed and looked into my eyes. "The cancer, Emily. It's terminal."

"But you said—"

"I know. And I'm sorry. I didn't want you letting me into your life just because you felt sorry for me. That wouldn't have been fair to you. I wanted us to come together on our own terms without the specter of death looming over us. I wanted to try to set things right, to make sure I hadn't destroyed your life with the things I'd done to hurt you. I wanted you to know that you weren't doomed to repeat my mistakes, that you're your own person with a beautiful future in front of you."

"But the doctors—"

"—have done everything they can," my dad finished my sentence for me, his tone gentle. "I was stage three when I was diagnosed, but I haven't responded well to treatments. I need to address the shareholders in my company very soon, but I wanted you to know first."

I began to cry, suddenly overwhelmed with a powerful sense of despair for a person I thought I'd lost years ago. He was slipping away all over again.

"I'm so sorry, Emily. So very sorry. For everything I've done. For being a fool for so long. For throwing away the most important things in my life. For being too late to fix things between us."

My father stood, pulled me to my feet, and enveloped me in a hug. I could feel sobs racking his body too, and I held on tight, wishing I could take away some of his pain but knowing that I couldn't. Sometimes, I realized, it's only by going through the fire that you can come out the other side, reborn.

"It's not too late, Dad," I whispered into my father's chest, hoping that somewhere up there, Peter Dahler was seeing this moment, and that he knew that one of his last acts on earth had led to this reconciliation. Yes, people leave. But sometimes, they come back. And when they do, maybe it's worth opening the door a crack to let them in. "It's never too late."

I stayed with my father for a long time that afternoon, talking about the past and what the future held for us. I wanted to hear optimism in his voice, a sign that perhaps his doctor's words weren't exactly the death sentence they sounded like. But instead, I heard resignation and peace.

"I'm so glad we've had these last few weeks together, Emily," he said as I hugged him good-bye just after twilight fell outside his office window. "I'll remember them as some of the best in my life."

I left the painting with him and promised to spend more time with him in the coming days. We parted ways after I had elicited a promise from him to meet for dinner the next night.

I cried all the way home, and when I got there, I felt exhausted and depleted. I sat for a long time in the kitchen staring at the painting in my kitchen, the one of my grandmother in the sugarcane field, the one that had started it all. I knew I'd be spending many nights in the future staring at the swirling purples, pinks, lavenders, and violets of the horizon in the background. It was the same sky my grandfather met my grandmother under. If that day hadn't happened, I wouldn't be here now. I knew I'd never look at a beautiful dawn the same way again.

I called Myra twice, leaving her a message the second time she didn't pick up. I sobbed my way through an explanation about my trip to Atlanta and my father's terminal diagnosis before asking her to call me back as soon as possible. I really needed someone to lean on. Finally, although it was only 8:30, I crawled into bed, exhausted, placing my phone on the pillow beside me with the ringer turned to high, just in case she called.

I was jarred awake by the doorbell ringing some time later. "Dad?" I asked aloud, remembering my father's news the second I was conscious. I glanced at the clock. It was 9:15; I'd only been out for forty-five minutes.

The doorbell sounded again, and I jumped out of bed, wrapped a robe around myself, and rushed to the front door. I looked through the peephole, expecting to see Myra or maybe even my father standing there.

Instead, I saw the last person I thought would ever be on my doorstep.

"Nick?" I murmured in disbelief as I opened the door. He looked tired and rumpled.

His face creased immediately with concern. "Emily? What's wrong? You look like you've been crying."

I wiped self-consciously at my eyes. "Oh. It's . . ." I trailed off into silence, because it was too much to explain right now. "I'm okay. But what are you doing here?"

He held up the note I'd sent him two weeks ago. "I got your letter. I needed some time to think, Emily. But I woke up this morning and knew I had to see you. I got things squared away at the office for a few days and left this afternoon." He smiled and pointed to the upper-left corner of the envelope. "Luckily, you included your return address."

I still couldn't understand what was happening, but I knew that I owed him another apology. Millions of them, in fact. "I'm sorry, Nick. For everything. I'm so sorry."

"The past is the past, isn't it? But you were wrong about something."

I couldn't help but laugh. "I'd say I was wrong about an awful lot of things."

"No, I mean in your letter. You were wrong. I'm not married."

I blinked at him. "But your wife . . ." I paused, trailing off. "It says on your website you're married."

He looked surprised. "Does it still? Obviously I need to change that. The divorce was final last year. Jessica wanted a different life, one that didn't include me, I guess. She lives in Arizona now. It's for the best. We weren't right for each other. We never were."

"Oh." I suddenly felt breathless. "I'm—I'm really sorry to hear that."

"Me too. But that's life, isn't it? We all take some wrong turns along the way." He took a deep breath, and when he looked up a moment later, he was looking right into my eyes. I could almost feel the years slipping away. "Did you mean the things you said in your letter?"

"Every word, Nick."

"Then I have a question for you. I know a lifetime has passed. But I never stopped thinking about you either, and that's got to mean something. And there has to be a reason that everything has felt different since you walked back into my life."

I didn't say anything. I couldn't. I just stared, my heart pounding.

"So I guess what I came here to ask you is, I mean, maybe it's a terrible idea . . ." He was blushing now. "But in your letter, you mentioned regrets, and Emily, I don't want to have any. I don't want to have to wonder what might have been. So what I'm trying to say is, do you think it would be crazy to see if we could try again?"

"I don't think it would be crazy at all." I paused, thinking of the life that might stretch before us, as wide open and beautiful as one of Ralph Gaertner's violet sunrises, full of promise and hope. "Would you like to come in?"

CHAPTER TWENTY-NINE

Three months later

On the third Friday in February, I woke up to a glorious rainbow stretching across a brilliant dawn, and as I stood on my front porch a few minutes later, stretching for my morning run, I was thinking about how beautiful and surprising the world was. The sky was the same blend of violets and lavenders that my grandfather had rendered so many times, and for a moment, I let myself imagine that I was inside one of his paintings. It was a beautiful place to be.

As I set out on my run, heading west toward Lake Eola with the rising sun behind me, I thought about how after my grandmother had died last year, Myra had told me that she believed you could see the people you'd lost in the magic of a rainbow. I'd thought that she'd just been trying to comfort me on one of my darkest days and hadn't meant a word of it. But then my father had died right before Christmas, and as I left the hospital on that terrible morning two months ago, there was a faint rainbow looming to the east. "Dad?" I had whispered, already doubting myself. But from that day on, there had been a part of me that believed.

This morning, as I ran with the rainbow looming overhead, I thought about how maybe I was seeing my father up there today. Or my mother. Maybe my grandmother and grandfather were together, looking down on me. Or perhaps it was just a trick of the light that meant nothing. Still, I felt a sense of peace, and I wondered if my grandfather had been right all along about the way the sky holds a certain kind of magic.

Nick and I were officially seeing each other now, but we were taking it slow. After all, we couldn't wipe away the nearly nineteen years that had passed between us, nor could we erase the nearly four hundred miles that separated us now. Nick's life and business were in Atlanta, and my life was here, in Orlando. I was still freelancing here and there, and although it wasn't the professional life I dreamed of, I was scraping by. I'd probably move back to Atlanta one day, if Nick wanted me to. We had talked about it a bit, dancing around the topic, and I think we both wanted to be together. Rushing into it didn't feel smart, but now that my father was gone, there wasn't much to stay for anymore.

At the beginning of December, I had introduced Nick to my dad, and they'd liked each other, which meant a lot to me. When I'd visited my father at his bedside the next afternoon, he'd squeezed my hand and said softly, "I'm happy to see you happy. Just don't let go of the way you're feeling now, the way you love him." He'd coughed, long and hard, and I'd ached to take away some of his pain. "Why is it only in the last few months that I'm realizing that family is everything?" he'd asked when he could breathe again. "It has been all along, hasn't it?"

I'd nodded, thinking about how nice it felt to be his daughter again. And I thought, too, that knowing we'd reconnected in the end might make my mother smile. I'd spent years thinking that a reconciliation with my dad would be a betrayal of her, but I now realized that she'd probably want most of all for me to be happy.

Two weeks before he died, my father had asked me about my daughter for the first time since we'd discussed her in Atlanta. "Did she look like you?" His skin felt cold and clammy as he reached for my hand, his grasp weak, and I knew he was slipping away.

"Maybe a bit. But I saw Nick in her more than I saw myself. She had Mom's nose and your facial expressions."

"She looked like me?" His eyes were suddenly watery.

"A little. She was healthy, Dad. Seven pounds, three ounces, even though she was three weeks early. She was due on October 31, but she arrived screaming her little lungs out on October 8." I smiled, and he smiled back. "I had her at Bayfront Medical Center in St. Pete, and I didn't know a soul in that city except for Grandma Margaret. I think the moment they came to take her away was the most alone I'd ever felt in my entire life. I hadn't realized during the time that I was pregnant with her how comforting it was to know she was right there with me. But having her taken was like losing a part of myself. I wish I'd understood that sooner."

"It seems like the most important lessons in life are the ones we grasp far too late," my father said.

"Yeah." I knew he wasn't just talking about Catherine. "You know, I went to Mom's grave a couple months ago. I asked her to help me find Catherine, just so I could know she was okay. Do you . . . do you believe in stuff like that?"

"That your mom can hear you in heaven? I think anything is

possible, honey." My father started to say something else, but whatever it might have been was lost in a fit of coughing.

Later, after I'd grabbed a soda from the machine down the hall and a nurse had brought in a glass of water for him, he'd raised his cup in the air. "To second chances, however they happen," he'd said, looking me in the eye.

"I can drink to that."

"You deserve every happiness, Emily," he'd murmured. Two weeks later, he was gone. And somehow, in the wake of his death, I had gone from having no family to connecting with the people who had once been a part of my grandparents' life, in one way or another. I had visited Belle Creek in January to tell Jeremiah and Julie in person about the true story of Peter and Margaret, and they'd both called several times since. I'd reached out to Franz, who sent flowers for my father's funeral, and I talked on an almost weekly basis to Arno Fromm, who loved to share stories of his memories with my grandfather. I felt like I was discovering pieces of my past at every turn, and it made me feel somehow like the circle of my family's life was almost complete.

Maybe that's what the rainbow this morning was trying to tell me—that it was okay to reach for all the colors of joy, all the happiness I could find, just like my father had said. The only thing missing was Catherine, but I knew that was something I'd have to learn to live with.

I did two loops around the lake and headed back toward my house, lost in thought. The rainbow had faded as the day grew brighter, but it was still just slightly visible, beckoning me home. I had just turned the corner from Shine Avenue onto my street when I saw a woman at my front door, her back to me. She was knocking, and in her left hand, she was clutching a piece of paper.

"Can I help you?" I called out as I reached the bottom of my driveway.

She whirled around, and I stopped in my tracks. I knew instantly who she was.

"Excuse me," said the woman—a girl, actually, an eighteen-year-old. "But I'm looking for Emily Emerson."

"That's me," I managed to say.

"Oh. Well, I'm, uh, I'm Megan Clark." She paused, seemingly unsure of how to continue.

"Megan," I repeated with a smile.

"Well, the thing is, I think you might be my biological mother." The girl held up the piece of paper in her hand and waved it uneasily. I took a few small steps toward her, my vision blurring as my eyes filled. "I got this letter a few weeks ago," she continued. "I'm sorry it took me so long to come, but I just wanted to think about some things before I met you. I hope that's okay."

"Of course it is. It's more than okay." I couldn't stop staring at her. She was beautiful; she had Nick's eyes, my high forehead, and a button nose that reminded me of my own mother. She had the same dimples as Nick's sister, Abby, and a narrow chin that looked just like my father's. She was the best of all of us, but she was her own person too. "You said you received a letter?"

"Yeah. From a guy named Victor Emerson. He said he's your dad. My granddad. Is that right?"

I stared at her in disbelief and took a few more steps so that I was standing just in front of her. I ached to reach out and touch her, to pull her into my arms just to make sure she was real, but I didn't want to scare her away. "Yes. He is. Um, he was. But how . . . ?"

Megan handed me the letter, which was dated December 15, just five days before my father died. "See for yourself."

I began to read, my heart in my throat.

Dear Megan,

I'm afraid that this letter probably feels very out of the blue to you. My name is Victor Emerson, and I believe I'm your biological grandfather. If you don't want to find your birth family, I offer my deepest apologies for contacting you; you are certainly free to discard this letter. But if you have ever wondered about where you came from, I'd love to tell you a little.

I found out only recently that my daughter, Emily—to whom I fear I've been a terrible father—had a daughter of her own and gave her up for adoption years ago because she thought she was giving that child a better life. I've hired a private investigator who tells me that child is you. Every day, Emily has wondered and worried about what became of you. So even if you're not ready to meet her—even if you have no interest in ever meeting her—please know that you've been loved deeply since the day you were born. I know she would want you to know that.

It may be difficult to understand, but regardless of the choices we make, love doesn't go away. I know without a doubt that Emily has loved you every day of your life, just as I've always loved her. Please don't feel any obligation to reach out to her—I know she doesn't want you to feel any pressure—but if you've ever wondered about the woman who gave birth to you, I know she would love to explain what happened, and I think you'll understand.

I used to believe that in life, we would always have a million more opportunities to make things right. "Why do the hard things today when I can do them tomorrow?" I would ask myself. But in recent months, I've come to realize that tomorrow is never a guarantee and that if we don't say and *do the important things in life now, we may never have the chance.*

Megan, I'm including Emily's phone number and address below, as well as the details of her child's birth so that you can confirm that they match the details of your birth. Again, you have absolutely no obligation here, and I know Emily does not want to interfere in your life. But if you've ever wanted to know about your past, and about the woman who gave birth to you, this should be all you need to reach out. Please know most of all that you are loved—by her, and now by me too— and if there's anything you ever need, you only have to say the word.

I wish I'd had the chance to meet you.

With love always,
Victor

When I was finished reading, I looked up at Megan, who had tears in her eyes. How strange and unpredictable life could be. "Megan, I'm so glad you came," I said, handing her the letter. "I've been looking for you for a long time."

"Really?" she asked in a small voice. "I always kind of figured you'd just forgotten and moved on."

"Not for a second."

"I just—I need to know why you didn't want me. I need to understand."

"It was *never* that I didn't want you. Never. But come in. Please. I'll tell you everything, okay?"

Megan looked at me for a long time. "Okay," she said finally.

I pulled the key from under the mat and opened the door. Megan took a deep breath and walked inside, then she stopped short, staring at the painting on her left, the one that Ingrid had given me, the one that hung on my father's wall until he died. "That looks like a Gaertner," she said. "Well, not the faces, obviously. But geez, it looks just like one of his skies. I actually wrote my college entrance essay about his art."

"You did?" My heart skipped. "It is a Gaertner, actually."

"But it's a print, right?"

"No. It's an original." I watched as her jaw dropped. "How do you know about Gaertner?"

"I paint a little. He's always been my favorite."

I stared in disbelief. "Would you believe me if I said art is in your blood?"

She laughed. "Really? That's cool. I'm going to the University of Florida in the fall to get a BFA in painting, hopefully."

I smiled. "I went to school there too. For journalism."

"You're a Gator? That's so cool. So can you tell me why you have a Gaertner original? I mean, this has to be worth like a hundred thousand dollars."

"I'll tell you the whole story," I said. "But first, can I ask you something?"

She nodded.

"Have you had a good life? I mean, your parents, are they good people? Are you happy?"

She reached out and touched my arm, the first time we'd made contact in more than eighteen years. "Yeah. Everything's been good. My parents are awesome."

"Good," I whispered. "I'm so glad."

And as Megan began to tell me, haltingly, about growing up in Sarasota, about her little sister, Anne, and their dog, Dexter, and about her mom, Heather, and her dad, Martin, I realized something. Although the reasons behind giving my daughter up were the wrong ones, the outcome was right. Maybe I was never meant to be her mother. She'd had a good childhood.

And finally, I could feel myself beginning to let go of all the guilt I'd carried for so long. Maybe I was never meant to bear it in the first place. And maybe in order to move into the future, I finally had to let the past stop controlling me once and for all.

"Victor," Megan said after a moment. "My grandfather, I mean. Your dad. Does he live around here too? He only gave me your number and address, not his."

I hesitated. "I'm sorry, but he died a few days after he sent you that letter, Megan."

Her mouth opened in a small *o* of surprise. "Oh my God. I'm so sorry."

"I'm sorry too. He would have really loved meeting you. I think it would have made him really happy to know that the two of us were standing here together now."

Her brow furrowed. "Were you real close to him?"

"Yes. In the end, I think I was." I could feel my eyes beginning to sting, so I changed the subject. There would be more time to tell Megan about my dad—and my mother and grandparents—later. "You know, your father's going to want to meet you too."

Her eyes widened. "He's here?"

"He's in Atlanta. But I bet he'll be on the first plane down once I tell him about you."

"Really?"

I nodded. I could hardly wait to tell Nick, but I wanted to stay here, in this moment, with Megan for as long as I could. "Do you want something to drink?" I asked.

She shrugged. "Just some water or something."

"I'll be right back."

When I returned a moment later with two water bottles, Megan was staring at the painting, her back to me. She spun around, a look of awe on her face, when she heard me behind her. "That's you in the painting. Isn't it?"

I nodded. "Me and your grandfather and your great-grandparents."

"For real? Ralph Gaertner actually knew you?"

I thought about that for a moment. "In a way, I think maybe he always did."

She shook her head and turned back to the painting. "It's beautiful," she murmured, and I didn't know whether she was talking about the painting or about this moment.

"Yes," I said to my daughter. The bright future I'd always searched for, the answer to everything, was finally here. "It really is."

ACKNOWLEDGMENTS

A huge thank-you, as usual, to two of my favorite people in the world: my amazing literary agent, Holly Root, and my awesome editor, Abby Zidle. I feel very grateful not only to have such a wonderful professional relationship with the two of you but also to count you as treasured friends. Thank you for believing in me, fighting for me, and helping me to become a better storyteller.

To my wonderful publicist, Kristin Dwyer: You are such a rock star, dude. It's not just the skillful and perfect way you spell your gorgeous first name—wink, wink—it's just your all-around coolness and generosity.

A huge thanks to the incredible Dana Spector, my film agent, who could probably negotiate a deal underwater, with her hands tied behind her back, if she had to. You're amazing, mama! And to the lovely Heather Baror-Shapiro, who has helped bring my books to the world: I can't thank you enough.

I'm also very grateful to Marla Daniels, Louise Burke, Jennifer Bergstrom, Jen Long, Liz Psaltis, Diana Velasquez, Melanie Mitzman, Mackenzie Hickey, Laurie McGee, Christine Masters,

Alexander Rothman, Chelsea McGuckin, Taylor Haggerty, Julianna Wojcik, Ashley Lopez, Kim Yau, and the rest of the wonderful folks I work with at Gallery Books, the Waxman Leavell Literary Agency, and the Paradigm Talent Agency.

To Eva Schubert (my first German editor) and Elisabetta Migliavada (my Italian editor): I can never thank the two of you enough for your support, your encouragement, and your friendship. Thanks also to the team at Blanvalet (especially Julia Natzmer and Nicola Bartels) and the team at Garzanti (especially Francesca Rodella and Ilaria Marzi), as well as my many wonderful foreign publishers, editors, and publicists. Special thanks to Bettina Schrewe and of course Farley Chase. I feel so lucky to have all of you in my life—and to be able to reach so many readers around the world with your help.

I had the wonderful experience of meeting screenwriter Heather Hach through my previous novel, *The Life Intended*, and I'm so lucky to count her now among my close friends. I'll always think of you as "the friend intended!" I'm so excited for all the wonderful things to come in the future, and I'm so grateful for your friendship and support.

I couldn't have written this book without the help of Butch Wilson at the Clewiston Museum and Gregory Parsons at the Camp Blanding Museum. The two of you were enormously helpful in helping me to understand the lives of German POWs in Florida during World War II. Special thanks to painter Melissa Wolcott Martino for providing some eleventh-hour art assistance.

Thank you to all my wonderful writer friends, especially my sounding board and writing soul mate Wendy Toliver, and the Swan Valley gang: Jay Asher, Linda Gerber, Alyson Noel, Aprilynne Pike, Allison van Diepen, and Emily Wing Smith.

I'm very lucky to have some of the best family members in

the world, especially my mom Carol, my dad Rick, Noah, Karen, Dave, Barry, James, William, Johanna, Janine, Donna, Wanda, Mark, Brittany, Jarryd, Chloe, Bob, JoAnn, Steve, Janet, Anne, Fred, Jess, Greg, Merri, Derek, Eleanor, the Troubas, and Courtney. And thanks to my wonderful friends, especially Kristen Bost, Eddie Bost, Colton Bost, Marcie Golgoski, Melixa Carbonell, Lisa Wilkes, Lauren Elkin, Scott Pace, Walter Caldwell, Jon Payne, Christine Payne, Brendan Boyle, Kelly Galea, Nick Harris, Sara Sargent, Amy Tan, Courtney Dewey, Amber Draus, Megan Combs, Scott Moore, Megan McDermott Lewis, Trish Stefonek, Robin Gage, Wendy Jo Moyer, Chad Kunerth, Gillian Zucker, Chubby Checker, Jay Cash, Pat Cash Isaacson, Andy Cohen, Sanjeev Sirpal, Kat Green, Ben Bledsoe, Joe Grote, Kathleen Henson, Andrea Jackson, Nancy Jeffrey, Karen Barber, Lauren Billings Luhrs, Zena Polin, Kerry Reichs, Daryn Kagan, Samantha Phillips, Kate Atwood, Christina Sivrich, Amy Ballot, Jason Cochran, Al Martino, Karen Leigh, and the rest of those I know and love. I know I left people out . . . I'm just so darned lucky to have so many great people in my life! I could go on for pages!

A special thanks to the lovely Aestas (of *Aestas Book Blog*), Jenny O'Regan, Melissa Amster, Amy Bromberg, and all of the other bloggers who have been so wonderfully supportive over the years.

And finally, to Jason: I'm so happy and proud to be your wife. I couldn't be more excited about the new adventures ahead.

WHEN WE MEET AGAIN

KRISTIN HARMEL

When a mysterious painting arrives out of the blue at Emily Emerson's door, all the heartache and uncertainties in her life bubble to the surface: she is out of work, her mother and grandmother are dead, she isn't speaking to her father, she abandoned the love of her life, and she gave up her only child for adoption. The painting, which depicts a familiar-looking young woman in a field under a violet sky, stirs a desire in Emily to reconnect with her long-estranged father in an effort to find the grandfather she never knew. Emily and her father travel from Florida to Germany to Georgia and back again, and along the way uncover a family history both beautiful and tragic. In the end, Emily learns about the healing power of art, forgiveness, and love.

WHEN WE MELT AGAIN

KRISTIN HARMEL

1. Our first encounter with Emily Emerson involves her lying in bed on a Friday morning, discouraged and alone. The scene is broken by a telephone call from her former editor, letting her know a package arrived for her—a package we later learn is the painting of Grandma Margaret. How did you initially characterize Emily? Did you feel sorry for her? Is she a likeable character? Without the arrival of the painting, do you think she would have snapped out of her depression? Why or why not?

2. Very early in the novel, the topic of abandonment arises. Emily's grandfather abandoned her grandmother and father; her father abandoned her; she abandoned Nick and her daughter, Catherine. Discuss this abandonment motif, considering how each of the characters reacts in the wake of being left behind. Does the title—*When We Meet Again*—hint at reconciliation? Do you think all of the characters find reconciliation in the end? Why or why not?

3. Discuss the structure of the narrative. How does the weaving between the past and present-day story lines affect your under-

standing of the characters? Do you think this "time travel" allows the story to belong to both Emily and her grandparents? How would the story change if we only had Emily's point of view?

4. On page 33, Jeremiah tells Emily, "sometimes, when one is living with a broken heart, it's too hard to give voice to the stories that hurt the most." Consider the ways in which silence shapes the lives of these characters. Is what is *not* said a defining aspect of life for Emily, her father, her grandparents, etc.?

5. "Do you really think one bad experience has the power to change a person's character . . . ?" Myra asks Emily, and she replies that yes, "if you love someone enough and they hurt you deeply, it can change you forever" (pages 70–71). Answer Myra's question for yourself. Did Grandma Margaret change as a result of her love affair with Peter? Did Peter? In what ways?

6. How is Margaret a symbol of American ideals—specifically life, liberty, and the pursuit of happiness? In what ways is she the antithesis of these principles? Consider her relationship with her family, Jeremiah, Peter, and Emily in your response.

7. Evaluate Franz Dahler's character. Do you blame him for allowing Peter to leave his family, his home, and his country? Do you think he could have changed the course of Peter's life if he had stood up to their father? Is he similar to many of the other characters in that he can "never forget that which you regret" (page 166)?

8. What role does World War II play in the novel? Do all of the characters' suffering and joy happen as a result of the war?

9. On page 184, Peter declares, "From this moment forward, I am no longer a Dahler." Consider the ways in which troubled parent/child relationships are the sparks that cause the characters to change their lives and their identities—in some cases very literally. Discuss in relation to the moment when Victor tells Emily, "That's what being a parent is: loving someone so much that they'll be a part of you forever, no matter what" (page 190).

10. Revisit the scene, beginning on page 306, when Emily goes to her mother's grave. Do you think she finds the closure she is seeking? In the end, does Emily "find [her] way back to who [she] used to be" (page 307)?

11. A possible theme for the novel emerges on page 329 when Louise asks Peter, "You ain't gonna hold a grudge, are you?" Which character seeks forgiveness most? You might consider Emily, Victor, Peter, Louise, Franz, Margaret, or Ingrid in your response.

12. Were you surprised when Nick arrived at Emily's doorstep? Do you think Nick and Emily are fulfilling the love story that Peter and Margaret never got to have?

13. Ultimately, do you think the painting is responsible for changing Emily's life? Reflect on the changes in her relationship with her father, Nick, Catherine, and herself. Do you think art has the power to transform the way we understand the world? Why or why not?

ENHANCE YOUR BOOK CLUB

1. Peter and Margaret share a passion for the works of Ralph Waldo Emerson—a poet, essayist, and philosopher who defined the nineteenth-century American literary scene. Spend some time with Emerson in your book club meeting, paying particular attention to his famous essay "Self-Reliance." Why do you think Peter and Margaret were so drawn to Emerson's philosophy? Does the pair embody Emerson's famous saying "A foolish consistency is the hobgoblin of little minds, adored by little statesmen and philosophers and divines," which suggests that we must always think for ourselves? Share with the group your understanding of Emerson's belief in the individual. Have you faced a moment in your life, like Peter and Margaret, where you chose to "be yourself in a world that is constantly trying to make you something else" (page 60)?

2. "I was floored to learn that nearly four hundred thousand Germans had been imprisoned in the United States during the 1940s, but that newspaper coverage of the POW camps was limited, so many Americans didn't even know about them. Most of the prisoners had been captured in battle or

on German U-boats and had been brought to the States to work" (page 65). Were you as shocked as Emily to learn about the POW camps in the United States during World War II? Consider reading a different take on this unusual piece of World War II history in *Summer of My German Soldier* by Bette Greene. Compare and contrast this book with *When We Meet Again*. What themes do the two share? Did the characters face similar prejudices?

3. The fictional Ralph Gaertner's paintings are compared to the realist twentieth-century American artist Andrew Wyeth, though Wyeth "painted subjects in a much different kind of landscape, mostly in the northeast region" (page 123) of the United States. With your book club, host an art night. Over appetizers and drinks, preview some Andrew Wyeth paintings (andrewwyeth.com). Do the paintings appear as you might have imagined Gaertner's? Are they different? How so? Does it seem that Wyeth agrees with Gaertner that "to paint a face was too intimate; it was like baring a person's soul to the world without their permission" (pages 123–124)? Why or why not?

4. Didn't get enough Kristin Harmel? Read another book by her with your book club, such as *The Sweetness of Forgetting* or *The Life Intended*. With your group, come up with a list of themes that seem to interest this author. How do the families in *The Sweetness of Forgetting* or *The Life Intended* compare with Emily Emerson's family? Do you agree that love and forgiveness are central to all the novels?

Printed in the USA
CPSIA information can be obtained
at www.ICGtesting.com
BVHW031641150823
668589BV00001B/1